BANE AFFAIR

The BANE AFFAIR

ALISON KENT

KENSINGTON PUBLISHING CORP.
http://www.kensingtonbooks.com

BRAVA BOOKS are published by

Kensington Publishing Corp.
850 Third Avenue
New York, NY 10022

All Kensington titles, imprints and distributed lines are available at special quantity discounts for bulk purchases for sales promotion, premiums, fund-raising, educational or institutional use.

Special book excerpts or customized printings can also be created to fit specific needs. For details, write or phone the office of the Kensington Special Sales Manager: Kensington Publishing Corp., 850 Third Avenue, New York, NY, 10022. Attn. Special Sales Department. Phone: 1-800-221-2647.

ISBN 0-7582-0668-2

First Kensington Trade Paperback Printing: October 2004
10 9 8 7 6 5 4 3 2 1

Printed in the United States of America

To Walt.
You always said I could.
And I did.
I love you.

Acknowledgments

Listing everyone who offered support and encouragement during the writing of this book would take as many pages as the story. I'll synopsize instead.

I owe the biggest thank-you of all to the most brilliant Kate Duffy, a goddess among editors, for believing that I could deliver on an idea unlike any I'd written before.

Additionally, I give credit to Karen Solem for the subtle-and not-so-subtle nudges that pushed me out of my comfort zone.

As always, Jan Freed reminded me that God is in the details.

This time around Jill Shalvis, Shannon McKenna and the Namumis provided the reads I needed, along with the hugs, laughter, and unmentionables that saw me through to the end.

Mike Stone provided much of the technical input. Any mistakes are my lay interpretation. And John Carbonaro came up with a B movie just when I needed one.

I thank all of you very much.

"The only thing necessary for the triumph of evil is for good men to do nothing."

—Edmund Burke (1729–1797)
Irish philosopher, statesman

Prologue

A fine horse, a fine cigar, a fine woman.

Two outta three wasn't half bad.

With a stopwatch dwarfed by his meaty left palm, Hank Smithson chomped down on the butt of a Montecristo Corona Grande and watched Maddy Bar None fly. The mare hit the quarter-mile mark; Hank hit the stopwatch, and hard. He rolled the cigar to one side of his mouth, rolled it back. The thud of the horse's hooves beat at the base of his skull.

Unbelievable. Dad-blamed unbelievable.

He grinned, watching as she slowed, as she tossed her head and sashayed her fine chestnut ass around the back side of the track. He glanced again at the time on the stopwatch, shaking his head, disbelieving. Life didn't get much better than this. Not to his way of thinking. Making it better wouldn't be possible without giving him Madelyn back—a thought that had his grin fading, that never failed to hit him where his heart refused to heal. She'd been a good woman, his Madelyn, and he missed her more every day.

The acres of prime Saratoga County pastureland beyond the barns and the track remained Crayola crayon green but for spatters of red-gold, orange-gold, and yellow-gold leaves blowing in from the wooded hills beyond. A chill was coming.

He felt it in bones that were growing brittle, in joints that were sorely in need of a good slowing down.

Thing was, slowing down had never been much in his blood. Madelyn had known that, had lived with that, and with him, for forty-one years. His boys knew that, too; every time he took on one of his SG-5 team's jobs, they threatened to hog-tie and sling him up in MaddyB's barn until the horse was too old to race.

That was when he reminded them who had nipped a couple of their courts martial in the bud, who had buried the dishonorable truth of a discharge or two. Or, in the Bane boy's case, who it was that had ponied up a future of honky-tonk bars and biker bars and sushi bars instead of the bars seen from the wrong side of a Thai prison.

Funny thing the way all those governmental special forces and their covert ops could get a man into trouble, yet none of 'em seemed to be able to find their asshole with a flashlight when it came to getting him out.

Hank didn't for half a second cotton to all that mission-critical, sealed-lips, country-first bullshit. The men always came first. *Always.* And that wasn't talking out of his ass. He'd done his time. Little places like Korea and Vietnam. Even served up a few off-the-record words of advice to Norman during Desert Storm.

Bottom line was, if there was no man, there was no country. At least to Hank's way of thinking.

MaddyB continued prancing, tail flagging, nostrils flaring. And then his own ears pricked, and at the sound of heavy boots crunching gravel behind him, he pocketed the stopwatch. Catching his unlit cigar between his fingers, he leaned into the practice track's railing, listened to the boy's approach, and figured it was time he stopped thinking of his SG-5 team as boys.

They were men, elite operatives who had served their country and served her well, yet were nameless and faceless and sharper than a tack knew how to be.

It was Hank's own soul-deep patriotism, his love for the land he'd risked his life to defend, that had driven him to put together the five-man Smithson Group in the first place. Discreet inquiries had taken him from military courtrooms to jungle prisons, searching for the type of man who would boldly go where law-abiding, rule-stickling, by-the-bookers wouldn't, and get done what needed to get done.

He'd hand picked all of 'em. And it hadn't taken a one of the five long to learn not to use their sneaky hush-hush shit on ol' Hank, no matter that he'd been around for three-quarters of a century. Now they let him know they were comin', fully appreciative of his own dodgy experience in the Pacific Theater beneath Westmoreland and Krulak.

And hell if he wouldn't give his right nut to turn back the clock about twenty years. He was tired of being tied out here to the farm. Or worse, to Smithson Engineering's offices in the city. Fuck the money the corporation generated, money that provided the horses and cigars, that would've provided the women had he an itch left to scratch. Doin' nothing was no way for a man to live out his life.

Ten more seconds of gravel-crunching and Christian Bane braced a boot on the lowest rung of the split rail fence, draping his forearms along the top and turning his intense gaze in MaddyB's direction. Hank shifted his bum hip to the side and took a moment to study the profile of the boy who was the quietest member of the team.

The one Hank had chosen first.

Taciturn wasn't the right word. Christian plain didn't have a whole lot to say. And that was fine. More than fine. Hell, Hank had known big talkers who never said anything worth listenin' to. At least with Christian, when he talked, a man knew to pay attention. Though Hank did wonder a bit if the boy's tendency to hang back and not speak until spoken to made him the right one for this job.

It wasn't going to be an easy lap around this particular track, impersonating Peter Deacon, the puppet doing the dirty work for the syndicate known as Spectra IT. Pulling it off believably put a whole lot of conversation—and other not so nice doings—in Christian Bane's future.

Looking out towards MaddyB as her trainer led her to the stables, Hank broke the silence by clearing his throat. "No passport this time, son. Figured that should make you happy." He narrowed his eyes, glanced to the side, waited for Christian's reaction. And there it was. That slow upward tilt of the right side of his mouth. "Matter of fact, you don't even have to leave the state. Couple of county lines is all."

And at that, Christian stepped back from the fence and turned. "I'd say that's the best news I've had in awhile, but I know you way too well."

He was a tall man, topping Hank's own five foot eleven by about three inches. 'Course, Hank had once been a bit taller himself, dad-blamed bum hip. He had to say he liked the military haircut Christian wore even if the beard stubble wasn't quite as clean-looking. And his eyes . . . yep. They were the same ones Hank had felt that day seven years ago like darts blown into his skin as the boy stared out from behind those bars deep in the jungle of northern Thailand's Chiang Rai province.

Spectra IT had put him there, had left him to die there, which made this whole affair one Hank wasn't thrilled about having to involve Bane in.

At Hank's continuing silence, a look came over Christian's face, a look speaking of the things he'd seen that no man should have to, drawing down his brows in that way he had of frowning so fiercely that even Hank considered taking a step back. Christian shook his head slowly, pulling in a deep breath as he cast down his gaze, shoved his hands to his hips, and braced against the coming blow.

It was when he looked back up that Hank stopped worrying. For all the boy didn't speak with his mouth, he said enough with his eyes. And it was those eyes Hank wasn't looking forward to answering to.

He'd take that look, that haunted look, that hunted look,

all the way to his grave. He'd take it because even knowing what he did about Christian's history with the dragon, Hank was still sending him deep into the beast's lair.

So when Christian finally asked, "It's Spectra, isn't it?", Hank nodded and answered, "They're holding another innocent man hostage. I need you to go in and get him out."

And nothing more was said.

One

Gothic mansion or gingerbread house.

Natasha Gaudet had never been able to decide.

Each time she approached her employer's home, an estate set on ninety-eight acres near Lake Placid in New York's Adirondack State Park, she was struck with the fanciful idea that she was entering an amusement park. Or a wickedly haunted house.

By daylight, the three-story structure twinkled as if sugared with white frosting, shingled with red gumdrops, and shuttered with slats of blue lollipops. The beds of peppermint geraniums scattered throughout the yard of green candy sprinkles provided the finishing touch. Alice would have thought it a wonderland. Gretel would have thought it dessert. Natasha simply thought it a hell of a lot of fun.

But after dark, shadows crept about with a menacing presence, turning the fairy-tale castle into a hulking creature whose hideous fangs gleamed in the yawning maws of its dormer windows, whose aura of evil pulsed from the depths of its sinister lair. Of course that was because Natasha had a ridiculously vivid imagination and rather enjoyed the idea of being at the mercy of such a villainous beast.

The fact that her employer, Dr. Wickham Bow, was also her godfather made the entire experience of working as his personal assistant the best of her life. Or at least a close runner-up, she decided, switching the headlights of her luxury SUV to bright, because nothing would ever compare to being a child and sitting at the feet of Wick and her father—even if where she'd really been sitting had been one floor above.

Vividly, she remembered sneaking out of her bedroom, gripping the railing that edged the landing, and pressing her face between the spindles. Her mother's television had blared from behind the closed door at the hallway's end, purposefully drowning out the very voices Natasha had stayed awake to hear. The voices of Wick and her father, boisterous with brandy and good conversation.

They'd talked of politics. Of religion. Of international affairs and the condition of the greenhouse flowers. More often than not, she'd fallen asleep there on the pillow she'd brought with her, waking only when her father cradled her in his arms and carried her to bed. Having tucked her in, he then retired to his own room at the opposite end of the second floor from where her mother slept. Even as a child who knew nothing about matters of the heart or the bedroom, her parents' estrangement had saddened her.

The one thing she was most thankful for—though she hadn't recognized the blessing until years had passed—was that neither parent had ever used her as a pawn, allowing her to remain close to both. As divorces went, theirs had been amicable, her mother raising no objections when, though only eleven, she had chosen to live with her father. To move with him, in fact, from their Boston home to New York City, where he had taken a job with NYC Department of Education.

Michael Gaudet had been blessed with the need to nurture—a trait which had made his passing five years ago so very hard to take. Unable to bear her grief, Wick had stepped in and offered her a job as well as a home. He'd allowed his love for her—his one seeming weakness—to override his life's tenets. This, the very same Dr. Wickham Bow, who expected everyone around him to be self-sufficient, short on emotion, long on logic, and free of any misplaced compassion for others.

After all, the formula had been the very one that had taken him from the South Bronx of the late sixties to Polytechnic as a tenured professor, and then to the global community of scientists and educators as a respected authority in his field of computer science. He was no different now than he'd been during those years she'd listened to him challenge her father on Buddhism and Vietnam and the grafting of hibiscus.

He was simply older, more deeply set in his ways, a bit of a curmudgeon—especially when crossed—yet she adored him without measure. And though she stayed two or three nights a week at his estate as work and his declining health demanded, she spent most of her time in her apartment on Manhattan's Upper West Side.

Making the final turn from the long private road off of Route 86 and through the property's gates, Natasha slowed her Infiniti FX45—oh, but she loved the extravagant toy—and made her way around to the back of the house, pulling to a stop next to the modified van that allowed Wick to drive when he chose.

He rarely chose. He preferred to remain underground, working in his state-of-the-art computer lab, or holding court in the lecture theater from which he broadcast via satellite, interacting with his grad students and research assistants, instead of communing with the general population or the great outdoors. For the former, he relied on his household staff. For the latter, well, he never had been much for nature.

She sighed, climbed from her SUV, and stretched before gathering up her suit jacket and the endless work and correspondence she'd brought from the university. She'd present it all to him at tomorrow morning's breakfast meeting, which meant organizing and prioritizing the bulk of it tonight. Definitely a long evening ahead.

Halfway up the inclined walkway from the garage to the back of the house, she stopped.

And turned.

And frowned.

Angling her computer bag's wheels on the slanted ramp, she set down her purse and the expanding files she carried, and draped her jacket over the telescoped handle. Her heels clicked sharply as she made her way back along the smooth sidewalk that appeared as an extension of the water garden between the house and garage.

Wick had a visitor. She'd been so self-absorbed that only her subconscious had noticed the low-slung import parked on the near side of her godfather's van. Upon closer inspection—because she had this *thing* for hot-bodied cars—she realized Wick had a very wealthy visitor.

She circled the Ferrari once, shaking her head and grinning like a besotted fool, leaning down to peer unsuccessfully through the driver's side window. Neither the light from the garage spotlight nor that from the moon was a match for the dark tint. No big deal, really, because she wanted to see the interior only half as much as she wanted a good look beneath the glass cover over the rear engine bay.

She made her way around the car slowly, fingers digging into her palms instead of testing the sleek surface of the composite and metal as she wanted to do. What she didn't want to do was set off the alarm. So at the two sharp shrieks of said alarm being deactivated, she jumped back, hand to her throat, pulse thundering. The rumble in her ears took long seconds to quiet.

Once it had, she blew out a breath, hearing footsteps, a slow but certain approach from behind. Footsteps, yet no familiar voice calling out to her to set her mind at ease. The owner of the car; it had to be. Busted by her own curious nature, Natasha turned.

The man she assumed to be Wick's visitor was tall and lean and frighteningly attractive—frightening, because the intensity of his gaze was not the least bit dimmed by the darkness or the shadows. If she'd been the type to shiver, her Jimmy Choos would not have been the best choice of footwear. The way he was looking at her? Looking into her? Looking through what she showed the world for what she might be hiding? She would have shaken out of her shoes by now.

He had to have come from the water garden. Perhaps he'd seen her stop on the walkway. The garden took up a good eight hundred square feet, and any number of the benches along the water's edge, as well as at least two Natasha could think of nestled deeper into the lush foliage, offered a perfect view of the path rising from the garage to the house.

Approaching from that direction gave him the advantage. She stood in the full fall of moonlight, yet all she could see was his eyes.

Well, that and his build, which had a lot to do with the buzz of energy sizzling at her nape. Hot-bodied cars. Hot-bodied men. Both hit her right where it counted. He drew closer, and she waited, her gaze taking in his long legs and his stride that made clear he was in no hurry.

He wore black dress pants and boots. Ostrich, she decided, as the leather appeared distressed rather than the gloss more natural to crocodile. Pricey boots, she knew, because footwear ran a close second to her love for cars. His shirt was dress white, with collar open and cuffs rolled to mid-forearm. He'd tossed his suit coat over his right shoulder and held it there hooked on his thumb.

A watch—platinum, she was certain—hugged his left wrist. No ring on that telltale third finger. That she noted right before his hand came up and his car keys came flying. She snagged the silver ring from the air, lifted a brow, and watched as his gaze dropped to the throbbing beat at the base of her throat.

"She's open," he said, now no more than ten feet away.

As much as Natasha longed to slide down into that smooth leather seat and get her hands on the wheel, she waited. She waited because no car could spike her pulse like a man. She slipped her index finger through the ring, spun the keys around and into her palm, keeping her gaze steady and losing the battle with a smile.

"Just like that? No terms? No questions? The keys are mine?" *Wow.* Not a crack or a waver. She actually pulled it off.

He grinned. Not broadly, nor with his eyes, which she thought might be a shade of aqua rather than the bright sky blue she'd first thought—oh, why couldn't this be happening in daylight? There was so much of him that she wanted to see.

And then his grin widened, the right corner of his mouth quirking upward. It was enough. She was in love. No, lust, she corrected, determined never again to confuse the two. Oh, but he was gorgeous.

"You caught me feeling generous."

"Generous?" She swung the keys around once, twice, catching them again as they smacked into her palm. He now stood close enough to touch, and having the key ring to hold onto was a very good thing. "I'm thinking more along the lines of insane. You just handed, what? Four hundred thousand dollars to a woman you've never seen before?"

"The professor asked if I would mind a delay in dinner as he was waiting for his assistant to arrive." The stranger tossed a quick glance toward the mountain of work she'd left stacked on the sidewalk with her jacket and purse. "I'd say those files make you the assistant. That means if you run off with my car, I'll know where to find you."

"Then run with me," she said without thinking. "Wick will kill me for my lack of punctuality. I might as well be granted a last request before he carries out the sentence."

"That's a hell of a stiff fine to pay for being late." He grinned again. This time with both sides of his mouth.

She saw the dimple on the left and was a goner. "For a ride in that car? I'll make the sacrifice."

He moved his left hand to his hip. The platinum case of his watch caught the moonlight and flickered. He gave a lift of his chin. "You've got the keys."

She opened her fingers, her gaze caught by his, her palm beginning to sweat as she offered up the ring. "You want them back?"

He didn't move. He simply stared, his gaze even more intense with so little distance between them. She wanted to ask what he was looking for, what he expected to find. She had no secrets, yet she kept her mouth closed. Intuition told her the thoughts going on behind his eyes would quickly dispel this two-strangers-and-a-Ferrari fantasy she wasn't finished living.

When he remained silent, she withdrew her offer, palming the keys. She wanted this ride in a very bad way. "I've never had an accident. I've never been ticketed. I've never been stopped. Not even for a warning."

This time when he shook his head, she swore he was also shaking off a chuckle. "I suppose you want the top down."

"Yes, though my stylist will *definitely* kill me."

He moved closer still. A flicker in his eyes was her only warning before he reached up to finger a lock of her hair. "Do your decisions always invite this hovering crowd of executioners?"

Her voice. Where was her voice? "What can I say? I enjoy living dangerously."

His touch as well as his gaze lingered there where he rubbed the strands between forefinger and thumb. "Then it seems we have more than a few things in common."

Heat lightning arced as the back of his hand hovered close to her neck. She watched as he caught sight of the popping pulse at the base. "Does that mean you trust me to drive?"

"No." His gaze came up to meet hers, hot and vivid and razor's-edge sharp. "And if you wreck my car, I'll personally escort you to the guillotine."

She could hardly breathe. And a part of her believed that he literally meant what he said. "Promise to make it swift and painless?"

He released her hair but he didn't lower his hand. Instead, he traced the line of her collarbone through her red silk shell. "And here I thought you were into danger."

She'd never been so glad for the shadows as now, feeling her nipples tighten. "So I lied."

At that, he laughed. And he stepped closer, reaching behind

her to open the driver's side door. She felt the brush of his chest to her shoulder, caught a much closer glimpse of the hard line of his jaw where golden brown beard stubble glinted. And his scent. Yum. Very warm and very woodsy, and oh, but she was in such big trouble here.

He gestured for her to get in, which she did before he shut her door and circled around to the passenger side. He slid down into the seat, taking up a whole lot of space in the intimately close interior. Only the console between them kept their thighs from touching.

She buckled her seat belt; he did the same, and then she turned the key. The car rumbled to life beneath her, behind her. The power of the engine tickled her legs where bare skin met luxurious Connolly leather. She moved her hand to the gearshift.

He draped his coat across his lap, settled back like a man without a worry in the world. Then he turned to face her, his grin having finally reached his eyes. "Let's see what you've got."

She was close to melting into the seat. Instead, she winked, kicked off her shoes, and tossed them into his lap. "Hang on."

Wickham Bow maneuvered his motorized wheelchair away from his desk and out into the foyer, certain that he hadn't missed Natasha's arrival, curious as to what could be keeping her. Her routine never varied, a habit he favored—one that allowed him the uncommon luxury of positive reinforcement as a controlling technique rather than being forced as he was by so many others to wield an iron fist.

Upon her arrival, Natasha would stop in her office to drop off the documents she'd couriered from the university requiring his attention. In the morning, she would organize them by priority before presenting them to him during their breakfast meeting. It was important to him that appearances and schedules were always maintained. She knew that, knew he valued consistency, dependability, and loyalty above all else.

Her tardiness tonight angered him.

He had watched the Black Forest clock above his fireplace for thirty minutes; he now checked the grandfather clock positioned at the base of the foyer staircase as well as the pocket watch he pulled from his vest. Intercepting Natasha upon her arrival was paramount. He had postponed the dinner hour, allowing for the time all females required to dress for a special occasion.

Tonight's dinner was a very special occasion. One vital to his future, yet one with an importance he could never explain. Using his goddaughter to further his cause was hardly a sin. She was quite dispensable. He had no trouble with any end justifying any means. The fact that she was late when he expected promptness left him at the mercy of his ulcer and vexed that his guest was having to wait.

Because Peter Deacon was not a man one kept waiting.

Two

Those unfortunate enough to work with the man behind the public mask knew Peter Deacon as a womanizing asshole. He was slick. He was a player. He brokered arms sales and drug deals, sold stolen bonds and human beings, excelled in extortion, forgery, and laundered money.

Interpol knew it. The Feds knew it. The Smithson Group knew it, as well. The rest of the world knew only the legitimate persona of the Spectra IT spokesman, that of a businessman: straightforward, scrupulous, as squeaky clean as any businessman got.

Christian Bane could think of no one he wanted to impersonate less, though right now he was hardly in a position to complain. Later, maybe. When the smells of the jungle blindsided him again. When he woke to the sensation of mud oozing between his toes.

When he licked his lips and tasted rank insect bodies that provided the protein rice gruel did not. Then he'd remember exactly what he'd suffered at the hands of Spectra IT and complain about this time spent living in Peter Deacon's skin.

It was hard to think of anything outside of the present when he was riding in a Ferrari 360 Spider with a pair of ridiculously sharp stilettos in his lap, the bare-footed wild woman at his side clocking close to one hundred ten miles per hour. At the moment, impersonation required less thought than breathing.

He didn't know a man alive who wouldn't pay him to trade places. Including Peter Deacon, though the other man would no doubt be holding more than the woman's shoes. By now, he'd have talked her out of her panties—a thought that had Christian cursing Hank Smithson for not the first time.

The hows and whys of the older man's logic for assigning team members to missions was a mystery not one of the group had solved. They joked about Hank's magic lotto balls but collectively owed him their lives. Each man did as he was asked to do because Hank had yet to be proven wrong. Just as he wouldn't be proven wrong this time.

It only felt that way to Christian, stuck impersonating a scumbag Don Juan whose conquests were legendary.

Here he'd been handed a beautiful woman to use at will, to exploit until she revealed all that he needed to know. A beautiful woman employed by a man whose dealings with Spectra had him holding a scientist hostage.

Christian's initial pause about taking her to bed hadn't been any misplaced sense of decency. Women who toyed with the wrong side of the law rarely had qualms about sex being used as a bargaining tool. And with Deacon's reputation preceding him, Natasha would be expecting no less than seduction.

No, it was simply that out of all the SG-5 operatives, Christian Bane was the least likely to score. Kelly John was the one with the notched bedpost. Julian left the string of broken hearts. Eli and Tripp both bagged their trophies when and where they could, considering sex a well-deserved perk of the job.

Christian preferred assignments that kept him under the radar. Just his luck he was the one who most closely resembled the Spectra spokesman. Not to mention the one who kept the organization's dossier tattooed like a rap sheet on the inside of his skull.

At least Peter Deacon wasn't having an easier time of it.

Christian wondered if the bastard had a clue where he was being held, or if the self-contained vault beneath MaddyB's stable had instilled the fear of God he was sorely lacking. He'd need it where he was going. And it felt damn good to be taking him down at last.

Natasha downshifted through the next corner, then floored the Spider and punched up into gear. Natasha Gaudet. The name had been one of several he'd memorized from the mission's portfolio. It fit her well. Exotic, as were her looks. Dark hair, dark eyes, skin as ivory as a pearl. Her photo had intrigued him; in the flesh, she blew him away.

Strange, because he'd given up his attraction to two-faced, gypsy-gorgeous whores.

She let go a loud "Whoo-hoo!" at the top of her lungs, the sound swallowed by the starry night sky. He shifted in his seat to watch her, figuring since she hadn't yet sent them skidding off the road and crashing down the wooded slope beyond, it was a safe bet she knew what she was doing.

Hell, the position she was in? Working for Wickham Bow? The professor might be her godfather rather than related by blood, but she obviously shared Bow's calculating mind, or so hinted the Smithson intel. And with the two of them now making deals with Spectra?

Who said pretty white girls couldn't be bad guys, too?

Natasha's cover was damn convincing and clever, going back as many verifiable years as it did. And Christian was going to enjoy blowing it. Taking her to bed in the meantime . . . Well, hell, he mused, unable to deny the jolt of fire to his gut, one he hadn't felt for a very long time.

Wasn't that exactly what Peter Deacon would do?

She hit the brakes, spun the wheel, took the car off the road; it fishtailed to a hard stop right where she'd no doubt intended. Christian swallowed his fast-beating heart and glanced up to see the low stone wall of the estate's private lake lookout point inches from the car's front grill. Then he looked at Natasha.

"Scared ya, didn't I?" she asked with a wink.

The move had been too skillfully maneuvered to be frightening, but he wasn't going to deny the rush of blood through his veins. Fast cars and fast women. A deadly combination.

"Not a chance," he said, hooking her slingbacks over one finger and offering them up as a bribe. She reached for the shoes. He held on, forcing her across the console and into his space. Her face was but a foot away when he growled, "But you lied about lying about loving to live dangerously."

"Why do you say that?" Her face was flushed, her voice breathless, her pupils dilated to the whites of her eyes. Her chest beneath her silky red top rose and fell. A thrill junkie through and through.

Talking her out of her panties was going to be a piece of cake. Now to find her weak spot and talk her out of the info he needed to locate the kidnapped Woodrow Jinks. "Your face." When she frowned, he added, "Take a look," and angled down the rearview mirror.

She glanced up. Her eyes went wide. Releasing the shoes, she sent her fingers combing into her hair. "I am such dead meat. Wick is going to have my hide. Not only am I late, now I look like cat draggings."

Christian played along. "Dr. Bow doesn't approve of cat draggings?"

"Something like that," she said with a laugh as she finished with her hair, grabbed her shoes before he thought to stop her, and opened her door. "Wick's my employer, yes. But he's also my godfather. He's quite stern about appearance and punctuality, not to mention being way overprotective. He treats me at times as if I'm still twelve years old."

"Instead of twenty-eight?"

Her legs out the door as she slipped on her shoes, she cast him a curious glance from over her shoulder, her eyes bright, a brow arched. "Nice guess."

He shook his head, watching for her reaction as he, too, pushed out of his seat. "It's not a guess. I investigate everyone with whom I consider doing business."

He climbed from the car, and she did the same, shaking her

head as she walked toward the stone perimeter and keeping the car's width between them. Once he reached the knee-high wall, he glanced briefly at the lake beyond before turning to face her, struck with the strangest sensation of seeing a creature of the night.

He couldn't imagine the sun glinting any more brightly off of her hair than did the light from the moon, and he forced himself to harden his heart, reminding himself of what she was capable, what she had done, what he had come here to stop her and her godfather from doing to anyone ever again.

She stood in profile, staring off toward the distant water, the surface of which rippled with the same breeze that lifted the strands of her hair and tugged her clothing tightly to her very fine body. "I had hoped you were a friend come to visit, though the car should have tipped me off." Her mouth pulled into a wry grin. "Wick doesn't have many friends who can afford Ferraris."

Now this was interesting, Christian thought, his intelligence radar blipping. The professor keeping his appointments from his assistant? Especially the timing of Deacon's arrival? "You prefer he conduct his business from the university?"

"I prefer he conduct no business at all except for his distance-education lectures. But he's hardheaded and refuses to take my advice." She crossed her arms over her chest as if chilled. "He certainly refuses to listen to his doctors."

Yeah, Christian knew about the arrangements Polytechnic had made for Dr. Bow to conduct his lectures via satellite. Unusual, but so was the man and his international reputation. The university wasn't about to lose a professor of Bow's regard. No matter the provisions they had to make to ensure he remained on faculty.

Christian stayed silent, waiting her out, gauging her reaction against what he'd learned of her in the Smithson portfolio. She was sharp and well-spoken; both qualities he'd seen for himself. She was loyal to her godfather, and protective, as well. It didn't surprise him to see either in action.

He was surprised, however, that she seemed so convincingly unaware of Deacon's scheduled visit or the identity of the man himself. Almost as surprised as he was to feel the sharply humming and purely sexual sensation centered at the base of his spine.

She turned to sit on the low stone wall, crossed her legs, and tucked windblown strands of hair behind her ear. "I'm Natasha, by the way. Natasha Gaudet, though if you know my age then I'm certain you know my name."

He did. What he wasn't certain about was if she was a better actor than he was. "Peter Deacon." Christian walked toward her, held out his hand, and lied again. "And I wasn't aware Dr. Bow was in poor health."

She shook his hand, her fingers lingering in his as she met his gaze. "His health should remain stable as long as he doesn't accept any more consulting projects."

Christian took in her pointedly arched brow and her denial; his thigh brushed her knee as he sat on the wall beside her, and he stayed where he was. Let her break the physical contact, he decided, waiting for her to scoot forward, to turn away, neither of which she did.

"Then we're good to go," he finally said, hedging with a vague, "This project has been in the works for awhile now. I haven't brought him anything new to take on."

He watched her eyes, looking for a hint of recognition. Surely she knew what Bow and Spectra wanted from the work Jinks was doing. *Had* been doing for a global technology firm until he vanished two months ago, turning up unexpectedly on Smithson's radar.

If Christian didn't have equipment monitoring Spectra twenty-four/seven from SG-5's ops center in the city, the reference to Woodrow Jinks might've been missed. What the crime syndicate and the good doctor wanted from the kidnapped scientist would be sorted out later. This mission was solely about setting the other man free.

"You came for a tour of the facilities, then?" Natasha asked him at last.

He braced his elbows on his thighs and leaned forward, looking down at the gravel and concrete. "Not exactly."

"Hmm," was all she said, and that brought his head up. Her eyes were a deep dark brown and flashed in the moonlight like sun on iced coffee. She gave a small laugh before saying, "Well, now you have me curious."

He kept his fingers laced together, kept his thigh pressed to her knee. He wasn't one to be taken in by a pretty face. Not any longer, and certainly not this face. In this light, at this distance . . .

He clenched his hands tighter and reminded himself who she was and where he was, what year it was and how many miles separated the Adirondacks from Thailand. Flexing his fingers, he breathed deeply and expelled the reminders she brought up of his past.

"A dangerous thing, curiosity," he finally said.

"And therein lies your proof." Her eyes flashed again, this time showing off what he sensed was a self-directed shot.

"Proof?" he asked, pressing his thigh harder to her knee.

Her lashes drifted down, drifted up. She shifted slightly, not away, but at less of an angle so that the length of her leg, from hip to knee, touched his.

"Proof that I was lying about lying." She smoothed down her short skirt with her palms. "Curiosity is my weakness."

"Tell me, then. How many lives *do* you have left?"

She shrugged, a slight lift of the shoulder closest to his. This time when she met his gaze, her irises glittered with a hungry need to know. Yet it was the tone of her whisper that gave away the extent of her interest when she asked, "That depends. How dangerous are you?"

He held her gaze, unspeaking and still, and after a long silent moment, she shivered, rubbing her palms up and down her biceps. Gooseflesh pebbled her arms in a breeze that wasn't really that cold. It was good that he made her nervous, he mused, his mind returning to her question.

How dangerous was he?

She'd do better to ask that question of Eli or Julian or Kelly John or Tripp. None of the four would mince the words Christian wasn't able to speak. He'd seen things, done things, made deals that were no better than Peter Deacon's, though he'd never willingly hurt anyone innocent, never killed anyone who didn't deserve to die.

He turned his gaze away, breaking the eye contact that had gone on long past what civilized conversation required. Natasha shivered again; he took advantage of the distraction, shaking out the suit coat that lay in his lap to drape it over her shoulders.

She pulled the lapels close and, smiling, snuggled deep. "Thank you."

"Not a problem." He left his arm behind her, his hand at her hip on the wall, his body offering shelter. No. It was Peter Deacon offering shelter to a beautiful woman. And Peter Deacon wouldn't give a rat's ass if Natasha knew what went on in the underground lab as long as she shared his bed for the duration of his stay.

The thought again gave Christian pause. "So. Where were we?"

She nodded briskly. "I asked you why you were here if not to tour the lab."

He caught her gaze and held it, one heartbeat, two, waiting, wondering, curious if she'd retract or stick to her guns. They both knew that wasn't the question hanging pregnant in the air, the one he hadn't answered and was sure she hadn't meant to ask. He knew that by her hesitation, the sense he got that she wanted to say more, yet she was the first to look away. Her eyelids came down to shutter her gaze, and the moment of heat finally fizzled.

Christian moved on. "Those details are for your boss to share, not me."

"Why?" She gave a wry grin. "Unless telling me why you're here means you'll have to kill me."

His free hand came up to finger the lapel of his jacket above where her hands held the fabric close. "Do you want to talk about this death wish you have?"

She stopped breathing as if anticipating his bolder touch. "I don't have a death wish."

He continued to stroke; her gaze on his hand never wavered. "Then why all the people in line to kill you? Your stylist. Your godfather." He moved his hand upward until his knuckles grazed her bare throat. "Me."

She laughed, a breathless, nervous twitter. "That's just a figure of speech."

"It's come up a lot in the last thirty minutes of this conversation."

"I swear I won't use it again." She drew an *X* over her chest, right above his hand. "Cross my heart and hope to die."

"Die. Right." He released her then; he'd pressed hard enough for now.

"Okay, okay," she said, once again exhibiting the self-amusement that he'd noticed—and appreciated—before. "I hadn't even realized. My guilt at keeping Wick waiting must be eating at me."

"Don't let it. Once we get back, I'll explain that you were showing me the extent of the estate."

Her brow arched. "And you think that will appease him?"

"I have every confidence that it will."

"You don't know Wick very well, do you?" she asked with a bit of a huff.

Christian leaned closer, forcing the contact of her shoulder with the inside of his and keeping his hand on the wall at her hip. Here it was. The test he'd been waiting to give her. "I know enough. He told me earlier that he plans to put you at my disposal for the length of my stay."

Her pulse fluttered. Christian watched it there at the base of her throat. Good. She wasn't unaffected, though he would have liked to be sure of the cause.

Was it being at his disposal and the intimacy that entailed? Or the realization that he knew of the deal she'd made to accommodate Deacon during his stay, a particularly telling detail she had yet to mention.

"How long will you be here?" she finally asked, her voice less steady than before.

"As long as it takes to get what I've come for." An honest and double-edged answer—and one she should have known. Her position as Bow's assistant should've given her the inside scoop as to why Deacon was visiting. There was a lot going on here that wasn't making sense.

Uneasiness begin to stir where he stored his gut feelings. "My firm is investing in a project in its final stages of development. I want to be here for a complete demonstration of the capabilities. Plus, it's easier to troubleshoot from on site."

"So . . ." she began, frowning while she processed what he'd said, continuing with, "you don't work with Wick at Polytechnic, then?"

He shook his head. "No, why?"

She shrugged again. "Most of his lab rats who spend time up here are graduate students. And if you're here to troubleshoot—"

"I'm not a graduate student or a lab rat, Natasha. And if the project continues at its current momentum," he added, shifting so he could better see her face, gauge her reaction, "your godfather will be a wealthy man when I leave."

He didn't need to see her face; her laugh gave away as much as her expression. This time he was the source of her amusement and, if he wasn't mistaken, a source of perceived insult. Interesting, that. Especially when he'd fed her the very least she should know as the employee who handled Bow's business dealings.

She got to her feet, pushed her hair from her face, stood her ground as she faced him. "Mr. Deacon, you don't know Wick at all if you think money is the goal of his research."

He hid none of Deacon's cynicism, which in this case mirrored his own. "Your godfather works in data encryption, Miss Gaudet. Not exactly a humanitarian effort. I don't buy the altruistic sentiment."

"It's not about altruism." She pressed her lips tightly together, paced a short strip of graveled parking lot while gathering her thoughts.

When she finally stopped, Christian was struck by the way her brows drew down, as if she wasn't at all pleased with her own conclusion. "It's about being able to say, 'I told you so.' About being right and proving everyone around him wrong."

And with that, she handed him his suit coat and headed for the car's passenger door without a single backward glance.

Christian waited, watching, taking his time shrugging into the jacket. He'd had but seventy-two hours to study her portfolio along with that of Dr. Bow. Deacon's hadn't even required a refresher.

But now he found himself blinking rapidly as he mentally scanned each page of information, looking for anything he'd missed. Anything to prove his intuition wrong.

Because right now, at this moment, his intuition had him swearing that Natasha Gaudet had no clue her godfather was making deals with the devil.

Three

The bank of security monitors behind which Wickham Bow sat was positioned at such an angle that he had no trouble viewing the floor of the underground lab from his raised platform in the room's corner. He could easily monitor the workings of the room at the same time he assured himself that his household staff aboveground was following his instructions to the letter.

Natasha knew nothing of the hidden cameras throughout the house and grounds. She made for a perfect pawn—a beautiful woman, innocent and guileless, caught unawares in a tangled web of high stakes. He might have felt sympathetic had not so much been on the line.

Had not his very life been on the line.

Before he forgave her tonight for being late—and how could he not, watching her climb from Deacon's Ferrari, seeing the other man guide her with his palm placed intimately in the small of her back?—Wickham would make his displeasure at her tardiness known.

He would relent once when she admitted her mistake, which she would in her efforts to please him. He only needed to decide whether his cause would be better served by chastising her privately or in front of his guest.

He flipped a switch on his control panel and brought up the

camera above the kitchen's rear entrance to follow the couple up the ramp from the garage to the back of the house. Natasha stopped to slip on her suit jacket and to quickly run a brush through her hair. Good girl, he mused with a nod, his gaze moving to the man watching his goddaughter as she saw to her appearance.

Peter Deacon had arrived only two hours ago and already the plan was coming together. Asking Deacon if he minded holding dinner for Natasha, then suggesting he might enjoy the water gardens while waiting, had been an ingenious stroke of luck on Wickham's part. His earlier irritation had eased once he'd realized the two were together. Both of his pawns were making the very moves he'd hoped for.

All he had to do was sit back and watch the games begin. Then . . . checkmate.

The fluid hem of her paisley Ralph Lauren halter dress flirting at her knees, Natasha paced the mauve carpet of her rooms, from window to door, settee to fireplace, wing chair to bed, her bare feet sinking into the plush wool fibers that offered the only familiar comfort she'd found since arriving for the second time tonight.

Something was wrong here. Very, very wrong.

Her godfather seldom invited colleagues into his home, but never did he invite men of Peter Deacon's character. The gothic gingerbread functioned as Wick's living quarters, yes, but the house also sat atop the computer lab that was the hub of the estate's activity and the core location to which the majority of his visitors migrated immediately upon arrival.

They didn't come for dinner. They didn't stay in the upstairs guest room suite. And they certainly didn't require her escort services—so to speak.

Most were the lab rats of which she'd spoken earlier, and lived the cliché, rarely sleeping, rarely eating, speaking to one another in binary instead of more accessible languages like Latin or Greek. Natasha seldom had reason to visit the lab. She handled her godfather's calls and correspondence—both printed and electronic—and made his appointments along with the few travel arrangements he still required.

Thinking about it in those terms, the job didn't sound like much until one factored in the global scope of Wick's reach. In reality, Natasha was as much diplomat or envoy as personal assistant. As busy as she was, as long the hours she kept, she never disturbed him when he was at work down below. Her arena was aboveground, both in the city and here at the estate, making her the least likely candidate for effective guide.

That said, she would hardly score points by refusing his request, though she did wish he had checked with her before he'd guaranteed her services to Peter. She had so much on her upcoming plate that required her time and attention. Yet, even drawing enough of a salary to afford Ralph Lauren, Jimmy Choo, and her Infiniti FX45, it wasn't enough to argue that one of the rats would make a better companion.

Wick ruled his castle as if he were king, his staff and houseguests his subjects. And that was the thing, she mused, squishing the carpet between her bare toes. She couldn't imagine Peter Deacon subjecting himself to any authority figure. Such an image, the man pledging fealty from his Ferrari, made no sense.

She'd known him less than two hours, hardly enough time to make his acquaintance, much less form a learned opinion. But that much she knew. That, and the fact that the man he was exquisitely reinforced how opposite were the sexes—and how dull her romantic life of late. A dullness to which she could see him adding a much needed shine. He was the quintessence of everything she loved in the male of the species—and she'd always been mad about men.

Tall and broad-shouldered and built. Blue eyes to drown in. A dimpled smile to knock her off her feet. But more than a compilation of all those clichés, he was confident. Successful. Powerful. He was observant, wrapping her in his coat when she was chilled. Generous. How many others would have let her behind the wheel of a nearly half-million-dollar car? Hot-bodied cars. Hot-bodied men.

She pressed both palms to the flutters in her belly, slipping her fingers down to the coiled tension between her legs, knowing the relief a quick orgasm would bring. She would . . . but she didn't have time. And if she wasn't careful, very, very careful, she was going to blow her good intentions not to fall into bed until she'd learned more about a man than how fully he turned her on.

A knock at the door brought her head up and her pensiveness to a halt. She hesitated briefly, then shook off the last few minutes of misgivings and headed for the door, slipping her feet into strappy black sandals along the way.

"Wick. Come in." Stepping back, she gestured him inside.

But Wick shook his head, his hands laced in his lap as he glanced up at her over the gold rims of his bifocals. "You seem to be ready. We can talk on the way to the dining room."

"Sure. Let me grab a wrap." The dining room remained perpetually cold, and she tossed the fringed silk shawl over her shoulders as she pulled the door closed behind her. She hadn't seen her godfather since returning from the spur-of-the-moment drive to Overlook Point, and an apology was in order.

"I met your guest earlier," she began, walking alongside Wick's wheelchair down the second floor hallway. "We drove out to the lake, so I'm to blame for dinner being late. I should have let you know before taking off like that."

"Mrs. Courtney has a sixth sense for timing her meals. I'm sure none of us will suffer for your . . . disregard."

Natasha cringed. "I do apologize. It's just that when I drove up, Mr. Deacon was outside. And he drives a Ferrari, did you know that?"

Wick seemed to hedge, but Natasha heard rather than saw his smile when he said, "No, but that would explain the impromptu drive to the point."

"You should see it. All that sexy metallic black and leather. And the horsepower." She reached down, vigorously rubbed his shoulder. "If you're undecided on what to buy me for Christmas . . ."

At that, Wick laughed; the deep, familiar, and humor-filled

rumble tickled Natasha's palm. "I'll be sure to let Mr. Claus know."

Natasha grinned, glad to be forgiven. And to see her godfather in good spirits. As his health deteriorated, so did the state of his moods, yet his mind remained as sharp as ever. Knowing the slow, wicked death he faced, becoming a prisoner in his own body . . .

She squeezed his shoulder again, dispelling what she could of her anxiety. "You know, I'll bet I could talk Mr. Deacon into letting me take you for a ride."

They'd reached the elevator door at the end of the corridor. Wick brought his wheelchair to a stop. He pulled his glasses from his face, then a handkerchief from his suit coat pocket, and cleaned the lenses.

He delayed a long, thought-filled moment before he looked up. "I depend on you too much, Natasha. You never fail to make me laugh when I disabuse myself of having reason to—"

"Of course you have reason to," she began, stopping once she realized the list she was getting ready to tick off was hers, not his. He lifted a brow expressively, forcing her admission of chagrin. "Well, you have me, anyway. Use me at will."

"I do hope you mean that, dear."

She studied his face; the grooves around his mouth appeared to be deeper now than when she'd been here earlier in the week, the sallow tinge to his complexion more noticeable. His eyes were as bright and expressive as always, but the tired circles beneath broke her heart.

Leaning down, she kissed his cheek. "I don't say what I don't mean as a rule."

Wick considered that, then said, "I'd like to hear your impression of Peter Deacon."

Natasha straightened, sighed. The hot-bodied part of her impression of their visitor was probably best not spoken aloud. That or the way he'd felt sitting there beside her on the wall at Overlook Point. He'd felt like a fantasy, as if he'd come out of the dark when she'd most needed to look up and find him waiting.

Funny, that, as she'd been reared to be independent, and had never needed to look up and find any man. "Actually, it was a quick drive. We hardly had time to talk."

"I don't need to know what you talked about," Wick said, his mouth grim now. "Merely your impression."

Yes, but the meat of her impression had been formed based on their conversation. Not so much on what he'd said but on the tone of his voice, the way he'd looked at her while speaking, as if he were trying to see beneath the surface of what she'd revealed to the truth.

A strange sensation, since she considered herself an open book and hadn't kept anything from him—anything beyond the urge to place her palm to his cheek, to feel the heat of his skin, his stubble, the strength in his jaw.

He, in fact, had been the secretive one, and she wondered if that was what Wick was asking. "He seemed quite intense, actually. Focused, I suppose," she added, recalling the other man's eyes. "I'd say he was evasive, but that's more than likely the response of my unsatisfied curiosity."

"A man able to resist your inquisitive nature?" Wick chuckled softly. "I'm impressed."

"*And* you're making fun of me."

"Only because I adore you and know I can get away with it."

Unfortunately, he was right. She adored him equally and always enjoyed their teasing thrust and parry. "So? Are you going to fill me in on why he's here?"

He wheeled his chair around to face her. "He didn't tell you?"

She shrugged noncommittally. "Not specifically, though I assume it has to do with Dr. Jinks's project."

"Why?"

"Why do I assume it has to do with Dr. Jinks?" she asked, and when Wick nodded she said, "Because Mr. Deacon mentioned the timing, the project reaching completion."

"That was all?" Wick's brow went up.

"About his reason for being here? Yes." She hesitated before saying more, staring briefly at the abstract pattern in the hallway's cream and wine-colored carpet before going on. "Though he did suggest that you've put me at his disposal for the duration of his visit."

Wick considered her for a long moment before saying, "I hope that's not a problem for you."

"It's not, as long as neither of you expect me to show him anything of the lab." She adjusted the shawl slipping from her shoulders. "Or at least to do more than a cursory walk-through."

"I'll handle showing Mr. Deacon the lab. What I'd like you to do"—Wick pressed his lips closed as he searched for the words—"is make him comfortable while he's here, provide him with anything—no, *everything* he might possibly need."

Everything? She felt the first stirrings of unease. "What exactly are you asking me to do here?"

"I can't emphasize how important this is to me, Natasha. How imperative it is that he enjoy his stay."

"Then I'll see that he does," she replied, frowning. She never questioned her godfather's requests, but this one had an added hint of desperation she hadn't previously sensed. A desperation that had her remembering their guest's comment about her godfather becoming a very wealthy man. Curiouser and curiouser as the night went on.

"Thank you, my dear." Wick reached out then and pressed the button to signal the elevator. "And I hope you don't mind, but I asked Mr. Deacon to wait for you at the bottom of the staircase. Please escort him to the dining room. I'm sure Mrs. Courtney is beyond ready to serve the four of us."

"Four?"

"Yes." The elevator car arrived; the doors opened, and Wick wheeled his chair inside in reverse, adding, just as the door closed, "Dr. Jinks will be joining us as well."

Christian leaned a shoulder on the wooden ball topping the staircase balustrade, stared at the grandfather clock at the base of the foyer stairs, and waited. He'd always assumed those dealing with Spectra's agent knew he was not a man one kept waiting. Yet all he'd done since arriving this evening was wait.

Upon returning from the drive with Natasha and checking in on the professor in his office, he'd headed for the suite where he was staying to set up his laptop and wireless connection. He'd had no need yet to contact Smithson and wouldn't do so from this location unless left with no choice, but he went nowhere without the secure and ready access to his files.

The cost of leaving himself vulnerable was too hefty to pay twice in a lifetime. Now he made sure every angle of his ass was covered all of the time.

This mission's main saving grace was Spectra's M.O. When Deacon or any of the organization's higher-ups traveled to the States from their headquarters in the islands of the Netherlands Antilles, they flew solo. No contact with the behind-the-scenes machine.

It was a cardinal rule of the operation, no different than it had been seven years ago when Deacon's predecessor and his team of Thai drug-runners left Christian to rot in the jungle's steaming heat—heat that crawled over skin with centipede feet, that seeped stinging into open and weeping sores.

Heat that stole a man's breath as it worked to steal his mind, to rob him of his sight until he didn't know if the things he saw were real or hallucination's monsters. If he'd dreamed the sounds he'd heard or dreamed that he'd dreamed them. If the prodding searches of his body, the invasions and assaults, had happened, or if he'd simply gone insane.

Christian pushed away from the staircase and was halfway across the foyer's marble floor to the front door before he pulled himself to a stop. He was so close, so goddamn close. Another few steps and he'd be out the door and sliding down into the Ferrari's leather bucket. He'd be back at the farm in no time, back to where he could tell Hank in person to take him off all Spectra scenarios, starting now.

It was the memory of the crude guerilla prison that had his jaw grinding, though his feet stood still. The prison, and how it had been Hank who'd freed him, Hank who'd left the barely recognizable Spectra agent in Christian's place, wearing what remained of Christian's clothing. Left the man behind his own bars to die of bullet wounds from his own men.

And that was why Christian would stay. His loyalty to the leader of the Smithson Group demanded no less.

He shoved his fists into his pockets. Making sure Spectra didn't get their hands on whatever it was they were forcing Jinks to do, while freeing the man at the center of their plan, was nothing. A walk in the park.

All he had to do was remember that he was taking that walk in upstate New York and not in the jungles of Chiang Rai.

At the sound of footsteps on the stairs, he swallowed his adrenaline-hyped heart, turned slowly, and watched Natasha descend. Earlier, she'd looked like the epitome of a corporate professional—or that had been his impression, seeing her climb down from her SUV before she'd been hit with Ferrari fever.

But now . . . Now she was all woman. Soft and flowing and female, the hem of her dress swinging around her knees and giving him a nice long look up her skirt at her bare thighs as she made her way down.

He walked toward her, toward the base of the staircase, settling one hand against the balustrade's finial as he waited for her, this nine-lived chameleon who was to be his guide. The heavy flow of his blood through his veins told him how clearly he was anticipating time spent in her company.

And he'd be lying to himself if he denied the source of the tingling buzz at the base of his spine.

He wanted to take her to bed.

She smiled down at him, skirt flaring, hair swinging, and the tingle took on an electric heat.

"I hope you haven't been waiting long."

Just long enough to regain his bearings, he mused as he shook his head. "It's been worth it."

"It's been worth what?" she queried, coming to a stop two steps from the bottom of the staircase.

Two steps that put him eye level with her chest. She was breathing as hard as he was, and she wasn't wearing a bra.

"Watching you." He waited a moment then gave a small nod. "Nice dress."

Her cheeks bloomed a soft pink; she tucked her wrap tighter around her arms and shoulders. If she was trying to blame her body's response on the room's temperature, he wasn't buying it. He'd followed her approach and knew exactly when her nipples had tightened.

"Thank you. Wick enjoys a more formal dinner hour. Or two." She canted her head and considered him. "You look quite dashing yourself."

He'd changed his shirt, added a tie, still wore the black pin-striped Armani and the boots. He hadn't bothered to shave. "Dashing. Hmm."

"You don't think so?" she asked, her grin getting to him.

"I don't think a lot about how I look." Aw, shit. *Character, Bane. Play the part.* Who knew how much her godfather had told her about Deacon's obsession with fashion and style? He moved up onto the step that separated them, ran a hand along the railing until his fingers touched hers. "Why waste the time when I can enjoy looking at you?"

She left her hand where it was, even as he waited for her to back away. She didn't, and in the next second she lifted two of her fingers, the first and the second, so that the tips brushed the vee between his forefinger and thumb.

"What's that they say about flattery?" she asked with a gently teasing lilt to her voice.

"That it's going to take me where I want to go?" Boldly, he moved his free hand beneath her wrap and settled it on the swell of her hip. She was soft; she was strong. He felt both in the long lean curve of her body. He felt her tremble, as well, and the tingling at his spine bored inward.

She cleared her throat, her eyes glowing brightly. "It might. Eventually. But right now, Wick is expecting us."

"And what Dr. Bow wants, he gets." Wasn't that what she'd said?

"Something like that," she responded, though she didn't move.

Christian did, raising his hand at the same time he lowered his gaze. He measured her ribs with his fingers, her ribs that expanded around her lungs and her deep labored breaths. When he reached the plump side of her breast, he stopped, his thumb resting beneath the full lower curve, stroking in a downward motion when what he wanted to do was stroke up.

"We could skip dinner," he suggested, his gaze returning to hers at half-mast as she leaned into the motion of his hand.

"I don't think that would be a good idea," she murmured.

"Why? Because you don't want to disappoint your godfather?"

She gave a noncommittal shake of her head. "That's part of it."

Christian's hand stilled. "Are you afraid of him?"

"Not at all," she said, her voice low and breathy. "Why would you ask that?"

He wanted to know what hold Bow had over her, the extent of her loyalty. How far she would go. He wanted to know if she was playing a part even now, or if what she was feeling was real, because that raw tingling buzz was now poker hot and flaring toward his groin.

He captured her gaze as he moved his thumb, this time in an upward sweep, over the firm swell of her breast to the center, where her nipple stood beaded and taut. His own breathing uneven, he said, "Does he punish you if you disobey?"

She laughed at that, then pulled in a harsh breath when he moved his thumb in a circle. "Wick doesn't punish me. He would reprimand me if he felt he had reason. But I don't give him reason."

And there was Christian's answer to the question of Natasha's loyalty, though the flush to her face, the glassy brightness of her eyes, told the truth of her conflicted desires. "I think you should give him one. Tonight. With me."

"I would never have taken you for the type to enjoy punishment, Mr. Deacon."

"Peter," he said, and tightened his hold on her ribs. The fire in his belly burned like coals from hell. "Call me Peter."

"Peter, then," she said, sliding her hand from the banister to rest on the back of his. "We should be going."

"After dinner, then," he pressed. He wasn't through with her yet. Not halfway through. But the break would give his blood time to return to the head where he needed to be thinking. "You *are* at my disposal?"

"Absolutely."

Her husky affirmation even more than her smile nearly sent him to his knees. What the hell was he doing? What the hell was going on? *Play the part, Bane. Play her and play the part.* This game wasn't about getting laid. Yet even as he served up the reminder, he slipped his hand around to the small of her back and pulled her flush to his body.

To Peter Deacon's body.

His mouth was but inches from hers when he said, "After you."

She took a deep breath and blew it out with a light shudder as she made her way to the foyer floor and stopped. "I'm sure by now Wick and Dr. Jinks are wondering where we are."

Christian stopped beside her, saw her mouth move, saw the sweep of her long dark lashes, saw the tiny flare of her nostrils—and saw all of it in slow motion.

What had she just said? "Dr. Jinks will be joining us?"

She frowned up at him. "Wick invited him, yes. I assume that won't be a problem? It is his project you're here for, isn't it?"

"You know about Dr. Jinks's project?" Christian swore his heart was seconds from bursting in his chest.

At his side, Natasha shook her head, confusion creasing her brow. "Not the details, no. I do know that he's finishing up the beta testing of what he's been working on. The timing is why I made the connection between the two of you."

The timing. Right. Not that she had been aware beforehand. Not that she knew the details. Not that she was up to her eyeballs in this scheme along with her godfather.

And no admission that Dr. Jinks was being held against his will.

Christian tightened his hold on her waist, determined to get to the truth. He turned toward her, one hand slipping around to her back and pulling her close, the other moving up to cup her jaw, her cheek, his fingers sliding into her hair. Her gaze grew sleepy, sexy. Her lashes fluttered down, then back up.

When she smiled, he felt it in the palm of his hand as deeply as in his gut, and swore her pleasure at the physical contact was only part of it.

Her enjoyment of the secrets she kept was the rest.

He touched his thumb to the corner of her mouth. "I hope I'm responsible for this."

"Oh, you are." Her smile widened.

"But?" he asked, since he sensed it coming.

"But I'm afraid it's not what you think."

He stroked the line of her jaw. "You know what I'm thinking?"

She nodded, briefly catching the lower edge of her lip with her teeth. "You're thinking that my working for Wick means I know all about his business."

"And you don't," he said, moving his hand to her neck to measure her pulse, which beat hard and fast. Not with the sure, steady pace of a consummate liar.

"Trust me. I'm no more involved with the lab work than Wick is with balancing his accounts." She took a deep breath and a distancing step away. "I hope that doesn't disappoint you."

"On the contrary," he said, returning his fists to his pockets. "It will make it much easier for us to separate business from pleasure."

Four

Never put off till tomorrow what you can do today.

Never bite off more than you can chew.

Never cross a bridge until you come to it.

Never try to out-con a con man.

His tie a choking hazard worse than any toy with small parts, Woody Jinks stuck a finger in his shirt collar and tugged, tuning out the voices in his head. It was like hearing his mother's child-rearing proverbs blasted in Dolby Digital Surround EX. Except the last one. The con man part.

That one was all his. It was also the very reason he found himself eyeball-deep in the worst crap he'd ever thought to see in his life.

"Natasha is on her way downstairs," Dr. Bow was saying as they made their way from his office into the dining room, where the table was set with a lacy tablecloth, tall skinny candles, napkins folded into fans, and as many forks and spoons as Woody had chucked into the trash during the years he'd eaten in Polytechnic's commons.

The floor here wasn't the same industrial-strength tile but a chessboard of slick wooden squares, and the rubber soles of his sneakers squeaked like farts when he walked. He was nervous enough to laugh, but he doubted Dr. Bow would think it was funny. The old man had, like, zero sense of humor anymore—a truth Woody had discovered when he'd hacked the lab's intranet firewall just to prove it could be done.

"Cool. It'll be good to see her again." He said it automatically, then realized he totally meant it. He hadn't seen her much since he'd been here. A real fuckin' shame, because Natasha Gaudet was amazingly hot.

"I'm sorry you haven't had time to enjoy more of her company." Dr. Bow wheeled his chair to the head of the table. "She's been quite busy these last two months at the university, as well as tied up with a personal matter she is helping to organize for me."

"No worries. It's not like I've had a lot of time to party anyway, right?"

"Well, soon you should have time to socialize to your heart's content." Hands laced over his puffy-looking gut, Dr. Bow offered up a fatherly sort of look. "And the money to enjoy all the women you want, yes?"

Woody nodded, saying nothing about their deal, which seemed to be the best way to make sure he didn't say anything he shouldn't. He'd never been good at keeping secrets, and this one was killing him in a very bad way.

He cast his gaze the length of the table and back. "Am I supposed to sit anywhere in particular?"

"To my left will be fine. Natasha always sits to my right." The older man gestured from side to side, and nodded toward the table's other end. "And Mr. Deacon can sit across from me."

At the mention of the Spectra IT rep, Woody swallowed and swore he was going to puke up his guts. If he made it through these next two weeks, he promised himself he would never again confuse reality with playing Counter-Strike. "Yeah, I'm looking forward to meeting him."

"And now you shall." Dr. Bow nodded toward the dining room's door.

Bouncing from the toe of one sneaker to the other, Woody turned. But he saw only Natasha. And either she was freezing cold or was really turned on because her dress had, like, these *huge* headlights.

She walked right up to him, her smile mystical and magical. He coughed once, twice, tugged again at the knot of his tie.

"It's good to see you again, Dr. Jinks," she was saying, and all he could do was nod because for a minute there he couldn't even breathe.

"You, too," he finally got out, shaking the hand she offered. It felt so tiny and so warm, and her smile was going to kill him even before lack of O2.

"I don't believe you've met Mr. Deacon yet."

"Uh, no. I haven't." He released her hand, though not her gaze, because looking at her was like seeing Zatanna Zatara come to life, and the guys on the comic book boards were so not going to believe it.

Too bad he wouldn't be able to post there ever again. Not as himself, anyway. Once he got hooked up through Iridium's satellite service, he'd have to come up with a new e-mail address and use an anonymous proxy for the IP.

"Dr. Woodrow Jinks? Peter Deacon. Peter, Woodrow Jinks."

Okay. He could do this. He could do this. As long as he didn't get stupid and start asking about the perks that came with a career in organized crime.

Swallowing the gagging ball of snot in his throat, Woody turned his attention to the other man. A nice enough lookin' guy. Younger than he'd figured—a thought that made him want to laugh since everyone he met said the same thing about him.

Except he suddenly doubted he'd ever laugh again. Not after getting a look into Deacon's eyes.

And then being twenty-four years old and having a doctorate meant nothing because he was back in first grade again, the big-eared, big-footed playground target getting slammed from all sides with the dodgeball. His palm was sweating when he shook the other man's hand.

"Nice to meet you, dude," he said and cringed. *Dude*. He'd

called him dude. He was such freakin' cement-shoe fish bait. Or whatever ways guys like those in *The Sopranos* did away with scum. He really should've boned up on the show and given up his Xena reruns before coming here.

Deacon's brow went up. His grip tightened. His expression cut into Woody's gut like the edge of Xena's Chakram. "Ditto. I'm looking forward to our association."

"Uh, yeah. Me, too." Woody ran a hand back over the hair he couldn't remember if he'd combed. "Should be a kick."

"Natasha? Please, come sit before Mrs. Courtney feeds our dinner to the dogs," Dr. Bow said.

Woody pulled out his own chair, then felt like a complete dork when Deacon walked Natasha around to hers.

Not that Woody thought he had a chance with her, but he would do just about anything to have her look at him the way she was looking at the Sopranos dude, her eyes all soft and her mouth open and sweet and wet.

He squirmed in his seat, tugged at the fly of his pants. Yeah. He'd do anything, he mused, smiling at the sick thought that he might even take a cue from the company he was keeping and knock off the competition permanently.

In this place? Surrounded by these people?

How hard could it possibly be to get away with murder?

Natasha lost her appetite ten minutes into the meal. An ebullient Mrs. Courtney served plates laden with poached salmon, mustard dill sauce drizzled over steamed asparagus, and garlic new potatoes. The aromas were mouthwatering. The ambience was tasteful. Dr. Jinks took one bite of his food and broke out in hives.

The following minutes were a flurry of activity as Wick excused them all in order to give Woody privacy, sending Mrs. Courtney for the younger man's medication. In the chaos, Peter vanished without saying a word. Once Natasha realized her charge didn't require her services and that Wick's nurse-cum-housekeeper had her new patient well in hand, she left the house for a breath of fresh air.

After the last few hours, air was the very least she needed. Sleep sounded damn good. Alcohol even better. But when she pulled her shawl tighter against the night's subtle chill, she had to force herself to admit it wasn't the weather responsible for the tremor running from her nape to her fingertips.

It was her intuitive sexual response to Peter Deacon.

Confined on the estate and assigned to see to his *every* need . . . She shook her head. Fate was tempting her cruelly, bringing him into her life after she'd determined to be more tortoise than hare when it came to taking any relationship to an intimate level. Yet she was quite certain that staying out of this man's bed was going to drive her mad.

Her heels clicked against the flagstones as she walked along the lower edge of the tiered terrace that wrapped around the front of the house like stair steps. She remembered the cocktail parties Wick had once thrown here, and her father, believing baby-sitters to be the devil's spawn, sneaking her in. What days those had been! Ladies in hats and gloves and smart dresses. Men in their same racetrack finery.

The talk had been of horses and handicaps, and Natasha had crouched beneath umbrella tables wearing yellow dotted Swiss and white patent leather, pretending invisibility as she soaked up the conversation, the bubbly laughter, the dynamics of power and position determined by love, lust, lucre, and loathing. The later those hours had reached into the night, the further from the hub of the parties she'd drifted. Her father, however, had always known where to find her once he'd deemed her bedtime at hand.

Today, Mr. Courtney, the gardener, still fertilized, weeded, and pruned, but the terrace gardens hadn't heard more than the chatter of chipmunks and squirrels for years. Instead of the occasional cigarette butt or soiled cocktail napkin, the ground was now littered with acorn hulls and birdseed. She hated the loss of Wick's social life, feared the effect on his emotional health, but selfishly enjoyed claiming the terrace as her own private retreat.

Reaching the half-moon bench farthest from the house, she

sat and slipped off her shoes. The flagstones beneath her feet held the warmth of the day's sun, as did the cement of the seat. But remembering her earlier encounter with Peter there on the foyer staircase, she couldn't help but shiver and draw her fringed shawl close.

"You're welcome to my coat if you need it."

His coat that smelled of a strangely exquisite herbal elegance and his body's heat. She staved off the shudders that threatened to permanently settle into her bones. "Are you following me, Mr. Deacon?"

"Peter."

"Peter, then."

"Following, no. I've been standing here watching you for ten minutes at least." He stepped out of the shadows, from the dark corner where the terrace ended and the dense woods began. "One might wonder if you were following me."

"One might." Though what she really wondered was what he was doing down here so far from the house. No one visited this corner of the estate any longer. And even with Dr. Jinks not feeling well, she didn't understand why Peter had yet to go downstairs and check out the lab.

Like she'd thought earlier, something here was very, very wrong.

She sat unmoving, barely breathing inside the half-moon's center, waiting as he walked behind her along the bench's long outside curve. To look at him now, she would have to turn her head. Instead, she crossed her arms over her chest and tightened the hold on her shawl.

It offered little in the way of a defense against the tug of attraction, especially when he sat down beside her, shoulder to shoulder, hip to hip, temptation so close she could taste it. She looked toward him. He looked toward her. Their gazes caught and held.

And she said the safest thing on her mind. "I wasn't expecting to see you again before breakfast. I assumed you had gone underground."

"The lab's not going anywhere." He reached his far hand

toward her and ran the backs of his fingers down her arm. "You, I wasn't so sure about."

She couldn't help it. She trembled. The sheer silk of her shawl only heightened the sensation of his touch. "Why would you think that when Wick made it clear I'm to be at your beck and call?"

He canted his head to the side; his eyes flashed. "Put like that, you don't seem thrilled with the prospect."

She shook her head, avoiding his searching gaze. "It's not that. It's just . . ."

His fingers made another trip from her shoulder to the bend of her elbow. "Just what?"

She had to fight her eyelashes from fluttering down. Repeatedly tonight, she'd fallen prey to his touch, his words, to the idea that he didn't know her from Eve, yet he wanted her. But there was the small matter of trust. Not to mention that tortoise thing.

Still, she'd always felt the pull of a mystery. And when it came with a man attached . . . "You're not a lab rat, but you're still here to do business with the boys in the basement. It would only make sense that you monitor your investment closely. Especially considering the money you claim is at stake."

For a long moment, he didn't react. He only stared into her eyes unblinking, leaving her again with the feeling that she was forensic evidence laid bare beneath his microscope. But then a chuckle rumbled low in his chest, and at long last she remembered that she needed to breathe.

"The boys in the basement," he repeated. "Is that what you call them?"

She nodded, fought a grin, leaned instinctively toward him, even though he'd blown off addressing the rest of her speech. Her shoulder brushed his as she said, "I've been known to call them worse. Especially when they keep Wick up all hours of the night. They forget that he's not as young as they are, or as invincible as they consider themselves. Though, since Dr. Jinks arrived, no one else has been up here to work."

His eyes narrowing, Peter seemed to mull over that tidbit before saying, "I'm not so sure Dr. Jinks is considering himself anything but human at the moment."

She sighed, shook her head. "It's a good thing he wasn't very hungry. I can't imagine how much worse his reaction would have been if he'd actually eaten more."

"It wasn't a lack of appetite that kept him from eating," Peter said, his voice having dropped to a low, seductive, toe-curling tone. This time when he touched her, he slid his hand beneath the fringe of her shawl, caressing bare skin from forearm to shoulder.

This time she allowed the resulting shiver to run its course, allowed the flutters between her legs to blossom. God, but she felt alive like she hadn't in . . . in . . . if ever. "What was it then?"

"It was the distraction of sitting across the table from you."

When he pulled the fringed silk from her near shoulder, she let him. When he leaned down and breathed in the scent of her skin, she watched him. When he parted his lips to taste her, to kiss the skin between her arm and the swell of her breast, she very simply wanted him.

"Am I a distraction?" she asked once he'd straightened and faced her.

He spoke with his eyes. The blue-green irises shimmered. The lids above grew heavy as if desire drew his thick lashes down. "Since watching you circle the Ferrari, I've thought of nothing but tasting you."

Oh, but she was in trouble, what with the images his claim brought to mind. She barely managed a whisper to ask, "And how do I taste?"

"Like I want more." He angled his body across hers then, trapping her with a hand on the bench at her hip. His biceps brushed the taut peak of one breast when he leaned forward and moved his mouth to her ear. "Like you're wearing too many clothes for me to get to you the way I want."

Her eyelids drifted down and her imagination ran wild, working to catch up with her body, which sizzled and steamed. This was insane, this physical need he inspired with his suggestively sexy words. Any other man she would've had the strength to push away. Inexplicably, she wanted to pull this one near.

She turned her cheek into his, rubbed her tender skin over his beard, which was coarse. His breath on her face was warm, as was the trail of nips he left along her jaw as he made his searching way to her mouth.

She opened her eyes only far enough to see his lips hover over her own. Her heart beat frantically in her aching chest. Her skin burned with the fire of anticipation. Her tongue slipped out to bathe her lips, and his parted. Yet when she would have leaned into his kiss, he pulled back.

"Are you sure this is what you want?" he asked, his voice low, his eyes dark.

Right here and right now? Yes, without question. She released her shawl, sensed it fluttering to the ground behind her, and pressed her hand to the center of his chest. "What do you want?"

"I want it all," he said, and then his mouth was on hers, his hand in her hair holding her head.

Her first thought was magic. Her second was thrilling fun. After that, she stopped thinking and lost herself in the kiss. He was hard even as he was gentle, both the pressure of his fingers and that of his mouth.

She parted her lips freely, welcomed the intrusion of his tongue, wished boldly, then shyly, to feel that same probing pressure between her legs. She kissed him back, sliding her tongue over his and filling his mouth as she worked to free the buttons of his shirt. Her hands shook, and she gasped with relief the moment her fingers found skin.

He ground his mouth harder against hers in response to her tactile exploration of his collarbone and the corded tendons of his neck. She cupped his throat, her thumbs humming with the reverb of his pulse. She drank of his mouth, loving the way he so expertly swept his tongue along the length of hers, the give-and-take pressure of his lips as he coaxed her to reach for more.

No other kiss, no other man . . . This made no sense, this

burning need to know him. Yet even more so, she wanted him to know her in ways they couldn't manage from here. And so, reluctantly, she reached for her inner tortoise and began to ease away. She wanted to go wherever he chose to take her, but sex on a cold cement bench held little appeal.

She wanted to explore him, to arouse him, to do so much more than get the both of them off with a quick groping fuck managed through opened flies and raised skirts, and told him by trailing her fingertips down the column of his throat, over his Adam's apple to the hollow beneath. His chest rose and fell like a bellows, and she quite enjoyed knowing she wasn't the only one struggling to breathe.

It was when she returned her gaze to his that she realized the good luck of her timing. Had she looked up first and seen that soulful hunger, she'd never have been able to tell herself no. He looked like a man longing for a woman's healing, soothing touch, and it was the hardest thing she'd ever done to make herself wait. She wanted more than anything to settle her naked bottom over his naked lap and rock his pain away, rock the both of them into a state of physical bliss.

"Want to know a secret?" she finally asked to break the darkly moody silence.

He lifted a brow, said nothing.

She tried the smile again. "I think the backs of my thighs have frozen to this bench."

This time it worked. The corner of his mouth crooked upward, and even his frown softened. And then he stood and straddled the bench, stepping across to the side where she sat and helping her to her feet with a hand at her elbow.

Her thighs, of course, were just fine. "Come here. I want to show you something."

She led him to the edge of the terrace and the waist-high iron fencing that separated the lawn from the estate's undeveloped acreage. The thickly wooded terrain seemed to fall away from the house and manicured grounds, leaving the gothic gingerbread sitting above as if on a pedestal cake plate.

Peter had released her arm as they crossed the short width

of the terrace, but she sensed him hovering when she leaned her forearms on the rail of the ornamental barrier. Her feet still bare, her shoes dangled from her fingers as she looked off into the distance.

"Between those two stands of trees?" She pointed in that direction. "Can you see the lake?"

"Sure. That's the lake from earlier."

She nodded. "It's not as easy to see as it was when I was a girl. The forest is so much thicker now. And I'm definitely taller. Anyway, this used to be one of my favorite spots to come sit when hiding from my father."

"You lived here then?"

"No. My father and Wick were friends long before he inherited this place. My parents divorced when I was eleven, and my father had custody. He used to bring me out here when he'd come to visit. I was pretty much a permanent fixture any time he and Wick got together, and they eventually forgot to censor their discussions." She chuckled. "That was when I decided my favorite hobby was eavesdropping."

"And when you started flirting with the first of your nine lives?"

She laughed again. "Could very well be. Eventually, though, either Wick or my father would snap back to reality long enough to order me to bed. I hated it. Absolutely hated it. It felt like punishment, not parenting."

"And you wouldn't go."

"I would, but I'd sneak out here later." She'd loved it out here, the darkness, the solitude, the time spent alone to pick apart and digest the questions raised by the conversations she'd heard. She supposed Peter was right, that those days had given birth to her curious nature.

"I'd be furious that I wasn't allowed to stay up as long as I wanted and just knew I was going to miss something good. So I'd come out here and pretend I was being held against my will. This fence was my prison. And if I could make it to the lake, I'd be free and never have to go to bed again."

She rubbed her palms up and down her bare arms, now

wishing for her shawl, or at least for Peter's coat; surely he could see that she was cold. Or maybe not, as the moon had dipped behind a bank of encroaching clouds.

Sighing, she turned with a smile to make her request—only to find him gone. Not walking away. Not returned to the shadows. Not sitting on the bench waiting for her to join him.

He was simply gone.

Five

Christian clutched a highball glass in one hand and braced the palm of his other on the window frame as he stared out from his second-story suite at the same view Natasha had shown him below. From behind the fence she'd likened to prison bars. Off toward the lake where she'd looked for freedom.

It was his second drink, and he was well on his way to a third, possibly a fourth. Or he would've been. Except that while he watched her cross the terrace for her wrap and head back to the house, the reality of where he was and why he was here came crashing in.

And goddamn if he didn't need to get a grip.

He was Peter Deacon. He was not Christian Bane. And he didn't like the fact that one night in Natasha's company was blurring those lines. A lack of focus was a death sentence for an SG-5 operative, but he had to face it. The facts of this assignment were no longer crystal clear.

Neither was his line of attack.

He'd admitted the absolute truth when he'd told her he'd wanted to get his hands and mouth on her from the moment they'd met. Making that admission hadn't exactly been a moment of thrilling self-enlightenment. Especially since he was the operative who avoided mission-casual entanglements with the opposite sex.

Hell, who was he kidding? His entanglements with the opposite sex had been nothing but mutually mind-bending and anonymous fucks for years now.

It wouldn't be that way when he took Natasha to bed. He would . . . and soon. As much as he was looking forward to enjoying her body as Peter Deacon, however, he was not the least bit gung-ho about the price he, Christian Bane, would have to pay personally, privately, and painfully for getting emotionally naked.

And it would happen. That was one part of who *he* was that no role-playing game could disguise.

Walking away without saying a word to her earlier had been a cheap trick, but she'd started talking about escaping her imaginary prison, and his past had rolled back in haunting, menacing waves, more powerful for their invisible undertow sweeping over him and dragging him down.

Still, personal issues weren't at stake here. And he wasn't going to get very far if he didn't keep that foremost in mind.

He had a feeling Natasha's curious nature was going to benefit his mission's cause. Though she seemed intent on prying out his secrets—*What was he doing here? How long did he plan to stay? Why hadn't he spent more time in the basement?*—she was much less reticent to reveal her own private thoughts.

Unless, of course, she was playing him to the same extent that he was playing her. Discovering that truth was now his top priority, a shift in strategy after what had gone down earlier tonight.

What the hell was Woodrow Jinks doing sitting down to dinner with his kidnapper?

Smithson's intel was never one hundred percent, but to have a mission's main objective blown out of the water less than twenty-four hours in? Uh-uh. Totally unacceptable. Christian needed to know where he was putting his feet each time he took a step.

And Natasha was going to be his ticket onto this runaway train.

He had to get to Hank, or to Tripp, who was monitoring the SG-5 communications while Christian was away. He needed sources double-checked, intel verified, rumors quashed, facts confirmed. He'd managed to relay most of that on the terrace earlier, contacting Smithson's gateway via his satellite phone.

The call would have been rerouted and bounced until even the NSA would be hard pressed to locate either the source or the target, as was the case on all missions. Hank didn't take his sense of duty lightly, or treat his operatives as anything but the invaluable commodities they were.

The one thing Christian would have to request in person, however, was his need to have every detail of Natasha's life laid bare. She was his in. And it was obvious that he was operating blind. Not unfamiliar territory, but it sure as hell wasn't where he did his best work.

The best laid plans of mice and undercover operatives . . .

Returning to the guest suite's bar, he refilled his tumbler and had just reset the decanter's stopper when a knock on the door brought his head up. He glanced at his suit coat draped over the sitting room's wing chair, his tie tossed in the seat, his boots beneath, a lock pick in the sole of the right, a switchblade in the left.

His phone and headset sat next to his laptop on the desk. His SIG-Sauer P-232 9mm was in his attaché propped against the chair leg on the floor. His .45-caliber Ruger P97 and holster were in his garment bag hanging in the closet. Nothing out of place. Everything accessible. He wrapped his hand around the cut crystal and headed for the door.

"I'm sorry to disturb you," Natasha said, standing barefoot on the threshold. "But I didn't think to mention earlier that I won't be available for most of this upcoming weekend. In fact, I'll be leaving early Saturday and gone until Sunday afternoon late."

He'd run out. He owed her an explanation. He'd slit his own throat before he gave her one. He was Peter Deacon, after all.

The fact that she looked like she'd come here to take up

where they'd left off, however, with her hair tousled, her eyes dazed, her lip color eaten away, made it hard to separate his two selves when both of them wanted her. "Does Dr. Bow know this?"

She shook her head, her grin wry. "Everything tonight happened so fast my plans totally slipped my mind. Wick rarely needs me on the weekends so I don't schedule my days off around him. And I wasn't aware of your visit, or had explained what was expected of me until, well, until you were here."

He gestured with the tumbler, filed away the information. "Don't worry about it."

"It's just that I'm getting together with a few of my friends to celebrate a birthday, and it's been on the calendar for awhile . . ." She let the sentence trail and finally shrugged, yet seemed in no hurry to go.

"Thanks for telling me. I'll find something to keep me busy."

"That's one of the other reasons I stopped by."

Christian waited, one heartbeat, two, *boom, boom.* Invite her in or send her away. Listen to his head or to the sweet siren of desire. In the end, she was the one who made up his mind, waiting as if she had more patience than any bloody saint yet looking like original sin.

He stepped back and ushered her inside, wondering with no small twist to his gut what she was doing here or if he even wanted to know. He shut the door behind her, leaning back with one hand on the knob.

Halfway between the doorway and the desk, she turned, a shoe held in each hand. "I *am* supposed to be seeing to your needs while you're here, so would you like me to arrange anything for you to do while I'm gone?"

He fought a grin at the possibilities. "Such as?"

"The library and the media room are off to the left of the foyer if a book or a movie interests you. The lake fishing is actually quite good. And Wick still keeps horses. Mrs. Courtney's husband loves showing off the estate on horseback."

"No, but thanks." He filed that away, too, wondering what about him made her think of fishing. Still . . . why not kill two birds with one stone? He stared down into his drink, swirled the remaining liquid around in the glass before looking up again. "I'm going to have to make an unexpected trip into the city this weekend anyway."

Her eyes lit up.

"My leaving makes you happy?"

"Of course not," she said shyly, dropping her gaze for a moment before going on. "I hate to sound stupid"—she glanced back up—"but are you familiar with the city? Wick didn't mention where you're visiting from."

"I know New York, yes. I have an office there."

"Okay. I just thought . . ."

Snap went his trap. "You thought we could make the drive together?"

"Well, that, yes."

He pushed away from the door, walked toward her. "And?"

She frowned curiously. "And?"

"Instead of a 'but'," he said, then downed the rest of his drink. "It sounded like you wanted to add an 'and'."

She took a deep breath. "I did."

"And?"

"And perhaps you might enjoy having a drink with me and my friends?"

He crossed behind her as he made his way back to the bar, refilling the tumbler with ice and scotch he didn't intend to drink. "As your date?"

"Or my escort. Turnabout, and all of that," she said, worrying her shoes from hand to hand.

He liked her show of nervousness. Liked it a lot. "Had you been planning on attending alone?"

She nodded. "It's not a big deal. I'm okay with doing things on my own."

"Miss Independent?"

"Something like that."

"Why?"

This time when she frowned her expression seemed to be one of confusion. "Why am I independent?"

"Why do you want me to go with you? If you're okay with doing things on your own?" He couldn't deny the small pleasure at seeing her squirm. Meant her façade was subject to cracks and fissures. Taking advantage of both was his specialty.

She squirmed her way into a careless shrug that he didn't buy for a minute. "Just part of making sure you enjoy your visit. That is my job, after all."

"Here, yes. Not on your days off."

"I'm not so sure Wick would see it that way."

"I'm more interested in how you see it." Leaving the drink on the bar, he headed toward her, stopping when they stood toe-to-toe. Hands at his hips, he drew his gaze with precision from her crimson toenails to her face. "If you're asking me because it's what Dr. Bow would want, then we're done."

"That's not the case at all."

He studied her closely, seeing a flash of desperate disappointment before she lowered her lashes. Good. She didn't want to go, making her vulnerabilities his to exploit. Besides, her nervousness intrigued him. Especially having seen her behind the wheel of Deacon's Ferrari.

"Natasha, why did you come here?"

Slowly, her chin came up, as did her lashes, until she returned his searching gaze. "Why did you walk out in the middle of our conversation?"

He blinked, and blinked again, the sound of his eyelids as loud in his ears as a gunshot. *Play the part, Bane. Play the part.* No bedroom confessions about his own prison experience proving her child's play on the terrace to be just that.

His gut knotted. "Why did you get cold feet when I kissed you?"

"It wasn't my feet that were cold, remember?" she asked, her voice having dropped to a whisper.

Yeah, he remembered that lie. "I was sitting beside you. I

had my hand at your hip. I don't buy for a minute your story of being cold. In fact"—he reached for the edge of her wrap draped loosely over her shoulders, toyed with the sheer fabric—"I know exactly how hot you are."

She shrugged, and the garment drifted to the floor. Her shoes followed, a soft *thud, thud* as she dropped them. Her gaze was the third thing to fall, from his eyes to his mouth to the front of his shirt that hung open, and the belt at his waist, still unbuckled. Her examination lingered, and the rise and fall of her chest grew rapidly as she returned her gaze slowly to his.

"How hot am I?" she asked.

He would choke on his voice if he answered. He swore he would fucking choke. The sharp stabbing blade at the base of his spine knifed its way to his balls; his sac drew close to his body instinctively, a self-preservation reflex kicking in.

What the hell was he doing, being afraid, or was fear even what he was feeling? Fear he knew. Fear he'd lived with. But this was a protectively primal urge to seek safety that made zero sense.

With her eyes flashing a challenge Christian was loath to resist, he closed the last few inches between them, raising his hand to the ties at her neck holding her dress in place. As he worked at the fabric fastenings, she moved her hands to his hips, hooking her fingers in his belt loops and holding him in place.

He backed up, bringing her along until his rump hit the desk. Once there, he opened his legs and pulled her between. One of her eyebrows arched, and he knew she was waiting for his answer, yet he still wasn't able to speak. All he was able to do was breathe, and not without effort.

When the ties came free in his hands, he played the loose ends over her neck and bare shoulders, her eyes closing then, her chin lifting as she leaned into the caress. Hot wasn't even the half of what she was. She was hungry, she was ready, she was his. He bent forward, touched his lips to the column of her throat and peeled the dress to her waist.

He explored the soft skin of her neck, nipping lightly, breathing in the scent of spicy florals while cupping both of her breasts. He took his time fondling her, stroking her, nuzzling her, giving her a moment to catch up when his body and his instincts wanted the burning fire now.

It had been so long. God, it had been forever. Or so the waiting caused it to seem. But then she moved her hands up his bare sides, shoved his shirt from his shoulders. And catching up was no longer an issue.

His elbows became trapped in the sleeves but no way was he going to move his hands from her body, even to cut himself free. Especially not when she was making these soft, mewling sounds, offering his hands and mouth complete access to whatever he wanted to take.

She had no idea the hunger ripping and roaring through him, the appetite he kept leashed that even now strained his reins of control. He wanted her heat, wanted her wet mouth and warm, willing cunt, wanted more than he'd wanted from a woman since . . . since . . . no.

Oh, hell no, he thought, as his world fell into the dark abyss of his past.

Not now. *Sonofabitch,* not now.

His heart thundered as he pulled his head away, as strands of her near ink black hair—too close in color, in texture, in scent to Malena's for him to separate one woman from the other—brushed over his cheek. He ground his jaw, certain the bone would shatter before he could see Natasha to the door.

She slid her hands from his shoulders to his elbows, over the fabric of his sleeves to his wrists, and covered his hands on her breasts with her palms. She was so full, so ripe, firm and beautifully rounded, heavy and perfectly real.

And when he would have let her go, she pressed harder into his hold. "Please don't tell me that you're going to turn me down."

He looked up. The challenge was still in her eyes, as was uncertainty and a flickering ember of downright mad. "The way you turned me down earlier on the terrace?"

"I didn't turn you down. I simply prefer soft beds to cement benches."

"I don't play games, Natasha." He was barely managing to play this part. Too much of Peter Deacon, the fabric of who the man was, rubbed against the grain of everything Christian considered decent. Even the bigger picture of bringing down Spectra IT wasn't making this deception any easier to swallow.

And now that he was seeing Malena in Natasha's eyes . . .

"But the rumor that I'll bed any woman given opportunity isn't true." He pulled his hands back to skate his palms over no more than the barest tips of her nipples. Around and around and around, until she shuddered and the peaks hardened. "At the very least, she has to want me, not come to me because it's her job."

He waited for her reaction because, the mission and all the lies aside, he had to know. Did she want him? Or was she selling her body for Peter Deacon's secrets? And what exactly was Bow hoping she'd discover once she took Deacon to bed?

Her expression, however, never wavered. Never grew shuttered as if to hide guilt. Never veiled as if to hide hurt. She seemed unflappable, that steel-willed nature a fascinating display of character. One that renewed the desire he'd never fully tamped down.

Her silence continued as she slid her palms to his wrists, encircled him with her fingers and pushed him away. He shrugged back into his shirt and watched as she snagged up her wrap and her shoes. Her breasts bounced as she bent and straightened, and it was all he could do not to groan.

But instead of heading for the door, she headed for the bar, where she set down her stilettos, freeing her hands to drape and settle the triangle of fringed fabric over her shoulders before she picked up the drink he'd abandoned.

She tossed back the fiery scotch and poured another, looking down as she swirled the melting ice through the liquid, while all Christian could do was stare. At her face, which was set in an expression he couldn't decipher. And at her breasts, which the sheer black material showed off like her dress never had.

Her nipples puckered and his mouth watered; he pushed off the desk and walked toward her. She picked up both shoes, warding him off with that hand while swallowing half of her drink and letting the burn toast its way the length of her throat.

Only then did she turn to face him and approach him, one measured step at a time until she stood but inches away. Fire burned in her eyes; her chest heaved beneath her ragged effort to breathe. And a corresponding coil of desire wrapped itself around the base of his cock and squeezed.

"If you can't tell the difference between a woman who wants you and one who considers sex part of her job, then you have no business bedding anyone." She pushed past him, her shoulder shoving him out of her way.

He didn't even stop to think. The lines blurred further between who he was and was not, and he reached out, grabbed her wrist, and pulled her flush to his body.

Six

His fingers tightened around her wrist until Natasha knew her choices were limited. She stayed, he let her go, or she broke bones fighting to escape.

Independence and feminism be damned, she didn't want to escape. She wanted every bit of what his eyes promised. Never in her life had a man looked at her with Peter's intensity, with a focus that saw all the way to the essence of who she was.

It took all of that strength, that confidence, that composure and independence to keep from offering herself up as the sacrifice that look made her feel. Made her long to be.

Made her *ache* to be.

She wanted him. God, but she wanted him. Wanted him so much and in so many ways—ways she feared could easily make her seem stupid for refusing to resist the temptation of their pull. She didn't care. She was the hare, racing toward the reward for which she'd been waiting. And right now she was beyond separating her body from her brains.

"Did you want something?" Good. Her haughty tone hadn't faltered or broken, allowing her to smoothly slide her gaze from his to the hold he had on her wrist and back again with a questioning arch of her brow.

He nodded, the tic at his temple telling of his battle for control. He hadn't dropped his gaze to her nearly bare breasts even once. "I want you."

She lifted her arm, the one he still held, her pulse beating wildly beneath the binding ring of his fingers as she moved her wrist into his direct line of vision. "This isn't the way to go about it."

A smile crept over his face, the right corner of his mouth crooking upward; the lines that fanned out from his eyes to his temples ran deep. But he didn't for a moment even pretend he would release her. In fact, he held her tighter, pulled her closer, and settled his lips over the soft inner skin of her wrist.

He kissed her there slowly, his eyes never leaving hers, drawing on her flesh like a vampire seeking blood, like he needed the simple contact if he were to remain alive. A fever raced over her skin, an awareness not unlike a current running overhead through high wires. She felt the same sort of deadly threat, the same sort of high frequency buzz in her ears, the same sensation of walking beneath the dangerous fallout.

Dear Lord. Dear God. What was happening here?

She dropped her shoes, slipped her free hand beneath his open shirt and around to his back. His skin was so warm and so smooth there where she spread her fingers, measuring the distance and the firm muscles between his shoulder blades and pressing him close.

He came willingly, and when she opened her mouth at the base of his throat, he growled, easing his hold on her hand—though he didn't release her. Instead, he moved her palm to his abdomen above the fly of his pants, and held her there.

She continued kissing her way over his neck, nibbling her way to his collarbone and then to his shoulder until he let her go and jerked out of his shirt. The slip in his control encouraged her; the feel of his body taut beneath her hands spurred her on.

He was a beautiful man, leanly muscled, his strength obvious but understated. He would not be the sort to flaunt his physical power; as secure as he was, he had no need. It was his sexual power, however, holding her in its spell, enchanting her, intoxicating her, rendering her incapable of even putting one foot in front of the other should she change her mind and decide to run. As if. She couldn't get to enough of him, taste enough of him. Thinking of the night that lay ahead left her breathless.

And then his hands were on her shoulders, wickedly kneading for a moment before he set her away, his chest rising and falling in perfect sync with hers. His silence continued, the moment suspended, his eyes sharply hot, alert, engaged. He had her full attention; she couldn't possibly look away.

He was the only thing in the room she wanted to see as he ran his fingers into her hair, his thumb along her cheekbone. His palm cupped the side of her face with a rare tenderness. God, but she was lost.

"You are a beautiful woman, Natasha Gaudet." He leaned forward, brushed his lips along her brow. And then he whispered, "I'm going to enjoy you in ways you've never thought to imagine."

She shivered. "I certainly hope that works both ways. It's been awhile since I've taken the time I like to take with a man."

"It's nice to know your curiosity extends into the bedroom," he said once he'd wiped a look from his face that she swore spoke of pain.

"And, lucky you"—she turned her lips toward his wrist, wet his skin with the tip of her tongue—"I haven't used up but one or two of my bedroom lives."

This time it took him longer to recover. She curled her bare toes in the plush mauve carpet to wait, dropping her gaze to the flat of his stomach, threading her fingers through the line of silky hair that grew there, scraping her fingernails along his skin just above his fly.

It would be so easy. His belt buckle hung open, after all. So easy to unhook and unzip and slip her fingers inside and take him into her hand. But she never had a chance.

He returned his hand to her shoulder, slowly slid his palms down her arms until he once again cupped her breasts. Cupped and kneaded, circling her nipples with the pads of his thumbs, sending her into a realm of heightened impulses. Arousal swept through her like a raging wildfire, leaving nothing but the ashes of her old self behind.

Eyes closed, she arched her neck and pressed herself more fully into his palms. Her hands sought out his biceps, her hard grip encountering even harder muscle. And then she felt his mouth seeking hers, his tongue pressing for entry as she parted her lips.

The kiss was amazingly tender, in perfect symphony with the sweeping brush of his thumbs. His tongue darted in and out, teasing hers with short light strokes before sliding long and deep. She whimpered, caught the lower edge of his lip with her teeth, swearing this kiss alone was enough to make her come. Swearing she wasn't going to last out the night.

She wasn't used to her knees being so weak, her thighs trembling so noticeably, her sex pulsing with the same beat as her heart while desire pooled between her legs. She needed relief from the heaviness, and wanted his hands on her hips, his mouth on her belly, his lips whispering kisses over the burning surface of her skin, his tongue lapping between her legs like a cat's questing for cream.

His hands left her breasts, moved to her waist, his fingers digging in and holding on. As if he was no longer able to breathe, he pulled his mouth from hers, his chest heaving. She spent another tense moment shuddering with Peter cursing under his breath, before he turned them both around, walking her in reverse until she felt the edge of the room's Queen Anne desk bite into the backs of her thighs.

When she'd gone as far as she could go, he reached behind her, pushed aside his laptop, and lifted her onto the cool polished surface, prying apart her thighs with his and wedging himself between.

"How do you want this?" he asked, dipping down and flicking his tongue over one nipple, sucking both her flesh and the silk fabric of her shawl into his mouth.

She gasped, locked her feet behind his legs and braced her weight in her palms at her hips. "That's definitely good for starters."

He chuckled, suckled one breast, moved to the other and continued to drive her insane, nipping at her full flesh, lapping at her areola, drawing her nipple between his lips, using teeth and tongue to torture. The added friction of the wet silk bordered on unbearable, and it was all she could do not to reach a hand between her legs and bring herself off. She was so ready for him, so open, her sex weeping with need.

Leaving her achingly, wonderfully abraded and sore, he released her nipple and kissed his way along the shawl's fringed hem toward her throat. She hated the material, wanted his mouth on her skin, and shrugged; the fabric slid from her shoulders, baring her to his gaze.

He took her in his hands, pressed her breasts together, creating a deep valley between. His gaze sparkled, his nostrils flared, his pulse beat visibly at the base of his neck. Beat as well at his temple, the hard tic pulsing as he ground his jaw.

"I know," she said on a strangled whisper as he stared. "I want you there, too." Silently, he raised his eyes to hers, and she nodded. "I can almost feel you thrusting."

He rolled her breasts together again. "Be careful," he said, a low growl humming in his throat. "Or this is going to be over before it begins."

"Would that necessarily be a bad thing?" God, she wanted him, wanted to feel him slide inside her, wanted to come around him. "I'm not going anywhere, and we have all night."

"Greedy wench." He stepped closer, but still not close enough. She desperately longed for him to grind himself against her, to ease the ache between her legs that had her squirming where she sat.

He chuckled again. "It's like that, is it?"

"Oh, yeah." She shivered. She sighed. "It's very much like that."

"What do you want me to do, Natasha?" He slid his palms

to her shoulders then down her arms to her wrists, trailing heated damp kisses over the swells of both breasts as he did. "Tell me what you want me to do."

She wanted all of him everywhere, doing anything he wanted to. And she told him exactly that.

He rubbed his face to hers, whispered into her ear. "I don't know if you're ready for that. You wouldn't be able to walk for days."

She couldn't even breathe. Couldn't even think. Couldn't imagine wanting anything more. "Show me."

He continued to nuzzle the skin between her neck and her shoulder, returning to her ear to softly ask, "Do you like toys?"

She barely managed a nod, thinking of sharing such an experience with this man she barely knew, this man whose touch she wanted so very much, whose scent she would never forget. He smelled of warmth and clean air and the woods beyond the window.

"Good. That's good." He nipped at her hard enough that she jumped. "And we know you like danger."

Another nod. Another shiver as he tasted his way down her arm, his tongue swirling over the skin inside her elbow. Anticipation held her immobile when she ached more than anything to move, to strip off her own clothes then go to work on his. That he'd made no move to undress either of them . . . Where in the world had he learned such control?

"You'll do what I say?" he asked, his voice ragged and raw and telling.

"You promise not to hurt me? To stop if I ask?" He nodded, brushed against her roughly, his beard leaving marks on her skin. "Then, yes. Anything." *Anything*. What she was giving away was nothing compared to the control she had gained, to the feeling of power now soaring through her on freedom's wings.

Peter stepped back, helped her down from the desk, set his hands on his hips. He stood and he stared and he made her shiver and sweat. When he finally twirled one finger, gestured for her to turn around, she did, holding her breath, her fingers laced tightly at her waist while she waited. And waited.

Waited until he moved to hover at her back. He never touched her, simply reached for the zipper at her waist and eased it down. Her dress fell to the floor, a puddle of paisley pooling at her ankles.

"Put on your shoes," he ordered, and she did, slipping her feet into the strappy black sandals while he picked up her shawl and turned off the lights. He made his way unerringly through the dark to the room's window, shutting the drapes and plunging the room into blackness.

"Come here," he said, opening the balcony's French doors. The moonlight shining through lighted her way. When she reached him, he draped the shawl over her shoulders, leaving her standing in nothing but the sheer silk, her lace panties, and her three-inch heels.

It was when he motioned for her to step outside that she had her first doubts. Uncertainty tiptoed down her spine on spider's feet, tickling and frightening and wickedly sexy as she thought of baring her body to the great outdoors. The hour was late, and she knew the habits of everyone on the estate.

And so she did as she was told, expecting him to follow her. He did, but not before she heard the slide of his zipper, the rustle of fabric as his pants hit the floor.

More compelling than the view of the lake in the distance was that of the man behind her, yet she didn't turn back. Instinctively, she knew he hadn't undressed until the lights were out and she had walked through the doors for a reason. A reason she would discover if not tonight, then by morning, unless she died of pure pleasure before dawn.

As cool as the breeze was, she felt little chill as he moved to stand behind her. The lift of her heels caused her hips to fit to his perfectly, allowed the prodding head of his erection to slip easily between her legs. She shuddered, feeling the bulbous tip weep against her inner thigh with wanting her. He was so warm, so hard, so thick and full.

Oh, God. What was she thinking? "Please tell me you have a condom."

"Neither one of us would be here if I didn't," he said, reaching back for one of the balcony's padded chairs before ordering, "Hold onto the railing."

She did, curling her fingers around the cold metal. He leaned over her then, his chest warm on her back, his arms circling around her. While she looked on, he wound the tie he'd been wearing at dinner between her wrists and the railing's bars, binding her tight.

Her breathing suddenly seemed just as confined. Her lungs refused to expand. She was naked, out of doors, and caught in a trap of her own making like a not so cunning fox. Oh, boy. She glanced from the bond to his profile. "Is this what you meant when you asked me about toys?"

"No. But it's all I have with me," he said, making a final tug to secure the knot, his expression fierce but his gaze avoiding hers.

Oh, boy—again, she mused and breathed deeply, staring off into the distance, toward the lake of her freedom, beyond the prison fence of her fanciful childhood imaginings.

All these years later, she stood here truly bound. The irony was strangely unnerving, as was the reality when the legs of the chair scraped the balcony's surface and he sat. She didn't have long to wonder what he had in mind.

"Back up."

She took a step in reverse; her upper body leaned forward, a move that she knew raised her backside and put it level with his eyes. The thought of him looking his fill from a distance that was no distance at all . . . She thanked her lucky stars for the canopy of darkness above.

Her luck, however, quickly ran out as he grasped the tops of her thighs and spread her apart. She closed her eyes, opened them just as swiftly—and widely—caught off guard by the tip of his tongue running along the elastic of her panties, as far between her legs as he could reach.

It wasn't far enough. He was barely able to tongue the

crease separating her sex and her thigh. She wanted more, wanted him deeper, and told him so with a whimper that sounded more like a cry.

"What are you doing?" she asked, knowing how stupid she sounded because the answer was beyond obvious.

He moved his mouth, replaced his tongue with roaming, probing fingers. "Tasting you."

Torturing her was more like it.

"You're not having a good time?" he asked when she squirmed away from his hand.

If by good he meant she was about to crawl out of her skin, then yes. Yes. Oh, yes. She nodded, gasping when he slid a finger deep between her legs and hooked it around the crotch of her panties. He pressed a knuckle upward. She pushed down, grinding hard, but he was already gone, leaving nothing behind but frustration. So much so that she felt the childish urge to kick him with one of her heels.

She was obviously out of her mind. This was only playtime; she shouldn't ache and want this fiercely. Shouldn't feel as if he was the first man to touch her, to truly touch her, a touch that brought her to life. Such a ridiculous thought when in reality he had hardly yet touched her at all.

He spread his hands, one over the back of each of her thighs, and massaged her, moving up over the cheeks of her bottom to the small of her back. It felt so good. *He* felt so good. The strength in his hands, the magic, the warmth of his fingers as he took hold of her panties by the waistband and peeled them all the way down, baring her completely except for the shoes and the shawl.

At his insistence, she stepped out of the scrap of stretchy black lace and looked down to see it lying on the balcony between her feet. Taunting her. Mocking her. The evidence of her indiscretion. She wanted to laugh. This wasn't her. This wasn't her at all. A silk shawl and stilettos and bound with a lover's tie. Yet at no other moment in her life had she felt more alive.

He cupped her bare bottom, his thumbs slipping between her legs and opening her. The night air blew over her intimately, cooling her heat with her own moisture, drying her out until Peter leaned forward and stroked his tongue the length of her slit. She cried out, a loud, desperate, wanton sound she tried to cut off but couldn't, and then it no longer mattered.

Her moans drifted into the night air as he licked her again, from her clitoris through her folds, spearing his tongue into her core, swirling and lapping, in and out, pulling back and pushing in. She sobbed from the pleasure that bordered on pain. Sobbed from the need to come.

"Are you having a good time now, Natasha?" he asked, his voice deep and raw and telling of his arousal.

She'd be having a much better time if they were in his bed, their bodies locked together. She so wanted to dig her fingers into his very fine glutes and pull him inside, to lose herself with him, to share instead of take. But she told him none of that. He was her captor, she was his slave. She wanted to live the fantasy, and so did no more than dutifully nod.

"Good. I want you to enjoy this as much as I do."

And then his hand was between her legs, his thumb inside her, oh god, *oh god,* two fingers sliding through her slick folds to squeeze the hard knot of nerves above. She thrust against him. Again he pulled away. She strained at her bonds, wanting to scratch and claw until he stopped with the teasing, but stomped one foot instead.

Behind her, he chuckled, and she felt the heat of his warm breath on her bottom. Apparently, they didn't share the same definition of enjoyment because his seemed to be coming at her expense . . . or so she thought until he sighed.

"Do you have any idea how gorgeous you are?" His whisper was ragged, harsh, sounding of pain. "Do you know how few women are this comfortable with their bodies? To be this uninhibited?"

"I'm not so sure that I'm either," she admitted softly. She loved sex, yes, but this was more about her fascination with him, and wanting him in ways she wasn't sure she would ever understand. Being here with him like this made no sense, which only caused her to want him even more.

"You should see the moonlight on your skin. Like alabaster. Like ivory." He rubbed both palms down the outside curve of her hips then over the round of both cheeks before pressing his thumbs into the cleft between and pulling her apart.

"And your cunt is absolutely exquisite." He sighed, leaned forward to breathe her in, to taste her with a long hard lap from the flat of his tongue that had her beating her forehead against her bound fists.

"You glisten. Like petals dripping with nectar. I can't get enough. You're so intoxicating. So sweet." Again he slid his tongue so deeply inside her she felt the bristle of beard scrape her flesh. He ate, he drank, he feasted from the rosebud of her bottom to that of her clit.

She was going to die. She wanted him, needed him, ached for his hard driving thrust, was insane with it all. Mad to get her hands on his body. Crazy to take his cock into her mouth and learn his texture and taste.

"Peter?" she began, hating the kitten-soft plea. She wasn't the least bit weak, simply out of her sexual league.

"Hmm?" he hummed in answer, leaving a trail of love bites along her plump lips.

She clenched her inner muscles, wanting the freedom to play herself into orgasm, to finger herself through the spasms. She had no patience to wait for him to take her there, yet instinctively knew the wait would be worth everything.

"I need you. Inside me. I can't wait anymore." Even the fringe of her shawl dangling and blowing in the night breeze was too much sensation for her live-wire skin. So when he got to his feet behind her, she swore her revenge.

Let him see what it was like to want this way for no reason, to be caught tight and unable to reach for what he wanted, to have his satisfaction, his desire, his completion held in another's hands. Her hands. Her mercy. She couldn't wait to have him there.

Neither could she wait to appease her curiosity as to how he would feel, how he would taste, how he had managed to make her feel as if she'd never known a man before . . .

The sound of a condom packet tearing brought her back to the present and into anticipation's clutches. Hurry, *please.* She didn't know how close she was to losing what remained of her mind.

He stepped toward her, his thighs aligning, his hips fitting, and finally, finally, *finally* the tip of his penis sought entry, rubbing through the sticky slick moisture coating her sex.

He thrust forward and filled her, and even her heels weren't a high enough lift. She swore he took her off the ground. The railing edges bit into her palms as she held on for what felt like her life. It wasn't a fear of falling over the edge, but one of tumbling into a well of bottomless need.

He gripped her hips, the fingers of both hands digging into her muscles with near bruising strength. She didn't care. She wanted it all, the powerful thrusts as his cock hit bottom again and again, the fullness, the feeling of being stretched beyond what her body was built for.

No, that wasn't true. She was built for *this,* for him, and pushed back as he pushed forward, the wild coiling tension tightening so deeply inside her body that she feared relief would never come. But then it did, a shattering, consuming burst of heat searing her nerves.

She couldn't move, couldn't stop moving. Squeezing, flexing, dragging him as deeply inside as she could with nothing but muscles in spasm. Her legs shook uncontrollably. She wanted to scratch and claw and, oh, again, she was coming apart, undone, thrashing, her throat raw, her chest burning, aching, the strain beyond what she could bear.

He waited for her to begin the long trip down, his strokes increasing in speed and in force the further she fell. He grunted, pounded, groaned, shoved into her with thrusts she felt all the way to her toes.

He came then. Almost silently. If not for the spike in the temperature as his semen spilled, she wouldn't have known. He slowed his movements, strained, then shuddered until it seemed he would collapse. She wanted to help, to soothe him, to hold him. She could do nothing without the use of her hands.

Another long moment, another quake that ran through his body and into hers, and he pulled free. She felt the loss immediately. She wasn't ready to let him go.

"Peter? Please untie me?" Her back ached. She needed to stretch, needed to turn and run her palms over his chest to his belly. She listened to him breathe, waiting. Finally, he loosened her bindings and set her free. She rolled her spine from base to nape, rubbed the circulation back into her wrists, and stretched into an upright position.

Then, pulling her shawl closer, she kicked off her shoes and stepped out of the emotional fantasy she always tended to weave out of good hot sex. She didn't hurry as she bent to retrieve her sandals and her panties. She'd heard him step back into the room, leaving her alone once again.

This vanishing act was a habit she wasn't going to put up with after tonight. Else he could find himself another tour guide and companion. Starting now.

Seven

Christian lay on his back on the bed in the dark, Natasha asleep at his side beneath the blankets he'd thrown back an hour ago. He hardly needed the protection from the cold. Not with his body bathed in sweat.

Why the hell did Peter Deacon's sexual preference have to be bondage?

All that talk on the balcony earlier of alabaster and ivory. Christian wanted to choke on the sleaze. Yeah, Natasha was gorgeous, beyond gorgeous, amazingly sexy, hot, and his dreams embodied. But he sure as hell didn't want to tell her that with words that would've come out of Deacon's mouth.

He wanted to tell her as himself. And was so fucking screwed with it he hurt.

He'd expected to come here, get in good with Bow, spring Jinks, leaving no one the wiser, and get out. He hadn't expected to be blindsided by one of the bad guys who happened to be female—and who his gut was now telling him wasn't a bad guy at all.

If nothing else, the number one thing he'd learned these last seven years was to listen to his unfailing gut.

He'd been prepped. He'd been briefed. He'd been forearmed, ready, and good to go. All of that, but he'd never been prepared for what taking her to bed had made him feel, for the fact that it *had* made him feel. And right now he wanted nothing more than to grab Hank Smithson by the throat and shove him into the nearest wall.

Staring at the triangle of light where the curtain's edge caught the windowsill, Christian admitted to himself that wasn't ever going to happen. He owed the old soldier too much. He loved him even more.

The complexity of his indebtedness to the older man was no secret in the ranks of SG-5. The rest of the guys had been in deep shit and on their way down when Hank had ridden to the rescue. How and when he'd learned about any of them, why the hell he'd gone to such extreme lengths in terms of cost and red tape in order to secure their futures and their freedom . . .

Hank refused to talk about any of it. He wouldn't even talk about his motivation for assembling the Smithson Group in the first place. Gratitude naturally fueled a big part of their individual loyalty, but there was more. A lot more. Christian couldn't speak for the others, but he doubted not one of the four did what they did, putting their reputations and often their lives on the line, because they were thankful.

No. He knew without being a betting man that it was because of what they saw in Hank's eyes. His ferocity of conviction, his willingness to wade into the thick of the bullshit, his compassion for what they'd each been through, and his sworn oath that he would never leave them alone to face a court or more deadly consequences made doing what they did second nature.

He was Saint Hank, and they were the lucky five over whom he'd chosen to watch—though right now Christian would have preferred a simple guardian angel to whom he owed nothing. And it was that personal reality, the full extent of that debt, the one hundred percent likelihood that he'd die still indentured, that had him in such a foul mood.

Yet none of that held a candle to the conundrum of why he'd gotten off so completely on the power of binding Natasha, when he loathed the idea of bondage, hated confinement, couldn't shake the Chiang Rai association no matter that doing so would be worth singing soprano.

Almost. But not quite. Because that would mean never again knowing a woman as intimately as he intended to know Natasha—and that was too much of a sacrifice to make when he'd just gotten started. He would've been a lot further along, in fact, if she hadn't fallen asleep.

Yeah. Asleep. He couldn't believe it. He'd come out of the shower to find her curled up in his bed, eyes closed, breathing soft and even. His own fault, really. They could've been going at it like rabbits for hours now if he'd invited her to join him and kept her wide awake. The hell of it was, even for hours of wild sex he wasn't going to expose himself like that.

To answer the questions he knew she'd ask about his deal with tight spaces, the fact that he showered with the curtain hanging open, or with the stall's frosted glass panel left ajar. Hell, most of the time he didn't even bother closing the bathroom door. But this time she'd been here, and he'd had little choice. The shot of scotch he'd downed standing in the cloud of steam had marginally helped.

He stared toward the balcony and the sliver of light knifing through the glass. The drapes over the window were drawn as well. He'd made sure of that, not wanting to take in the view of the lake again until he was bloody well forced to. At least the next time he looked that way he'd have the visual memory of Natasha's bare body silhouetted against the scene, her legs spread wide, her ass in the air.

He reached down to his crotch, scratched, adjusted, stroked his hardening cock once, twice, more than ready to have her again—and this time to have her his way. Fully involved bodies, tongues and fingers and teeth. Enough with the props and the power plays and the fetishistic exposure. Enough with sex being no more than a game. That wasn't what he wanted, what Christian Bane wanted.

Because Christian Bane wanted it all, to explore the connection he was already feeling with her, to see where beyond the bedroom it might lead, to find out why. Why her, why now, and why after all this time.

Yeah, he'd made her come. The least he could do considering the way she'd questioned nothing of what he'd asked, the way she'd bent over and bared herself, opened up, grown wet. She hadn't even fought the bonds, a thought that had him stroking faster, harder, cupping his palm over the head of his dick, rubbing in a firm circle until it was almost too late to stop himself from shooting his load.

He pushed out of the bed quietly, picked up the glass of melted ice and watered-down scotch Natasha had left on the bar hours ago, and finished it off. A check of his watch on the desk told him dawn was at least two hours from reaching the horizon.

If she hadn't been sleeping behind him, he would've used the time to pull up his files, scan the mission's portfolio for details he might've missed connecting her activities and Bow's deal with Spectra. He didn't want to risk an uplink to the audio files stored on Smithson's secure communications server, but reading the transcripts would've made for a good use of his time if his body wasn't hard with other ideas.

He turned back to the bed where she faced away from his side, lying on her stomach, one leg extended, one knee drawn up, her arms wrapped around her pillow, her ass temptingly raised. The blanket covering her did little to hide the rounded curves he'd grown so familiar with on the balcony while using her in a way he wasn't particularly proud of.

Being pissed at himself because of that, because he'd used sex to further a cause, to break his enemy, to take her down . . . he poured a half shot, downed it, hating how much he was drinking tonight. Being pissed at himself because all of that didn't mean he wasn't going to take full advantage of her very fine body and the fact that she was naked in his room.

He fought off a shiver as he crossed the room and returned to the bed. Not a shiver resulting from cold but one brought on by the sort of fear he'd thought himself beyond feeling. Yeah, he knew all about cold sweats, about panic, and had a healthy respect for his body's fight or flight response. This wasn't the sort of adrenaline-charged alarm that had kept him one step ahead of Spectra in Thailand until hit square in the face with the shovel of Malena's betrayal.

The woman in his bed now was Natasha, and this fear was about how vulnerable wanting her left him. Yet he hesitated no further in rejoining her, slipping his fevered body between the cool sheets and spooning up against her, damning himself all the while for this primal need that had him rutting like a buck on a doe.

His erection prodded her hip; he wedged one leg between hers, spreading her open with his knee, molding his palm to the round of her rump and massaging the toned muscles he found there.

She lifted into his caress, whimpering in her sleep and cuddling back against his chest. His head braced in one hand, he leaned over her, rubbing tiny circles in the small of her back above the cleft of her bottom before his fingers drifted down to explore, first the round bud of her ass then seeking below, her moisture easing the slide of his fingers deep into her folds.

She arched her back, raised her lower body far enough off the bed for his hand to slip beneath and cup her sex. The tips of his fingers teased the fluff of hair hiding her clit. She was already aroused, the knot of nerves engorged, the surrounding lips of her pussy plump and soft. He teased her, soft brushes of his fingers over and around even as he pushed his thumb inside of her, past the barrier of her clenched muscles and found her swollen G-Spot.

She gasped, caught her breath, moaned into her pillow, and tried to turn toward him only to find herself trapped by the weight of his leg. And so, instead, she thrust her sex into his hold, pumping her hips in a hard mating rhythm as he fingered her clit and fucked her with his thumb.

She was so hot, so responsive, so unrepressed. His cock pulsed and he shoved his hips forward, getting off to the slide of his flesh against the curve of her bottom, the crease of her thigh. And then the bed became frenzied, the mattress heaving beneath his pistonlike thrust, the bucking of her hips against his thumb, the grinding of her clit against his fingers. When she came, she convulsed and shuddered, reaching between her own legs to apply the pressure she needed to finish.

Feeling her there, her small fingers winding through his to add her own pleasure to that which he gave, slicking her moisture around and around, making soft throaty sounds as she slid her thumb along his into her cunt . . .

Christ, but he wanted to taste her, wanted to drive his cock as deep into that gorgeous juicy pussy as he could, to come all over her and watch her eyes as he did. He jerked away, rolled to his back, grabbed the sheet in his dry hand, grabbed his cock with the one wet with her cream, stroked hard and stroked fast.

But she was faster. On her knees and between his legs, her hands beneath his thighs forcing him open. And then he was in her mouth. All of him. The capped head of his cock rubbed the back of her throat as she pulled her lips the length of his shaft, sucking him back in to repeat the torture again and again.

She held one hand wrapped around the base of his cock, sent the other exploring—his balls, the hard extension of his erection, the puckered entrance to his ass. She played with him and sucked him and never let up, blowing him below the belt but blowing his mind as well.

He'd think about that later. Wonder later how she'd gotten to him. Later, that's when he'd figure out when he'd let himself become susceptible, putty, at risk. But right now the moment was all about relief. And so he let himself go, pulsing his release into the warm wet heat of her mouth, shuddering as she demanded every last drop until he was spent, and he collapsed.

She let him go then, reached for the blanket and sheet that had been shoved to the foot of the bed, and pulled both with her as she crawled up beside him and sighed. She didn't say a word. In fact, in less than five minutes she fell back to sleep, her knee cocked over his thigh, her arm draped across his belly, her face nuzzled close to his armpit as he pillowed his head on crossed wrists.

She lay there sleeping, having just wrung him dry and asking nothing, satisfied with what he'd given her, so content that when he reached over to tuck the covers around her shoulder, she didn't even stir.

Peter Deacon, hell. It was Christian Bane up to his eyeballs here in horseshit.

The next morning, Christian met Natasha in front of the second-floor elevator just before ten. He'd dressed and gone out to the water gardens before the sun was even up while she'd continued to sleep in his bed. He'd thought about waking her, but then had thought better. He might be playing the part of Peter Deacon, but he was first an SG-5 operative and he had a job to do.

This mission, unfortunately, was no longer cut and dried, leaving him with too many loose ends and no clear picture of what it was he needed to sew into a neat package for delivery to the Feds. Woodrow Jinks was obviously working with Bow of his own accord, which meant Christian's next move was to discover what Spectra wanted from the two men—and discover what he could of their connection.

He'd hoped to do that while eating breakfast with Dr. Jinks while Natasha simultaneously had her meeting with Bow. But Christian had arrived at the appointed hour for guests, only to be told by Mrs. Courtney that Jinks had mixed a protein shake in the kitchen at daylight, leaving his usual mess for her to clean up, mind you, and that Dr. Bow had called down and had her bring a tray to his room earlier. Poor man was barely able to lift a fork and spoon some mornings.

While eating the cheese and spinach omelet Mrs. Courtney eventually prepared, Christian had made a mental note to find out more about Dr. Bow's illness. The files from Polytechnic had made mention of a motor neuron disorder, and Christian couldn't help but wonder if Bow's health wasn't having an impact on the decisions he was making these days. Dealing with Spectra IT seemed way out of character for the respected professor profiled in the mission's portfolio.

At the subtle sound of footsteps on the plush hallway carpet, Christian glanced up from his musings and watched Natasha approach. Today she wore another pair of stilettos with a funky pink suit. Classy and hot, through and through.

The fabric was tweedlike, a light background striped in a darker, nubbier weave. The skirt was tight and hit her midthigh. The button-front jacket's sleeves ended in ruffles just below her elbows. And her hair swung above her shoulders like strands of the finest black silk.

Knowing exactly how that hair felt sliding over the skin of his thighs, tickling his belly and his balls, had him shifting from one foot to the other and wishing he could turn away and adjust the hardening goods.

"You should have woke me when you got up," she said softly, smiling and stopping no more than two feet away.

He wanted to reach out and haul her into his body, to drag her close and grind his mouth down on hers, to taste her sweetness and remember how far she'd taken him last night. But that was Christian Bane's reaction, one he didn't have time to analyze because he was Peter Deacon and he was here on Spectra business. He didn't have time to scrutinize the sex, simply time to engage.

So what he did then—as Peter—was move closer, one slow step then another, until his lips grazed the shell of her ear. "Did you know you had kicked the blankets to the floor by the time I got out of the shower?"

She shook her head, her breathing quickening, and so he went on, creating a gulf between the two men that he was and the ways both of him wanted her. Making sure she knew Peter Deacon because she would never know Christian Bane.

"I watched you while I was getting dressed. You were cold. Your nipples puckered like ripe cherries on your tits," he added, skating his palm over the center of her breast that was hard even now.

"Why didn't you cover me up?" she asked once she had found her voice.

"Because then I wouldn't have been able to see your beautiful cunt." When she pulled in a shocked breath, he slid his hand from her breast to her waist and held her still. "Were you dreaming about sex, Natasha? About my thick cock buried inside you? I think you were. I could smell you. And I kissed you before I left."

She raised trembling fingers to her lips; he in turn slid his palm over her firmly rounded ass and squeezed. "I leaned in right here and ran my tongue all over you. I shoved a finger into you. I fucked you with it until you rolled over and stuck your ass in the air. Is that what you want, Natasha? You want me to do you like that?"

"Stop lying," she whispered sharply.

He grew very still. "What do you mean?"

"Besides the fact that I would never have slept through you touching me"—she lifted a hand, adjusted the points of his shirt collar—"I don't believe for a minute that you would ever use a woman while she slept."

She sounded so certain, she looked so sincere, that a part of him ached to confirm her faith. The rest of him screamed to stick to the plan. It was his only rational choice, his only true salvation.

The elevator car arrived then. He stepped back, took hold of her waist, his gaze locked with hers as he dragged her inside. She hit the button for the basement, her chest rising and falling as rapidly as his. So he hit another button and stopped the car between floors.

He'd started this as Peter Deacon, being as crude and raw and coarse as he knew the man to be. But her trust in his basic decency joined the mental picture he'd painted . . . Well, it was his own erection now straining at his zipper, his own lungs heaving like a bellows. He needed to push her away, to regain the control he'd so obviously lost before they reached the lab.

He allowed a smile to lift one side of his mouth. "You're right. I am lying. But a thousand dollars says your panties are as wet as my cock is hard."

That, of course, was the wrong thing to say. Her eyes sparked with anger. She shoved away from the wall on which she was leaning and approached. "Okay, tough guy. We can do this your way. Just be sure that's what you want."

Either he made for a worse Peter Deacon than he'd realized, or she was the most fearless, the most foolish, the most utterly fascinating woman he'd ever met.

He was rapidly beginning to believe the latter, what with the way he couldn't get his mind off her body long enough to focus on the job. That and the way she seemed to feel exactly the same.

This time she was the one who leaned up and whispered into his ear, wrapping her fingers around his shaft and squeezing as she said, "Keep your thousand dollars. I'll take this instead."

He turned his head, ground his mouth to hers and gathered up the fabric of her skirt until his hands were on her bare bottom, his fingers sliding between her legs, pushing inside the strap of her thong to find her soaking wet.

Just because he no longer bedded women who crossed his path on the job didn't mean he couldn't tell an honest response from a fake. Natasha's body was telling the whole truth about her desire.

"I want to eat you," he said, because right now he wanted nothing as much as getting between her legs.

She widened her stance, her feet on either side of his as she rubbed her lower body to his. "I want you in my mouth."

He groaned, growled. "You can have me anywhere. Just say the word."

Her hands freed his belt from his buckle, released the button beneath, slid his zipper all the way down. She tugged his pants over his hips, took his shorts down next. But instead of wrapping her lips around his swollen head and sucking him into her mouth, she hiked her skirt up to her waist and pressed her body to the wall.

He took one look at the offering of her bare ass and stepped in behind her. He bent his knees, spread hers, sent two fingers exploring, and followed with his cock. He drove deep, drove hard, covered her hands on the wall with his palms, and laced their fingers together. She was so tight, so wet, so hot. So incredibly hot. The sounds she made, the panting, the gasps drove him out of his mind.

And then it was over. Not thirty seconds had passed and she came. Her contractions gripped him, pulled him, squeezed him. He angled his shaft, rubbing upward against her clit as she cried out. She spread her fingers wide.

He clutched her hands tightly, keeping their fingers meshed. She brought a pair of their joined hands down between her legs and played her clit as she finished, shuddering, trembling . . . and that was all it took.

He followed her over the edge, spilling himself in waves that threatened to tear him apart. He thrust once, twice, then didn't move, couldn't move, stood tensed and still while she milked him dry. Moments passed, moments of recovery, of coming down from a high he wasn't sure he'd ever reached with another woman, a moment that rapidly brought recriminations.

What the hell had they just done?

He stepped back, eased out of her, realized he was caged with a beautiful woman he dared not trust, whose loyalties he had not yet determined. He needed to know, needed to settle this, needed to get out of this fucking goddamn cage. Sweat broke out on his forehead and beaded his upper lip as he tucked himself back into his pants.

Natasha settled her skirt around her hips, smoothed it into place, then turned. He offered her his handkerchief, held onto her hand as she took it. "Tell me there's not going to be a baby from this."

The flash of hurt in her eyes stung more than a slap to the face. Her chin lifted with a haughty indignation. "A little late to be thinking of that, wouldn't you agree?"

He deserved the how-dare-you but repeated his demand just the same. "Tell me."

"No. There will not be a baby. Now, you tell me you didn't

give me anything *I* don't want." And this time it wasn't indignation but fear he saw in her expression. Fear and regret and, yes, there it was, the shame he'd wondered if she'd feel. The shame that told him he'd managed to make her feel used.

The shame that shamed him to the core for using her. He suffered the cut of that emotion more deeply than he'd thought possible, and Peter Deacon or not, on this he had to set her mind at ease.

He raised his free hand to caress her cheek. Her skin was so smooth and so soft. "The only thing I gave you, Natasha Gaudet, was a very good time. Like giving you the keys to my Ferrari." He tweaked her nose. "Only this ride was a whole lot better."

As intended, his teasing did the trick. She rolled her eyes before offering him a weak smile and gesturing with his handkerchief. "Do you mind turning around so I can . . . ?"

He turned before she finished the request. There was that ladylike decorum again, the class he found so irresistible in such a sensual package. No, this woman was not one who sold her body for any cause.

Which left him wondering what in the hell she was doing here sleeping with Peter Deacon.

Eight

The elevator opened directly into the underground lab. Praying that her skirt was less rumpled than her composure, which she swore had fallen to her feet, Natasha stepped out onto the white tiles of the raised platform built against two walls of the room.

Peter followed, moving immediately to the safety railing along the platform's edge and taking hold of it with both hands. He leaned forward, arms bracing his weight, indomitable will marking his territory as surely as he'd claimed her body just minutes ago.

Natasha watched his gaze slowly canvass the room of computer stations, servers, and monitor banks. He was all business, playing it cool. Masking the passionate—and equally compassionate—nature he'd just demonstrated so fully. Fine. She'd go along for now, though she couldn't help but wonder what he was covering up with the distancing act that was as annoying as his habit of walking away.

Looking around, she tried to view the lab through objective eyes. To the right of where they stood, the platform slanted down into the room, creating a wheelchair-accessible ramp onto the main floor. To the far left was the corner Wick had claimed as his own, the elevated stagelike setting giving him a bird's-eye view of the lab's activity—appropriate, since his workstation resembled a predator's nest perched strategically above a field of . . . rats.

None of it was anything she hadn't seen before, and so she returned her attention to the man at her side, wondering if he was seeing what he'd expected to see. Glancing now at his face, she could hardly believe how they had spent the last five minutes. He looked like a man who had room for nothing on his mind but the deal he'd made with her godfather.

Yet she wondered . . . and so she stepped up beside him, not touching him, just close enough to hear that his breathing hadn't quite settled, to see the lingering sheen of sweat on the backs of his hands where his fingers curled around the railing, to feel the heat pouring off his body in waves.

Good, she mused wryly, more than a little bit pleased to confirm her instincts. She'd hate to think that she was the only one here who wasn't so quick to recover, who'd been caught off guard by an attraction that seemed to defy such a simple definition.

Most of all, however, she'd hate to find out that his mask of cold indifference was no mask at all. She wasn't sure she could bear that.

Except for Dr. Jinks, wearing a "Got Milk" visor and headphones, his head banging side to side to his own private beat, the lab was empty. She gestured expansively to encompass the whole of the room and broke the silence first. "I'm sorry, but there's really not much here to see. Wick isn't feeling well this morning, and there haven't been any of his grad students up here to work since Dr. Jinks arrived."

"Why is that?" Peter asked, lifting a hand when the other man caught sight of them and hesitantly did the same.

Natasha waved as well, watching as Woody's attention was snagged again by his monitor. He grabbed a CD from a stack on the desk behind him, snagged the pencil stuck behind his ear in the visor's band. Though Peter's question triggered a vague unease, she gave a small shrug. "I assume because of the project that brought you here. That Wick wanted to give Dr. Jinks the full run of the lab without the distraction of having the rest of the rats underfoot."

Peter let that digest, remaining pensive several seconds longer before asking, "Where do the grad students stay when they're here?"

"They bunk at the carriage house. Wick had it converted into a dormitory during the summer semester. But a few always seem to be underfoot at the main house around dinnertime . . ." She trailed off and frowned. Now that he'd brought it up, her subconscious recalled the almost eerie quiet of the last two months with no one else around.

"Having them underfoot is a problem?" Peter prompted.

She forced a smile that she didn't feel. "They forget that Wick's strength is limited. They can't resist the chance to pick his brain. He's a world-renowned scientist, not your average professor, which translates into your not so average learning experience."

Peter straightened then and turned to face her, one hand braced at the waist of pin-striped navy pants, the other still gripping the rail. He was so amazingly sexy as he stood there, the epitome of masculinity, doing nothing more than looking at her, that her spit dried in a flash of heat. His expression gave away nothing of what he was thinking. It certainly didn't hint that he was having the same trouble she was having focusing on the here and now.

Then again, he wasn't the one with a trickle of semen running down his thigh.

"Tell me about him." He lifted his chin to indicate Wick's corner workstation. "Tell me about Wickham Bow."

She crossed her arms over her chest, settled her weight into one hip, and returned the pinpoint directness of his very business-intensive gaze. "You've worked with him now long enough to form your own impression. I don't see that I have anything significant to add."

"Perhaps. But I'd like your opinion. You know him better

than anyone." His voice gentled along with his gaze, and just like that, his mask lifted. "I'd appreciate your input, Natasha."

This was the man in the elevator whose eyes had been filled with teasing tenderness. This was the man who'd handed her his handkerchief to use and then turned his back with a gentleman's respect. This was a man whose every question she found herself compelled to answer—yet one who disappeared again before she drew her next breath.

His eyes flickered dangerously, a deep sea blue where she thought she might drown. "How did he come to be based way up here? Why not closer to the city, what with the university in the Bronx?"

On this she didn't hesitate. With her godfather's emphasis on the importance of this deal with Peter, anything that was public knowledge was fair game. "I mentioned last night that he inherited the property. The accompanying trust has paid the taxes and the maintenance as well as allowed him the luxury of the live-in staff. When he was still in the city, having the Courtneys on the place meant he didn't have to involve himself except to approve their expenses."

"That doesn't answer my question," he said rather brusquely.

She frowned up at him, biting down on her tongue when she would have reminded him who he was talking to—right before she reminded herself who she was talking to and her charge to see to his needs. "Renovating his apartment to make it wheelchair-accessible would have been impractical. The cost was beyond prohibitive."

He seemed to let that settle in, moving along the railing until she had to back up or be run down. "Tell me about his illness."

She took a breath, willed a calm to replace the tightness in her middle brought on at the thought of Wick's future, and glanced back toward the near empty lab. "He has good days and bad."

"Get more specific, Natasha. I'd like to know how his health is going to impact our dealings."

Was it her imagination, or were dark secrets creeping back

into the mask he'd pulled down? "I don't talk about Wick's private life with anyone." On this, she wasn't going to budge. Wick could damn well fire her if he chose. "If he wishes to share the details, that's up to him."

Peter let that sink in, waited a moment, and asked, "How long has he known Dr. Jinks?"

She took a deep breath. "Wick actually mentored him during Dr. Jinks's years at Polytechnic. He was only sixteen when he enrolled—"

"Jinks was Dr. Bow's student?" Peter interrupted forcefully.

She frowned. "His protégé, yes."

"Have they kept in touch in the years since?"

Noting his expression that seemed to harden even further, she sighed.

"Is that a yes or a no?" he demanded.

Irritation descended in a tsunami wave. "That's an 'I don't know,' damn it. If they kept in touch, it wasn't so regularly that I took notice." She turned on him then, arms crossed, stance wide, prepared for battle. "What is this? Twenty questions? The Dr. Peter Show?"

He lifted his chin toward Jinks. "I need to know what makes him tick."

An evasive answer if she had ever heard one, she mused, following the direction of his gaze toward Woody. "Why?"

"He seems nervous. A little unstable." A pause, and Peter's voice dropped. "A lot is riding on the kid's shoulders, Natasha. I need to know if I can trust him."

She shook her head, glanced up again in time to catch a flash of what she swore was calculated concern. Curiouser and curiouser yet again. "So you didn't include him when you had Wick and I investigated? You know. The way you investigate everyone with whom you consider doing business."

He'd told her that less than twenty-four hours ago and now she waited for him to react, wishing they'd had more time together so she might be somewhat clued in as to what he was thinking, why he was asking about Woody's relationship with Wick, what it was he really wanted to know.

He reached out, circled the gold button between her breasts with one finger. "Perhaps I wasn't as thorough as I should have been, no. But there were a few players involved who interested me more than the others. One in particular who intrigued me enough to sidetrack my attention."

"You're full of crap," she said, removing his hand from her clothing. "You're hiding something and distracting me with sex whenever I get too close."

"Distracting you?" His gaze crawled up to hers. "Tame words for what I make you feel. And that scares you to death, doesn't it?"

"Your ego is monumental."

"Just answer the question."

"Hey, Mr. Deacon." Woody's call from across the room was an interruption Natasha had never thought to welcome. "I've got something here you really ought to see."

Peter waited a moment before retreating, looking down into her eyes that she was certain hid nothing of her store of insecurities, the fears she wasn't ready to confront, the sticky and sordid truths that sent her too soon and too often into a man's bed.

It was so easy to bare her body, to pretend that was enough, that she needn't bare anything more . . . oh god, what was she doing? What was she thinking? She took a deep breath, then a step in reverse, seeking out the solid ground that had seemed to drop away.

Hell yes, he scared her! There, she admitted it. He was an enigma, and he had her thoughts racing in directions she'd never wanted to run, had her heart racing, as well.

He turned his attention to Dr. Jinks then, backing away and leaving her shaking in her shoes. She watched him hop down the four steps from the center of the platform to the lab's floor, watched as he rolled up a chair to Woody's workstation and devoted one hundred percent of his attention to the other man as if she wasn't even standing in the room.

"Who are you, Peter Deacon?" she whispered to herself.

Whoever he was, whatever he was hiding, she vowed to find out even if it killed her.

"Good afternoon, Dr. Jinks."

Woody looked up from his monitor as Dr. Bow wheeled his way down the ramp along the side of the room instead of to his workstation in the room's raised corner. Smiling at his partner in crime wasn't coming easy for Woody today. Not after what he'd witnessed last night or even this afternoon. But he gave it his best shot.

"You don't look so hot, Professor." And the older man didn't. His face was pale, making his stubbly black and white whiskers look like crap. The dude really should've shaved, Woody thought, rubbing his own face that produced little more than scraggly fuzz.

"A restless night and a bit of an uncomfortable morning. That's all." Dr. Bow pulled off his glasses, cleaned the lenses on the tail of his shirt left untucked on one side. "I'll get to bed early tonight."

"Yeah, you should." And hopefully no one would be fucking their brains out on their bedroom balcony and Woody could get the sleep he'd missed out on, too. He reached down, tugged on the fly of his pants. "Making this deal with Spectra isn't going to do you much good if you're not around to get what you want out of it."

The older man's mouth grew grim and tight, making his whole face look like it belonged to a cadaver. "Lest you forget, I won't be the only one getting what I want out of this deal. Your percentage will be substantial, allowing you to start your new life wherever your heart desires."

Dr. Bow settled his glasses back in place, staring until Woody couldn't take it anymore. He returned his gaze to his monitor, unable to blink though the dry burn in his eyes felt like sand needles shoved to the back of his skull. He was so going to fry before this scam was over. The look on the old doctor's face was enough to snap him in half like the scrawny twig he was.

Then again, scrawny or not, *he* was the one who had the goods. He was the brainiac, the one who'd written a third of the encryption program the CIA's analysts were using to transmit data to their agents in the field, the one who'd left a back-door crack that only he knew where to find. That put him in a position his gamer buds would envy.

Whoa! That's all he had to do. Think of this with a gaming strategy. He'd reminded himself earlier that this was reality; that didn't mean he couldn't *think* like the gamer he was. He sure as hell wasn't getting anywhere thinking like a criminal.

He nodded, turned a sly gaze back to Bow. "I've always wanted to visit Bora Bora."

"I was thinking of Tahiti myself," the doc said with a bit of a grin.

"What about Natasha?" Woody asked before he remembered that his foot had a hard time fitting into his mouth.

Bow's smile vanished. "What about her?"

"You taking her to Tahiti, too?"

He looked away. "Natasha isn't part of this."

"I'm not so sure. I think she's pretty involved. At least that was how it looked when I was out"—*smoking a joint,* Woody'd almost said—"uh, getting some air on the terrace last night. I couldn't sleep. The meds and all."

"What does that mean? What did you see?"

Duh. Now what was he supposed to say? "She may not be part of this deal, but she's definitely mixing it up with Deacon."

Bow rolled his chair closer to Woody's workstation. "Listen to me, Dr. Jinks. I need to know exactly what it was you saw."

Obviously it wasn't a good idea to talk about her tits or her ass, he thought, tugging again on the fly of his pants. And he sure as hell wasn't going to spill the beans on the way she'd been tied up. Even now it had him thinking of another shower with a whole lotta soap.

He shrugged, grabbed hold of his Dr. Pepper. "The two of them were pretty hot and heavy there on the balcony."

"Whose balcony? Which room?"

"Uh, second floor. Far side of the house looking up from the bench at the end of the terrace."

"Deacon's room."

Woody shrugged. "You say so."

Dr. Bow drummed his fingers on his wheelchair's control panel, his eyes blinking rapidly. "Have you managed to capture any of the CIA transmissions?"

"Getting there. Got some good pieces of code that I'm working on," he said, congratulating himself on his brilliance since he wasn't getting stroked here. "I was about to show what I had to Mr. Deacon this afternoon but lost the feed"—oh so conveniently, too, he snickered to himself—"and never got it back."

The thought of the government dudes finding his Counter-Strike strategy zooming along their wires gave him a case of the giggles. He hadn't messed with any of their current transmissions, of course. He wasn't going to do that until Deacon was around to see a real-time demonstration and everyone involved knew what was going down.

And then he'd have some sort of immunity from prosecution or whatever, right? As long as he cooperated and swore he'd been held against his will? Threatened at gunpoint? Or—even better, he thought, getting into this criminal stuff now—had a bomb strapped to his chest with the detonator in Bow's shaky hand?

"Good. Very good." The doctor backed away. The washed-out, beat-up, done-in look on his face vanished to be replaced by a victorious halo, as if Woody's news was the best thing Bow had heard in his lifetime. "Natasha and Mr. Deacon will be traveling to the city for the weekend, some nonsense about a birthday party she's required to attend."

"Deacon's taking her to a birthday party?" One night of pussy and she was treating the dude like her bitch. Woody straightened his shoulders. He had way too much pride to be ruled by his dick. He liked the idea of that making him a better man than the Spectra dude. "Didn't seem like a party guy to me."

"No." Dr. Bow shook his head. "Mr. Deacon has business to see to. They'll be back on Sunday. Does that give you enough time to prepare a live test?"

It would be cutting it close considering the contacts he needed to warn. Sweat sprouted in Woody's pits; he wished the other man would roll his decrepit old self out of here so he could head for the shower.

He wanted soap, couldn't stand smelling himself any longer, and got to his feet, praying the professor didn't notice that he couldn't keep his own hands from shaking. "Plenty of it. But if you don't mind, I've gotta jet before I take a leak all over myself."

Nine

They made the drive to the city two days later on Saturday morning, and made it with the Ferrari's top down.

The rush of air was cool but not frosty, yet due to the speed at which they traveled, the wind bit sharply at Natasha's cheeks. Studying her reflection in the car's passenger-side mirror, she couldn't decide if she looked more like a victim of sunburn or frostbite.

Unless she wanted to spend the entire evening deflecting teasing accusations of carpet burn to her face and how *were* her knees, by the way, she'd need a full facial before going out tonight.

Funny how she hated the idea of her girlfriends' harassment while not minding as much that Peter witnessed the Rudolph-the-Red-Nosed-Reindeer effect of the elements. Wednesday night spent in his suite and Thursday morning's elevator escapade had certainly stripped away any worries that he might find her physically unappealing, she mused, sinking even deeper into the plush leather seat.

Well, okay. She did care, but she wasn't going to obsess. At least no more than she normally obsessed—a woman's prerogative, right?—when in the company of a man she was interested in attracting.

Today she'd dressed to emphasize her coloring and—yes,

she admitted it—her breasts, which he seemed to find fascinating, wearing wide-leg designer corduroys in navy and a skinny sweater in variegated reds, both pieces which she'd picked up at Daffy's on Broadway at the end of last season. She'd clipped her hair up but found herself fighting rogue strands determined to blow into her mouth anyway.

Honestly? She really didn't mind. In fact, earlier, when Peter had offered to stop and put up the top, she'd simply shaken her head.

The wind in her ears, even if it was also in her hair, made talking impossible—a good thing since she and herself were already deep in an exhausting discussion and she wasn't sure she had the mental energy to expend talking to him, too. Who would've imagined she had so many arguments—both pro and con—for continuing this affair they'd begun?

And what a beginning. Even when she'd been involved and sleeping with a man on a regular basis, *that* sex, the sex they'd shared during those three amazing encounters, wasn't at all what she was used to. It wasn't the bondage or exhibitionism, the positions or the way bodies were pleasured and explored. Not at all.

She'd known from the moment she'd first seen him that his appetites would be nothing if not intense. His needs and responses, as well.

No. It was the secrets. Why had he not invited her to share his shower? Why had he not fully undressed until she'd been on the balcony? Even in the elevator he'd allowed her to see nothing of his body. He was avoiding exposure and she wanted to know why.

But more than the secrets, it was the way the intrigue between them had heightened her desire—a state of affairs that went against the honesty she so highly valued and left her quite vexed at herself. Since that morning in the elevator it had been nigh on impossible to keep her distance. But she had. She needed to know more about him before taking their relationship forward.

She certainly wasn't going to become involved long-term in

anything that required dark rooms and shadows, drawn curtains and closed doors—conditions that bred dishonesty and a clear lack of trust. He hadn't asked her to join him in any such relationship, no.

And when she stepped outside her fantasy world, she knew this *thing* between them was temporary. But she did need to make that secrets-and-lies business clear with herself before the two of her fell in over her head.

She grabbed another handful of wild hair and tucked it beneath the teeth of her clip. Peter glanced over, and though he wore sunglasses in sleek pewter frames, she swore he arched a questioning brow her direction. She smiled, shook her head again.

Oh, but she was tired. The two-lane road screamed beneath them, a rush of greens and reds and golds flashing by as they drove, the kaleidoscope of colors and the wind in her ears lulling her to sleep.

She didn't want to go to sleep. She hated the idea of waking groggy and disoriented when discovering whatever it was this man was keeping from her required wits she wasn't even sure she had. Still, if this was no more than the fling she was certain it was, his secrets shouldn't matter.

And they didn't. They didn't matter at all. It was just her damnable need to know everything, and to never be deceived or used again. . . .

When she next looked up, Peter was making his way through the Upper West Side toward her 73rd Street apartment, and the Ferrari's top was up. Her exhaustion had been more serious than she'd realized for her to have slept through him stopping the car. Then again, riding in the heated and padded leather bucket was akin to being rocked to sleep.

Another moment spent rousing herself to wakefulness and it hit her. Hard. Her stomach clenched around a knot of suspicion as she realized that she'd never given him directions or even told him where she lived. Yet here he was, pulling up to her place with a confidence that told her he hadn't once made a single wrong turn.

She shifted in the seat, turned her gaze his way. "I wasn't aware I talked in my sleep. And coherently enough to tell you exactly where to drop me off."

He draped an arm over her headrest, toyed with the clip on the back of her head until she reached up and shook her hair free. That seemed to please him, and he stroked the strands, smoothing down the flyaway wisps. "I know my way around the city."

His touch was so simple but so intoxicating. Doubts were quickly swirled up in a soft stirring of desire. "Right to my front door? When I haven't even told you where I live?"

He shrugged one shoulder. "Like I said, I thoroughly check out everyone with whom I intend to do business."

No. He wasn't getting off that easily, she decided, worrying her hair clip with both hands. "Wick I understand, but his personal assistant? That's going a little bit overboard, don't you think?"

He smiled, a lift of his lips that didn't manage to reach his dimple. "You're much more than an assistant though, aren't you, Natasha?"

His fingers in her hair were distracting enough that she almost missed the nuance of suspicion in his tone. She supposed wariness was required by whatever business he was in, but she bristled anyway. "Other than being his goddaughter, no. With Wick's contacts and his work being on a global scale, it may seem so. But I simply manage his affairs. I don't involve myself in them."

Peter's hand had stilled while she talked, and she could read nothing of his expression beyond the set line of his mouth. Still, she sensed that he didn't believe her, that he was looking to her for an admission, a confession, when she'd already given him the full extent of her truth.

She didn't like being disbelieved. "Would you mind taking off your sunglasses?"

He hesitated for a moment, then dipped his head, pulled the frames from his face, and returned his gaze to hers.

If she'd hoped to see suspicion in his eyes, she'd hoped in

vain because all she saw was need. The caress of his hand over the back of her head was no longer so simple, but sensual, a reminder of the night they'd spent in his bed, of the passion they'd shared, of the reason she would no longer think of a man's silk tie as simply an article of clothing. The knot in her belly tangled and tightened; she feared if she didn't leave his car now she never would find the strength.

And so she said, "I'm meeting my friends at ten, the second floor of Slick Velvet. I have to let the club's doorman know you're with me or they won't let you in, membership required and all that. So just meet me out front. I'm assuming you don't need directions?"

He stared into her eyes, trailed his fingers through her hair until he reached the skin of her neck just beneath her ear where he rhythmically, hypnotically stroked.

It was all she could do not to lean forward and kiss him, not to take him by that very same hand and lead him upstairs to her bed. Her body came alive under that touch, sparking off a sizzle capable of burning up her skin.

She had to get the hell out of here. Now or never.

And so, reluctantly, she reached for the door handle and climbed from the car.

Her heart racing madly, she stood there in the middle of the street watching as he sped away.

It wasn't until he slid sideways around the next corner, gunned the engine and disappeared, that she realized he'd never assured her she would see him later at all.

Christian left the Ferrari with the valet at the midtown hotel where Hank kept a penthouse suite, grabbed a taxi, and made his way the dozen or so blocks to Smithson Engineering's offices. Hank's legitimate business, which provided the SG-5 team cover and made him a buttload of money building dams, roads, and bridges worldwide, occupied the twenty-first through twenty-third floors of a financial district high-rise.

The layout was typical for a corporation Smithson's size. The corner offices, those with the best views, the ones with the most square footage, etcetera, belonged to the executive officers and department heads, with the clerical pool on the floors beneath sharing space with the information technology support team and accounting staff.

Though Christian officially worked for the firm as a project consultant and had every legitimate reason to enter through the lobby and take the elevator up, he didn't. He was undercover, and though the likelihood that he'd run into anyone in Bow's employ was virtually nil, he had no story to explain what business Deacon had in the building should anyone approach him about seeing him there. Especially on a Saturday.

Besides, he was headed for the twenty-fourth floor.

To keep his nose clean and his story on the up-and-up, he had the driver make the corner, handed him a twenty, and ducked into Brighton's Subs & Spuds. Wearing Perry Ellis pants in olive green and a geometrically patterned silk Prada shirt—both duplicated in Christian's size from Deacon's wardrobe—he easily blended into the smaller than usual lunchtime crowd of corporate professionals dressed down for a weekend spent in the office.

Or he would have blended if Kelly John Beach hadn't been standing in line to order and staring toward the door as Christian walked in.

He caught the other SG-5 operative's gaze but for a moment. Both men had been doing this long enough to know never to make extended eye contact or any gesture a tail could construe as communication. Christian simply glanced at the stylized poster of a Rueben and vinegar chips before exiting through the glass doors that opened into the parking garage between the buildings housing the sandwich shop and Smithson Engineering.

Once across the main floor, where a parking attendant pointed out the 'No Pedestrians Allowed On Driveway' sign, he headed for the service elevator instead of the building's lobby and punched the button for the twenty-fourth floor.

The boxy cage clattered and groaned. Christian closed his eyes, shoved his fists into his pockets, and conjured up the safest picture that came to mind: Natasha between his legs, going down.

Yeah, well, maybe not so safe, he admitted, a tingling settling in behind his balls, but it beat the hell out of the memory of what had spawned the flare-up of his boxy cage phobia. And since the ride up was already over, he didn't have much time to think of it either—a very good thing since he needed one hundred percent of his brain cells for the task at hand.

The elevator opened into a closetlike space. He pushed open the swinging doors and walked down the floor's long silent hallway carpeted in boring dirt brown and painted industrial tan. Halfway down the corridor, a single glass door led into a reception area, sans receptionist.

The walls here were papered in a textured bamboo. A black-lacquered, chrome-legged table sat in the center of the room on the same brown carpet, a cordless single-line phone the only other accoutrement.

Lettered on the door behind the table was the name DATA 2 TECH. That and the two twelve-inch windows on either side, through which visitors could peer at the banks of servers behind, told them the floor was indeed a data farm. What no one could see unless they made it from the reception area into the racks of warehoused equipment was that the floor was also the ops center for the Smithson Group.

No one ever made it that far.

Christian punched the security code into the lock and walked through the heavy bulletproof door into darkness. Once it latched shut behind him, overhead lights switched on to reveal a high-ceilinged, four-walled enclosure outfitted top to bottom in soundproofing tile.

The exit out of the confining cell and into the floor's true nerve center required a thumbprint scan. He rubbed the sweat from his palm onto his thigh then pressed his dry thumb onto the biometric authentication pad installed in lieu of a knob onto the second door.

Mechanized bolts and pins disengaged and the door swung open. He stepped into the ops center sweating like a pig. He understood the need for security, had no problems with the precautions taken, agreed with every aspect of the infrastructure designed to keep the SG-5 control room impregnable—all but one. The size of the goddamned safety vestibule.

The walls separating the tiny chamber from the ops center were constructed of sixteen-inch steel, which meant any uninvited guest who got in wasn't getting out. That didn't mean he had to like it. He didn't. And he prayed every time he walked inside for the scan not to fail.

Struggling to steady his breathing and pulse, he headed for his bank of terminals in the circular workstation that was half the size of a baseball diamond. He dropped into his chair, dropped his head back, and closed his eyes. Less than five minutes later, Kelly John tossed a sack from the deli into his lap.

"A Reuben and chips. That's what you wanted, right?"

"A beer would be good," Christian said, giving himself another ten seconds before sitting up to the sound of a bottle striking his desktop. "You're a good man, K.J. Don't believe anything Tripp says."

"What the hell are you talking about?" Across the room, Tripp Shaughnessey gave a hard shove against the foot of the workstation. His chair rolled to within five feet of where Christian sat. "Piece of shit. I swore oiling the wheels would help."

Leaning his backside against the edge of Christian's desk, Kelly John shook his head. "You need inline wheels if you're ever going to make it this far. Oh, wait. I said that last time. And the time before that."

"Yeah, yeah, shove it. And fork over the food."

Kelly John hefted a second sack to Tripp. "Smoked turkey, avocado, sprouts, and Dijon mustard. A wuss sandwich. Hell," he amended, chucking a bottle of Evian in the same direction. "A wuss lunch."

Tripp cackled. "Embarrassed you to order it, eh? Bet that red hot little Glory of mine teased you while she packed in the turkey."

A wide grin broke across Kelly John's face. "Glory wasn't

in much of a teasing mood. And she knew the sandwich was for you. So she packed in a little something special."

Tripp stopped chewing and nearly choked. "Whaddaya mean, something special?"

"Stop talking with your mouth full and maybe I'll tell you."

"Stop acting like your mama and I might."

Christian looked from Kelly John's black Irish blue eyes to Tripp's surfer dude looks and shook his head. Out of the four SG-5 operatives who were also his four best friends, these two were the mouthiest, both as tall as he was, though Tripp was lanky while K.J. was built like a bull. They were also the two with the tightest bond.

He supposed that had a lot to do with the reason they rode each other as hard as they did, picked and bickered like two old women, took crap from one another they'd take from nobody else. Yet any time bad shit went down, times that mattered more than others, each had the other's back. Always.

A small part of him envied that bond. But the other part, the biggest part, the part responsible for his still being alive knew he was a hell of a lot better off on his own. Hank seemed to sense that as well, sending Christian on assignments requiring an operative to fly solo.

Assignments like the one he was fighting to get back under control even now.

Biting off enough sandwich to keep him chewing for awhile, he turned to his keyboard, punched in his security code, and watched his monitors come to life before spinning his chair back to Tripp. "Nothing new between Spectra and Bow?"

Swallowing a mouthful of water, Tripp shook his head. "Not a scratch or a peep. You weren't expecting anything, right?"

Another bite of sandwich before Christian answered. "Bow's contact was Deacon, so no. You shouldn't have picked up anything."

"But for some reason you thought I might have," Tripp stated, tucking into his sandwich again.

Christian thought for a moment, back to last night's drive

in the Ferrari and their visit to Overlook Point, and Natasha's persistent questioning as to Deacon's reasons for being there. "Nothing at all from Bow's estate then? Not just from the doctor. From anyone. The staff. The lab."

"Trying to reach Spectra, you mean? Nope. With the real Peter Deacon gone underground"—Tripp chuckled at his own joke, which was pretty funny considering Deacon was being held in the vault beneath MaddyB's barn—"Spectra's channel's been dead as a corpse's dick."

"You're sick, man. You're twisted fucking sick." Kelly John planted a foot on Tripp's chair and with one hard shove sent him flying. Tripp yelped, scrambling to stay upright and salvage his sandwich as K.J. turned his attention to Christian. "What's going on, Bane?"

He glanced up at the big man's question. "Bow's goddaughter."

"She onto you?"

He shook his head. "No. It's not that. I'm beginning to think she's not onto Bow."

"Whoa. You're kidding." Tripp left his chair at his desk and returned, crossing the room under the power of his own two feet. "Intel said she was up to her eyebrows in his dealings."

"His legitimate university dealings, yeah. His consortium lectures and seminars. But not in whatever it is he's doing with data encryption." Christian grabbed his beer from his desk. "She has nothing to do with the lab. She doesn't even go underground unless running an errand for Bow."

"She doesn't have to know any of that encryption shit herself to be in on Jinks's kidnapping," Tripp said.

"I was thinking the same thing." Christian looked from one man to the other, the two standing side by side blocking the view of his monitor bank. "Until Jinks sat down to dinner with us the other night. And until she asked me the next morning why I—why Deacon—wouldn't have investigated Jinks as well as her and Bow before coming in."

Shaking his head as he polished off the rest of his sandwich,

Kelly John wadded up the waxed paper wrapping with one fist and brought his knuckles down against the desktop. "That is seriously fucked up, man. Seriously. The dude know you're there to spring him?"

Christian dropped the second half of his sandwich back into the sack half eaten, tossed the sack to his desk. He leaned back in his chair, laced his hands behind his head. "I don't think the dude needs to be sprung."

"Then he's in on Bow's deal." Tripp crossed his arms over his chest, rocked back on his heels. "That's the only thing that makes sense."

"Yeah, but what's he gaining by helping to stage his own kidnapping?" K.J. asked.

Tripp pushed away from the desk, turned back. "The money, man. Those are serious dollars Spectra's handing Bow. Jinks has to be in on the take."

Christian scrubbed his hands down his face. "I want to think so, but I'm not so sure that's all of it. He started to show me something a couple of mornings ago. A transmission he was trying to capture. He lost the feed, never could get it back."

"No idea what it was?" K.J. asked.

Christian shook his head, shrugged. "I couldn't decipher a thing of the code on his screen."

"Well, we've got the tape with the money details, at least, so there's something going down," Tripp reminded him. "You heard Bow verifying the amount with Deacon. We're not talking Cracker Jacks here."

"Yeah, I know. But there's too much that doesn't make sense. This scenario's fucked worse than anything I've seen in a hell of a long time."

A tense moment passed; neither Tripp nor Kelly John said a word. They simply stared at Christian, each man's expression a mirror of the other's. A disbelief that with Christian's history he would be so gullible as to look for zebras instead of horses at the first hard strike of hooves.

He didn't blame them. He was having a hard time with his

own rejection of the obvious. Especially when doing so was the first step down a short road to trouble.

Tripp took a deep breath, exhaled. "You're talking about the goddaughter again, aren't you?"

Thankful for the room's low lighting that hid the pulse pounding at his temple, Christian gave one quick nod. "She said I didn't know Bow very well if I thought anything he did was for money."

"And you believed her?" K.J. asked with a snort.

"At the time, no."

"But you do now that you've stuck it to her, right?"

Clenching his hands into fists, Christian said nothing in answer to Tripp's accusation, afraid the other man had hit too close to the truth.

"Christ, Bane. What's it going to take, man?" Tripp asked, his voice cracking with his concern. "Even I can see that it's Malena fucking you up all over again."

And so the story goes.

Christian hated that he'd ever told Tripp about Malena. Hated it because Tripp had told K.J. and neither of them would let it go. Hated it, too, because there had been so much alcohol involved that night, Christian couldn't remember half of what he'd said. Or if he'd really cried like a baby into the bottle of Crown he'd downed.

"Believe me. The comparison has not slipped my mind." Except during the time Natasha had taken his body apart. Then there had been no doubt who it was sharing his bed. Malena had never loved with him like that. "And as similar as the situation seems, there's too much of Natasha in real time that doesn't jive with the intel."

Kelly John shoved hands to his waistband, hooked his thumbs through the belt loops of his jeans, and stared Christian down. "You're screwed, Bane. You are flat out screwed."

Elbows braced on his knees, Christian dropped his forehead against his stacked fists. His head ached for no reason but that he'd driven too many hours after too little sleep, spent too many hours staring at his computer monitor, and tossed way too few ice cubes in his scotch. Ached, as well, because these two dickheads were hammering him with the truth.

Only his dickhead was the cause of the real trouble here.

"Yeah. I know," he finally said. "And I've got ten hours max before I see her again. Ten hours to listen to hundreds worth of audio and find something to use to trip her. Now, you guys can stand here and keep beating me up, or you can help."

Ten

Natasha climbed from the cab and waved at Susan as the other woman hurried across the sidewalk, giving up her place in the line of mostly women waiting for ID checks at a separate roped-off entrance to the club.

Tonight, access to the Slick Velvet's second floor required a membership to Club Cake, a female-focused entertainment company allowing women to comfortably explore their sexual culture.

Natasha had a membership, as did Susan, Yvonne, and Elaine, though none of them seemed to find the time or coordinated nerve to attend the group's events together. Well, except for Elaine. She was all nerve, all of the time.

"God, Nat. I didn't think you were ever going to get here." Susan smoothed her short black skirt down her hips, her shoulder-length white blond hair swinging forward as she bent her head. "And I still can't believe I let you guys talk me into this. I would've been more than happy to go dancing at Show."

Natasha leaned in and paid the driver, straightening to give Susan a distracted smile while glancing around the crowd milling on the sidewalk. A quick scan of the queue for the second floor revealed a few male faces, but no Peter. Neither did she spot him in the even longer line waiting for entrance to the nightclub's main floor.

She'd told him what time to be here, told him that he couldn't get in without her. She wasn't going to deny her disappointment but refused to stand out here and wait when he'd never guaranteed that he'd show. Especially not when this was Susan's night to celebrate, not Natasha's night to get lucky.

"Hey, you. Remember me? The birthday girl?" Susan waved a hand in front of Natasha's preoccupied face.

Clutch in one hand, Natasha draped her free arm over her girlfriend's shoulders, bared in a silver lamé bustier, and headed for the end of the rapidly moving line. "Sweetie, you are shaking like a leaf."

Susan gave in to a full-body shiver. "You've known me as long as you have and you expected anything less? I'm the one who thought Elaine's vibrator was a tampon case, remember? I belong here about as much as Elaine belongs in a nunnery."

Natasha adored Susan's dismay at her own innocence. "Well, consider this the first step toward the rest of your sexual life."

"It's kinda hard to think of it like that when I don't have a *date,*" Susan leaned over to whisper.

"No, no, no. That's the entire point of this exercise. You need to relax and release your inner sensualist. No pressure to perform and impress. It's all about being yourself with trusted friends who won't judge you on the length of your legs or the size of your ass."

Susan held up one finger. "Or try to get me drunk."

"Or try to get you naked." Natasha held up another finger as they counted off the ways of men's evil.

"Oh, good grief, yes. None of that groping and grabbing and getting into my pants business."

"Exactly," Natasha said, guiding the other woman toward the doorman working the entrance for the private upstairs party. "So, no men. At least for you."

Susan glanced to the side from under lowered lashes as they

left behind the noise of car horns, tires striking manhole covers, and sirens wailing in the distance for hard-driving house music and conversations shouted above the drums and the din.

"What's that supposed to mean, at least for me?"

Side by side, they climbed the carpeted stairs, the spinning disco ball above the downstairs dance floor sending shards of pink and red and orange light bouncing off Susan's bustier and into Natasha's eyes.

Funny, but all of a sudden she couldn't see Peter Deacon fitting in here at all. He was much too urbane, too refined, too . . . cosmopolitan for disco balls.

That didn't mean she wasn't rather depressed that he'd chosen not to come. She took a deep breath. "Obviously, he's not going to show, but I did invite a guy I met Wednesday night."

"Three days? That was fast."

"You have no idea," Natasha muttered under her breath.

"Ooh, details. I want to know everything." Susan fairly tittered.

And Natasha laughed. "See? I knew you had a voyeuristic streak. Now to get you upstairs so you can give it the exercise it deserves."

Susan wiggled both brows over her big baby blues. "Are you sure you don't want to wait for your new boyfriend?"

Boyfriend? Was that what Peter was? After knowing him but seventy-two hours and spending how many of those with her panties down? If she were to judge on appearances, she'd have to say no. He wasn't a boy, and nothing about him brought to mind the idea of holding hands and going steady.

What he brought to mind she wasn't able to articulate. She was only able to feel it, and feeling it here by herself, in a room of lowered inhibitions and scantily clad bodies, of throbbing music and alcohol buzzing through blood, made her itchy and frustrated, and yes, okay, she was edging toward becoming quite horny.

"Forget him," she shouted above the racket, knowing her

body never would and her mind wouldn't have it much easier, but thankful that at least she hadn't been stupid enough to involve her emotions. "Let's dance."

"What?" Susan shouted back. "Who are we supposed to dance with?"

"Each other, silly."

"I thought we were going to hook up with Yvonne and Elaine."

Natasha grabbed Susan by the hand and hauled her out into the middle of the crush of hot, sweaty bodies. "That's what we're doing."

"Nat, wait. What!" Susan wobbled on her heels as Natasha swung her around and into Elaine, who had a martini in one hand, her other raised overhead while she ground her pelvis against Yvonne's butt.

Susan gasped, cackled. And then, as the two women caught her between their sexy bump and grind, covered her shock with a hand to her mouth. Her silent surprise only lasted another two seconds, turning into a screech when Elaine leaned forward to run her tongue down Susan's neck.

Laughing, Natasha wrapped the three of them in a huge bear hug, stole away and downed Elaine's martini, and swore not to think about Peter Deacon for the rest of the night.

She had her girlfriends, good booze, and good music; she needed nothing more, though she would hold tight to the memory of her time spent naked with Peter.

She'd hold tight and add it to her mental reminder file that smart women did not involve themselves with men who kept secrets.

Tripp Shaughnessey jerked his headphones from his head, tossed them to clatter across his desktop, stretched out in his chair, and sighed. The sound was loud enough to echo above the constant hum and buzz of computer fans and hard drives in the cavernous room, muffled only by his hands scrubbing over his face.

Christian, listening to his set of recordings with his headset held to one ear, paused the audio playback on his control panel and swiveled his chair to take in the other man's exaggerated exhaustion. The room's high, open ceiling allowed for the rise of heat from the high-tech equipment, yet provided minimal lighting.

Instead, low-hanging lamps suspended on cables spotlighted each of the six desks in the circular workstation. The lack of viable windows inside the core of the server farm added to the cloistered feeling while providing one more necessary element of security.

The light was still enough to see the exhaustion wasn't exaggerated. Tripp didn't look so good.

They'd been listening now for eight hours to weeks of conversation from Bow's estate and university office—the lines having been tapped after the first contact with Spectra—as well as from Natasha's West Side apartment. None of the audio had been obtained legally and could never be used in court.

Then again, the Smithson Group wasn't about going to court. They were about doing what needed to be done, the good guys versus the bad guys, white hats sticking it to the black hats, the end justifying the means.

And, yeah. Once reaching that end, making sure to leave plenty of hard evidence laying around.

From the look on Tripp's face—or at least judging by his body language since his face was behind his hands—he wasn't having any more luck than Christian was finding evidence damning or even circumstantial enough to put Natasha away. It was a hell of a fucked-up situation, giving him cause to wonder a lot of things.

Such as, did he want to bust Natasha because Malena had so pulled the wool over his eyes. Or if he was looking for a legitimate reason to put a stop to what they'd started. Neither rationale would fly with Hank. Which meant Christian needed to get his act together and now.

"Tell me something, Bane."

"Shoot."

"How many years you been monitoring Spectra's communications?"

Too many. He should've wiped the bastards off the planet by now. "It's been seven years since . . . Thailand. Took a couple to get back up to speed. So"—he shrugged—"five at least."

Actually, it had been four years, eleven months, and seventeen days since Hank had handed him the assignment to dog Spectra's heels when the operative who'd been at the helm went down in the fiery ball of a sea plane in Prudhoe Bay.

"Okay, then." Tripp straightened in his chair. "I trust that you know their MO. And I know you were in the field when Hank caught first contact and the deal with Bow went down. But remind me again what convinced you that his goddaughter knew what was going on?"

Christian had been back from London for a month now, and the hell of it was, he couldn't pinpoint anything specific tying in Natasha. It was more a case of experience and heeding his unfailing gut instinct that told him a woman that close to the source was not uninvolved.

During his time away, it had been Hank himself who'd manned the audio surveillance, Julian and Eli who'd then snagged the Spectra front man when he'd entered the States. Once Hank handed down the mission, Christian had spent his prep time eating, breathing, and sleeping Deacon's portfolio and listening to the same recordings he and Tripp were going over now.

Yet he couldn't put one of his ten fingers on anything specific that had raised his suspicions anymore than he could now find what he needed to clear them.

"I mean, you of all people know that guilt by association is bullshit," Tripp was saying.

And, yeah. Christian should know that. He did know that. He was losing perspective, and shit was getting skewed when he should've had his head on straight enough by now to keep that from happening.

"I hate to say it, Bane. But we could be frying our brains here for no reason."

Not just no, but hell no. It would never be for no reason. Not when destroying Spectra for good was the endgame. Still, he'd be a fool to discount Tripp's frustration. Frustration and exhaustion made for sloppy work, missed opportunities, too many cases of jumping the gun. Patience was never such a virtue as during surveillance.

Tripp pushed up out of his chair and stretched side to side, popping joints and vertebrae until Christian found himself gritting his teeth at his partner's pain.

"Hell," the other man said, going on and knowing Christian well enough to expect no response. "If she's not a part of the deal, then bring her in and use her. She may know a lot and not even be aware. You know how that works. What she thinks are throwaway tidbits might be the information nail in Bow's coffin."

Christian knew that, too. He moved beyond the recorded conversations and thought back to the ones he'd had with her, real time. And this time he was the one leaning back and dragging his hands over his face, digging the heels of his palms into his eye sockets, hoping the outside pressure would balance the internal that was about to blow.

"I mean the only reference I've heard to your Ms. Gaudet is Bow telling Deacon she would be available to see to his needs, which sounds pretty kinky to me. I can see why you—"

"Wait, wait." His heart misfired. His adrenaline popped. He shot up straight in his chair, narrowed his eyes. "She didn't know that."

Hell, he hadn't even known that until he'd arrived that night. How had he missed that? Stupid shit, going in unaware of a detail so obvious even Tripp in his exhaustion had picked it up. "She didn't know that."

"What?" Tripp asked, dropping flat out on the floor to stretch his aching back.

"When Deacon—when *I* got there, she didn't know that. Bow didn't tell her until later that night."

"Or so she says."

"Yeah. But why the pretense? If it was prearranged, why

not be up front with it? I mean, she acted like she didn't even know Deacon was coming."

"Unless she's lying about it all."

"Again, why would she?" He surged to his feet, paced the floor in front of his desk. "If this deal is that important to Bow, so important that he's handing Natasha to Deacon, then she would've known he was coming. She would've been prepared. She would've been waiting for him."

He stopped, stared down at Tripp. "Right? Right?"

Tripp simply shrugged.

"What reason would she have to pretend she didn't know who the hell he was? I was?"

"I dunno."

"Give me a reason, Tripp. I need something to chew on here."

"Bad taste in your mouth?"

Actually, no. Christian was tasting Natasha along with what seemed like the truth. "Think about it. If she knew she had this deal to do for Bow, why plan tonight's party the same time Deacon would be visiting?"

"She can't exactly pick and choose birth dates."

"No, but birthdays aren't always celebrated on the exact calendar day."

"It's a stretch, Bane."

Yeah. He knew that. But Natasha knowing who and what Deacon was hadn't worked for him now for seventy-two hours. The tapes were doing nothing more than confirming what his gut had been telling him since he tossed her the keys to the Ferrari.

Natasha Gaudet was being screwed by the man pulling the strings of her loyalty. And for too many reasons that he didn't want to examine, because of too many nightmares that he didn't want to relive, that pissed him off more than anything.

She was an innocent standing in the crossfire of danger. And he had to get her out.

Eleven

An hour later, the four women managed to claim a half-moon booth in the quietest corner of the club and collapse.

Natasha had long since stripped off her sheer black one-shouldered pullover, and still perspiration had her black Lycra tank clinging like a second skin. Her low-rise swing pants were loose enough to be breezy as she danced. Sitting, the bright red rayon swathed her like wet blankets.

She stretched out her legs beneath the table, her arms along the top of the red and gold striped and padded bench. "Remind me next time we do this to come in nothing but my undies."

"Strip down now." Leaning into the elbow she'd propped on the circular table hardly big enough for four drinks, Elaine swirled her index finger in her sour apple martini, then lapped the drink from her skin. "It's not like anyone would notice."

"Tell me about it," Yvonne piped in, fluffing up her bouncy golden brown curls. "I haven't seen this much skin since, well, since ever. Mmm-mmm-mmm. So many chests to ogle, so many fine asses to grope. And no expectations at the end of the night. Could it get any better?"

"Depends," Elaine said, one dark eyebrow raised over a dark brown eye, her beautifully elfish face belying the workings of her kinky mind. "Are you ogling the men or the women?"

"Both, actually," the other woman answered before the two-of-a-kind pair collapsed back against the booth and dissolved into silly drunken giggles.

Natasha rolled her eyes and glanced around the club where, indeed, a good portion of the women wore next to nothing as they danced, drank, and partied with one another as intimately as did the few who had brought along men—most of whom were quite undressed themselves by now.

She couldn't help but wonder about those men, if they'd perform as well in bed later, or if the pressure of a one-on-one with a confident successful woman—a woman such as any one of the three sitting with her—would have them running for a dose of Viagra.

Why were men so challenged by a woman who knew her own mind?

At times she was certain that all the headway made in the name of women's independence had backfired. After all, here she and her girlfriends were. Accessible. Available. Alone.

All four of them living in a city where the single women outnumbered the single men, reducing the chances of ever finding that one special man to wake up to, to anticipate seeing at the end of the work day, to laugh with over dinner, to cuddle with during late night television, to make love with and fall asleep with. . . .

Sighing, she shook off the ridiculous burst of white picket fence melancholy just as Susan tittered and grabbed her glass of white wine. "I think, actually? That Nat's holding out until she gets home to strip. Just in case her new boyfriend is there waiting."

Elaine and Yvonne immediately sobered, sat up, and leaned forward to get a better look, as if Natasha were some sort of highway accident and their necks were made of rubber. She narrowed her eyes and glared at Susan's angelically innocent expression as Elaine asked, "Boyfriend?" Yvonne adding, "And we're the last to know?"

Natasha pulled her arms from the back of the booth and tucked both hands beneath her thighs. She bounced her heels, her knees bumping the table, and met each woman's inquisitive gaze in turn.

Her entire body was suddenly rife with a strange energy. Nervous, yes. But more than that.

Edgy.

Uneasy.

She didn't want to explain anything at all about Peter. What they'd shared belonged solely to her. Mentioning him to Susan had been a mistake; the club's atmosphere was hardly conducive to conversation. Not that they'd stopped dancing long enough to talk. . . .

Damn it. She needed to talk. Needed her girlfriends' advice. Perhaps discussing him in abstract was the answer. Vague responses. Anonymous queries. No details that could smack of self-betrayal.

Sighing deeply, she stretched her legs out and stilled. "He's not a boyfriend. I only met him Wednesday night."

"Wait, wait, wait." Elaine shook a scolding finger, frowned at a passing server who jostled her shoulder. "You've known him three days? And you're already including him in our group?"

"Sounds like she wanted to get him here and get him out of half of his clothes," Yvonne suggested.

Susan snickered again. "Why bother with half? Why not the full monty?"

Natasha remained mum on the question of Peter's nudity, picked up her wineglass, and said, "I don't think he's the party type anyway. I'm really not all that surprised he didn't show up."

Ever helpful, Yvonne offered, "Or else he likes to keep his parties private."

"And what about that full monty business?" Elaine asked. "Are you getting busy with him already? Because, if you are? I'm seriously going to have to kick your ass. You know better, Nat. Really."

Natasha swirled the last of her wine in the bowl of her

glass, signaling to the server for another. "Does that really sound like something you can see me doing?"

"I don't want to see you doing it, no." Elaine turned down the offer for a refill. "But I *can* imagine it."

"Especially since it's happened before." Yvonne handed the server a twenty to cover her and Natasha's drinks.

"Pet—uh, this guy," she quickly corrected, "isn't like Keith at all."

"Keith, who was going to be"—Susan clasped her hands beneath her chin and took on a dreamy-eyed expression—"the one."

"The one you connected with like no man before," Yvonne added, lifting her glass in a toast.

"I did. I still do." Ugh. This was not going well, Natasha grumbled to herself, rubbing at the strap of tension binding her temples. "Just not on a level that works in the bedroom."

Elaine snorted. "Well, it might work there if he didn't have a wife."

God, did Peter have a wife? One he left at home while visiting lovers in every port?

Nice time for her curiosity to take a vacation; the thought had never even crossed her mind. "Okay. I realize that I tend to jump first and ask questions later—"

"That's putting it mildly." This from Elaine.

"—but I have a sort of sixth sense about this guy. That he's worth jumping for."

"Jumping into bed?" This from Yvonne.

"Maybe, yes. But not just bed." This wasn't exactly easy to explain, to the girls *or* to herself. Making such a judgment after only three days? No wonder they all stared at her as if she were daft. "I know. It sounds loony. I'm not even sure I can make it make sense."

Shaking her head, Elaine helped herself to Susan's untouched cosmopolitan. "Let me guess. You felt an instant connection."

Natasha gave into a spontaneous smile as she thought back. "Even before he tossed me the keys to his Ferrari."

Three pairs of eyes made up in glittery metallic shadow

widened. It was Susan who finally squeaked out, "A Ferrari? He drives a Ferrari?", and Elaine who interrupted with, "Wait. He let *you* drive his Ferrari?"

Yvonne simply pressed the backs of her fingers beneath her chin to close her slack jaw.

"It's not about the money," Natasha insisted to a round of rolled eyes and shaking heads. "It was every single moment together being about me."

"Oh, now *there's* a surprise," Yvonne teased.

"No. *He* made it about me. He walked up and saw me drooling over his car and let me take it for a drive. When we stopped at Overlook Point, he gave me his jacket the second he noticed I was cold. And we're talking quality. Gorgeous Armani that smelled so fine."

Even now Natasha found herself breathing deeply and remembering the warmth of Peter's scent. "He asked questions and talked about me. For the first time in forever, instead of a man feeding me line after line—or lie after lie—all about himself," she corrected to nodding heads and knowing laughter, "he was interested in me. Which means, unfortunately, I know almost nothing about him."

"Including whether or not he's married." Yvonne's emphatic statement required no response. So Natasha didn't give one, turning instead to Susan, who asked, "So you met him upstate, not here in the city?"

"He's doing business with Wick and has an office here, but I get the impression he lives abroad."

"Well, that explains it," Elaine said. "He's not caught up in this ridiculous competition that's corrupted every man I've met lately. It's all about out-climbing, out-witting, out-maneuvering, out-spending, and out-fucking the rest of the male population."

Yvonne turned her gaze on Elaine. "Bitter much?"

Elaine snorted, finished off the rest of Susan's drink, and drilled Natasha with a gaze that was surprisingly sharp for the amount of alcohol she'd downed. "Just do me a favor, Nat. Do yourself a favor. Find out if the bastard is married before you tumble head over heels."

"I know. I will." The matter of discovering Peter's matrimonial state was first on Natasha's "to do" list.

"I'm serious, Natasha. We're here for you. We'll always be here for you." Elaine went on, both Susan and Yvonne nodding their agreement. "But after the shit you went through with Keith? Don't expect us to be quite so gentle the next time we have to shovel you up off the floor."

"Trust me. There won't be a next time." And there wouldn't be. She was done falling in love at the drop of a hat—or a pair of Armani pants. She lifted her wineglass to seal her own personal relationship bargain. "No more confusing lust with love for this girl."

"Good. Because we're going to hold you to that," Elaine said, as she and the other two women hooked their pinky fingers in a show of solidarity that had Natasha on the verge of tears—partly because she loved her friends so dearly.

But also because they looked so damn silly. "C'mon, you guys. Enough about me. This is Susan's party and she needs to dance!"

Wickham Bow sat in the far corner of the terrace that edged his property's landscaped yard.

Natasha had insisted last year on renovations to make the area wheelchair accessible. He'd argued at the time that the expense would never see a return as he seldom felt the desire to spend time out of doors.

Now, however, he had to admit a bit of a grudging—and ironic—pleasure in her efforts. Being able to access the terrace gave him a choice view of the guest suite's balcony and the opportunity to imagine the intimate assignation Dr. Jinks had witnessed.

It pleased Wickham to no end that Natasha had followed his instructions so implicitly in regards to seeing to Mr. Deacon's every need. She had even, it seemed, gone above and beyond. His goddaughter's judgment had always been impeccable; he expected no less from the lessons she'd learned sitting at his own feet and those of her father.

A gust of wind swept over him, and he turned up the lapels on his suit coat. Michael Gaudet had been a true friend, and Wickham missed the other man sorely, the way he would miss a brother, the way he missed his good health. The sort of friend who would no doubt advise him to seek psychological help or don a straightjacket were his plans discovered.

But Michael was no longer here, and Wickham was facing a crisis unlike any he had known in his life. A life that was growing more painful to live. That he refused to live with no hope beyond his current prognosis.

To be confined to a body that no longer functioned. To be unable to voice his theories. To be forced to communicate by blinking his eyes. And how long he'd be able to do that much . . . he didn't even want to think that far ahead.

"Desperate times call for desperate measures, my friend," he said, wishing Michael were here to respond. A rousing good argument was what he needed right now.

A challenging debate on the federal policy regulating research involving human participants. A heated discussion of a man's theological right to determine his own fate, to use and abuse his own body at will.

He could just see Michael's face when he argued that Christian apologist C.S. Lewis had been out of his mind to claim that pain allowed one to see joy more clearly. Wickham had been blinded to joy now for months.

He'd been following the advancements in research on his neurodegenerative disease since being diagnosed, but time was not on his side.

Yet now . . . Now he had been given an opportunity that he had to take, an opportunity that he knew he would regret not embracing. The possibility that he would die?

Die as a result of a procedure that, no matter its promising results in unsanctioned clinical trials, would never receive governmental approval and was costing him more money than he'd see in his lifetime?

He laughed to himself, huddled deeper into his suit coat as the wind from the woods cut across the terrace, whistling in the boughs above his head. He would die regardless, as was man's destiny. Yet because he was slated to die sooner than his time, reflecting on his past had become a near daily and proliferative waste of time he could be devoting to work.

It was that reflection that had brought to mind the years he had spent mentoring Woodrow Jinks. A great fortune, when combined with Wickham's own recent work and resulting papers published on data encryption. Work that kept his name on the international radar as an expert in his field. A radar seen by both friend and foe alike.

What wasn't on any radar but his own was the fact that the encryption work Jinks had done while under his tutelage was now in federal hands. The software had been purchased by the government along with that of other developers, and was part of the package protecting the transmission feeds sent by the CIA's data analysts to their agents in the field.

No one man, no one team had written the encryption program that guaranteed the security and authenticity of the transmitted data. The software had been amalgamated, certain functions of the individual programs utilized, others discarded, giving none of the original developers ownership or authorship of the product in its final form.

Neither would they be able to access the original programs via the original commands. Exactly as it should be, Wickham had noted at the time, pleased to have a small part in his country's defense and wondering what his recently deceased friend, Michael Gaudet, would have said had he witnessed Wickham's ridiculously uncharacteristic display of patriotic schmaltz.

It was only years later, after the diagnosis of his illness, following months of research into possible treatments and his discovery of the radical institute testing an experimental procedure, that he remembered Dr. Jinks's penchant for hacking, for gaming, for leaving back doors into his own work.

Patriotism did a man no good if he wasn't alive to benefit, or so Wickham would have argued with Michael. And there were always men willing to pay another for his treachery to give him that chance.

This was Wickham's chance. This experiment that might offer his only prospect for a life worth living. It was a hefty cost monetarily, an even heftier one should his treason be discovered—though the possibility of a death penalty was hardly a deterrent when he was living with one as it was.

It seemed Wickham had been right about Dr. Jinks. And now it was simply a matter of the younger scientist giving Mr. Deacon a proper demonstration of his capabilities. Wickham glanced up again at the guest suite's balcony.

Once Spectra IT's representative was satisfied that the encryption software had indeed been cracked, and the transfer of funds had been authorized, then Wickham would set into motion the rest of his plan.

The part involving Natasha and her lover.

Twelve

Arriving home exhausted, Natasha tossed her clutch to the corner of her blue and beige plaid sofa, kicked her shoes off and up against the base. She needed a shower, a fat dose of aspirin with hot herbal tea, and sleep. The recipe was a sure cure for avoiding tomorrow morning's guaranteed hangover.

A hangover would only double her grumpiness at having to hire a car to drive her back to Wick's estate. Thankfully, his department's travel budget made it possible for her to write off such an expense. Obviously, Peter's business dealings with her godfather meant he would be returning, too.

But just as obviously she couldn't count on getting a ride back with him. Stupid of her not to have asked for his cell number. Stupider even to think she wouldn't need it since she'd be seeing him later at the club. And if that wasn't the most stupid assumption of all, then she truly was the ass assuming made of "u" and "me".

Way too pleased with her tipsy and self-directed humor, she headed for the kitchen, shook out three aspirin from the bottle on top of the microwave before filling a mug with filtered water from the tap. After downing the meds, she stuck the mug in the oven for a quick blast and dug a tea bag from the pantry. She watched the mug rotate, grabbed it on the oven's first "all done" ding, and had just dunked the bag of aromatic herbs when she heard a sharp rap at the door.

Since she wasn't missing any clothing and had made it home with only her own, she doubted her visitor was one of the girls. Unless Yvonne had lost her keys, or Elaine had forgotten her address, or Susan was too depressed about being a year older to spend the night alone.

Of course it could be Keith, lonely Keith, promising that this time he was leaving his wife. For real. He swore. Setting the tea on the counter, Natasha tiptoed her way to the door in the dark. No sense broadcasting that she hadn't yet gone to bed if it was indeed Keith and he'd been watching for her to come home.

It took but one bleary-eyed peek through the peephole to identify her visitor and set her traitorous heart to pounding. She stepped back, swiped at her hair, sniffed her pits—ugh, she'd been sweaty—before deciding that any man who stood her up wasn't worth primping for.

She unlocked the door, pulled it open, but did not swing it wide and invite Peter in. "If you're looking for your watch, I'm sorry but I haven't seen it."

He blinked slowly, lazily, his blue eyes sparkling even at this late hour. "My business took longer than I expected. If I'd had a way to reach you, I would have called to keep you from waiting."

That was so close to an apology she wasn't sure what to say, so she simply told him, "I didn't wait."

"Good." He stood with one hand on the doorjamb, lifted the other to tuck her tangled hair behind her ear. "A woman as beautiful as you are should never wait for a man."

God, he was doing it to her already. Doing it to her again. Barely touching her and making her want him. Her girlfriends were right. She hadn't needed them to remind her how weak she was, how susceptible to falling too hard and too fast, but the reinforcement could not have come at a better time.

She drew on it even now. "Were you wanting something?

Other than to let me know what time tomorrow you're thinking of leaving?"

The light in the landing shone around his head like a halo, limning him with a surreal golden glow, but casting his face into shadow as if to hide the truth. This man was no prim and proper white-winged angel. He looked mysterious standing with his head bowed, daunting when she took in the breadth of his shoulders, intimidating in that way he had of seeming to hold himself in check when he was capable of doing any damage he damn well pleased.

She did her best not to shiver. She failed.

His hand lingered, toying with the ends of her hair, using the tips of the strands as a paintbrush along the line of her jaw. "What time would be convenient for you?"

"Wick's not expecting us until early evening. So, noon would be fine. That would give me time to run a few errands." When he stopped stroking her, she lifted her chin, unconsciously reaching for more. "Besides, if I get up too early I'll be worthless tomorrow. After tonight out with the girls, I've got to get some sleep."

He let her hair go; his hand hovered at the neckline of her tank before he dropped it to his side. "Then I hope that tea you're drinking is decaffeinated."

Her tea. Right. She cleared her throat and stepped back as if she'd never begged him to touch her. She wanted him to touch her and admitted then that desire was a bitch. "It's herbal. Would you like a cup?"

"I would, yes." He moved to block the doorway, both hands now braced on either side of the jamb, and loomed over her. "But if you invite me in, I'm going to stay the night."

"I see," she said, swallowing hard and reminding herself of the secrets he kept, arguing back that she would never have a better chance to ferret them out than here and now, the two of them alone without the interruption of his business with Wick. "The sofa's quite comfortable, though admittedly short. But I have plenty of blankets and pillows—"

Peter cut her off with a shake of his head. "If I stay the night, I won't be sleeping on the sofa."

She knew that. She knew that. And she let him in anyway. Doing what she could to justify her actions with reasons that even she would have trouble believing on a good day. Like entertaining Peter was all part of the job Wick had given her. Like she enjoyed Peter's enigmatic personality and wanted the quiet time to figure out why. Like she wanted to hear what he'd like to do in the days ahead so she could schedule her time accordingly.

The truth was much more simple, as truth usually was. She let him in because her body steadfastly ignored the good intentions of her head, refused to listen to the warnings of her common sense, denied giving credence to rational thought, which insisted she didn't know what she was getting herself into.

So what if a previous leap or two of faith had ended badly. She was learning life's relationship lessons along the way, was stronger and smarter these days, less likely to be duped now that she lived with her eyes wide open. Right? *Right?* "I'm drinking honey chamomile. But I also have straight Darjeeling if you'd prefer."

"The Darjeeling, please," he said, closing her door and locking both of her deadbolts before following her to the small combination kitchen and eating alcove. There, he crossed his arms, leaned a shoulder on the long edge of her pantry door, and watched as she reached for the tin of tea. "This place suits you."

She stopped herself from rolling her eyes, lifted a brow instead. "You haven't even seen it. And you've only just met me. How do you know what suits and what doesn't?" She filled a second mug from the tap, set it in the microwave, and turned toward him as the water warmed. "And don't give me that crap about thoroughly investigating anyone you're doing business with. I don't buy it for a minute."

"Why not?" he asked smugly.

"Because if you've gone so far as to check out my decorating tastes and hatred of all things knickknack just to work with Wick on data encryption—"

"I thought you said you didn't know the details of your godfather's work," he said, cutting her off sharply, his suspicious tone of voice bringing her chin up defiantly.

"I don't." The microwave dinged, but she didn't punch it open right away. She didn't know what his deal was, repeatedly challenging her on her involvement with Wick and the lab rats, but she was pretty much fed up. "But I'm not stupid. And considering the correspondence I handle for him, the conversations I have with experts from all over the world, the gist of what he does is not lost on me."

When Peter didn't immediately respond, Natasha turned back to his tea to regain her bearings. She couldn't imagine that her godfather would've said anything to give Peter the impression that she was any more than an administrative assistant.

The fact that he thought she might be involved in the programming and software development was, she supposed, a backhanded compliment; it took a hell of a genius to work with binary data. But repeating herself, defending herself was rapidly getting old.

"You're right," Peter finally said as she removed the tea bag and offered him cream and sugar. "Black, a teaspoon of sugar, thanks. My thinking this place suits you is based solely on how it makes me feel."

"How it makes *you* feel?" she queried with no little sense of righteous skepticism, as she stirred the sugar into his tea. Why should the place where she lived give him cause to feel anything? "I don't understand."

He canted his head, frowning in thought. "Tell me something. Are you most comfortable when you're here or when staying in your rooms at your godfather's estate?"

Though she'd never really thought about it, the answer came to her without a moment's consideration. "Here, actually. But that's because this is my place, you know? I have free reign when at Wick's, of course. And he's never made me feel as if I have no right to be there. But when I'm here there's no question of anyone looking over my shoulder. Besides," she went on, offering up a small shrug, "I get homesick for the noise and the bright lights if I stay away too long."

"Is that what you feel when at Dr. Bow's place?" Peter's gaze slowly hardened. "As if you're being watched?"

"No. Not at all." She handed him his tea, his fingers warm as they covered hers; the strange look in his eyes—guarded? protective?—told her he would have held her longer if she hadn't pulled away. She picked up her own mug, blew over the steaming surface. "At least not watched like being spied on. It's just hard to have any privacy with the lab rats coming and going and the staff in and out doing their thing."

He held his mug in one hand, fisted his other and shoved it into his pants pocket. She had no idea what he was thinking, though the fact that he seemed to be fighting for control caught her off guard. And then remembering how this conversation had started quickly became a lost cause. He was looking into her again with that intensity that hummed over her skin like the wind racing before a wildfire.

She watched him raise his drink to his mouth, watched him blow lightly then sip. She mirrored his actions, using two hands to hold her mug while he managed with only one. Funny, her sudden awareness of their disparity in size, as if she wasn't intimately knowledgeable already. And before that train of thought took her into territory best avoided, she asked him, "So, what *does* make you think this place fits me?"

"I'm not sure." He stared into his mug's dark liquid. "Or at least not sure I can explain."

"Uh-uh. You started this. I don't buy that you don't have some clue."

His head came up at that, his expression saying "fair enough." "I work a lot of hours, at least half of them while traveling. I stay in rooms that cost what is a monthly mortgage payment for many."

"And that's what suits you?" she asked when he seemed to grow lost in thought.

"No," he said, shaking his head. "I don't think it does. Not anymore."

"Good. That means you're still human. And as long as you don't demand bowls of nothing but green M&M's when you're staying wherever it is you stay, then I don't think you need to worry."

And then he laughed. "That's it. That's why your place fits. It's no frills and straight to the point. Just like you are."

Her heart turned over with what she swore was an audible thump. She might feel most alive when in the city, but she was still a big fan of simplicity. And the fact that he had noticed . . . *tha-dump, tha-dump, tha-dump*. "So, then, you find my Spartan furnishings appealing."

He smiled, almost tentatively. "Perhaps I do."

"Well, Spartan or not, the sofa is much more comfortable for conversation than standing here in the kitchen," she said, taking her mug of tea and leading him to the sofa on which he'd refused to sleep. And besides, if he laughed like that again, smiled like that again, looked into her eyes again as if searching out all of her thoughts, well, they needed more space between them than her kitchen allowed.

"How was your party?" he asked, choosing to sit in her side chair instead—a choice that could have been devastating had she not just reined in her lust. Devastating, because sitting the way he was, one ankle squared over the opposite knee, the fabric of his clothing clearly showed off the build of his most amazing body and she was not as immune and strong-willed as she'd thought.

"It was fun," she said, smiling, staring down at the surface of her tea to regain her bearings, and realizing that she really had enjoyed the raunchy fun—and needed the ass-chewing—of her girl's night out. "You didn't miss anything but a lot of girl talk and wild girl-on-girl dancing action."

He didn't say a word. For a very long moment he simply sat

there in a chair she'd never thought very comfortable, his elbows on the padded arms, his big hands enveloping the mug he balanced on his belt buckle. Devastating, yes, that was definitely the word, because she felt her will to resist him crumble into tiny particles of resolve.

And then the corner of his mouth lifted. The right corner, revealing that dimple in his cheek she wanted to measure with the tip of her index finger. Measure and poke and feel the bristle of beard he wore.

"I'm sorry I missed that," he finally said, lifting his tea to hide the full tilt of his smile. Typical man. Caught virtually speechless by the mental picture of writhing female bodies she'd painted. Or so she thought until he added, "The talk more so than the dancing."

"You're kidding, right?" She tucked her legs up beneath her. "You would rather listen in on a conversation between four women than watch them dance?"

"Dancing only tells me how your body moves," he said, completely serious. "That I already know. What you choose to talk about reveals so much more."

They'd talked about other men. They'd talked about him. They'd talked about her need to curb her physical needs long enough for her brain to engage and involve itself in her relationship choices. She couldn't imagine him sitting in on any of those conversations.

"So, we talk now. I'll reveal all." She allowed herself a private smirk as she lifted her mug to her mouth. "Of course, that means you have to do the same."

"Or we could simply go to bed," he countered, his expression near enough to neutral that she sensed he was baiting her more than issuing an invitation.

"We could, yes." Think fast. *Think fast.* "But how much more pleasurable to"—she stopped herself from saying *make love*—"share that intimacy with a partner you know."

"I don't think either of us have missed out on any pleasure recently."

Oh, but he was good. Seducing her with nothing but memories and the silky tone of his voice. "Perhaps not," she whispered, her hands trembling around her mug. "But we'll never know without giving it a try."

"Curiosity killing you again?"

Of course it was. And she liked that he remembered more of what had gone on between them than the sex. "Well? Is it a deal?"

He shook his head. "We can talk in bed."

She heard hushed sex words, softly spoken requests, pleas disguised as rough demands. Her breathing quickened, as did her body, the rush of blood through her veins a singeing furnace blast that had her ready to strip naked then and there. "That's not the kind of talking I meant."

"No clothes. No barriers. Both at our most vulnerable. Dangerously exposed. Perhaps saying more than we should."

A little late in the game to be asking, but she had to know. "Peter, are you married?"

A winged brow lifted, he murmured, "Would it matter to you if I were?"

"Yes. It would. I'm not in the habit of sleeping with married men."

"Are you sure?"

Would he have investigated her that deeply? To have found out about Keith? "I made a mistake. I won't make it again. And, if I have? Then I need to correct the situation, don't I?"

"No. I'm not married."

She couldn't believe the relief that swept through her. Oh, but she was in deeper here than she'd thought. Wanting to do exactly as he'd suggested. Bare his body and work her way into his mind. "I have to shower."

"Then we'll shower."

"We?" she asked before wondering why she was questioning him when he was giving her what she wanted. The eroticism of skin on skin. Of steam and heat and slick soap.

"Yes. We." He paused, added, "Unless you have some female ritual you'd rather take care of in private."

Was he talking about shaving her legs? Douching? Masturbating? Or was he simply giving her a way out? "No. No rituals but those involving soap and shampoo."

"Okay then." He uncrossed his leg, leaned forward, and set his mug on the coffee table. Elbows braced on knees, he met her gaze and waited, his patience making her jumpy and insane.

"You know," she began, placing her mug next to his, feeling strangely shy all of a sudden. "This seems almost too . . . calculated."

"You prefer to be impulsive?"

"Yes. I suppose. Doesn't everyone?" She shrugged, rubbed her cooling hands together and laughed softly. "I love spontaneity, the excitement of it. Like the other night."

He watched her for a moment that grew long and heated, his expression darkening, kindling the room's tension to a combustible point. "Are you so sure what happened that night was spontaneous? We kissed on the terrace, Natasha. You stopped us then from going further, but I wasn't the only one aroused while it happened."

What could she say in response? Admit he was right? She *had* put him off on the terrace. She'd wanted privacy, wanted the intimacy she hadn't thought possible when faced with the fear of discovery. Even now arousal returned. A flush warmed the skin of her chest, crept upward in a tingling, tickling rush of sensation until even her ears felt the burn. Until it hurt to breathe!

"If you tell me that when you came to my room you'd already put that kiss from your mind, I'll believe you. But I don't think it happened that way." He took hold of the hands she'd laced together, rubbing his thumb over the backs of her fingers in long smooth strokes and with a hypnotizing pressure so intense she feared she would follow him anywhere. "I know it didn't happen that way for me. When you knocked on my door, I was debating whether to go to your room or to make do with a hot shower and soap."

She pictured him naked, using her tactile memories of his body to imagine him taking hold of his erection and stroking himself to completion. Stroking while he thought of their kiss, thought of the way he'd thumbed her nipples there on the staircase. She couldn't help it; she wanted to watch. Oh, how she wanted to watch.

But she wanted to watch less than she wanted to touch, to take him in her hand, into her mouth. To bend over for him there in the shower, to back up and offer up all he might desire to take.

"So, tell me the truth, Natasha. Is it the spontaneity that turns you on, or is it me?"

Thirteen

It was him. Without a question. Without a doubt. Oh yes. The spontaneity meant nothing in the end, and he knew it. She saw that awareness along with every bit of his arrogance when she forced her gaze from their joined hands to his eyes.

Cocky, egotistical sonofabitch, manipulating her into a silent confession while totally turning her on. He knew exactly how rapidly her pulse was racing, how warm her skin had grown. How could he not when he held her hands there where her skin perspired, her blood ran heavy and hot?

She'd never known a man like this one even while she didn't know him at all. And she couldn't believe how much she wanted him.

Oh yeah, she wanted him, wanted to laugh from the giddy expectation, wanted to cry out with the frustration of being so expertly played, wanted to push him down onto her sofa, climb on top, and have him until he cried out for mercy.

That thought more than any other was the basis for the smile she gave him. She wanted to witness him break down and beg.

Still holding both of her hands, he got to his feet, pulling her up against him. For a second or two, she swore he was going to kiss her. He had that look in his eye, that haunting need she'd seen before, an expression so unbearably sensual that she guilelessly parted her lips.

She watched him touch the tip of his tongue to the edge of his teeth, watched as he weighed his decision, watched it all unaware of holding her breath until he pressed his lips together and backed a step away.

He led her unerringly around the sofa, through her bedroom to her bathroom, large enough for only a shower. He seemed so out of place, the epitome of sophistication in his designer labels and Italian car, moneyed and well-traveled, by his own admission used to staying in places she could never afford without winning a Powerball lotto.

Yet here he was, undeterred by her shower enclosure's very modest size. She liked that about him. Liked it a lot. More than she should be thinking of liking anything considering this was no more than a fling. And it was just a fling, right?

Right?

She hugged her arms to her waist, glanced from her pedestal sink and the mirror above to the shelf of towels and toiletries and the frosted glass front of the stall while she waited.

He closed the bathroom door; she heard him take a deep breath and blow it out slowly. At the catch of the latch, she flinched, more nervous now than she'd ever been on the balcony. On the balcony, she hadn't had time to think, only to feel.

It came to her then, way too late. *That* was the beauty of spontaneity. Leaping into the heart of the fun without making this endlessly long critical analysis prior to launch.

"I'm sorry the quarters are so cramped," she said at last.

"Don't be." He moved in behind her, rubbed his palms up and down her bare arms before bodily turning her around. "Don't be sorry. And don't be nervous. We're both here because we want to be. That's the only thing that matters."

He sounded so certain and so confident when she was neither. She was, in fact, on the verge of shaking out of her skin. What was it about him that made her so edgy? She'd never been the sort to get caught up by feelings she couldn't define.

Yet here she was, a casual affair held in one hand, the need to know the secrets he kept in the other, and no way to balance the scale of contradictions.

"I'm not nervous," she said, and shivered. "I'm just... cold."

His expression softened, the lines at the corners of his eyes fanning out as he smiled, seeming to relax even further the deeper her tension set in. He reached around her into the stall and turned on the water. From the corner of her eye, she watched clouds of steam roll and rise, the humid air swirling, settling on her skin and, when she inhaled, reminding her of why she was here.

She retreated a step within the confining space. "Uh, you probably don't want to get too close. I did quite a lot of dancing tonight."

He moved nearer anyway, one brow arched with interest. She backed up further until she hit the wall of white and blue tiles, raised a halting hand to the center of his chest. "Trust me on this. Space right now is a very good thing."

"Consider me warned." He spread his legs, using his body as a barrier to prevent her escape, braced both palms above her shoulders on the wall and leaned in, nuzzled her neck, hummed against her skin. "You smell like you've been having a very good time."

The man was obviously too horny to think straight. "I smell like a locker room."

He chuckled. Her nipples hardened. His heart beat a tom-tom rhythm into her palm. "It's a hell of a turn-on, Natasha, knowing a woman isn't afraid of working up a sweat. Makes sex all that much better not having to worry about messing up her hair."

Natasha snorted. "You mean it's better because you don't have to do all the work."

"That, too," he said before he bit her.

Not too hard and not to hurt her. Only to let her know he was there. As if there was a chance she could ever forget. Especially now that he was tasting her, drawing the skin he'd nipped into his mouth and healing it with his tongue, the tip that was teasingly gentle, the flat that was firmly intent.

She dug her fingers into the hard muscles of his chest, groaning, then fumbling with the buttons of his shirt, tugging the tails from his waistband, finding skin—yes, there he was. Warm and smooth. Hard beneath flesh that was resilient. His pecs. His abs. The round of his shoulders. The strap of muscle supporting his spine.

She couldn't get enough of touching him, or of his mouth kissing and nibbling and no doubt marking her neck black and blue. He smelled so good, like dark woods and desire, and she smelled like . . . ugh. No. Not yet. *Not yet.* Palms flat to his pectorals, she pushed him away.

His eyes flashed brightly, and she loved seeing the evidence of how much he wanted her. Loved the power inherent to sex. Wondered not for the first time if her fascination with men wasn't as much about that sense of control as it was about their bodies.

"Peter, I need a shower," she said, reaching for the hem of her tank and whipping the shirt over her head. Her breasts bounced; she watched him watch her, saw his ragged intake of breath, took note of the tightly clenched line of his jaw, the tic of pulse at his temple.

Grinning to herself, she ducked out from beneath the bridge of his arms and reached for her pants' rear zipper. He stepped in behind her, and before she knew to struggle, bound both of her wrists in one hand. She was no match for his strength, had she wanted to fight. She didn't.

She simply closed her eyes, raised her chin, and let him win this first battle. Mist from the shower settled over her skin, beading and running in rivulets that dampened her throat to her belly.

She arched her back, thrust her hips into the cradle of his, wanting, aching, needing him to release her, to slip his hands around and cup her breasts, to slide his fingers between her legs and discover how ready she was. To press the heel of his palm to the mound of her sex and grind down hard. What she needed was for him to be naked.

Her impatient tugging of her hands from his hold only served to tighten his one-handed grip. "You're hardly playing fair."

He chuckled, toyed with her zipper, inched it down just far enough to dip a finger beneath the elastic of her thong and into the crevice between the curve of her cheeks. "Isn't all fair in love and war?"

This wasn't about love. *It wasn't.* He knew it as well as she. This was about using his strength to get what he wanted. About her willingness to easily give in. "Sure. The same way paybacks are hell."

He laughed at that. A belly-deep laugh. The sound burst free before he could stop it, as if he'd held the emotion prisoner too long. "Natasha Gaudet, you are a hell of a woman. You try a man's control in dangerous ways."

He didn't know from dangerous, she mused, squirming against his hold. "What exactly are you trying to control back there, mister, because I can't imagine anything being more dangerous than a dissatisfied woman."

"You think I would ever leave you dissatisfied?" he asked, his voice low and soft against the shell of her ear. He settled his free hand on her belly, spreading his fingers wide. She sucked in her stomach; he took advantage of the gap, slipping into her pants to cup her sex through the textured lace of her thong. "Making you happy is all that matters."

"Then let me go," she demanded, pressing herself into his hand and wiggling until she felt that first sexy zing of heated sensation zipping all the way to her core. She trembled, and then she said, "Because I'm not the least bit happy, I guarantee you that."

"Are you sure?" He eased a finger into her folds, found her moisture, slicked it in a circle around her clitoris until she writhed against him and moaned. He responded with a chuckle, along with a whispered, "I thought so."

"Damn you," she said with a whimper. She hated how effortlessly he aroused her. She loved how effortlessly he aroused her. "I want a shower."

"I want you." He pulled his hand from her panties, made quick work of her zipper. But when the low-riding waistband refused to slide from her hips, he had no choice. He had to let her go, needing the use of both of his hands.

She shimmied out of the clinging red rayon, and before he could stop her, she stepped into the shower wearing only her thong. She turned, victorious—a feeling he doused immediately when he reached back and flipped off the lights.

She heard the rustle of clothing, saw shadows cast by the night-light plugged in on the one bare wall, the shape of a shoulder, an arm, the muscled curve of a hip as he shed his pants. She wanted to see him. God, but she wanted to see him. What was his deal with letting her see his body?

She had no time to ask. He blocked what light there was when he stepped through the enclosure's door, which he never did close. And then his hands were on her shoulders, his mouth grinding down on hers, his erection a heavy solid weight pressing into her belly's soft give.

With the glossy tile behind her, she had no place to go, nothing to hold onto. Nothing but Peter's body. She reached up, took hold of his biceps, and returned the kiss, drawing his lower lip between hers and keeping her eyes wide open.

It was an erotic sensation, looking up and seeing him in the abstract while feeling him tangibly, with her hands, her belly, her breasts. He opened his mouth, and she followed his lead. He tasted like Darjeeling tea, smelled like the woods in the rain. His tongue rubbed languorously over hers; he seduced her with sweeping strokes and his lips' soft suction.

She moaned, deepened the kiss, digging her fingertips into the hard bulge of flexed muscles he kept in check. He had her where he wanted her, where she wanted to be, and possessed the strength to do anything. Yet he simply made love to her using no more than his mouth.

He was supposed to be vulnerable. She was supposed to be prying out his secrets while all barriers were down. She was too busy to pry. Too busy falling hard for a dangerous man. It didn't matter that she'd sworn earlier, to herself and her girlfriends, that she wouldn't let this happen.

It *was* happening. Later she would be a big girl and swallow the bitter pill of repercussions, as long as he didn't stop touching her, kissing her, loving her now.

He slid his hands from her shoulders to her neck and then her jaw, cradling her face tenderly, dropping kisses along one cheekbone, the bridge of her nose, her eyebrow, the dip of her temple. She shivered beneath his touch, certain she had never felt so much from such a slight caress.

It was simple, innocent, no more than a soft kiss good night, a mellow good morning, a lovers' affection gesture. She swore she would melt from the pleasure. Her limbs grew languid, her breathing shallow, though her skin began to sizzle and burn.

The night-light blurred an orange glow through the frosted glass, casting him in silhouette. Hot water stung like bullets striking the tops of her feet, a contrast to the sweet brushes of his mouth. She whimpered, wanting more, searching with her lips, which reached no higher than his collarbone.

She kissed him there; tickled by the damp dusting of hair in the center of his chest, she wiggled her nose like a bunny. That made her laugh, a laugh that was in no small part panic over how hard and how deeply, how completely, how madly she was falling for no reason that made any sense.

"You're laughing." His voice rumbled low against the shell of her ear.

"You noticed." She found the disc of his nipple and laved it with the flat of her tongue.

He growled, the sound rising from the base of his throat. "I'm hoping that means you're happy."

Happy. He had said her being happy was all that mattered, yet she'd let him get his way. "You know what would make me ecstatic?"

"Tell me," he said, trailing kisses and nips down the side of her neck all the way to the curve of her shoulder.

He kept that up and she wasn't going to be able to tell him anything. She wasn't going to be able to think.

She did manage to release him, however, long enough to reach for the wire rack hanging from the showerhead and her bottle of shampoo. "To start with, washing my hair. Then cleaning my body. You know, those female rituals you were so worried about witnessing."

He moved away—not far because there was nowhere to go—but far enough that she missed him. She sighed, shivered, and raised her face to the spray. He took the bottle of shampoo from her hand, and once she'd thoroughly wet her head and body, he pulled her back into his warmth.

He washed her hair, working up a lather with his fingertips, massaging her skull from her forehead to her nape, rubbing circles of varied pressures over her scalp until keeping her eyes open was not the battle but the war. She moaned, caught up in the sensation of coming undone.

"You have no idea how good that feels," she mumbled, her head moving side to side then up and down in response to his kneading hands. "My stylist can't even compare."

He chuckled. "Do you get naked with your stylist?"

"Hardly. Mmm. I'm not so sure her husband would go for a threesome. He's pretty possessive. Not to mention old school when it comes to relationships." She quivered with sensation as suds ran down her neck and over her breasts in a sensuous trail. "They make an interesting couple."

"How so?" he asked, holding her now with a forearm to her chest while massaging the base of her skull. And he expected her to carry on a lucid conversation when she was melting faster than any wicked witch.

She cupped her hands beneath the water and splashed her face free of lather. "Ione's as punk as it gets. Piercings, tattoos, leather. Hair that's a different color every week. And Rey's a circulation assistant at the city library. Very brainy and bookish-looking in his oxford shirts and sweaters. Not that Ione's any less intelligent. It's just strange seeing them together."

"You don't believe that opposites attract?" he asked, turning her to face him and backing her under the spray.

She held her breath and squeezed her eyes shut as he rinsed the soap from her hair. When she came up sputtering, she wrapped her arms around his waist, pressed her cheek to his chest, and sighed. "Nothing about attraction surprises me at all. It's totally unexplainable, the emotion or experience or events that draw two people together."

His hands settled in the small of her back. "Are you talking about Rey and Ione? Or you and me?"

"Oh, the you and me is obvious. You wooed me with your Ferrari." She chuckled, then yelped when he smacked her on the ass. "No, I'm not into spanking, thank you very much."

He grabbed her by the bottom and hauled her as close as he could. His erection, having softened, settled into her belly and started to throb. "What are you into, Natasha? Tell me what turns you on."

Anything two consensual adults find pleasurable, she wanted to say. Instead, she chewed at her lip for a moment before giving him an answer. "Honesty." She moved her hands to his chest and pushed back, looking up at him but seeing no more than the shadows of his face. "Answers."

"To what questions?"

"Anything I ask you."

"That's right. A mutual give and take."

"I have nothing to hide."

He laughed at that, but she sensed uneasiness more than humor. "So you keep telling me."

"Ask me anything." She reached for her squeeze bottle of shower gel, trailed a line across his collarbone, and went to work with her sponge. "Anything you want to know."

He remained silent, his body tensing as she worked the lather in ever widening circles, over his pecs, his shoulders, down to the flat of his abs. When his penis bobbed, the swollen head tickling her hipbone, she grinned. And then she washed him, taking his breath away when she enclosed his shaft in the glove of her joined hands.

He sucked in air sharply. "You keep that up, I won't be asking you anything but to bend over."

She stroked him once, twice. "That doesn't sound so bad, you know."

He gave a strangled laugh, raised his arms, and laced his hands atop his head. "You think I'm kidding."

"Not at all," she said, finding the sponge she'd tucked between her thighs and scrubbing it up over his arms. "Though I do hope you brought condoms."

"Plural?"

She found herself smiling. "Did I mention that a shower always seems to wake me up?"

"Apparently," he responded, groaning when she dropped to her knees and took her sponge to his legs. As hard as it was to resist, she avoided wrapping her mouth around his begging cock. Instead, she ordered, "Turn around."

He did, allowing her to make her way north again, even spreading his legs when she reached her soapy hands between. She fondled his balls as she bathed them, loving the hard ridge of flesh that had risen behind. Loving the way touching him brought her own body to life.

The response was sexual, yes, but it was more about knowing that she pleased him, that he enjoyed her touch. That he had the patience, the control to stand still while she played—even when she took her playtime higher, sliding the soapy length of an index finger upward between his cheeks. He shuddered, and she got to her feet, her own breathing harder than his.

She washed his back and his shoulders; he felt amazing beneath her hands, taut and fit and so beautifully smooth she wanted to touch him forever. Instead, she reached for the shampoo, squirted a circle into her palm, and scrubbed her hands over his short-cropped hair.

It tickled her fingers and palms, much as his beard had tickled her chin when they kissed. Had tickled her thighs on the balcony when he'd pleasured her with his mouth. Oh, but she wanted him.

Holding both of his elbows, she stepped back into the water, pulling him with her to rinse. Once under the spray, he turned to face her, his shadowed form advancing, looming, his arms rising, head lowering, breath blowing like a bellows as he struggled for control.

She didn't want him controlled. She wanted him wild and untamed. She wanted him to let himself go. She wanted him in ways she'd never before wanted any man.

And she wanted him now.

Fourteen

He didn't take her until they were in bed.

He'd been thinking about her all day. Hearing her voice on the tapes he'd listened to, wishing perversely that he could have known her in another time and place. Though they'd easily guessed the truth, he hadn't wanted Tripp or K.J. aware of the fact that he'd slept with her, because what he'd been feeling while listening to her talk wasn't about the sex.

It was about a fantasy he hadn't entertained for seven years. A woman wanting to be with him, wanting nothing from him, wanting only the pleasure they made together, the chance that pleasure might grow into more, into something worth fighting for, worth living for.

And that's why he didn't take her until they were in bed.

That and the reality that the shower was barely larger than a cage. Hell, the entire bathroom was barely larger than a cage. The fact that he'd been able to breathe, that he hadn't panicked and run, that he'd been able to get it up at all in such close quarters, said more about her effect on him than he'd had time to process.

The fact that he hadn't even realized it until he was out of his clothes scared him half to death.

She lay on her back in the center of the mattress. The pillows had long since been tossed to the floor, the top sheet and comforter, too. He liked the simplicity. Nothing but the two of them, their bodies warmed by the shared heat of skin-on-skin contact. No tangled snarl of limbs and bedclothes. No cushions to soften their joining.

Palms flat on either side of her head, he loomed above her, rotating his hips and pressing upward, grinding hard against her with the base of his shaft. She whimpered, her head tossing right then left, her arms thrown out to the side, her fingers clutching handfuls of sheet for purchase.

She was so gorgeous, so uninhibited, caught up in sexual abandon. Sweat beaded on his forehead. He was too close, wasn't ready, had to stop. His cock throbbed, his balls ached, and he sat back on his heels to center himself.

The room was dark. Light from the street lamps shone through her sheer curtains, casting the room in an eerie blue-green glow. It wasn't much, but enough so that he could see her. Her body, which glowed with perspiration. Her face, which glowed with bliss. Her sex, which glowed with her slick musky juices that smoothed the way for his cock. She wanted him. And he groaned at the truth of how much.

She raised up on her elbows and smiled. "You okay?"

Her voice was breathless, the question strangled. She was doing better than he was; he wasn't even sure he could talk. He nodded, then braced his hands on her knees and forced out a harsh, "Yeah. Maybe."

She laughed. A sexy guttural sound that turned him to putty. "We can take a break, you know."

"I am taking a break."

Shifting her weight to one elbow, she slipped her free hand down into the heat where their bodies were joined, sliding the vee of two spread fingers around the base of his cock. "I don't want to wear you out."

The only thing here being worn out was his self-control, but damn if he was going to come before he was ready. He let her play, grinding his jaw until he swore he felt a molar crack, and deciding then to get even. His slid his palms from her knees over the soft skin of her thighs to her center, stopping only when he could part the lips of her pussy with his thumbs. Exposing her, spreading her wide, rubbing the skin stretched taut at the entrance to her sex where he filled her.

She moaned, fell back on the bed, and arched her hips until the head of his cock hit her womb. He throbbed, pulsed; his balls tightened and drew up into his body. He wanted to come, ached to come, *needed* to come. But he continued to play, stroking the soft outer skin she'd shaved bare then back through her slick inner folds.

He loved touching her, the feel of her flesh beneath his fingers, loved hearing the tiny sounds that she made. She amazed him, her unbridled response, and he rubbed upward in circles, working the hard knot of her clit between the press of his thumbs. She cried out, thrust her hips upward.

It was then that he let her go, guilt slicing through his gut like a razor. He owed her. For all the ways he would soon be destroying her life, he owed her now. He pulled out, knelt between her legs and, before she got out more than a whimper, settled his mouth over the mound of her sex, sucking her between his lips lightly, then with more force, easing two fingers into her gorgeous cunt, fingering her, stroking her.

She was so hot and so tight and so wet. She smelled like the sea, tasted salty and warm and alive, and like he'd known her taste forever. He ate her, he fucked her, he drove her hard and fast. She came then, convulsing around his fingers, tearing the sheet from the bed, sobbing as she thrashed side to side.

He stayed with her, ignoring the hammering pulse in his ears as he tendered his touch, bringing her down slowly from her orgasm's high. She was all that mattered. Her completion, giving her what she wanted here and now because this was real, this moment, this joining. Nothing about their being here together was a lie, he realized, struck hard by the reality of what he was feeling in the mangled knots of his gut.

"Why did you do that?" she finally whispered, strands of hair clinging to her damp forehead. "Why didn't you stay with me? I love to feel you come."

He crawled up over her, pushed himself inside; she wrapped

her legs around his hips, her heels pulling him deep. "I'm with you now." She gripped him. Her muscles tightened around his shaft until he wanted to die. His balls ached fiercely, yet he didn't move except to lower his weight to his elbows and push her hair from her face.

"Do you know how beautiful you are?"

"Right now?" She smiled, shook her head. "I don't think so."

Again with the self-deprecation. Who in the hell had convinced her that she had to be neat and orderly and perfectly put together all of the time? "If I didn't have to move the both of us, I'd smack you on the ass for that."

She thrust her hips upward; he sucked in a breath and held it. "You have a thing for my ass, did you know that?"

He pulled back slowly, eased back in until she shuddered. "No. I have a thing for you."

"And here I thought it was all about the body parts," she squeaked out when he shifted up onto his knees and crushed their lower bodies together.

With Peter Deacon, it would've been. And Christian was beginning to chafe beneath the weight of this masquerade. "I like your body parts a lot. But you're a lot more than tits and ass and a pair of long legs."

"True." She moved her hands to his shoulders, massaged his muscles there. "But this is all you know of me."

He had to be careful here. He knew so much more, very little of it that he'd learned from her. "It's a good place to start, don't you think?"

"I do think, though a lot of people would say we got it backwards. Intimacy before friendship."

"Do you agree?"

"No. Not really. It's just that starting here"—she rotated her hips, pushed up to grip him, to pull him down with her as she pressed her spine to the bed—"tends to get me in trouble."

Christ almighty, but he'd never seen this kind of trouble before. He bit back a curse, his neck aching with the strain of his reach for control, and finally managed to ask, "You start here a lot, do you?"

The more intimate details of her love life had never been part of his investigation. He hadn't needed or wanted to know about the men she'd been with. It was bad enough to have her think he was Peter Deacon, to not be able to tell her about Christian Bane.

And the fact that he wanted to, that he desperately wanted to, was proof positive insanity was rapidly closing in.

"I wouldn't say a lot." She shuddered at the shift in his hips. "It's just that I love intimacy. I love sex. It's when I feel closest to a man. It's probably the time I feel closest to myself."

He was crazy, mad. Insane in ways he'd never before been. Not even . . . then. He refused to think about *then,* to allow that time in the jungle with Malena to invade the present. That time meant pain and betrayal. Yet now he was the betrayer, Natasha the betrayed. God, what was he doing here?

He couldn't allow her to feel close to him. He needed distance, to keep his head straight, to keep her from getting hurt. But it was too late. There was no distance between them. Not physically. Not emotionally. They had both reached that place of vulnerability from which there was no turning back.

He pulled out, pushed in, slowly, rhythmically setting up a pace that seemed so right, so perfect, he knew this was it. He wasn't going to stop. He couldn't stop. He wanted her and needed her in ways as vital as they were dangerous.

His speed increased, as did the force of his thrusts and the intensity of Natasha's response. She drew her knees to her chest, held her ankles to her sides, giving him access to whatever he wanted to take. He pumped harder, struck by the strength of her trust, her willingness to share her body while finding her pleasure in his.

"God, I could fall in love with you so easily."

She hadn't meant to say it; he knew that. He could tell that she'd spoken to herself more than to him. It didn't matter. He didn't want to hear the words. Couldn't hear the words. They were Malena's words, the words of his betrayal. And, like the flip of a switch, they spurred him to seek revenge. He reared back, held her ankles, moved her feet to his shoulders before driving himself home.

She cried out, and he listened, but she didn't tell him to stop. He wasn't sure he'd ever be able to stop. He thrust into her, hammered her, used her. This wasn't about love. It was revenge and atonement, penance and duplicity—all the things he'd kept bottled up for so long.

When he came, he swore he was being ripped in half, that he was pouring out blood and guts along with his semen. What should have been pleasure was pain, a fierce ache that burned from belly to balls. And then Natasha came again, crying out, and he continued to pound her, his mind and his body no longer working in tandem, his soul torn to shreds.

Eventually he finished, so drained he collapsed to the bed at her side. He lay there without speaking, without moving, listening to her suck in a sharp breath and groan as she got to her feet. She showered again, no doubt washing away the very idea that she'd allowed him to ever touch her while bathing the skin he'd abused.

And then he felt it come over him, exhaustion that wiped all cognizance from his mind, stealing his awareness of his surroundings, robbing him of conscious thought. It was the exhaustion he'd learned to welcome, to embrace, to give himself up to instead of giving into the long torturous months of pain. He had no idea if Natasha planned to return to bed and order him out; if so, she'd have to shovel his ass to the floor.

He knew only the bliss of sleep.

"How did you come to live with Dr. Bow?" Christian asked, dodging Natasha as she exited the kitchen, cup of coffee in hand, and headed back toward the bedroom.

She'd slipped out of bed twenty minutes before. Lying still, he'd listened as she'd made her way barefoot across the hardwood floor to the bathroom, opening one eye only when she tiptoed past him again on her way to the living room.

Once he heard the hiss and steam of the coffeemaker, he'd rolled up to sit on the side of the bed and grabbed his pants from the chair beside it, buttoning and zipping and slipping into his shirt before leaving the room.

He'd never been a man to use a woman. Not for sex. Not for getting what he wanted. Not for anything. Ever. Period. Peter Deacon, on the other hand, wouldn't think about it twice. The bastard deserved an eternity of rotting in hell—for Natasha, yeah. But for Christian, as well.

He was tired of living in the other man's skin, tired of living a lie bigger than any Malena had ever perpetrated during those weeks before literally selling his crew up the river.

He'd been working in Thailand a year when he'd met her. He'd been assigned to a military detail guarding a Doctors Without Borders humanitarian team. The relief workers had been dodging bullets and malaria to bring medical aid to impoverished villagers caught between rival warlords in a guerilla-warfare zone. Malena had been the liaison between the locals and the doctors who arrived in the villages looking much like guerillas themselves, armed to the teeth in camouflage gear.

It was only later, maybe the fourth trip that year up the Mae Kok river, that he learned of her true affiliation with Spectra IT. He'd learned it while he and two of his men stood at gunpoint, while three others from their squad bled out onto the ground, their throats slashed by village elders under the direction of the man who'd been Deacon's predecessor.

Malena hadn't been assigned to liaise by the Thai government at all. She hadn't fallen in love with him at all. She hadn't needed him at all, meant any of the promises she'd made when they'd slept together on the hard-packed ground and counted the stars in the sky. She'd simply been playing a part, using him as a means to an end, the same way he was using Natasha now—only not.

Because he wasn't getting her hopes up about the future,

painting pictures of the life they'd live together once their tour of duty was complete. And he wasn't leaving her to stand in a pool of blood shed by her closest friends, a fate he'd wished for months that he'd suffered instead of being tossed into a dung heap and forgotten.

"It was after my father died," she said when she finally returned. "The month before graduation." She set her coffee on the circular table in the small dining area, dropped a stack of clothing into a chair, gave him a raised brow. "But having investigated me so thoroughly, surely you knew that."

He did, but he liked hearing it firsthand, listening for the nuances of voice, tuning in to the feelings behind the facts. "Only that your father was deceased, and that your degree is in economics."

She shook out a pair of folded khakis and tugged them on beneath her robe. He swore it was one of the sexiest things he'd ever seen, her dressing without revealing but the barest amount of leg. "Fifty bucks says you know more than that."

He sipped his coffee, watched her hook her bra around her waist and pull the straps over her shoulders, never showing a bit of skin but the strip above her waistband until her bra was in place. Only then did she shrug out of her robe, tug her slip-like nightgown over her head, and pull on a high-necked, long-sleeved dark brown sweater that hid everything even while hiding nothing.

Fifty bucks, hell. He'd pay ten times that right now to bury his face between her breasts. He took a sip of coffee before he answered. "Watching you dress is worth far more than that."

She rolled her eyes. "That's only because you're a perv."

Right now, he wasn't sure he could argue. "I'm only a man, Natasha."

"Same thing," she said, snorting playfully and grabbing up her socks and boots that looked like brown suede high-tops from the chair before sitting. "Don't forget, Mr. Know-It-All, that I grew up in a house full of your kind."

"My kind?" He leaned a shoulder against the kitchen's arched entryway. For a woman who enjoyed men the way she obviously did, her cynicism—though good-natured—intrigued him. "Care to elaborate?"

She went about putting on socks and boots without ever meeting his gaze. "What's to elaborate on? Men will be men. You know what you want and go after it, whether it's a woman, a political position, a career advancement, or a Ferrari."

"You do have a thing for my car."

"No more than you have for my ass." She straightened, shook her pants legs down over the boots and finally reached for her coffee. "We're not going to get out of here without talking about it, you know."

"About what?" he asked, playing dumb and knowing she wouldn't let him get away with it for long.

"About why you don't want me to see you naked, for one thing. But also about me saying the L word"—she paused, one heartbeat, two, her big brown eyes tossing down a gauntlet—"and you trying to kill me."

"I wasn't trying to kill you," he said, just as a knock sounded at her front door.

"Okay. Now this is totally unfair," she grumbled, glaring at him before heading across the room. "You arranged this somehow, didn't you? To get out of talking to me?"

He chuckled to himself because she tickled him and it was all he could do. Well, that and breathe a sigh of relief that he'd escaped having that particular conversation. He wasn't ready to talk about the emotional impact of last night or share the reasons he feared exposure and wrapped himself in the safe cloak of darkness.

He backed another step into the kitchen and out of sight of the door. He'd just as soon keep the fact that he was here between himself and Natasha, but then above the hush-hush chattering of two female voices he heard her call out his name. Shit, he thought, wishing for his bomber jacket, shoulder holster, and Ruger .45-caliber he'd left in the car. The SIG-Sauer 9mm in his waistband beneath his untucked shirt wasn't as accessible as he'd like.

"Peter?" Natasha said, meeting him as he stepped around

the corner into the eating area. She took hold of his free forearm while he held his coffee in the opposite hand. "This is Susan Anderson, my roommate from Brown. Susan, Peter Deacon."

"Susan," he acknowledged with a nod.

"It's nice to meet you," she returned, studying him as he supposed women studied their friends' male specimens. "I'm sorry to bother you guys, but I'm off to spend the day with my parents. It's their day to pamper their"—she hooked her fingers into air quotes—"birthday princess, but I wanted to return the necklace Nat let me borrow last night."

"That's right. Happy birthday," he said, hoping he sounded believably apologetic. "I'm sorry I wasn't able to make it for drinks. Work kept me at the office until midnight."

Susan blinked. He watched her process his explanation, strangely edgy as he waited for her response, relaxing only when she laughed, rubbing a hand over her forehead. "Last night. God. I barely even remember it. I'd forgotten Nat said you might be there."

"Judging by that green glow you've got going, I'd say that's not all you've forgotten about last night," Natasha teased, hooking the slender silver chain around her neck and tucking it under her collar. "No more drinking for you, sweetie."

"At least not for another year," Susan said with a laugh that quickly turned sour. "I really wasn't feeling this bad until I got out of the cab and started using my feet. Oh, crap. The cab. He's waiting."

"Then you'd better go." Natasha wrapped an arm around her girlfriend's shoulders and walked her to the door.

Susan turned and offered Christian a weak lift of her hand. "It was nice to meet you, Peter."

"You, too," he said, returning the wave as she left and only then pulling in a full breath.

Natasha closed the door. "Let me straighten up the bathroom and change the sheets and we can go."

Her words returned him vividly to last night, to the beauty

of having her naked, to the near violence of their joining. He upended the last of his coffee and swallowed before responding. "If you're done with the coffee, I'll clean up the kitchen."

The beatific smile she gave him then nearly knocked him to his knees. "You've got yourself a deal."

Fifteen

Natasha had just slid down into the Ferrari's comfy bucket and was waiting for Peter to walk around to his side after shutting her door when her cell rang. She glanced at the number display. Susan again. Miss Nosy Nature calling back to get the skinny, no doubt.

"I think you're old enough now to know not to repeatedly interrupt your best girlfriend's hot date," Natasha teased, smiling across at Peter as he climbed in, buckled up, and put the car into gear. The engine roared to life behind her and she covered her free ear with her palm in order to hear Susan's response.

"Listen, Nat. This is going to sound like I'm trying to screw things up for you and really I'm not. But I'm not so sure about Peter."

Natasha couldn't help it. She bristled. She loved her girlfriends dearly, but hated their insistence on butting into her life. "Not so sure in what way?"

"Not so sure that his name *is* Peter."

Okay. That sure wasn't what she'd expected to hear. She switched the phone to her left ear, angling to face the window on the right as they drove out of the neighborhood. "Say again? I'm having trouble hearing."

On the other end of the phone, Susan sighed resignedly.

"Okay. I could be totally wrong, but I don't think so. Just ask him. I think his name is Christian."

"And why would you think that?" Natasha asked, doing her best to keep her tone light.

"Nancy? This girl in my Pilates class? She works in the same building that he does and talks about him all the time. She has a huge crush. He's an engineer or something."

An engineer? Named Christian? This was making no sense. "I'm sure Nancy's got it wrong, sweetie."

"I'm not so sure, Nat. I've seen the pictures."

Natasha shifted in her seat, cast a quick glance at Peter, forced a smile and nodded when he mouthed, "You okay?"

She studied his face for a moment, recalling the last thirty-six hours she'd spent with him. The conversations they'd never really taken anywhere. The questions he'd evaded, the answers he'd persistently pursued.

She curled her toes, or tried to; her feet had gone totally numb. "You need to give me more than that, Suz. What exactly did you see?"

"There's a fountain in the square across from her building. She eats lunch there a lot and people-watches. She always has her digital camera with her." In the background, a tea kettle whistled, and Susan's mother called her name. "I'm pretty confident it's him. That thing he does when he smiles? The right corner of his mouth?"

"Yes. I know it."

"So ask him."

"This isn't a good time. I'm on my way back to Wick's."

"I'd think it would be a perfect time. Before you're out of the city. Tell me where you are. I'll call nine-one-one."

"Susan, sweetie. That's hardly necessary." And it wasn't. Wick would not do business with anyone he wasn't sure of. She wasn't going to blow this off, no. But calling the authorities based on thirdhand tales told by a woman with a camera and a crush seemed a case of paranoia. "Let me think about it and I'll call you when I get to Wick's."

"I'm having dinner tonight with my parents, then seeing a

show. The birthday dinner and all, so I won't have my cell on. There had better be a message on my machine when I get home or I will call the cops. I swear."

Natasha wasn't the least bit worried that tonight she'd be anywhere but safe in her own bed at the estate. "And I swear that I'll call."

"Okay, then. I'll talk to you tonight," Susan said, and clicked off.

Natasha snapped her own phone shut and continued to stare out the Ferrari's passenger window, the silence in the car growing tense. Peter didn't say another word; she supposed he was allowing her time and privacy to stew over her conversation, not wanting to pry into what she and Susan had talked about, being a gentleman and all that.

She still couldn't believe it. That Peter wasn't Peter? That she'd once again been duped? No. It was too ridiculous. Susan had only seen him briefly. Surely she was confused, and Peter only resembled this other man. The right side of his mouth tilting up when he smiled was not a unique trait. There had to be hundreds of men, thousands, with the same facial feature.

So why the hell did the argument sound so lame?

They headed out of the city over the George Washington Bridge and onto the Palisades Parkway, Natasha wondering all the while what she should do and fighting the urge to turn and confront him.

Waiting until they arrived at Wick's seemed the smartest move. Once there, her godfather would have her back. She wouldn't have to worry about pissing off Peter—Christian?—and being thrown from the car and left for dead on the side of the road.

But her curiosity was killing her. And bailing out on him now meant she was close enough to the city to easily get a cab back. . . .

"Natasha? Did Susan have bad news?"

She shifted in her seat so that she could see his face. "That depends. Is your name really Peter? Or is it Christian?"

* * *

Christian watched the road rush by beneath the car, the roar in his ears much more than that of the engine or the tires. He should have trusted his instincts earlier. Susan turning green wasn't about the amount of alcohol left in her system at all.

He held out his right hand, gripped the steering wheel with his left. "Hand me your phone."

"Why?"

"The phone, Natasha." He didn't have time to argue. Didn't have time to explain. Had time to do nothing but react. An exit loomed to the right. He downshifted to slow the car and swerved across two lanes to take it. Ahead and behind, the road was blessedly free of traffic. "The phone, now, please."

"I don't think so," she said, yelping when he reached across and grabbed it out of her hand.

She slumped defiantly into her seat, arms crossed over her chest. Checking again for oncoming vehicles, he pried open the phone and removed the battery, tossed the case over the top of the car toward the ditch, the power supply to the side of the road a quarter mile away.

"What the hell are you doing?" she screamed, whirling on him, fists flying, nails raking, grabbing for the steering wheel.

He hit the brakes, whipped into the skid. The fast stop and shoulder strap slammed her back into the bucket. He kept her there with the barrel of the Ruger .45-caliber he snatched from beneath his seat. "Sit down. Nothing's going to happen to you if you sit down and be still."

She didn't say a word, but he heard her hyperventilating panic above the roar in his ears.

"Calm down. Natasha. Listen to me. No one's going to get hurt." His pulse pounded. His mind whirred. "I just need you to be still and be quiet."

"You're pointing a gun at me and you want me to be still and be quiet? You fucking piece of shit." She swiped back the hair from her face. "Don't tell me to be still and be quiet. In fact, don't tell me anything at all. When Susan doesn't hear from me later, she's calling the cops. She knows exactly where we are and what we're driving. So whatever the hell you think you're doing here, you're not getting away with it. You lying, fucking bastard."

He caught her gaze, saw the glassy fear, the damp tears she wouldn't shed, the delineated vessels in the whites of her eyes like a roadmap penned in red. He wanted to tell her the truth, that he was one of the good guys, to reassure her that she could trust him, that no harm would come her way—but he couldn't tell her any of that and he refused to compound his sins with yet another lie.

And so he issued a growling order. "Shut the hell up, Natasha. Now."

Grabbing his phone from his belt, he punched in a preset code. The phone rang once. Julian Samms picked up the other end. "Shoot."

"I need to get to the farm. Where's Briggs?"

"Hang," Julian ordered, and Christian waited while his SG-5 partner contacted Hank's chopper pilot, waited and watched Natasha hug herself with shaking hands, tears finally and silently rolling down her cheeks.

"I've got you on GPS. Briggs can be there in thirty, but you need to bank the car. And he needs a place to land. Hang."

More waiting. More looking for approaching cars. More watching Natasha glare, shake, and cry.

Christian switched from handset to earphone and lowered the gun to his thigh, keeping his gaze on Natasha while waiting for Julian's instructions. She seemed so small, so wounded, and he kicked himself all over again for failing to make it clear that their involvement was purely physical.

He should have spelled that out from day one, made it more clear that Peter Deacon took trophies, not lovers. But he'd never given her any such warning. Not that it would've done any good. Hell, he knew the lay of the land and here he was, so tied up in knots over what he was putting her through that he couldn't even think straight.

"My name is Christian Bane," he finally said, owing her that much. "That's all I can tell you right now."

She snorted, flipped him the bird, and turned to stare out her window.

"Bane."

"Yeah." Hand to his earpiece, he turned his attention back to Julian.

"Two miles ahead on the right," Julian said as Christian shifted into gear and accelerated, "there's a cutoff. Through a gate. Looks like a dirt road, rutted as hell."

He brought the car up to speed, scanned the landscape. "Got it," he said, and made the turn, nearly bottoming out on the first bump.

"Half a mile, make another right. Other side of a stand of trees."

"Almost there." He reached the cutoff and turned again, caught sight of the tumbled down barn and stables, the flat pasture beyond. Perfect. Plenty of room for the chopper and cover for the car. "Tell Briggs we're waiting."

A short couple of seconds, and Julian said, "He says make it twenty. K.J.'s with him. He'll bring back the car. I'll keep the line open. Hank's expecting you."

"Thanks, J."

Christian maneuvered the Ferrari down the road that wasn't much more than a trail of flattened grass leading to a clearing surrounding the barn. Once he'd circled behind it, he tugged the wire from his ear, cut the engine, and pocketed the keys. When he opened his door, Natasha finally looked over.

"Going someplace?" she asked snidely.

"We both are," he bit back. "Get out."

"You can go to hell, but I'm not going anywhere."

"Actually, you are. And you're going with me." He reminded her that he was the one with the gun.

She got out of the car, slammed the door, and was off like a rocket back down the road. Shit, shit, shit. He checked the safety, shoved the Ruger into his waistband next to the SIG, and took off after her. She was fast, but he was faster. He closed in, but she never slowed, leaving him no choice.

He grabbed her arm. She spun toward him. He took her to

the ground, bracing himself for the blow. He landed hard on his shoulder, doing what he could to cushion her fall. She grunted at the impact, and he rolled on top of her, pinning her to the ground with his weight and his strength.

Her adrenaline made for a formidable foe. She shoved at his chest, pummeled him with her fists when he refused to move. He finally had no choice but to grab her wrists, stretch out her arms above her head, hold her there.

Rocks and dirt and twigs bit into his fingers. He knew she felt the bite in the backs of her hands, but still he straddled her, capturing her legs between his.

"You want to wait like this? Twenty minutes? Because we can." His chest heaved in sync with the rapid rise and fall of hers. "Or we can get up and wait at the car. I'm good either way. You tell me."

"Get off me." She spat out the words.

He rolled up and away, kept his hands on her wrists and pulled her to her feet. Then he tugged her close, making sure he had her full attention, ignoring the stabbing pain in his shoulder that didn't hurt half as much as the one in his gut. "I'm not going to put up with any shit here, Natasha. Both of our lives are very likely in danger."

"Oh, right. I can see that. You being the one with the gun and all." She jerked her hands from his.

He let her go, walking a few feet behind her as she made her way slowly back to the barn and the parked car. She had nowhere to run; hopefully, he'd made his point. He had no intention to harm her, no *reason* to harm her, but he needed to finish this job, to make sure Spectra didn't get their hands on whatever it was Bow had to sell.

And now that he'd been stupid enough to get his cover blown . . .

"Where are you taking me?" She splayed shaking palms over the Ferrari's engine bay, staring down at her skin, which was ghostly pale against the car's black sheen.

"To get the answers you've been asking for," he said, guilt eating him from the inside out, and looked up with no small bit of relief at the *thwup-thwup-thwup* of an approaching chopper.

Natasha kept a death grip on the straps belting her against the helicopter's seat for the whole of the flight. She'd never been a big fan of air travel, but this time not only was her stomach in her throat, her heart was there, as well. She couldn't swallow. She couldn't breathe. She couldn't even think.

She wore the headset as Peter—*Christian*—insisted, but when he asked if she was okay, she didn't speak into the mike. She barely even nodded. She had nothing to say to him. Now or ever again.

They followed what she assumed was the Thruway due north then veered off to the east—or so was her best guess. It was tough to use the sun as a compass, what with it directly overhead in an overcast sky.

Listening to the brief snatches of conversation between Christian and the pilot named Jack, she determined they were heading for Saratoga County, where a man named Hank would be waiting. Waiting for what, she had no idea. She didn't want to know. Knowing would distract her from the only thing that mattered.

Escape.

Unfortunately, she didn't even have her purse. Not a credit card, a phone, or a dime to her name. Her shoes were good for walking, but even if she'd had a clue where she was and where to go, she wasn't dressed for the temperature expected tonight. Which meant finding a safe place to hole up before sunset. She didn't see that happening when she didn't know where she'd be an hour from now.

"Uh, Jack," she heard Christian say. "Can we have a minute here, please?"

"Switching you now."

A clicking sort of noise, a shift in the level of static, and then apparently she and the bastard were secured on some sort of private channel. Didn't matter. She wasn't talking. A cold day in hell and all that.

"Natasha."

She continued to stare out the window.

"I don't blame you for being pissed."

He'd better not blame her for a goddamn thing. He was the one responsible for this big fat mess she was in. Pissed wasn't even half of what she was feeling.

"I swear this will all be cleared up soon. And nothing's going to happen to you, I promise."

"And I'm supposed to believe that?" She sounded like a shrill harpy and didn't even care. "After you pull a gun on me and tackle me like I'm some sort of monster?"

"I'd tell you everything if I could. I just can't."

What? He didn't have the luxury? He was waiting for an engraved invitation? *What?* she wondered as stands of trees, one indistinguishable from the next, sailed by beneath them. There wasn't a house, a road, or identifying signage of any sort to be seen.

"But I don't want you to think the time we've spent together . . . what we've done . . . shit," he muttered, his voice cracking before he came back with, "what we've shared—"

She whipped around on him, cutting him off, feeling the heat as her nostrils flared. "What have we shared, *Christian*?" She practically spat out his name. "What exactly have we *shared*?"

His eyes darkened, the grooves at the corners gouging deep. His lips flattened, his expression stabbing her with his sharply felt pain. Good. Let him hurt. Let him feel what she was feeling. The betrayal. The deceit. God, why couldn't he have simply been married instead of . . . whatever the hell he was.

"Who are you?" she asked, her voice raw in her own ears. "*What* are you?"

He looked down to where her knuckles were white against the straps, but when he reached for her hand, she jerked away—and watched slashes of red flush over his cheekbones.

"Christ, Natasha. I'm not going to hurt you."

Right, she thought, even while she believed him. She wondered what he considered "cleared up." And then shifting in her seat, she was reminded by the sharp sting between her legs exactly how screwed up things were.

"Are you sure you're okay?"

No, goddammit. She wasn't okay. She was bruised and scraped and her heart was in pieces. "Yes. I'm fine."

She heard him clear his throat then swallow. "I just wanted you to know that it wasn't nothing. What we did together. It meant . . . a lot."

She snorted. "A lot of kinky getting laid and getting lucky, you mean."

"No. That's not what I mean," he fairly growled. "I haven't been with anyone in, well, it's been awhile."

"For who? For Peter? Or for Christian?" Not that she cared.

"For me."

"Well, then. Glad I could help with the dry spell." And now she really couldn't tell a thing about the landmarks below. Everything was a blurry, teary wash of green.

"Don't do this, Natasha."

"Don't do what?" She wasn't going to sob. She refused to sob. "Don't be honest when I say I wish I'd never met you?"

And, at that, Christian jerked the headset off and turned away.

She kept hers on, listened to the static, needing the buffer to keep the hard silence at bay. Peter Deacon had been the most amazing thing to happen in her life.

And she hated Christian Bane for stealing him away as much as for the danger and the lies.

Sixteen

Hank Smithson stood at the corner of the helipad and watched Jackson Briggs set the chopper down. He chomped down on his unlit cigar and jammed a hand to the top of his head to keep his ball cap from flying off and getting chopped like beef. He liked this hat. He'd worked years to get the bill bent the way he wanted, and he'd open a ski lodge in Hades before he'd give it up without a fight.

'Course he was that way about most everything he considered his. Including his boys. And dad-gum if he was going to let a wisp of a girl destroy Christian anymore than she'd already managed to do. He'd heard it earlier in the boy's voice. Even over the static crackling between the chopper and the ground, that tone was as hard on the ears now as it had been all those years ago.

A tone that spoke more of giving up than of living. And Hank wasn't having any of it.

Briggs cut the bird's engine; the whine and whir of the props wound down. Hank shoved the cigar back between his teeth, crossed his arms over his middle, and rocked back on the heels of his boots to wait.

Christian climbed out first, decked to the nines and looking enough like Peter Deacon to give even Hank's cast-iron stomach a turn. Natasha appeared in the doorway next. Pride kept her from accepting the Bane boy's help. She just up and jumped to the ground.

Hank had to admit he admired the way she held her head high as she followed Christian away from the chopper, not walking behind, just far enough to the side so that no one would make the mistake of thinking they were together.

Though he still planned to read her the riot act, Hank couldn't help but chuckle. It was like watching his own Madelyn, that way she'd always had of refusing to back down when she felt she'd been done wrong, and it hit him again how much he missed her.

He took a deep, aching breath, glanced back as Jackson Briggs raised a hand to signal he was shuttin' her down, and gave the pilot a thumbs-up. He didn't figure anyone would need to go anywhere in a hurry. In fact, no one would be leaving for a good little while. Snagging his cigar between two fingers, he pulled his ball cap from his head and returned his attention to the matters at hand.

"Miss Gaudet," he said as she stopped a good couple of yards away and hugged her arms tightly over her chest. "My name is Hank Smithson. And I have quite a story to tell you."

"Thanks all the same," she said, tossing her head to get her hair out of her face with the same sassiness he so loved in MaddyB. "But I'm too old for story time. I'd much rather have the truth."

He liked her plucky spirit. He did. He liked it a lot. What he wasn't feeling so kindly about was the tension hovering between her and the Bane boy. Christian looked to be on the edge, hands on his hips, standing and staring at the ground, his mouth drawn tight, leaving Hank to fight the churning in his middle that told him the boy had run face first into a wall even harder than Spectra IT.

He turned to Natasha with a little less admiration than he'd been feeling before realizing the damage she'd caused. "Then why don't we head back to the house and see about getting you what you want." He offered his arm. It took a minute, but she finally accepted, hooking her hand beneath.

He patted the backs of her fingers as they started off, Bane following while Briggs ran through his shutdown and maintenance routine. " 'Course, I was just about to sit down to a late lunch. It's not much. Tomato soup and grilled cheese. How does that sound?"

She hesitated a moment, as if weighing whether or not the offer was one she couldn't or shouldn't refuse. Finally she gulped down a nervous breath and said, "That would be nice, thank you."

"Good," he said, grimacing as he stepped badly on a tuft of grass and pain shot through his hip. The joint caught, bone grinding on bone grinding on metal, and then Christian was there, an arm around Hank's back for the support he hated to admit he needed for a second or two.

"Hank?"

"I'm fine. I'm fine." Hank caught his balance and waved Christian away. "Nothing a little replacement surgery won't take care of."

Christian raised a brow behind the fancy sunglasses he wore. "And you're going to take a break here soon and have it done, right?"

Hank snorted, picked up the pace. "Stormin' Norman's still usin' both of his legs. I think I'll manage with the original equipment a might longer."

"The general's managing because he hasn't been living with a piece of shrapnel buried in his hip as long as you have," Christian remarked, as if Hank needed the reminder of how his military career had ended.

"You know Stormin' Norman? As in Norman Schwarzkopf?" Natasha asked.

Good. The lady knew her history. Easing into an explanation of who were the good guys and who were the bad might not be the challenge he'd originally feared. "That I do, Miss Gaudet. Would've served alongside him in Desert Storm if I hadn't run into a speck of bad luck in Panama."

"The shrapnel?" she asked, her voice softer now, losing the uncertainty he sensed in her trembling fingers.

Hank nodded. "Dad-blamed ambush during Operation Just Cause. Jeep in front of me hit a land mine. Lost my driver but managed to hold my own against the guerilla bastards, excuse the vulgarity, before air support arrived."

"I'm impressed."

"No real need to be. A soldier knows the dangers going in. Just as this man here knows what he'll be facing when I send him out on assignment," he said, gesturing toward Christian with the cigar still held between two fingers. "That doesn't stop him from doing what he's called to do."

"And what exactly is that?"

They'd reached the back of the one-story ranch that at three thousand square feet was at least two thousand too big without Madelyn to share the space. Hank pulled open the storm door. Christian took it out of his hand, allowing Hank to push on the heavily reinforced door leading into the kitchen. He gestured for Natasha to go ahead, then followed her in.

Christian closed up behind, and Hank heard the boy mutter a coarse, "Christ," under his breath before raising a hand to greet another member of the Smithson Group who sat at the end of the table, nursing a mug of coffee, a bottle of brandy half an arm's length away.

SG-5 operative Eli McKenzie dragged a hand over his bearded face, and grunted when Christian clapped a hand to his back and asked, "Hair of the dog, eh, Eli?" before circling the table to sit behind.

"Leave it alone, Bane," Eli growled in answer, shoving his chair back as he did. Lumbering to his feet, he grabbed the coffee, left the brandy, then left the room. Christian watched him go. Natasha, too. Hank simply shook his head.

"You'll have to excuse our Mr. McKenzie," he said to Natasha. "I just pulled him off assignment in Mexico. He hasn't quite recovered his usual good humor. Give him time, and he'll charm you down to the toes of your socks."

Frowning, Natasha pushed Eli's vacated chair up beneath the table, one hand curled over the back to hold on. "I'm really confused. These assignments you're talking about . . ." She let the thought trail, tugging with her free hand on the silver chain she'd pulled from beneath her collar.

Gesturing for the girl to follow, Hank made his way to the fridge, pulling out mayo, butter, sliced cheddar, and a loaf of Rainbow bread. "There are some bad men in this world, Miss Gaudet. Living in New York City as you do, I'm not telling you anything you don't already know. What I am saying here is that too many times these men don't show their true colors until it's too late for countermeasures to be taken."

"What do you mean, countermeasures?" she asked as he offered her a knife. She took it, spread mayonnaise on the eight slices of bread he'd pulled from the wrapper and set on a cutting board.

After situating a warped griddle over the stovetop's low flame, he poured soup from a jar into a saucepan to heat. "I spent forty years of my life serving my country. It pained me to have to retire. But I couldn't get around anymore to do anyone any good. And then my wife took sick."

Ten years gone, and even a small reference to Madelyn's illness cut him to the bone. He flicked his wrist sharply, slinging a pat of butter from his knife to the griddle, where it sizzled and spread.

"Hank?" he finally heard Natasha ask, and he turned. She handed him the first sandwich; he slid it to the heated surface to cook.

"Being alone gives a man too much time to think. Too much time doing nothing. And nothing much to lose. I started checking the wires. Got wind of a soldier in trouble in Thailand." Hank paused to look after the sandwich, heard the scrape of Christian's chair on the old linoleum, the boy's footsteps heading for the back door, the door opening and closing as he walked out on the conversation.

Hank cast a glance to the side, where Natasha was staring at the sandwich makings, her eyes wide, her mouth plain ol' grim. "He was a young man who'd been part of a military detail escorting a team of doctors up the Mae Kok River. Seems the medical supplies being delivered on up to the Akha hill tribes in the Chiang Rai province were actually drugs headed for Myanmar."

"What happened to him?" she asked after a few seconds passed, handing him a saucer and a second sandwich. "And please make sure it has something to do with the reason I'm standing in your kitchen making lunch instead of on the road to Lake Placid."

Pluck and mettle. He could grow to like this girl. "Pretty simple. He was caught, accused, tried, and convicted of trafficking illegal drugs, and was left to serve out his sentence."

Frowning, she shook her head. "But you just said he didn't know what he was transporting."

"That didn't make him any less guilty, did it?" Hank remarked, raising a brow and hoping her indignation was at least a bit on behalf of Christian and what the boy had suffered. "Not to local law enforcement. Especially with the organization supplying the drugs paying the village elders to make sure he never again saw the light of day."

"You've got to be kidding." She took the second sandwich, handed him a third. "How sheltered have I been that I thought that only happened in fiction?"

"No, Miss Gaudet." Hank took a deep breath and prayed none of his boys ever suffered Christian's fate again. "It happens in the real world more often than anyone ever knows."

"You went to get him, didn't you?" she asked softly a minute or two later, her words nearly disappearing in the emotion of her voice.

"I did indeed. Then I recruited him." They switched out sandwiches again. Waiting for it to cook, they said nothing until Hank slid the fifth from the spatula to the griddle. "I recruited him and now he works under my command rescuing others."

"But you're retired military."

"Exactly so. Which means I have no one but myself and my maker to answer to."

"You do this on your own, then? Like a team of mercenaries?"

Hank screwed up his mouth, shook his head. "The idea of mercenaries leaves a bit of a bad taste. None of what we do is done for money."

"I still don't see what this has to do with me," she said, her frustration having grown by leaps and bounds while the soup and sandwiches heated.

Hank turned off the fire beneath the griddle and the saucepan. No need to grill up any more for now, considering no one was going to have much of an appetite when he was done saying what she needed to hear.

"I need to tell you about your godfather. You need to know the truth about Dr. Wickham Bow."

Two hours later found Christian standing in a dark corner of Hank's office-cum-satellite ops center, Eli McKenzie propped against the paneled wall at his side. The two had said nothing since returning from an equally silent stint watching MaddyB take a turn around the track.

Eli's eyes were red and bleary, and as much as Christian wanted to ask what he could do, he didn't. Because the truth he well knew was that he couldn't do a goddamn thing. This trip was Eli's to finish. And coming home was often the hardest leg to make.

When Christian had returned to the kitchen earlier, he'd found leftovers still on the table. Two glasses of milk, one half full. Two bowls of soup, both empty. One plate of nothing but crusts and crumbs, a triangle of toasted bread and melted cheese gone cold on the other.

He'd moved the dishes to the sink, dumped the milk, tossed the sandwich half into the trash. The idea of Hank telling Natasha the story of Thailand—even a simplified, Disney-rated version—had driven him out of the room. The thought of her learning the truth about Wickham Bow brought him back.

And now here he stood in the dark, the office lighted only

by the lamp on the desk where she sat flipping through transcripts, headphones delivering the audio of Bow making his deal with the devil. The very same devil who'd cost Christian well over a year of his life, who was now a part of stealing away so much of Natasha's.

Protect the innocent, his conscience shouted, his mind recognizing the reality that it was too late in the game.

There was no innocence here.

And then he startled, brought back to the present by Natasha shooting to her feet. She jerked the headset from her head, freeing strands of hair caught in the cord's coils, knocking the portfolio of transcripts she'd been following to the floor in the process.

She stared at the binder as if it would bite off her fingers should she reach down and pick it up. And so she didn't. She stood there like the clichéd doe caught in headlights, her chest heaving, tiny, injured animal sounds spilling from her throat.

It was all Christian could do not to go to her, to stay where he was, to let the ugly truth of what she was facing sink in. Nothing he could say or do now would ease any of what she was suffering. The pain of having her entire life, everything she'd thought she could count on, all of what made her feel safe and secure ripped away . . .

He literally flinched when she bolted from the room and slammed the door behind her. He glanced at Eli, who did no more than shake his head, push off the wall that was holding him up, and follow. It was all Christian could do not to head out after the both of them.

Had he been able to breathe without feeling the knife of betrayal sink deeper into his gut, he would have. Instead, he glanced across the room to where Hank sat in a worn leather recliner, the only nod to comfort or personalization in the high-tech surroundings.

"Let her go. Briggs is outside, and Eli will see that she doesn't go far."

Christian crossed his arms over his chest, then dropped his

head back and beat it against the wall. "Eli's in no condition to chase down more than roadkill."

"He's got a hangover to walk off. Keeping an eye on Natasha will give him a reason to shake his drunk that much faster."

Christian snorted. "I'm not so sure I want him anywhere near her."

"Soundin' a might possessive there, son."

"Protective, not possessive."

"And what are you lookin' to protect her from? An operative whose judgment is so far off that no hair of any dog is going to set it right again?"

Christian shook his head. He'd been in Eli's shoes more times than he wanted to remember. "He come in on his own, or you bring him?"

"A little of both. He didn't much like the idea of quitting. I reminded him it was better than being dead."

Christian closed his eyes. "I guess that depends on what it is you're quitting, doesn't it?"

Hank pushed up out of the chair amid creaks of joints and worn springs. "You listen to me, son. You never quit on those men. You saw them through to the brutal end. And I hear tell that you tried to sell your soul to take their place."

A lot of good it had done him, too. Offering his life for those of his men. No enemy wanted to kill a leader when he could be imprisoned, mocked, humiliated, and degraded as an example to others. "They got more bang for the buck their way. Though I imagine they'd rethink that strategy if they could see me now. My soul doesn't feel worth more than a bad penny these days."

"Why?" Hank asked, lifting a hip to the edge of the desk. "Because doing your job means you've had to deceive that girl out there?"

Christian took a deep breath. "Puts me in the same league as Malena."

Hank snorted. "I think you need a lesson in rights and

wrongs. You went in to rescue a kidnapped scientist. The lies you told were part of saving the life of an innocent man. Or so you thought going in."

And what a moral contradiction that was. If it was only the lies, Christian would be having a hell of an easier time. Because he hadn't simply glossed over the truth or involved her in a deception he could correct with a quick reveal of the facts.

No, he'd sucked her fully into the lies. Her body, her mind, her emotions. And he knew too well the way it felt when a lie like that blew up. His psyche was riddled with the shrapnel, and his explosion had happened seven years before.

He pushed away from the wall and crossed the room. "Yeah, well, it's too bad Natasha's world will end up a pile of shit in the process."

"Hmm. The girl's done some growing on you, has she?"

Growing. That wasn't the word he would've used, but having Hank say it felt right somehow. Hell, Christian reflected. He'd showered with her. He'd taken off his clothes and bared his body in an enclosed space no larger than the cage he'd lived in for months.

Yeah, having the lights off made it easier to pretend otherwise, pretend that beyond the darkness lay wide open spaces, as did having Natasha there with him. But even one week ago he wouldn't have been able to put himself through that torture. And that said a lot—too much maybe—about her impact on him.

"I don't like innocent people ending up in the cross fire. That's all." It wasn't all, but this wasn't the time for getting into any more of it.

Having made his way the width of the room, Hank clapped a hand to Christian's shoulder and squeezed. "I'm thinking it might be in the best interest of that innocence if she has a few more hours to let this sink in. Realizing the truth of what her godfather is doing has to have hit her like a fat ton of bricks."

"Deception does have that flattening effect."

"And that's why we have our friends, Christian. To pump

us back up again." Hank paused a moment, searching out Christian's gaze while the boy let that stew. When Christian nodded, the older man added, "Good. Now, let's go over what you've got and see if we can figure out the truth behind this sham of a kidnapping."

Seventeen

Natasha stood at the split rail fence that circled what appeared to be a racetrack, praying that the food in her stomach stayed put.

While eating the lunch she'd helped Hank prepare, sitting and listening to him tell her about her godfather's deal with this syndicate, Spectra IT, the tomato soup and grilled cheese sandwich had tasted like a feast for the desperately starving. Thinking about it now, she was surprised she'd been able to taste it at all.

A programmed response, more than likely. The same way mourners made their way through a buffet of tuna casserole and carrot salad, dinner rolls and chocolate sheet cake. Eating because the feeling of being full and satisfied was so much more comforting than an empty sense of being abandoned, that hollow sadness that would linger for the rest of one's life.

How was she going to move on?

She had no idea what Wick could possibly have been thinking. She'd listened for years to him expound eloquently on not only morality in a global dynamic, but on personal choices, rights and wrongs, codes of ethics. If what he was being accused of doing was true—and obviously it was; she'd been shown the proof—he had betrayed not only her.

He had betrayed himself, had in one fell swoop destroyed

the reputation he'd spent a lifetime building. That of a man with quirks like any other, but a good man, a man to count on, to never doubt. A man who, along with her father, had provided the education that had made her childhood one of defining beliefs as much as dodgeball and baby dolls.

She hugged herself tighter and sniffed, leaning her chest into the fence railing and staring down at the dying grass on the other side. The tufts seem to be struggling with their own disastrous truth, the fact that winter was coming and their blissful days of basking innocently in the sun were gone. Innocence. Bah humbug crock of fucked-up shit.

The sound of steps scraping over the gravel behind her wasn't enough to make her look up. It was easier to let gravity take care of her tears when she didn't have a tissue. If she'd had a change of clothes, she would have blotted her face with her sleeve, but her overnighter was still in the Ferrari that was still MIA. . . .

"I'll leave if you prefer not to have company."

What the hell did it matter now? she mused. And why did that deep male voice ring with a song so familiar, so comforting that she wanted to weep again? Instead, she drew in a deep breath and shrugged. "Stay. Go. I don't care."

It was a lie, of course. As perverted a reality as it was, Christian was the only thing here that was even halfway familiar. Not soothing. Not welcome. But the only thing to which she had a connection. Basically, he was better than nothing. Certainly better than being alone.

"I want to apologize but I'm not sure where or how to start." He placed a boot on the bottom rail of the fence, propped his forearms on the top and laced his hands together. He didn't look at her, though. He didn't touch her.

And she wasn't sure if she was happy or sad. "Starting with 'I'm sorry' is always a good bet."

"I'm sorry, Natasha."

"Okay," was all she could think to say because she didn't know if she was ready to forgive him anything yet—or if she wanted to wait until the grass was once again green.

He went on, no acknowledgement of her response, nothing. "It's funny, but every time I come here I'm almost able to forget what it is I do the rest of the time. This is about the only place I can breathe and think."

He was silent then, staring off in the direction of the woods beyond the track and stables, and she wondered what it was he actually saw. She curled her fingers over the fence railing, rested her cheek on top of her hands, and studied his profile. "What do you think about?"

He shook his head evasively.

"No. Tell me. I want to know." It was better than sinking any deeper into the quicksand of self-pity sucking her down. Besides, she still was who she was, which meant a man who would do what he did still intrigued her.

"Stupid shit. What kind of life I'd have if I really was an engineer." He shrugged.

"What? You don't enjoy chasing people down and jumping them?"

"Some are more fun to jump than others." He glanced in her direction then and frowned, straightening to dig into his pocket for a handkerchief. "Here. You've got . . . your face is . . ."

She sighed, cleaned the tracks of her tears, continued to stare at him. The setting sun cast rays of light at such an angle that he was left in silhouette. Strange how she saw him so clearly, no matter. "In another lifetime, I suppose I would have laughed at that."

"It really wasn't that funny."

"Sure it was," she said, uncertain why she had this need to soothe. "I just have a compromised sense of humor today."

He turned fully toward her, his eyes so bright and so clear, but most of all sad. "I hate to say this, but I don't see it improving much the next few days."

"Yeah. I pretty much came to the same conclusion after talking to Hank." Strangely, she longed to stay here and never go home again. Or click her heels three times and end up someplace even better.

"I wish I could make this easier for you." He started to

reach for her, one hand moving toward her cheek, but seemed to consider the wisdom of second thoughts and tucked his fingers into his pocket instead. "Hell, I wish I could make it go away."

"That would be nice, thanks." And then she couldn't help it. As hard as it was to say, she admitted the truth. "Having you there with me when I return will make it easier, Pet—uh, sorry. Christian."

He looked off beyond the track again. "Deacon really is a bastard."

"Then you're a terrible impersonator because you haven't been a bastard at all," she said, and didn't bother to hide the slight smile that appeared.

His smile was even wider, his eyes twinkling as he said, "I'll remind you of that next time you cuss me out for lying to you."

She wanted to be angry—at him, at Wick, at the world—but anger required too much energy and she was so very, very tired. Too tired to trust anything she felt. Too numb to feel much of anything at all.

She'd gone to his bed willingly. She'd enjoyed herself immensely while there. She only wished she knew who it was she'd slept with, how much of the sex had been business and how much pleasure.

She toyed with the soiled handkerchief. "Did you lie to me about everything?"

"No." This time he allowed himself to reach out and tuck her hair behind her ear. "Making love with you was never a lie."

She swallowed hard at the gentleness of his touch, fought to breathe at the tenderness in his expression, the break in his voice. "You don't think it's a lie to call it making love? When there was no love involved?"

"The first time?" He shook his head. "The first time was . . . complicated." Christian paused, continued. "On the terrace? I still wasn't sure of your loyalties."

"What about on the balcony?"

He took a deep breath. "That one's tough. I couldn't deal with what seducing you as Deacon would mean. But seducing you as myself . . ."

"What about last night?" she asked when he left the thought unfinished.

He hadn't wanted to talk about it this morning before they'd left the city. He'd tried to bring it up during the flight, before she'd been handed the indisputable evidence of Wick's betrayal.

Yet she couldn't help but wonder if last night's intimacy hadn't been more dream than reality, if yet again she'd been so overwhelmed physically that she'd lost all perspective on what had happened in bed.

So it surprised her when Christian moved his hand from her ear to cup her jaw, stroking her cheekbone before rubbing his thumb across her lips, staring down as he did, his pulse beating visibly at his temple. "For a long time now I've made sure sex was only about the physical act. I've kept my head out of the equation."

"Because of your work, you mean?"

He shook his head. "Because it's been the only way to stay sane."

"And now?" she asked breathlessly because the look in his eyes said the state of affairs had changed.

"Now all I know is being with you has been more than I ever expected."

She wasn't sure how she felt about his use of *has been.* Or what it was he'd been expecting. Right now, she wasn't sure how she felt about anything, and that was probably for the best.

She was in no shape for any sort of rational thought and wouldn't be until sleep cleared her head. She sighed heavily, leaned into the fence instead of succumbing to temptation and leaning into him.

He stepped away as if he realized he'd said too much. As if

he, too, needed the distance. "If you want to come back to the house, I'll show you where you're going to stay. And you can call Susan and Dr. Bow."

"Okay." She straightened, shook back her hair, cleaned her face one last time before returning his handkerchief. "I wasn't sure if you and Hank decided we would stay here tonight after all."

"It was my decision, actually," he said, stuffing the handkerchief into his pocket. "You haven't slept much this weekend, and I'm speaking from experience when I say that being rested up makes for a much more believable liar."

She shook her head, rubbed at her temples. "I don't know how I'm going to pull this off. To go back to Wick's place and act like everything's normal? Like nothing has changed?" She rubbed harder. It didn't help. Her head verged on exploding. "How exactly am I supposed to do that?"

"With a little help from your friends," Christian said, hooking an arm around her shoulders and guiding her back to the house.

Walking numbly beside him, she blinked back the threat of tears. Friends, huh? She supposed she could live with that—especially considering the mess she was in.

Keeping their relationship to friendship might be her best chance to stay alive.

Wickham Bow was not happy with this newest delay. Natasha should have been here hours ago, yet she had only just thought to call.

Though he had been pleased with her previous attention to Mr. Deacon, this jaunt to the city she'd taken with the Spectra representative had pushed Wickham's patience to the edge. Dr. Jinks had been working all night and was ready to give Mr. Deacon a live demonstration of what he had achieved.

Now, however, they would all be waiting another day. No, Wickham was not the least bit happy with this newest delay.

At a knock on his open office door, he looked up. "Yes, Dr. Jinks?"

"You got a minute, uh, sir?"

No, he did not have a minute. He did not have a second. He had no time to spare, no time to waste at all. "Of course. Come in."

"Uh, thanks." Dr. Jinks entered the office, lollygagged around in front of the bookcases along the front wall, touching the embossed spines with his unkempt fingers, nails chewed to the quick, cuticles ragged and raw.

Wickham found himself cursing his body, which kept him bound to this chair when he wanted to snatch the valuable volumes away from this . . . this *boy* who had no appreciation for life's finer moments. Who took for granted his brilliance, and was throwing it away for money.

A true conundrum, hating the very man he needed for his plan to work. The very man whose genius was providing the technology—and therefore the funds—which would buy the year of institutional care, the experimental treatment and unsanctioned clinical trials guaranteed to return Wickham's life to rights.

He laced his hands together atop his desk blotter. "What can I help you with, Dr. Jinks?"

The boy continued to wander. "I was just wondering what was up with giving Mr. Deacon a show of the busted encryption tonight."

"It appears Natasha and Mr. Deacon have been delayed and will be returning tomorrow rather than this evening."

Dr. Jinks snorted his response, scuffed his athletic shoes over the polished wood floor.

Wickham found himself grinding his jaw and breathed deeply to relax. "What's the matter, Dr. Jinks? You seem rather impatient, less than your usual jovial self."

"I dunno. I'm just ready for this to be over and done with. It's been two months now. I thought—"

"You thought what? That our agreement was on a strict time schedule? That you would have your money in hand and immediately be on your way to a new life?"

"Two months isn't immediately. Two weeks maybe."

The younger man hadn't once looked Wickham in the eye. He had to admit to a bit of creeping unease at this change in Dr. Jinks's demeanor. A change that was not for the better, and would now require a lighter hand to manage. "I forget how young you are, Woodrow. Once you are my age, months do seem to pass like weeks."

"Yeah, well, right now these months are passing like years." More scuffing. More fingerprints left on the leather bindings.

More disquiet with this turn of events. "Are you perhaps homesick?"

Woodrow was uncomfortably slow to respond. "Not so much homesick as bored. Ready to get this over with."

Get this over with? What sort of a comment was that when *this* would never be over? "I predict tomorrow will be a very productive day for both of us. Once Mr. Deacon is shown the extent of what you've accomplished, once he has seen a successful test of your capabilities, we will be one step closer to our goal."

"Yeah, I guess."

Wickham understood for the first time the purpose of rolling one's eyes. "I am sorry circumstances don't allow you to slip away for a night on the town. But it would hardly be wise for you to show your face and risk being recognized, however unlikely the possibility."

"I gotta say it's been pretty weird having free run of the place with everyone thinking I'm missing. I wonder if anyone is still waiting for a ransom note," Woodrow said with a bit of a laugh, then quickly quieted. "You sure the Courtneys haven't talked?"

"My dear boy. The Courtneys run in no circles where your name would come up. And your kidnapping has been kept out of the press per our—per *your*—instructions." As incommodious as the younger man's obsession with role-playing games was, Wickham had to admit Woodrow knew how to strategize. He had done a remarkable job arranging his own disappearance.

"I hope so, 'cause I'd really hate for this whole thing to blow up after all this time and effort."

Wincing, Wickham watched Woodrow pick up and shake the jade abacus dating from the early Qing Dynasty which Michael Gaudet had presented him years ago. The boy's disrespectful handling of a gift with incalculable sentimental value was too much. He motored his wheelchair away from his desk.

"I'd thank you not to touch that, please." He kept his voice toneless, even, not wishing to startle Dr. Jinks. "It was given to me by a dear friend."

"Oh, sure." He shrugged, passed the abacus to Wickham when he held out his hand. "I guess I'll head to the media room, check out a DVD or something."

"Certainly. Whatever you wish," Wickham said, but his comment was made in the abstract, his attention on the abacus he held and the refusal of his fingers to work.

He tried to grip the lower deck; the abacus bobbled in his palm. His heart lurched. He worked to slide the precious gift into his lap, to use his arm to gather it in. Nothing. Nothing. His extremities refused the signal from his brain. He couldn't even find his voice to call for Dr. Jinks.

All Wickham could do was watch the abacus fall to the floor and shatter, jade beads rolling across the hardwood, rods jutting from the frame like so many useless fingers.

Eighteen

According to Christian, Hank's Saratoga home had been remodeled after the death of his wife, one long wing converted into a dormitory. Three good-sized bedrooms had been cut into six, giving his SG-5 operatives a place to come in from the cold or whatever.

Natasha felt as if she was in a bad spy movie. Or, she supposed, a good spy movie, since these men were apparently the ones wearing the white hats. Unlike her godfather, who was equally apparently black through and through.

Shivering, she stared down at her overnighter, which had appeared earlier when another of Christian's cohorts, Kelly John Beach, had driven up in the Ferrari. She could keep staring for the next twenty-four hours and nothing would change.

She hadn't packed anything warm enough to ward off the cold she was feeling.

A bone-deep cold. No, a soul-deep cold. A cold that no wool or thermal weave would stave off. She needed a hot shower, a hot bath, a hot tub in the middle of a jungle. . . .

Thailand. The operative Hank had rescued had to be Christian. She supposed it could be Eli McKenzie; he was one very scary-looking man. But instinctively she knew Hank had been telling her Christian's story.

A story she might never have learned if Susan hadn't blown

his Peter Deacon cover. Christian sure hadn't offered up any of the details. Not that he'd been able to, seeing as he hadn't been Christian until a few hours ago.

What a big fat mess of secrets and lies. Natasha pulled the white chenille spread from the bed, wrapped it around her body, and crossed the short width of the room. Shoving the curtains aside, she leaned her forearms on the sill and stared out the chest-high window.

After a terribly overcast day, the night sky was clear, the moon bright, the view beyond nothing but silhouettes and shadows. The woods, the stables, the helicopter. All in shades of gray. Even the man pacing the perimeter of the house was a muscled bulk of black.

She wondered if Eli was still walking off his hangover, assuming that's what he'd been doing when he'd followed her earlier, though now he seemed to be doing a penance of sorts, his gait measured, his head hung low.

She couldn't suppress her curiosity, wondering if he'd suffered in Mexico what Christian had suffered in Thailand. And suddenly she had to know.

What was it these men did? What horrors had they suffered? What qualities had Hank Smithson discovered in them that made them who they were, made them live these deceptive lives?

But when she opened her door to go to Eli and ask, she saw light shining and shadows moving from underneath that of the room opposite. Christian's room. Christian's shadow. Eli could wait.

She knocked once, lightly, and had just stepped back to go on her way when she heard the doorknob turn.

"Hi," she said, catching Christian's frown immediately, as well as his concern.

"Are you cold?"

"Actually, I'm freezing." She tugged the cape of her bedspread tighter and laughed softly. "But I don't think it's about the temperature in here. The house seems quite comfortable. I'm pretty sure it's just me."

He hesitated a moment before opening the door wider. "Do you want to come in?"

"Yes, thanks. I'd like that." She made her way into the room and across to the window in time to see Eli walk by. She glanced back to Christian, who'd obviously been watching the other man, too. "Is he going to be okay?"

Christian leaned his backside against the doorjamb, arms crossed over his chest, and studied her. "Hard to say. He's strong. He's got it together. He should be."

That rationale would have worked if Eli had been suffering anything logical. These men and this place? She knew that wasn't the case at all. "How long did it take you?"

"To do what?" Christian asked blithely.

Hmm. So it was like that, she thought, pressing straight-forwardly on. "To get over Thailand?"

He stared at her for several long moments, the slow blink of his eyes his only response. And then he shifted his weight from one hip to the other, and lifted a questioning brow. "Who said I'm over Thailand?"

Okay. Well. That hadn't been what she'd expected. Now she wasn't quite sure what to say. "I'm sorry. I have to keep reminding myself that you're not who I've been thinking you were all this time."

"You're right. I'm not," he said with more bitterness than she'd ever heard in his voice as he pushed away from the door and returned to the small desk in the corner where a laptop screen glowed.

She wondered what it was he hated. The fact that she knew a part of his past? Or didn't know enough and was asking questions he didn't want to answer? "So, tell me who you are. Introduce me to Christian Bane."

He shook his head, punched a combination of keys to shut down the computer. "I don't think so."

"Why not?" she asked, brows lifted. "It only seems fair when you think about it."

He glanced up as the screen blinked off, his face going from light to dark just like that. "Think about what?"

"That you know everything about me, and I know nothing about you." Nothing beyond how he made her feel in bed, the ways he took her body apart. Nothing more than how much her stomach ached with the despair of his deception.

Nothing that wasn't about the attraction between them that even now buzzed overhead in the room.

"I needed to know you for this job." He stored the laptop in its case, then moved to the closet and unzipped the garment bag hanging on the door. "You need to keep thinking of me as Peter Deacon for that very same reason. It will make things a lot easier on both of us if you remember that."

"Right. I'll just act like everything's normal, like this whole day never happened." She followed Eli as he crossed her line of vision, wondering if walking for hours on end would give her the peace to move on after her "assignment." "Nothing matters but the job. Nothing but bringing down big bad Wickham Bow."

She supposed she should think about packing up her room there at her godfather's estate, about getting her résumé together, figuring out how to move on with her life. Then again, thinking about anything beyond getting through tomorrow hurt her head.

Her heart was thankfully numb. It would take seeing Wick again, confronting him, before the reality of his treachery hit.

She reached up to rub the bands of tension binding her temples, wishing away the hollow sensation that had returned to suck her down. She was so far out of it she barely registered Christian moving to her side.

He didn't touch her. He leaned an elbow on the wall beside the window, massaged his neck, and stared out, yet his closeness still gave her comfort.

"I've known your godfather barely a week, and the mission's portfolio is nothing but facts. As tough as it is for you, and trust me, I know that it is, I could really use any help you can give me."

She shrugged. She was as clueless as he was. And she'd known

Wick for more than half of her life. "I don't know what to tell you. I don't know what to think. What it appears he's guilty of here is so unlike him . . . I don't know. I just don't know."

"Has anything happened recently? A change in his routine? More demands than usual from the university? I know they've made special arrangements to broadcast his lectures, but is he under other pressures? Conferences he's scheduled to attend? A paper he has to present?"

She shook her head. Just stood there and shook her head. None of Christian's questions brought anything to mind. Wick's schedule had been business as usual for weeks now, months even. "The only thing going on with him lately is that he's pushing himself too hard. He's not taking proper care of himself and he doesn't like that I nag."

"Men facing their own mortality have been known to lose judgment and perspective."

"Which would make sense if we were talking about anyone else." She shook her head slowly. "I can't see Wick going this far off the deep end. Not after the stand he's always taken on morality."

Christian stiffened. "Taking a stand doesn't mean shit when a man's out of his mind, Natasha. Morality doesn't put food in his stomach. Principles and ethics don't put salve on open wounds."

He paused; she heard him swallow before he cleared his throat and went on. "Don't think you know what does or doesn't make sense."

Interesting. "Is that what happened in Thailand?"

"Which part of it?"

"Any of it?"

"Try all of it." He propped an elbow on the windowsill, leaned his forehead into his hand and scrubbed his palm back and forth over his head as if rubbing away the torture of his thoughts.

When he spoke again, his voice echoed with a tangible anguish. "This is why you're better off thinking of me as Peter

Deacon for the rest of our time together. Christian Bane isn't worth getting to know."

More and more interesting. Even as Peter Deacon, Christian had never struck her as the type to think so little of himself, to feel sorry for himself. She nodded toward the window. "What about Eli McKenzie?"

"What about him?"

"Does he possess any redeeming qualities?" She turned so that she faced Christian fully. "Or have you cornered the market on losing them all after living through hell?"

He shook his head, smirked more than smiled, and snorted.

Now she was getting somewhere. "What about Hank? Seeing his driver blown apart and living all this time with a piece of shrapnel grinding his hip into sawdust doesn't sound like a walk in the park."

Still he said nothing.

"I'm not trying to diminish your suffering. But you had your life ripped apart seven years ago. I'm not even up to seven hours here." She struggled to breathe, feeling as if she would never be able to fill her lungs. Feeling as if she had to strike out or explode from the anger building inside.

"I haven't been physically tortured or starved, no. But I'm standing here afraid if I unwrap this bedspread that I'll tumble to the floor in a pile of bones. So don't tell me what does or doesn't make sense."

His silence was a beat too long.

She turned to go but didn't make it very far. Christian put a foot down on the trailing end of her bedspread, ordering her, "Don't go."

She continued toward the door, the bedspread sliding from her shoulders until she felt completely exposed standing there in the khakis and sweater she'd been wearing all day. A ridiculous sensation since she was covered from head to toe, but she still felt as if Christian had stripped her bare.

"Please stay," he said, and she stopped.

One hand on the doorknob, she stopped and stared down at her pale fingers curled around the brushed brass ball. All she had to do was twist it to the right, pull the door inward a foot, and walk straight out of the room. A simple motion. That was all that stood between escape and letting him see the true extent of her vulnerability.

"I'm an ass, Natasha. I'm sorry. Now come here and warm up, or you'll never get to sleep."

In the end, she stayed because of the cold. She wanted to go, to spend the night alone, to use the silent time to dig for the inner strength the next few days would demand of her. But she was so cold. Cold to the bone. Cold to the very deepest parts of her heart.

Christian offered her use of the bed's sheet and blanket, insisting he'd be fine in his T-shirt and sweats. She chose instead to sleep on top of the covers, under which he finally slid. She was dressed, too, and had the nubby warmth of the chenille to cocoon herself in.

All she needed from Christian was the heat of his body as it warmed first his blankets then hers. That was all she needed.

She needed nothing more.

She woke in the middle of the night curled into a fetal position, having dreamed that she was hiding beneath the terrace tables from Wick.

He had wanted her to entertain his guests, to stand on the table's surface beneath the wide patio umbrella and tap-dance in her white patent leather shoes. She hadn't wanted to dance, hadn't wanted to be found.

Hadn't wanted to hear him making illicit deals behind her back with men she couldn't see while she played the part of entertainer.

And so she'd curled up tighter, tucked her hands between her thighs, her chin to her chest, and drifted between her dream world and the alien one into which she had briefly opened her eyes.

When she woke a second time, her dream was less specific, more ethereal, and she still didn't feel rested at all. Every bone in her body ached. Stress gripped her tendons and muscles so tightly she felt like a rubber band waiting to snap. She needed to ease the tension, needed to fall into an exhaustive sleep, knew the quickest way to both.

Still muzzy, she released the button on her waistband, lowered her zipper, slipped a hand into her panties and pressed a finger to one side of her clit. She shuddered, shivered, her eyes rolling back at the impact of the stimulation, her questing finger slipping deeper between her legs.

And then she remembered where she was.

How boneheaded could she possibly be, masturbating in her sleep while sharing his bed? She pulled her hand from her pants, reminding herself that this was her body reacting to the fantasy of her dreams. She settled back down to sleep, reaching and searching for . . . *what* she couldn't recall.

But the longer she lay there unmoving, the itchier she got. Awareness of the man sleeping at her side, his breathing deep and even, sparked like lightning over her skin, raising the hair at her nape along with her temperature. She rocked her lower body slightly, her breathing quickened, her sex grew heavy with need.

She had to get out of here now. Too much of her bedspread, however, lay caught beneath the weight of Christian's bulk. She left the covering, slowly swung her legs over the side of the bed, and sat up.

Christian reached out and snagged her wrist before she moved any further. "Stay."

She shook her head, certain he'd been sleeping, that it was her wrangling with the bedspread that had woken him up and not . . . "I have to go."

"Stay, Natasha." He eased up on his hold but he didn't release her. "I'd feel better having you here."

The comment put her on the defensive. She wasn't even sure why. "Afraid I'm going to bolt?"

"No. Afraid you won't get back to sleep if you go." He tugged lightly. "I know I won't."

"Why's that?" she asked, not quite ready to give in.

"Worrying about you," he said without hesitation.

See? Why was she expecting the worst from him when he'd never been anything but considerate? Well, except for the fact that everything between them had been based on lies. "I'm not sure I'll be able to get back to sleep. And I don't want to keep you awake."

This time he tugged a bit harder, his hold more insistent. "Stay. Please."

Once again, the magic word. Denying him anything didn't seem to be in the cards. Funny enough, however, giving in didn't seem like a capitulation at all. It simply seemed like the thing to do. Slowly, she lowered herself back down to lay on her side.

Christian wrapped an arm around her waist and pulled her and her bedspread close. "Much better."

God, but he made her feel so good. Protected and comfortable. Hopeful. Warm. "I'm embarrassed to admit this, but I can't remember ever sleeping with a man before."

"You've slept with me twice now."

She snuggled deeper into the spoon of his body. "Yes, but we did more than sleep both times."

"You haven't been in a relationship where you just slept with your partner?"

It did seem strange when she thought about it that way. "I've never lived with anyone, no. So, nights spent together always meant . . ."

"Sex," he finished for her when she suddenly grew too uncomfortable to go on.

She didn't want to talk about sex with other men, didn't even want to think about it, being with Christian here and now. They weren't committed. They had no understanding, no arrangement. Nothing about their intimacy meant anything—yet it meant everything.

It meant more than she'd let herself realize until now, because accepting that truth brought home the awareness that she was involved with another unsuitable man—and growing comfortably used to having him near.

"It's nice, you know. Being with you like this. Not to say

sex hasn't crossed my mind," she admitted with a bit of self-deprecation and a chuckle.

Christian tightened his hold around her middle. "Believe me. You're not the only one with the dirty mind."

She laughed again, enjoying that they could talk easily and feel no pressure to act on their shared desires. "My girlfriends give me a hard time about having a man's sex drive. Too much testosterone, I guess."

"Hmm. I was beginning to wonder about that mustache of yours."

She bit back a chuckle and jabbed her elbow in reverse, catching it in her bedspread and his blanket and sheet. "That was not funny."

"Hmm. I thought I heard you laughing," he said sleepily.

She should let him go back to sleep. Keeping him awake had not been her intent when she'd decided to stay. Yet while slumber seemed so elusive when he was here in her grasp, the anger and hurt were easier to bear.

She sighed. "That's because laughing isn't as painful as crying."

For several long minutes he remained silent, his hand slowly stroking over her hipbone and thigh. She waited patiently, loving the calming sensation of his touch, the soothing, repetitive motion that quickly lulled her like her own thoughts had failed to do.

Yet when his hand stopped moving, she inexplicably found herself holding her breath for the revelation to come. She wasn't disappointed.

Christian blew out a heavy breath. "I wasn't sure I'd ever be able to sleep with anyone again once I got home. I wasn't sure I'd be able to sleep at all."

"Home from Thailand, you mean?" she asked in a soft whisper.

He barely nodded. "I came here, actually. I didn't know Hank from Adam, but he knew I was going to need some serious time. You think Eli looks bad? You should've seen me."

"A mess, huh?" She didn't want to pry for fear of turning him off from sharing more, now that he'd finally started.

"Like you wouldn't believe. About forty pounds lighter. Hair longer than Julian's."

"Julian?"

"Sorry. A partner of mine. Thinks he's Sampson."

"Ah. It would've been interesting to see you with long hair."

He snorted. "Maybe if I'd been a head banger. But the hair I came home with was more like one big nasty dreadlock. I couldn't wait to shave that bitch off."

She stifled a giggle. "That bad?"

"You can't imagine."

"I'm sorry you had to go through that."

She felt him shrug against her back. "I survived. It sucked, but I survived. Even if I've pretty much given up on ever sleeping through a night again."

"I'm sorry I woke you. I should've just stayed where I was."

He shook his head, cuddled closer. "You woke me before that. You must've been dreaming."

God, please don't let him mention her having her hand in her pants. "I was. Strange stuff about Wick and the parties he used to throw. But it was all mixed up with what's going on now."

"Pretty normal, it sounds like. Your subconscious pulling the past into the present."

"Did that happen to you? Did you dream a lot during the time you were . . . ?"

"The time I was in hell?"

She nodded, wincing at the raw expletive that followed.

"I'm not even sure I slept, never mind dreamed. There were stretches when it felt like I hadn't closed my eyes for days. Other times I wasn't sure whether I was asleep or awake even with my eyes wide open."

He swallowed audibly and Natasha cringed, fighting the

nerves churning in her middle. She couldn't stand it any longer.

She needed to be nearer, to hold him, to comfort him, to let him know it was safe to close his eyes. That he wasn't alone, that she'd be with him as long as he wanted to have her around.

She squirreled around in the tangled covers and turned.

Nineteen

A thin strip of moonlight came in through the room's tiny square window, the sheer curtains over which Christian had never drawn.

"If you want to tell me, I'll listen," Natasha said softly, keeping her hands to herself when she wanted more than anything to touch him. His cheek. His forehead. The curved shell of his ear.

The fact that he didn't immediately say no, that his body seemed to relax as he settled beside her more comfortably, gave her hope.

And so she gently pressed. "I'm a good listener, Christian. I don't pass judgment or butt in with my opinions. Well, unless it's with one of my girlfriends but they usually deserve it."

He chuckled at that, one of his feet seeking out one of hers. "Tough on the girls, are you?"

She snuggled up, placed a palm in the center of his T-shirted chest. His heart beat hard; his heat warmed her. She spoke softly as an overwhelming and unfamiliar emotion began to weave a web around her, catching her unsuspecting and barely able to breathe.

"I won't be tough on you, Christian," she promised. "I'm pretty sure you've already been too tough on yourself."

He huffed. "I wondered if you picked up on that."

And how could she not? "It's not hard to miss."

He flopped over onto his back then, tossed a forearm over his eyes, his wrist up, his fingers tightly clenched. She stayed close, close enough to notice the grim line of his mouth in the moonlight.

A grimness that she feared meant he was through talking for the night. But then she caught the shift in his breathing, and her own pulse started to race.

"It was a tiny cell," he said. "A cage, really. Not even worthy of an animal. A lot of bamboo and rope and the bugs that came with both. Especially considering the whole thing was open to the elements."

"Oh my God." She wasn't sure whose heart was now beating the hardest. "Are you serious?"

"Oh yeah. And not the walk in the park sort of elements, either. For one thing, there wasn't any room to walk."

"What?" She breathed out more than voiced the question. He'd been caged like a rat for a year? And he was still able to function?

"Maybe six feet square?" He cleared his throat, once, twice. "By the time I was out, I would've sworn it was six inches."

She doubted her limbs would ever work right again. She wanted to hold him, to stroke him, to take away the memories of his suffering, to end the pain that still lingered. But she couldn't move, frozen by the horror of his story.

"God, Christian. I'm so sorry." She rubbed circles there in the center of his chest. "I'm so sorry."

"Yeah. Me, too." He placed his hand on top of hers to still her movements. "Just don't *feel* sorry for me. I don't need that. I don't want that."

"Oh no." She spread her fingers; he laced them with his. "Trust me. You're hardly an object to be pitied."

He grunted, seemed to consider what she'd said, and responded with, "As long as I'm an object to be worshipped, we're good to go."

She pinched him. It wasn't easy. He was nothing but muscle there. He yelped anyway, and turned a playful glare her way. His eyes sparkled brightly with such boyish, amazed humor, she had the feeling no one ever teased him. It was all she could do not to raise up and kiss him senseless.

But then he sobered almost instantly, staring into her eyes until her heart thumped so hard she feared her ribs would break. He squeezed her fingers, rubbed the tips over his closed lips before lacing his with hers and resting their joined hands on his chest.

"I've never known another woman like you, Natasha Gaudet. You make me smile when I'm pretty damn sure I'm not in the mood."

"You should always be in the mood to smile, Christian." She did then, though she felt like crying because of the tenderness with which he spoke, with which he held her hand. "It's a lethal weapon. No well-prepared spy should leave home without it."

He turned to face her, drew her arm around his neck, moved his to her waist, and opened his palm in the small of her back. "Nothing could have prepared me for you. For the way you make me forget things I thought I would never shake off."

"That's a good thing, yes?" she whispered, massaging the base of his skull.

"Truthfully? I don't know." He kneaded the muscles on either side of her spine, making his way up her back. "Drawing on the past helps me remember what I'm doing here in the present. And why. I don't want to lose my edge."

"And you think you will if you let the bad stuff go?"

He snuggled further down into the bed so that their noses almost touched. "I'm afraid it could happen, yeah. That I'll let my guard down and be blindsided."

What were they talking about here? More than just physical danger, she was certain. Was he afraid of her?

Afraid of *them*?

"I'm afraid, too," she admitted, surprising herself as much

as him. "And you know what? I don't like being afraid. Maybe we should both start trusting ourselves a little more than we do."

"Maybe I should just kiss you."

Her hand stilled. Her eyes widened. His lashes drifted down as he focused on her mouth. "Are you sure that's a good idea?"

He mumbled something in return, continued to stroke his way up her back, pressing a hand between her shoulder blades and pulling her close. "The best one I've had in awhile."

"Does this mean you're letting down your guard?" she asked breathlessly as his mouth drew close.

He touched his lips to hers lightly, never pressuring her to kiss him back, once, twice, this time running the tip of his tongue along the seam of her lips. She did her best to keep her breathing even, to keep from tugging him bodily forward, sensing that this kiss—so simple, so gentle, barely a kiss at all—meant more than the others they'd shared.

And then he nodded, and whispered, "Yeah. I think I am," and covered her mouth completely.

She shuddered with what he made her feel, the beauty of being cherished, of partaking in a moment so special, this new beginning for them both. When she kissed him back, she did so tentatively for fear of destroying this feeling of joy.

He chuckled. "It's okay. It's just a kiss."

"I know," she said. A big fat whopping lie. It wasn't just a kiss at all, but she wasn't sure how to explain what was going on with her, this unbelievable sense that what they shared could never be more right.

Despite her bold talk of trust, she'd never been so frightened. Considering what they still faced, right could go wrong in a heartbeat.

They finally arrived at Dr. Bow's estate around noon the next day. Christian pulled the Ferrari through the circular drive in front of the house and parked it there. His arrival last week had been about rescuing Jinks and taking down Spectra, Natasha, and Bow in the process.

Today he arrived with only one thing on his mind. Finish up with Bow and set Natasha free.

He cut the engine, glanced across the cockpit to where she sat staring straight ahead, her hands laced tightly in her lap, her eyes wide, her face pale. This wasn't good. Bow would suspect things weren't right if she walked inside looking like death warmed over.

Christian curled his hands around the steering wheel until his palms began to sweat. "Are you ready for this?"

"No, but I'm going to do it anyway."

He was in no frame of mind to smile but found himself unable to fight what she made him feel. He'd never known a woman to take on the world the way this one did, no matter how much she'd rather party the night away with her friends.

He liked that about her, her gustiness, her grit. "All I have to do is figure out what it is Bow has brought Jinks here to do. What it is they're selling to Spectra. If I can found out the way, all the better. If not, I'm still taking them out."

"Right. Get into the lab and snoop around without Woody or Wick catching you in the act. How simple could it be?"

"This is what I do, Natasha. I'm trained for covert ops. I don't make up this stuff as I go along."

She snorted her frustration. "Then I guess it's a good thing one of us has a clue because I can't guarantee I won't hunt down Wick and demand answers the minute I walk through the door."

"You know as well as I do that can't happen." He turned his full attention her way, shifting his hips in his seat to better face her, to better gauge her response.

Her response was a sigh, a heavy exhalation of the breath she'd drawn in as if she were blowing out all doubts and fears of what lay ahead. He knew what she was facing, knew he couldn't protect her from the emotional devastation, wondered if he'd even be able to keep her from any physical harm since his safeguarding record wasn't exactly squeaky clean.

What he could do was let her know he'd be there, that she wasn't going to have to do this alone.

And so he did, putting his arm around her shoulders and pulling her close. She glanced his way briefly, her eyes bright and liquid coffee brown, before her lashes came down. A shudder coursed through her; she rested her cheek on his chest, tucked her head up beneath his chin.

"I know," she finally said, the two words so simple and so soft as they blew over his skin that he held her tighter, held her longer than was probably wise considering that what he was feeling wasn't simple at all.

He tried to tell himself that he was doing no more than offering her the support she needed to get through the next few days. That he wasn't remembering holding her long into the night, just holding her while the bricks protecting his emotions began to fall.

But then he looked up to see her godfather sitting in his wheelchair in the house's open doorway, waiting for them, his expression smug at seeing them in the intimate embrace.

Christian couldn't lie to himself any longer. This return mission was more about keeping Natasha out of the bastard's clutches as it was about the parts they were both playing.

In fact, now that Bow looked so pleased, his hands folded in his lap, his mouth set in a grin that had Christian making a fist, it seemed the perfect time to get Natasha in on the deception.

He took hold of her laced hands, rubbed his thumb over the backs of her fingers. "Don't look now, but we have an audience."

"Wick?"

Christian nodded. "He's at the front door. He must have been waiting for us."

Natasha tilted her head back, lifted her chin, looked into his eyes. "Then why don't you kiss me like you mean it, and let's give him a show."

He didn't need a second invitation. He lowered his head, crushed his lips to hers. She opened without hesitation, bringing up one hand to hold the back of his head as she slipped her tongue into his mouth. She turned her body into his, poured all that she was into the kiss.

She blew him away. That was the only thought that came to his mind as he kissed her back, slanting his head first one angle then another in an attempt to get as close to her as he could. The car didn't offer a quarter of the room he needed. But it was enough for this kiss.

This kiss was for show, scene one, act one of the play they were here to perform. He told himself that again, tried to convince himself the rush of sweet relief he was feeling was fallout from having her soft lips searching, her bold tongue tangling with his, her hand sliding from his shoulder up his neck to cup the back of his head.

He convinced himself of nothing but how close he was to falling for her hard.

She held him as if she never wanted to let him go. As if she needed the same assurance from him. It was all a lie, all part of the deceptive display of affection, but still he gave her what she wanted, whispering promises and sex words and the truth of his desire into her mouth while he kissed her. She whimpered, took the hand he'd clenched against the console between them and opened his palm over her breast.

He fondled her for only a moment, and then he pulled away, setting her back into her seat and looking into her eyes, which broadcast sadness and fear mixed with arousal, and he smiled in an effort to set her at ease.

"That ought to convince him that our being late is no reason to worry."

"I wish it convinced me," she said softly, and the only thing Christian could think to say was, "Trust me."

"You called so late, I couldn't help but worry."

Wick sat just inside Natasha's bedroom doorway, watching as she put away the clothing she'd brought with her, and stored the travel bag of toiletries in her private bathroom's closet. She scurried back and forth, looking for both her courage and her voice.

This was it, her first starring role, her chance to convince her godfather that she had returned from the long weekend away no wiser to his nefarious dealings than before she had left.

She didn't know how Christian made a living doing this. "Why would you worry?" she asked with a frown. "I come and go all the time."

"Yes, but usually you're on your own."

She raised a brow, cast him a look. "I would think the fact that I wasn't alone would have set you at ease."

"Come now, Natasha," Wick said with more than a hint of condescension. "Mr. Deacon is an unknown element."

Hmm. This was interesting. And the perfect segue into a subject about which she'd been curious before ever knowing the truth. "You obviously know him well enough to invite him to stay in your home."

"You know I no longer travel well, my dear. And the technology Mr. Deacon is interested in is being developed here. Having him commute or stay in the carriage house, or even in one of the motels in Lake Placid when I have room here, hardly makes sense, don't you agree?"

She supposed so—the latter part, anyway, because she ignored the first, which was a bid for sympathy over his declining health. Funny how she had little feeling today to spare. "I still don't understand why you're using the lab here for something so obviously important. I would think Mr. Deacon would be more interested in the full scope of what the university offers."

"If this were a university project, then I would agree. But this is a private venture, one I've brought Dr. Jinks in to consult on." Wick frowned. "I'm not sure I understand the basis of your complaint. Unless you're finding entertaining Mr. Deacon too taxing."

She knew that, of course. The project was Wick's and not Polytechnic's. Even before hearing the details of what Wick was doing from Hank Smithson, Christian—as Peter—had told her that very thing. But she still wanted desperately to catch Wick in a lie, to trip him up and expose him even though Christian had insisted she not rock the boat.

So she tackled the second part of his comments instead. "Oh, I'm not complaining at all. Only curious as to the reason for my good fortune. Spending time with Peter has been anything but a chore."

She moved to put her underthings away in a bureau drawer, watching from the corner of her eye as Wick removed his glasses to clean them. Without turning and being more obvious, she couldn't tell if he was pleased by or uncomfortable with the implications.

And so it caught her off guard when he next said, "I've been thinking a lot about Michael recently."

"Michael? My father?" And had he really? Or was this just another diversion, another tug on her heartstrings so she wouldn't think badly of him once his treachery made itself known?

She closed the bureau drawer, turned slowly to face this man who had always meant so much to her but was now no more than a stranger. "Why would you be thinking about my father?"

She hadn't meant for her voice to quiver or her words to come out so softly, but Wick noticed and offered her a smile that spoke of a shared sadness, a suffering that only the two of them knew.

It took willpower she hadn't known she possessed not to scratch out his eyes.

"Wick?"

"Oh yes, my dear. I'm sorry." He settled his glasses back in place, repositioned his chair to better face her. "It seems that with Michael gone, I've not found any challenging conversation. Your father was the best at making me think."

"I don't believe for a minute that you've given up thinking, Wick," she said, more sharply than she'd intended. "But I do understand missing the conversations. I have never known two men more capable of talking two women under a table than you and my father."

He lifted a brow behind his gold frames. "Disparaging your own sex, Natasha?"

She shook her head. "Just playing to the stereotype."

"And here I thought Michael and I taught you better."

"You did, actually. You taught me everything that makes me who I am. It was like growing up with two male parents." And this wasn't the first time she'd thought as much. "Mom did little more than to make sure I knew that babies were not found under cabbage leaves."

"That's more than many mothers do." He canted his head to the side and considered her. "Do you talk to your mother often?"

Natasha both loved and hated how easily they slipped into the familiar comfort of their shared history. Loved it because Wick was the only father she had left. Hated it for the obvious reasons.

She returned to the bed, double-checked her overnighter, and folded it for storage. "We talked every week after the funeral, but that only lasted for a couple of months."

"I thought I might invite her out to visit for a few days. I know she and I have never been close—"

"Close? Try continents apart," she called before stepping back out of the closet. "Why would you want her to visit?"

"The visit wouldn't be for me, Natasha."

She paused for a moment halfway between the closet and the desk where she had Wick's university e-mail to check. "What's going on, Wick? You know my mother and I are both fine with things as they are. There's no animosity, but we never have been close at all."

"And, for that, I often fear I may be at fault."

Once her laptop had finished booting up, she turned to him, torn completely in half by her feelings. She wanted to rail at him, to demand answers for his involvement with a syndicate like Spectra IT. Yet she wanted just as much to hug him and set whatever fears he was suffering at ease.

"My mother's envy of the closeness you shared with my father is her problem. Not yours and not mine. She is the only one at fault here." She pulled out her desk chair and sat, gripping the arms to keep herself grounded when the ache in her chest and the burning lump at the base of her throat had her wanting to sit at his feet again, to listen to his words of wisdom, to find the same assurance he and her father had always offered that all would be right with her world.

Her world, which was now so very, very wrong. "You know that. We both know that."

Wick wheeled his chair further into her room. His gaze, usually so clear and so sharp, was fuzzy, unfocused, even uncertain, which despite all her intentions to harden her heart caused her no small amount of alarm. "We both know, as well, that had Michael and I not been closer than brothers, he and Gail might have never divorced."

"That's possible, yes, but again, their divorce wasn't your fault any more than it was mine." Why did it feel as if she was the one consoling a child at the heart of the parents' split?

"Perhaps not. But it would please me to know that there remain no hard feelings. Which is why I thought I would phone her and suggest a visit."

This sounded as if he was making amends. Or settling his affairs, putting things in order. The lump in her throat rose until she was no longer able to speak. Anger or not, she had no wish to lose him to his disease.

"Do you think if I telephoned her today, she might make arrangements to fly out for this weekend's ball?"

The ball. Natasha had been so caught up these last few days with Christian, she hadn't checked in yet with Mrs. Courtney on the preparations for this sudden party Wick had recently insisted on. And now with this trip down her old family lane, it was almost as if he were saying good-bye.

This time she did get up and go to him, kneeling at the foot of his chair, the carpet a soft comfort beneath her. "Wick, have you had news from the doctors you haven't shared with me? This talk of my mother and father, this party"—a party to which he had invited every longtime friend she'd ever known him to have—"you're starting to worry me here."

He frowned for a moment, then his eyes cleared and brightened almost immediately. And his smile spread over his face until she swore the only thing from which he was suffering was an overdose of joy.

He reached out and playfully tugged on a lock of her hair. "I'm fine, Natasha. Perhaps a bit melancholy at times, which I believe is my right as an old man. But there is absolutely nothing for you to worry about."

"Promise?" she asked, though she knew exactly the full extent of what she had to worry about, what she had to fear.

"I promise," he said with a simple nod. "I admit the idea of having stolen away years you might have spent with your mother has haunted me, but I will do my best not to give it another thought. As long as you promise me that you are truly happy."

She pushed to her feet then, patted his knee, putting the distance she needed between them again. "I am happy," she said, mixing truth with lies. "Why wouldn't I be? I lead an incredible life here." For one more week anyway. Who knew where she'd be once Christian's SG-5 group put her godfather away?

"And Mr. Deacon?"

She settled back down at her desk, swallowed the butterflies turning her stomach into a mess of fluttering, tickling nerves. "What about Mr. Deacon?"

Wick's chair whirred as he approached. "You spoke earlier of your good fortune. May I assume he is a part of that?"

Natasha smiled for her godfather's benefit but also for her own. "Yes. You may assume."

"Well, that is excellent news. I quite like the man myself."

"Too bad he's not going to be around much longer. He might turn out to be that good conversationalist you've been missing," she said, laughing at the idea of Christian ever saying more than he had to. Or volunteering information without prodding from a pitchfork.

"Yes, you're right. Too bad indeed. Too very bad indeed."

And then without another word, Wick turned and left the room, leaving Natasha to wonder what had just happened, what their conversation had really been about, and if Christian needed to know.

Twenty

Later that afternoon found Christian in the basement lab, on edge like he hadn't been in almost a week, rolling his chair up to Woodrow Jinks's workstation just as the other man rolled away. Jinks grabbed a CD from a spindle on the table behind him and wheeled back, gearing up to demonstrate a beta test of his model before taking it live.

The live part was what had Christian itchy. Going live was the endgame, that much was obvious, and he had to keep Jinks from getting that far. First, however, he had to know what the hell it was he'd come here to stop. If any other scenario had ever come so close to burning a hole in his ulcerated gut, he thankfully couldn't remember.

"You gotta know this whole business of cracking encryption isn't as simple as busting DVDs or hacking the Federal Reserve's wire system." Jinks loaded the CD and pulled up a DOS window of code Christian couldn't have read with a gun to his head—though he sure as hell didn't need any such encouragement to latch onto Jinks's remark about cracking encryption.

That one Christian filed front and center.

"Are you warning me to watch my step or bragging about what you can do?" he asked, watching Jinks's hand begin to tremble over his mouse.

"Not bragging. No way. Just letting you know this is serious stuff. Life sentence stuff. Traitorous, terrorist stuff." Realization dawned on the young scientist's face and he smirked. "But then I'm not telling you anything you don't already know, am I?"

"You're not, no." Christian's gaze drilled into the other man's, which interestingly enough never wavered. The kid had grown some balls. "And I assume you know you're risking the rest of your life here, as well."

"Oh yeah." Jinks cocked back in his chair, hands laced behind his head, and swiveled side to side. "But winning is like gaming. It's all about risks. Accepting challenges. Kicking ass. Biting the bullet and all that."

Balls and then some, unless the kid was so full of shit he'd actually convinced himself he could pull this off. Christian couldn't help but admit his curiosity. "You sure you can get your mouth around this one?"

"Are you kidding? For the money you're paying Bow?"

"And he is paying you."

"Oh yeah." Jinks blew out a heavy breath and shook his head. "Keeping my mouth shut about this has been the hardest thing I've ever done."

Interesting segue. Christian raised a brow. "But you have kept your mouth shut."

The shaking hands again as Jinks sat up and stared at the white cursor blinking on the black screen. "Not a peep to anyone."

Christian wondered who it was Jinks wanted to tell. "And what do you do when this is over?"

"Since I can hardly show up back in Seattle, you mean?"

Seattle. Hmm. "Right. You going to buy yourself a new identity?"

"Got it picked out already." Jinks smiled, rubbed his palms together gleefully, his momentary case of nerves long gone. "A nice beach in Bora Bora. John Smith from New York City."

"What about your family? Your friends?" Christian pressed.

"I don't have much of a social life. I pretty much hang out on-line," Jinks said, frowning as he typed another series of commands. "And on-line I can be anyone I want to be."

"You're right about that." The kid didn't seem the least bit fazed, Christian mused. Too bad he was going to have to sacrifice his brilliant mind because he was so stupid. And too bad none of what he was saying or showing off made a goddamn dent in Christian's need to know.

Jinks shoved his keyboard away. "Man, I think we're going to have to do this another time. I can't get a connection to hold."

Christian nodded. A connection. Cracking encryption. But nothing about the who or the how or the why. "Tomorrow then?"

"Yeah. It's been hinky all day. Too much line noise. And I'm betting that's not sitting well considering the money this so-called secure network must be costing taxpayers—not to mention the Agency."

They met in the kitchen at dawn the next morning, Christian ridiculously distracted by Natasha wearing Spandex when his mind should've been on the fact that Jinks and Bow were fucking with the CIA—a fact he'd passed along late last night in a phone call made from the woods beyond the terrace to the SG-5 ops center and Kelly John Beach.

But now frustration was eating at Christian's head, messing with his mind, and Natasha was screwing up his focus. It was like he'd never seen her body before. Like he'd never realized she had legs. Or that ass.

He didn't know why she couldn't run in sweats, or why he was in such a foul mood except for the fact that he didn't have enough of a grasp on the case to move forward, even while what he knew was enough to make him break out in cold hives when he considered the implications.

And considered Jinks's use of the word terrorist.

Christian squeezed the hell out of his water bottle as he

grabbed it off the countertop, pushed open the door out of the kitchen, and headed down the walkway alongside the water garden, leaving Natasha midstretch.

Bracing a foot on the seat of the closest bench, he continued his warm-up, breathing in the cool air's sharp tang and watching the sluggish Koi swim in place. He could think better out here without the distraction of the woman he wanted to strip bare.

Christian Bane, the SG-5 operative least likely to mix business and pleasure. And this was one of the biggest reasons why. He needed to concentrate. He didn't need to have to watch more than his own back.

He didn't need the burden of having to protect the innocent because he couldn't guarantee he'd come through. Natasha deserved better than that. She was a good woman. One he didn't want to see hurt more than she'd been hurt already.

He straightened, stretched his arms overhead, switched to his other leg. He was really in a world of trouble here, caught between wanting to send her back to the city and out of harm's way, yet knowing such a move would arouse Bow's suspicions.

Especially with the older man so obviously pleased by and encouraging of Natasha's relationship with Peter.

There had to be something there. Something Bow wanted to happen between them. Not the obvious physical relationship but a tie he could bind them with. Christian had nothing to go on here but gut instinct, but he'd learned the hard way to listen to his gut.

"You prefer doing your warm-ups alone?"

At the sound of her voice behind him, he dropped his foot to the sidewalk and turned. "I'm not much for the buddy system."

Her smile was just short of a smirk. "I can't say that comes as a shock."

"It shouldn't."

She shook her head, lifted her water bottle. "Ah, but a buddy can keep you from getting yourself into trouble."

"Remind me to tell you how I ended up in that Thai cage one day," he said before thinking better of it.

She froze, water bottle halfway between waist and mouth. "I'm listening."

"Remind me some other time to tell you about that Thai cage one day."

"Why not now?"

"Do we know who's listening?"

She glanced side to side, up down and around, lifted a brow and answered, "The Koi?"

He bit down on a grin. "What do you know about the estate's surveillance system?"

"Security system, you mean."

He held her gaze and repeated, "Surveillance."

When her eyes widened and she started to once again look around, he reached out and grabbed her wrist, giving her a quick shake of his head and taking the water bottle from her hand. He raised it to his lips and talked from behind it.

He doubted anyone was listening, but he didn't know who might be reading lips. "Two feet above the back door. Beneath the awning."

"The bird's nest? Wick won't let Mrs. Courtney touch it."

"How long has it been there?"

"I don't know, why? Awhile."

"Ever see any birds?"

"Making sense would be nice here."

"It's not a bird's nest. The darker twigs are filament. It's a fiber-optic camera."

He handed her back the water. They turned together, heading down the drive for their run. Natasha cast a brief glance where he'd indicated, never breaking stride, never looking back.

He wanted to give her a big high five for being such a trooper. He wanted to pull her close and tell her everything would be over soon and life would get back to normal, but he knew that wasn't the case.

And so he fell into step at her side, neither of them speaking until she made a turn off the long private road onto a dirt trail that led into the heart of the estate's wooded acreage.

She waited a hundred yards before speaking. "Are there cameras like that throughout the house?"

"I've seen several."

"Can you tell if they've been there long?"

"They don't appear to be particularly new."

She let that sink in, her feet thudding on the hard-packed surface in sync with his. Another few steps and she faltered to a stop. "Please don't tell me there's a camera on your balcony."

Her eyes were wide. Her lips trembled. On this, at least, he could set her at ease. "The foyer, the kitchen, the dining room. The other common areas. It seems to be more of an internal system than anything external."

He spared her the knowledge of the one he'd found in the corner of the guest room's armoire. Fortunately, the evening he'd arrived, he'd tossed Deacon's workout duffle on top of it, where it had stayed until this morning.

The dangling strap had obscured the camera—a discovery he'd made when finally pulling down the bag.

"Surveillance. Is that visual only? I'm assuming this is Wick's doing, but can he hear what he sees?"

"No. It's strictly visual. At least this version. He's got quite the bank of monitors in that basement corner of his. I'm going to assume that's where he receives the feed."

Hands on her hips, she stared down the trail in the direction from which they'd come. Her breath swirled and vanished in tendrils of wispy fog, and a moment later she turned and began to run.

"I wish I could help you but I've never had reason to work at his desk in the lab. I do know there's nothing obvious in his office. And no evidence of secret panels or sliding walls where he'd have installed any equipment."

Christian couldn't help but smile at the picture her imagination painted. "Been watching a lot of James Bond lately?"

She cast him a sharp glance. “That’s not funny.”

“I know. I’m kidding.” He looked over to see her stick out her tongue. He winked in response. It was tough to keep things light, but if it helped . . . “I’m sure the lab is where I’ll find the broadcast.”

“You’re going to look for it?”

“I’d like to know when he had it installed. I can get a date from the capture software’s registry.”

“I can’t imagine any reason he would’ve needed it before now. I can’t imagine why he would need it at all. Then again, the whole idea of what he’s done . . .”

She let the sentence trail and they continued to run in silence for several minutes. When they reached a small clearing, he slowed, catching her elbow and insisting she stop. “How has he seemed since we’ve been back? Have you gotten anything from him?”

“Anything like what?”

“Any strange vibes? Has he questioned you about me? About anything I might have said?”

“No. Nothing about you. He’s mostly talked about my father.” She dropped her gaze to the ground, lowered her voice. “And my mother, of all things.”

Christian’s radar blipped. “Why do you say that? About your mother?”

“Her relationship with Wick was never more than amiable. They were on speaking terms, of course, but if my father hadn’t been in the picture they never would have been friends. They had little in common besides their affection for him.”

“What was the context of him talking about her? Why bring her up?”

She paced a few steps away, pulled in a breath that caused her whole body to shudder. “I hate to say this or even think it, but it’s almost as if he’s gathering the people who’ve been important in his life for a final good-bye.”

Christian’s pulse began to race. “Gathering? Literally?”

“Yes, Saturday.” She rubbed at her forehead. “God, I haven’t even mentioned it to you, have I?”

"Mentioned what, Natasha?" he asked, his heart thumping even harder now.

"A party. A ball, or so he calls it."

"Here. This weekend."

"Invitations went out a month or so ago. Most have accepted. I think they realize this is the last time he'll be well enough to entertain . . ." Natasha left the thought unfinished and paused to gather her composure, pulling in a deep breath and blinking away the moisture that had welled in her eyes.

It was all Christian could do not to go to her. Not to pull her into his arms and soothe her pain. Soothing her would dilute the impact of what she was feeling when her suffering was the very source of the strength she needed. And so he let her work out the emotion alone, his muscles cramping like hell as he held his arms at his sides.

Her voice was steadier when she went on. "Mrs. Courtney has a cleaning service coming in today to air out the ballroom and start in on the windows and fixtures, the floors, the carpets, everything. The landscaping crew was to have started yesterday. The terrace still needs a few repairs.

"The exterior of the house could have used painting, but there just wasn't time." She shrugged then and turned toward him. "Other than that, the estate will look much the way it did years ago when a weekend without a party was the anomaly."

"So he is saying good-bye," Christian said after letting that sink in. When she nodded, he asked, "Where do you think he's going?"

His question caused her to frown. "I don't think he's going anywhere. I assume by good-bye—"

He cut her off with a shake of his head. "Think again. Bringing together years worth of friends. Restoring this place to its original state. The money Spectra is paying him. He's got plans to leave."

"I never even thought . . ." She rubbed at her forehead again. "What good is leaving going to do him? Unless he's going away to die alone. And if that was the case, if he was planning his suicide, he wouldn't need the kind of money he's making from this deal."

"I don't think it's about killing himself. He could do that here," he assured her. "Jinks talked yesterday of moving to Bora Bora and assuming a new identity. I've got to think your godfather is doing the same."

"Bora Bora? You've got to be kidding me."

"Nope. Quoting him word for word."

"This doesn't make any sense, not with the little time he has left. Another few months and Wick will no longer be mobile." She met Christian's gaze; her breath hitched as she pulled it in. "So what do we do? How do we find out? I mean, this is where you'll stop him, right? His leaving will help get the evidence against him you need?"

"I don't know. Obviously he wouldn't have had you make travel plans." Christian began to pace. He wasn't ready to share what he'd learned from Jinks. Not until he knew more, until he heard back from K.J. "I need to contact the ops center. See what they can find out. If he's chartered a plane or made other arrangements."

Natasha dropped down to her haunches, buried her face in her hands. "This is totally insane. This is so not like Wick, all this subterfuge. I don't know how I'm supposed to continue as if nothing's going on."

Christian stopped in front of her and held out a hand. When she took it, he pulled her back to her feet, settled his wrists on her shoulders, laced his hands at her nape. He waited for her to meet his gaze, needed to make her understand that he was here for her, that he believed in her.

That he needed her.

"You'll do it because you have to," he said when she finally looked up. Looked up and made him wonder what it would be like to know her away from this place, what it would be like to love her. . . .

He swallowed hard, fought back the emotion balling up in his throat. "You'll do it because you're strong and fearless and capable."

"Yeah," she answered, rolling her eyes. "Capable of arranging satellite conference calls and carting paperwork back and forth."

"You're capable of a lot more than that." He tugged playfully on her ponytail.

"But I'm not very fearless at all," she admitted softly. "And I don't think I have the strength to see this through to the end."

She did, and they both knew it. Knew, as well, that he wasn't going to let her give into her doubts. "Then you'd better run another mile or two. Work on those muscles. Build up that stamina."

"Slave driver," she said with a grin.

He couldn't help it. He grinned right back. "You betcha."

Twenty-one

The return run was silent but for the sounds of thudding feet and labored breaths, yet nothing about it was the least bit peaceful. Christian felt assaulted on all sides, felt the division of his loyalties in ways that caught him off guard. He was first and foremost bound to Hank Smithson, bound to righting the very bad wrong that was named Spectra IT.

For seven years nothing else had existed on the scope of his personal radar. Spectra had hands in more criminal activities than SG-5 could ever hope to bring down. That didn't stop the group, Christian specifically, from pulling plugs, making dents, and generally hammering one nail at a time into the syndicate's coffin.

But now he found himself considering Natasha, as well. Considering her to an equal extent, which meant less focus on the bad guys. And this was where he feared screwing up. One wrong move, one mistake made, and he missed the opportunity he'd spent all these years chasing. A weeklong fling was hardly worth that high a price.

A fling. Right. This hadn't been a fling since the night she'd first crawled on top of him and taken him boldly into her mouth. Since she'd trusted him completely, seeing beyond the Peter Deacon act to Christian Bane beneath.

He slowed enough to give her a short lead and watched her

ponytail bounce. He thought of her hair's softness tickling his skin, of the moonlight shining on the strands, of the wind whipping it like a horse's main into her face as they drove with the Ferrari's top down. She'd never complained. Ever.

She'd pushed back the tangled mess, laughed about her stylist's reaction, clipped it up on her head, and slept like a baby while he drove. She was absolutely gorgeous in the way that she didn't care about coming undone. She'd been just as beautiful with mascara-stained cheeks as she'd been clean-faced and wrapped in nothing but a bedspread and gruelingly honest curiosity.

That night at the farm when she'd shared his bed had been nearly impossible to get through without tearing her out of her clothes. He'd felt the same unrelieved tension simmering in her body when he'd held her close, yet had also sensed her shared realization that sex as a panacea would've lessened the intimacy of the night.

She cut in front of him as they left the wooded trail for the estate's private road, casting him a smile and a wink. He returned both, amazed again by her resilience in the face of what she'd been through this last week, especially knowing all that lay ahead.

His mind switched gears then, shifting forward to the weekend's party. Natasha had to be right. Bow had to be saying good-bye. But Christian didn't believe for a minute the other man had planned anything as maudlin as suicide. Especially after Jinks's talk of a tropical paradise.

No. What Bow was planning was his own disappearance. A big fat getaway financed with Spectra's hefty contribution to the cause. The one thing Christian didn't get, however, was how the other man planned to accomplish anything in his physical condition.

The money had to figure into this whole scenario in a way that Christian had yet to work out. A man who couldn't get around on his own, who was destined to get worse, never better, who was living beneath a death sentence . . . What the hell was Bow doing with all that cash? Buying a miracle cure?

The party would be the key. Bow would be involved with old friends and no doubt have Natasha at his side. And even though Jinks would have to stay out of sight, Christian doubted the kid would pass up the chance to indulge in the free-flowing booze, leaving the lab wide open.

Knowing what he now did, he figured it wouldn't take him long to follow K.J.'s instructions on how to patch into Jinks's system, capture the data from the CIA feed, and transfer the batch to the ops center for analysis.

"I can't believe it," Natasha said under her breath.

"What?" Christian glanced her way before following the direction of her gaze. Her godfather sat at the edge of the terrace while a half dozen laborers toiled under Mr. Courtney's orders to clean and landscape the flower gardens, to replace the broken terrace stones.

"He hasn't been out here in months. Even knowing what I know, I still swear something even more bizarre is going on with him." Natasha veered off the private drive and crossed the yard.

Equally curious, Christian followed. Bow looked up at their approach.

"Natasha. Mr. Deacon." He nodded at them, then up toward the clearing sky. "Enjoying this beautiful weather, I see."

Stretching out the kinks from the run, Natasha lunged forward on one leg then the other. "I'd ask if you were doing the same but I can't imagine you venturing outside for anything as mundane as blue skies."

Christian walked to the edge of the terrace, feigning interest in the cleanup, his attention on the two people at his side. Natasha had told him more than once that her godfather rarely left the house.

The fact that Dr. Bow had done just that was one more behavioral anomaly Christian couldn't afford to overlook.

"I was just recalling the parties we once had here," Bow was saying. "The feasts, the music, the conversations, Natasha? Do you remember?"

"Of course I do. I'm the one who still spends time out here, you know."

"Reconnecting with your past?"

Bowing out of the tête-à-tête, Christian walked several feet down the side of the terrace, appearing to give the pair privacy yet focusing on their conversation and wishing more than anything that Natasha was wired.

Getting this on tape, getting analytical feedback from Julian or Tripp—but he was on his own and sharpened his listening skills accordingly.

"I do. At times. I think about my father. About all the ways the two of you could argue and call it a friendly debate. There were nights I swore one of you would literally snap off the other's head."

"Ah, but those are the best sorts of discussions. Even if there is no more than ego at stake."

Natasha hesitated. Christian heard it in the way she breathed, and held his own breath as well. "Is that why you're out here, Wick? To reconnect with your past?"

"In a manner of speaking, I suppose. I would like to have the terrace restored to its original condition. Or as close as is feasible in time for the party."

When Natasha didn't immediately respond, Christian scrambled to cover, to continue the conversation, taking two steps in her direction. At this point in the game, every opportunity to gain information counted, and he didn't want to lose what this one might give.

He needn't have worried. Whether she was acting or honestly feeling the sadness he heard, her sharply inhaled sob seemed to do the trick. Bow turned his wheelchair toward her; Christian stayed where he was.

"What is it, my dear?" Bow asked.

"This whole party, bringing your friends together, thinking of my father"—she sobbed again—"I can't bear the idea of losing you, too."

"Ah, Natasha. You of all people should know that death is not to be feared."

"What frightens me is the idea of being alone. Of you not

being here." Her voice grew muffled. "You've been everything to me for so very long."

"You'll go on just fine without me. As we both did after Michael left," he replied in a voice that hit Christian as rather cold considering the circumstances. "You do have your mother, my dear. And my demise is hardly imminent."

"I know," she said with a sigh. "I just don't like that I do know. And that we can't do anything but wait."

Christian turned from feigning interest in the gardeners' work and caught Natasha's eye. She stood at her godfather's side, her hand on his shoulder, her expression giving nothing away.

She could have been acting. She could have been genuinely grieved. The fact that he couldn't tell which left him simply amazed. Left him wondering how quickly he could get her the hell out of here.

Left him wanting her and straight-up scared to death at the Achilles heel she'd become.

Laughing chatter drifted up into the vaulted, chandelier-festooned ceiling along with music from a harp and accompanying violins. A small chamber orchestra played in one corner of the ballroom. The caterer's tables sat in another, covered in white linen and set with crystal, silver braziers, and one gorgeous champagne fountain.

Natasha wove her way in and out of the crowd of university alumni, foreign diplomats, a herd of lab rats and their interesting—and unexpected—significant others. A similar crowd of old friends mingled on the terrace outside. Others strolled through the water gardens, and she'd directed an adventurous few to the stables.

Overall, the party seemed to be a hit. And strangely enough, Wick seemed to be in his element. Wick, who avoided any soiree that wasn't a command performance, who had never cared a whit what others thought of his reclusive curmudgeonly habits. Wickham Bow, who had little in his life to celebrate, was doing just that, as if nothing in the world mattered but this night filled with fun.

Natasha didn't think she'd ever seen him act so out of character—much as she and Christian had predicted would happen. This get-together was significant in ways her godfather hadn't seen fit to share. He had, however, made sure "Peter Deacon" was introduced to everyone as the business partner giving Wick a new lease on life.

That more than anything gave Natasha pause. Wick was facing a death sentence. An agonizingly slow and painful loss of his ability to move, to swallow, eventually to breathe. The claim of a new lease was bullshit, plain and simple. Her research would've uncovered any new treatment available and nothing had surfaced.

The longer she mingled with her pasted-on smile, the more desperately angry and hurt she became, the more tangled her emotions and loyalties. She needed a break before she slipped and said something she shouldn't, before her mood set off an alarm.

Ducking out of the ballroom, she made her way behind the foyer staircase and into the kitchen through the staff's entrance. The caterers were busy in the center of the room where Mrs. Courtney hovered.

Natasha didn't want to get drawn into the melee of dirty crystal and china being replaced by clean, of coffee being brewed and champagne replenished, of desserts being sliced and cubed into individual servings, and so she crept out the back door to the water garden.

At the first turn along the winding path, she ran unexpectedly into Christian and gasped. "I thought you were down on the terrace."

"Just walked back up." He took hold of her upper arm, led her further into the gardens. "Jinks is down there off in the corner and pretty much wasted out of his gourd. Where's your godfather?"

"Holding court in the ballroom. Or he was when I left. He had quite the audience for his exposition on encryption." She sat on the bench Christian indicated, smoothing her skirt as she did. "God, he's such a hypocrite."

"Why a hypocrite? He is an expert."

"I mean acting as if nothing is wrong." She leaned forward, buried her face in her hands, shivering when Christian placed his palm between her shoulder blades, her skin bared in the low-hanging cowl neckline. "Thanks, but I don't think anything is going to help. If you hadn't noticed, I'm an unraveling basket case here."

"You're holding up beautifully." He massaged circles in the center of her back. "I wasn't sure you'd handle things this well, but you've gone beyond proving me wrong."

She lifted her head enough to turn it and give him a one-eyed glare. "What did you think I was going to do? Hyperventilate or blubber like a baby?"

This time he reached over to push loose strands of hair from her face. And then he smiled, breaking her heart as he did. "I don't think I've seen you cry once through all of this."

"Sure you did," she said, frowning. Did he actually not remember? "At Hank's place. When you came out to the track. I was crying then."

"You'd pretty much dried up when I got there."

She shook her head, closed her eyes. "I was a wreck. A raccoon-eyed mess."

"You make for a beautiful raccoon, Natasha," he said softly. "You're gorgeous, makeup or not."

She sat all the way up then, loving him for teasing her, seriously considering smacking him for doing the same. Loving him, loving him . . .

She swallowed hard, afraid she wouldn't be able to draw another breath. Her chest ached as if turned inside out. A breeze flirted with the leaves overhead, rippled across the surface of the pond. The moon wasn't quite as bright as the first night they'd met, but it was bright enough that she feared he would see the emotion that surely shone in her eyes.

"Yeah, well, if you're flattering me hoping to get somewhere . . . I think you know it's hardly necessary." It was so much easier to relegate their relationship, and this conversation, to sex when she really wanted to ask him where they went from here, if she would see him again once he'd finished this assignment.

If that's all she was to him—an assignment.

But she didn't because she wouldn't survive any crushing blow he delivered. Not right now. Not in this moment. Later she'd be stronger, better able to separate this time out of time from reality. But now here. Not now.

Christian shifted on the bench, leaning toward her and reaching out one hand to lift her chin. "That day in the helicopter." He stopped, glanced away, his nose crinkling as he took a breath. "I told you then that I hadn't been with a woman in awhile. That wasn't a lie," he said, looking back. "I don't sleep with the women I deal with when in the field. I never have. Not since Thailand."

There had been a woman in Thailand. Oh God. Had she been the cause of what he'd suffered?

Christian glanced down to where he now held her hand in her lap and let go of the thought. Natasha boldly picked it up. This one thing she wanted to know. She'd heard much of it from Hank. She wanted to hear it from the source.

She laced her fingers through his. "What haven't you told me about Thailand, Christian?"

He shook his head. "Not now."

"When?" she persisted.

"Later. Maybe. I don't know."

"Okay, then. Tell me this. Why me? Why break your rules for me?" She wanted to know because she had never had the feeling that what they'd done together had been anything he'd gone into unwillingly, anything he'd forced himself to go through with.

Yet when he pulled his hand from hers, she knew she wasn't going to like what he had to say. And she was right. She didn't.

"Because it's what you should've expected from Peter Deacon," he said, his tone of voice as telling as his words.

"Deacon's reputation is no secret to anyone running in the same circles."

She let that sink in—a sinking that didn't take long. Her stomach rolled up into a hard ball of disgust. "So, Wick gave me to you knowing the sort of man you were?"

"Not me, Natasha. Deacon."

"But Wick didn't know that."

"No, but it's important that you do."

Oh no. Oh no. She couldn't take this, couldn't deal with it. She pushed to her feet, wrapped her arms around her middle to keep what little food she'd eaten today from coming up. It was no use. She was going to be sick.

"I can't believe this. That he knew the sort of man you were and he still gave me to you to use." She laughed as hysteria rose in waves. "And I was right there, ready to do his bidding. Ready to do yours. God, I took one look at you and was more than ready."

"Natasha, listen to me."

Christian was there now, standing beside her on the walkway, the water in the pond gurgling, the boughs sighing overhead. She'd loved this place once, but nothing about it soothed her now.

She turned to flee; Christian stepped into her path.

"Hey. I need you to listen to me." He gripped both of her shoulders. "You cannot beat yourself up over this. You need to have your head on straight now more than ever."

Oh, but she hated practical, bossy men. Especially this one she feared she had fallen in love with. She was so screwed. Loving a man who she knew was using her. Had used her. Who harbored more secrets, told more lies—justified or not—than any man she had ever known.

She pulled in a deep shuddering breath and thrust out her chin. "I know what I have to do. I don't need you telling me. I know how I need to behave, the act I'm required to put on. That doesn't make it any easier to face the fact that I am little more here than a whore."

Christian bit off a harsh curse. "Don't say that. Do not ever say that."

He held her so tightly she swore he would leave her shoulders bruised. If her girlfriends could see her predicament now. . . . "Why not? I've prostituted myself just as Wick planned the night you arrived."

Christian released her, moved one hand to his waist, rubbed at his temples with the other. "He actually planned it long before that. It's on the tapes we have of his discussions with Spectra IT."

The ground opened up to swallow her whole. "I didn't hear him say anything about me."

"I asked Hank not to play that one."

"Why? Why would it matter?" She was losing it. Losing it. "I was going to find out anyway."

"I was hoping you might not have to."

"So why tell me now?"

"Because I want you angry. I want you to know the full scope of Bow's treachery."

"So I can hurt even more?" Or so she could hurt the same as he did from whatever had happened in Thailand? So she could pay for what had gone wrong?

"No. So you won't soften. Won't feel sorry for him."

"So I won't screw up your mission, is that it?"

"No. Fuck. *No*. I want you to be tough. You need to be tough. To be strong. Stronger perhaps than you've ever had to be in your life." He got in her face then, moved to block her from escaping or turning away. "We've got to stop him. To shut him down and do it now. I'm going down to the lab. I need you to keep an eye on Jinks and Bow."

What? He wasn't making any sense. "Why would finding you in the lab make them suspicious? That's why you're here."

"I'm not here to dig into their files when they're not looking. Do what you can to keep them out of the basement."

She couldn't believe he was going to leave her like this; she had too many questions left unanswered. She crossed her arms over her chest, backed a step away. "Go. Do whatever you need to do. I'll make sure you're not bothered."

When he stepped toward her, she warded him off with one raised hand. "I'm fine. I need to see if Mrs. Courtney needs any help."

"Natasha—"

"Here's what I don't get, Christian." Why couldn't she let this go? "When we were at Hank's place, you told me what we'd done was as real as it gets. But you haven't even wanted anything to do with me since."

"It's complicated," was all he said after several moments of hesitation. "And that's not exactly true."

"Complicated because I know who you are? Because you're afraid my knowing means I'm going to expect something of you?" She feared she was going to push him even further away if she didn't get a grip. And the fact that she was worried about that very thing . . .

"I'm sorry. Forget I said that." She forged past him and headed for the house.

She didn't get far, brought up short by one very large hand coming down on her shoulder. She didn't turn, she couldn't. Right now she was certain looking at him would cause her to crumble like a rose petal crushed in a fist.

"You've got it all wrong, Natasha. It's what I expect from myself keeping me out of your bed. I'm not sure I can deliver what either of us wants. And I don't want to disappoint you more than I already have."

He wasn't talking about sex. She knew that without having to think twice. What he was talking about went deeper. To a place neither one of them would be ready to visit until they were done here, until her godfather had been put away and justice served.

Until the woman she had been all these years no longer existed, her foundation, her belief system destroyed at Wick's hands. Exploring anything with Christian would have to wait. Perhaps they would reach the perfect time and the perfect place once hell had frozen over, once pigs had flown.

"I understand," she finally said, though she doubted the dust of the last week and a half would ever clear. "I've got to go."

She ducked away, changed direction, headed for the terrace instead of the house. She needed air and time to let the events of the evening settle. Checking on her godfather was suddenly the last thing she wanted to do. She'd start with Woodrow Jinks.

Twenty-two

She said hello to the few clusters of people still remaining outside, forcing herself to smile as she inquired after their evening. By the time she made it to the far corner of the terrace, having stopped to gather two champagne flutes and a plate of discarded hors d'oeuvres, her only company was a passed-out Dr. Jinks, who Mrs. Courtney told her earlier had stolen a bottle of very expensive champagne, mind you, from the kitchen and disappeared.

The man obviously knew to make himself scarce, and was just as obviously no threat to Christian or anyone in his current condition. She set the flutes on the end of the half-moon bench where he lay on his back snoring, and crossed to the waist-high iron fencing. She tossed the food into the woods and stared at the lake beyond, trying to dredge up some emotion, any emotion, but all she felt was numb.

She supposed in this case numbness was a good thing. Numb would get her through the next few days while Christian worked his Smithson magic. Numb would even ease the transition of packing the things she kept here, of looking for employment elsewhere. . . .

"Miss Gaudet?"

Hand to her heart, she turned, smiled falsely again. "Yes?"

"If we could talk privately for a moment?" the man asked, a man she'd never seen before but who immediately raised her suspicions. She'd obviously been hanging around Christian too long.

This one was tall, as tall as Christian, though a bit broader in build, filling out the designer suit he wore as if it had been custom-made. It probably had. He stood with his hands in his pockets, an unthreatening stance, she supposed, the tails of his jacket flaring behind him like bat wings.

Unthreatening or not, he still presented an intimidating presence, and she was suddenly aware of how alone they were here away from the crowd. She stepped away from the fencing and started back along the terrace. He moved into her path.

That was when her heart started to race, her fingers to shake, the hair at her nape to rise. "Mr.—"

"Samms. Julian Samms."

Julian. Christian had mentioned a Julian. Still . . . "I'm not sure we have anything to talk about."

"I need to find Christian."

Natasha pulled in a huge breath and glanced up. "Who are you? How did you get here?"

His mouth quirked into a grin that seemed to be more a test of his patience than anything. "Protective of Bane, aren't you?"

She shrugged. "I'll answer your questions after you answer mine."

"I really don't have time to waste with your games, Miss Gaudet."

Bristling, Natasha pulled herself up. "And I have nothing to say to you, Mr. Samms. I'm sure you can find your way off my godfather's property. Good night."

She only made it three steps before his hand came down on her shoulder. She jerked away, angered, and turn to stare him down. But she wasn't prepared for the menace hovering above her, the dark eyes glittering down.

"Spectra is looking for Deacon," he said in a voice that froze her blood in her veins. "I need to find Christian now."

* * *

In his next life, Christian swore he was going to come back speaking and writing binary, living and breathing DOS. He really could've used K.J.'s help right about now, Kelly John being SG-5's computer expert, though the other operative had been pretty clear in his instructions.

Load the CD into Jinks's computer. Connect the external drive via USB. Reboot into Linux and he was good to go. Good to *grep,* anyway. Grep around and find Jinks's files of captured CIA feeds, copy them to his own hardware, and get it all back to the ops center ASAP.

His own specialty often seemed to be no more than staying alive, Christian mused as he watched the machine boot up in the new operating system. And since survival was a big part of every mission, he supposed it was a good thing on which to be an expert.

He also supposed it had been that particular skill Hank had talked about seeing in Christian's eyes when they'd first made contact in Chiang Rai.

That seemed so long ago, even while it seemed like yesterday. Strangely enough, however, having talked to Natasha about some of what happened in Thailand had helped ease the hold of his past.

As if sharing even those small bits and pieces had loosened the constriction that kept him from drawing a full cleansing breath.

He wouldn't have thought it possible. He'd never been one for saying much about what he was thinking or feeling, figuring he only had himself to rely on, preferring not to burden anyone else. Which was why he'd had such a time getting used to Hank demanding he open up.

He was surprised doing so had come so easily with Natasha.

It was a damn good feeling being able to breathe.

He typed a series of search commands and listened to the hard drive cook, flexing his fingers, waiting, waiting, wishing he was done here and able to whisk Natasha away. To where, he didn't know.

Just away from here, away from Bow. . . .

His head came up sharply as the machine's clicks and whirs were drowned out by the sound of the elevator coming down. Shit. He dropped the external drive into the seat of Jinks's chair, pushed it up beneath the workstation, and shut off the monitor.

He headed for the platform's stairs, took all four in two quick leaping steps, hit the switch for the overhead lights. The room plunged into an eerie darkness, the white floor reflecting a rainbow of colored beams glowing from the room's equipment.

His back to the wall beside the elevator, his hand on the gun at his hip, he waited, praying that when the doors opened Natasha stepped out. Yes, he had every legitimate reason to be down here, but he did not have reason to be ripping off data—a fact both Jinks and Bow would know.

Staying out of sight was the goal here. Keeping his visitor in the dark while he slipped into the elevator for the return trip up. Praying he didn't have to use his gun. The car stopped. The doors opened. A man stepped out, stopped, crouched and whipped to his left in one smooth movement, gun drawn and barrel inches from Christian's own.

Seconds ticked by. Half seconds. Less. And then, "Goddammit, Bane." Julian grumbled, scrambled, getting to his feet and holstering his gun. "Leave a light on for a guy, would you?"

"Julian. Sweet Jesus Christ." Christian tucked away his own gun and wiped the sweat from his forehead with the back of his wrist. "What the hell are you doing?"

"Looking for your sorry ass."

Christian hung his head, took a minute to remember how to breathe, then made his way back to Jinks's workstation. Julian followed, hands at his hips as Christian picked up the hard drive and sank down into the chair. "I have a phone. Learn to use it."

"Hank didn't want me to call."

At that, Christian looked away from the monitor to the man sent to deliver the blow requiring face-to-face contact. The very bad news Hank hadn't wanted Christian to be alone to hear. And when Hank got that worried . . .

Christian's heart thundered. "C'mon, Samms. Don't pull this dramatic shit on me. I'm all drama'd out."

Julian met Christian's gaze directly, solemnly. "Spectra's trying to reach Deacon."

What the hell? Thunder and lightning both this time. He wasn't even sure he could draw a breath to speak. "What do you mean, trying to reach Deacon? Spectra doesn't contact their field reps." He paused, then bit off, "Ever."

Julian raised a brow at Christian's tone then leaned further over Jinks's chair to get a look at what had pulled up on the screen. "They're sending Benny Rivers to find him. That's all Tripp picked up."

Spectra looking for Deacon meant something nasty was going down. Something ugly. Something deadly. Sweat gathered between Christian's shoulder blades. If Rivers picked up Deacon's trail . . .

He slammed a fist on the table. "Fuck it. Bring him on. I'm not coming in. I'm not leaving this unfinished. Not when I'm this close to taking these bastards down."

"What have you got?" Julian nodded towards the twenty-inch flat panel monitor.

"I won't know for sure until K.J. takes a look at this, but the scientist I came here to rescue? Woodrow Jinks? The kid has managed to crack the encryption on some feed from, get this," Christian added with a huff, "the CIA."

Julian cursed more often and more creatively than anyone Christian knew and did so now, muttering about donkeys and apes and higher powers. "You get this to K.J. and then what's the plan? How much more time here do you need?"

"Less than I'd planned for if Rivers is on his way." Christian shook his head. He removed the hard drive, handed it to Julian, pocketed the CD and USB cable. "Get that back to the ops center. If the information is viable, then we figure a way to get it into the right hands. A day. Two, tops."

"And then what?"

Christian checked that Jinks's workstation was put back to rights then headed for the exit, gesturing for Julian to follow. "Then what what?"

"Eli said you hooked up with Bow's goddaughter."

Christian swore to kick McKenzie's ass the minute he got back to the farm. "The shape he's in and you believe anything coming out of his mouth?"

"Knowing you, no. I didn't believe him." Julian paused. "Until I met her."

He would have to have met her to know to find Christian in the basement. "Yeah, well. You know how it is."

"Actually, I don't." Julian's dark brow winged upward; Christian saw it even in the minimal light. Saw as well the other man's mixture of disbelief and disappointment.

Julian went on. "I figured if you hadn't learned your lesson in Thailand, you would've at least picked up on the fact that none of us ever hook up with women we deal with in the field. Bed 'em, yeah. But that's it."

"That's all this is," Christian lied.

Julian's expletive proved that a lie told to another operative was no more believable than one told to oneself.

"I need to get back up to the party," was all Christian said. He wasn't admitting anything to Julian about what he had with Natasha until he settled it with himself.

Julian bit down on what was no doubt another lecture and patted his pocket instead. "I'll get this to K.J. tonight. Hank will be in touch later."

"Tell him to make it sooner if he has to. Whether it's what's in those files or news on Rivers. I need to know." Christian hit the button. The elevator door opened.

Both men stepped inside, Julian clearing his throat. "Look, Bane. The woman is none of my business. That's your call. Just don't flush the last seven years down the drain for what might be no more than a nice fringe benefit."

Christian bit down before saying a lot of things he knew he'd regret. He met Julian's gaze squarely. "I'll keep that in mind."

Julian nodded, appeared ready to say more, but then the elevator reached the first floor and the door opened.

"Mr. Deacon. I was wondering where you had gone." Dr. Wickham Bow's gaze moved from Christian to Julian. "And this must be your associate. Mr. Rivers, I believe it is?"

Natasha knocked softly on Christian's door but didn't wait for him to answer, turning the knob instead to let herself into his room. As expected, the suite was dark, the curtains over the balcony doors letting in but minimal light.

The bed was made, his suit jacket and tie tossed across the spread. She went further inside, found his shoes kicked off, one here, one there, his pants where he'd stepped out of them discarded in front of the bathroom door he'd left cracked open, the shower running behind it.

It was then that it hit her, how often he showered, and how he always left the curtain open or the door ajar. Even the night they'd stood under the spray in her apartment's miniscule enclosure, he'd shut the bathroom door but hadn't touched the sliding glass panel.

It had been the next morning when she'd mopped up the mess before she'd even realized it hadn't been closed. Then she'd been more aggravated at herself for not noticing than curious as to why he'd left it open. Now she knew.

The sense of confinement.

He hated anything that resembled a cage. How he'd managed to make love to her that morning in the elevator. . . .

She drew a shaky breath at the memory. God, but that seemed so long ago, yet it had been barely more than a week. Time did indeed fly—even when one's fun had been brought to a screechingly ugly halt.

She hadn't seen Christian tonight since directing Julian Samms to the lab hours ago. Julian was long gone, as were the rest of Wick's guests. She'd waited in her room as long as she could after the last had departed, pacing for what seemed like an eternity until she heard Wick's wheelchair in the hallway and knew he'd retired.

It was now almost five A.M.

She stopped outside the open bathroom door, staring down at the wedge of light shining on floor tiles a shade of mulled cider, uncertain whether to announce herself and enter, or wait in the bedroom until he was done.

"If you're going to come in, then come in."

She didn't hesitate any longer, pushing open the door into the room of creamy and tawny-soft marble accented in deep chocolate brown. "How did you know it was me?"

"Because I'm a good spy."

Grinning to herself, she stopped near the center of the long vanity counter, flattened her palm on the stack of plush hand towels Mrs. Courtney always left for guests. "I dunno. Your door was unlocked, and you're bare-ass naked."

"If anyone but you had come in, they'd be wearing wet footprints in the middle of their back."

Thing was, she didn't doubt it for a minute and rolled her eyes accordingly, but then just as quickly sobered. "What was Julian doing here?"

Christian shifted around beneath the spray, spattering her as he did. "Delivering intel Hank didn't want put in a phone call."

She frowned at that, brushed the mist from the sheer sleeves covering her shoulders. "I thought you had a secure satellite link or something."

"We do," he said, and left it at that.

Natasha moved further into the steamy room, reaching back to close the door on their conversation before she did. "I don't get it."

"You don't need to."

Oh, but he was wrong. So very wrong.

She turned her back to the long mirror, crossed her arms over her chest, and stared a hole through the shower curtain to the man behind. "Then the fact that my godfather thought Julian worked for Spectra is no big deal?"

"Shit," she heard Christian mumble before sputtering out water.

Just as she'd thought. "You weren't going to tell me, were you?"

"No reason for you to know."

No reason? Her fingertips bit into her upper arms as she tightened her hold on her sanity. "Jesus, Christian. My life is being screwed all to hell here. Why wouldn't I need to know?"

"It doesn't change anything."

"That's a load of crap. Even I know it ups the stakes here." Forget it, she grumbled to herself, kicking off the three-inch heels she still wore to pace the bathroom in bare feet. She wasn't going to stand here and pretend nothing had changed.

And after another long moment, Christian gave in. "It's upped the time frame, yes."

And that meant he would be walking out of her life soon because nothing between them was settled. She stopped pacing, leaned her backside against the vanity, her hands at her hips on the countertop.

She wanted to cry and scream and smack him senseless all at the same time. Upping their time frame was not the good news it should've been.

"Natasha?"

"What?"

"Just seeing if you were still here."

Like hell. "You know when I come into your room but can't tell when I leave?"

"So I'm not always a good spy."

And she was in no mood to be soothed with his teasing. "Did you find anything you could use in the lab?"

"Julian's taking several megs worth of data back to the ops center. I should know something later."

"And then what?" She brushed the spray of water from her arms again

"Depends on what Kelly John finds."

So her future was in the hands of an unknown SG-5 operative in the bowels of some ops center in the heart of the city. Yeah. She was screwed.

"Natasha?"

"Still here."

"Are you still dressed?"

She rolled her eyes. "Why? Were you waiting for me to leave so you could get out?" Obviously so. He couldn't stay in there forever. And he sure as hell wouldn't be getting out to dry off until she left the room. Couldn't have her seeing him naked now, could he?

When he didn't answer immediately, she thought he must be thinking of how to kindly give her the ol' heave-ho. So her knees threatened to give way when instead he asked, "Actually, I was hoping you might want to join me."

Long simmering seconds ticked by before she found her voice to answer. "Join you? In there?"

"Yeah. In here."

She waited again, hesitating, thinking he'd change his mind, that the water would shut off any moment and he'd order her out of the room. But he didn't.

He said instead, "Natasha?"

"Still here," she managed to reply.

"Is that a yes or a no?"

"It's a bit of wondering if you're sure."

"I wouldn't have asked if I wasn't. If I didn't . . ."

She held her breath, listening, closed her eyes so she could better hear over the water and over the beating of her heart.

"If I didn't want you."

A shudder of emotion coursed through her, a sensation that was not unlike tripping and falling with no chance to catch her herself on the way down.

She loved him. It was so easy to admit.

What wasn't easy was holding back when she wanted to

say it out loud, wanted to hear the words back from him. With the end they were facing soon, there existed the real possibility of never seeing him again.

"I want you, too," was what she finally said, reaching back to lower the zipper on her long-sleeved little black dress.

Twenty-three

Christian needed something other than slick brown and beige marble to grab hold of if he wanted to maintain any semblance of balance. Waiting for Natasha to make up her mind was about to drive him out of his own.

His invitation had come out of nowhere, yet he'd never considered taking it back. Not when it felt so very right to want her here with him, the way he hadn't wanted a woman in more years than he could remember.

And even if it meant exposing—

"Oh God."

Her gasp when she pulled back the curtain was much as he'd expected, though it didn't hurt that this time he heard concern more than horror.

A nice change, he admitted, watching her eyes widen, her fingers cover her mouth, from the reactions he'd received in the past. The ones that had kept him in the dark and eventually convinced him that celibacy wasn't any tougher to handle than a woman turning up her nose.

"Christian. Your legs. What happened?"

Thailand happened. Malena happened. That six-foot bamboo cage happened. He shrugged because he couldn't talk through gritted teeth. "I didn't have the luxury of a cinder block wall for marking off the days."

"So you used your legs?" she asked, her pitch approaching hysteria.

His thighs, to be exact. They were covered from knees to groin with tick marks. Four vertical, one angled across in a bundle of five. A lot of bundles of five.

"It got hard keeping track in my head," he finally answered, having realized she hadn't run. She hadn't turned and run.

Neither did she appear to notice that they were both naked, but dropped to her knees in front of him. He, on the other hand, noticed plenty; the spray pummeled his back as he blocked the flow from her face.

He noticed the curves of her hips, that valentine shape of her bottom as she sat on her heels, and wanted more than anything to pull her up and fill his palms with that very firm flesh.

To bury himself inside her body and forget he'd ever had reason to mark his legs, to scar himself permanently so that any woman he was ever with would bring to mind the one who had taken him down.

When Natasha—*Natasha*—kissed his right thigh, strands of her hair matted to her face and obscuring her eyes, it was all he could do to hold steady. Clenching every muscle in his body, however, drew that much more of her attention.

She kneaded and pressed and whispered healing words and tendered kisses over the damage he'd done. By the time she moved from his right leg to his left, he couldn't take it anymore. He reached down, hooked his hands in the hollows of her armpits, and urged her to her feet.

She pushed up slowly, her fingertips lingering, shaking, the tremors traveling upward, settling into her shoulders. He felt her shudder. It nearly killed him, and he had to let her go.

"I'm so sorry," she said, her lower lip quivering, tears mixing with water drops on her face. "I'm so very sorry. I wish"—she looked down, scraped his legs with the tips of her nails—"I wish I could make you forget."

He lifted her chin with his hand. Enough was enough was

enough. "I won't ever forget. Just like you'll never forget. Betrayal is like that."

"Who betrayed you?" she asked, her lip still trembling.

He shook his head. "It's not important."

"How can you say that? Look at your legs! Of course it's important."

Once it had been. But standing here with Natasha now, Malena no longer mattered. She didn't matter at all. He felt seven long years of tension seep away, felt peace descend. The tension that for so long had bound the muscles in his neck and shoulders drained until he couldn't remember how it had felt to be unable to move.

He closed the curtain Natasha had left open, curled the fingers of one hand around the rod, planted a palm on the wall at shoulder level. "What's important is that we don't waste what time we still have together."

She closed her eyes then, slowly shook her head. "Because you're going away."

"No. Because we're here. Because right now it's just you and me." God, but he wished that was the truth. That he wasn't standing here looking down at her and telling a big fat lie. "And because nothing else but this moment matters."

She looked up then, and he saw in her eyes that she didn't believe him. She knew the same truth he knew. That this moment was nothing but a stolen piece of time neither of them could afford to spend so selfishly.

He also saw her make the same decision he'd made when he'd invited her into the shower. A decision to blow off the rest of the world and prove what amazingly adept thieves they could be.

She settled her hands at his waist; he continued to stand with one splayed on the wall to his left, the other wrapped around the curtain rod. He was surprised he hadn't yet pulled it off the wall, and he gripped it even tighter as his erection began to rise.

The simple touch of her skin to his and he was ready to go.

Well, it wasn't really that simple. Not when her breasts rose and fell as she breathed, the cherry-ripe tips grazing the center of his chest.

He hooked an arm around her neck and drew her bodily forward. Her lashes, which had drifted down, lifted slowly until she met his gaze, understood his need and intentions, and questioned neither.

He didn't think he'd ever seen unspoken emotion so clearly in any woman's eyes, and what he saw in Natasha's knocked the wind from his sails. She wasn't here for sex, for comfort, for solace or relief. She was here because she loved him. Him. She loved him.

And oh, goddamn, but he loved her, too.

He swallowed hard, once, twice, worked to dislodge the lump burning from his gut up into his throat. And then he closed his eyes to squeeze the building moisture and lowered his mouth to hers.

She parted her lips. He did the same, kissing her with a tenderness that came from a place in his soul he'd long since locked away, a place he wanted to offer her, that he wanted her to know. She brought her arms around his waist and kissed him in return.

It was the softest kiss he'd ever known. It spoke of promises he knew he shouldn't make, ones he was wrong to ask of her. He asked anyway, asked that she trust him, and understand when he walked away that it was what he had to do.

As if she heard what he was thinking, she tightened her hold and increased the pressure of her mouth until he felt the edge of her teeth. She smelled like warm sweet honey, like spiced harem flowers. He couldn't get enough of her no matter how he tried. His desperation grew.

He'd promised himself to take this slowly, to savor this time as their last. Her insistent hunger made it impossible for him to do anything but feast. He pressed forward; the water striking the skin between his shoulder blades hit his waist with his first step, the small of his back with his second.

When he had Natasha where he wanted her, trapped between his body and the wall, only then did he raise his head. "It's going to get ugly from here on out."

"I know," she whispered, water beading on her lips.

He licked his own instead of licking hers. "If I seem cold and distant, it's all part of the act."

She nodded. "I understand."

Did she? Did she really? And how much of any act was he going to be able to pull off when she looked at him like that? "I don't mean to be all doom and gloom here."

She brought up her hand, placed it against his cheek. "Christian, please stop talking and make love to me."

He slid his hands from her shoulders down her arms and wrapped his fingers around her slim wrists, one near his face, the other not quite as close as he would have liked to the place where his blood was beginning to boil.

And so he took it lower, helping her close her fist around the base of his shaft.

One of her brows lifted archly while he was staring down into her eyes. "Talking with your hands now?"

"Women," he said with a smile. "Can't make 'em happy. Can't trade 'em in on a used car."

"I don't think I've ever heard that version."

"Glad to dish up a new experience for you."

"Ah, well, that you've definitely done. I've never had a spy before."

He fought a broader grin. He was sucker enough already. "And how would you know that? A good spy doesn't broadcast what he is."

"Hmm." She let go of his penis, moved both palms to the center of his chest, sputtered as water hit her in the face when he moved. "What he is. Not what he does. Is that how you think of it?"

The lightness of the mood began to fade, as did the smile he'd been feeling. "I have to if I want to walk away from a job in one piece."

She shook her head. "I don't know how you do it."

"Someone has to," he said simply, because that was long

since what he'd come to believe. That he was meant to give back, to do for others what Hank had done for him, to use the skills he had to wipe syndicates like Spectra IT from the planet's face.

He waited a long tense moment for Natasha to respond verbally instead of simply touching him the way she was, counting his ribs, the washboard slats of his abs. If she didn't want to be here, if who and what he was was too much for her to handle, if she wanted to break things off now instead of later . . .

"Christian?" She looked up at him, her eyes softening to match her tender tone of voice.

He answered her by cupping her head, stroking his thumbs over her eyebrows, her cheekbones, learning her, memorizing her, outlining her jaw, her lips . . .

"I love you."

The last time a woman had spoken those words his life had gone up in flames. This time was no different, only it was. Because this time it was his heart that was burning. And he answered the only way he knew how to do. He covered her mouth with his, holding her face still for the words he wasn't yet able to speak.

She wrapped her arms around him so tightly he could barely breathe, and he wondered if she truly believed he was worth holding onto, that he could give her the support she needed when he wasn't even sure of that himself.

She kissed him back with none of the tenderness he'd heard in her words. She kissed him with a sad desperation, with a need that hit him like a fist to the gut. He hadn't been ready for this woman to come into his life. And he feared failing her now.

He let his hands roam over her back, wanting to touch all of her at once, settling finally on squeezing her bottom, lifting her to her tiptoes so that he could touch her in the only way that mattered right now. The most basic, elemental way man knew to show his feelings to a woman.

She hooked her knee over his thigh, offering him access to the parts of her body he sought. He slipped his fingers deep between her legs; she moaned into his mouth. Moaned and whimpered when he found her slick entrance and pushed two fingers inside.

He stroked in and out gently, setting a pace she matched with the responding thrust of her hips. But impatience soon got the best of her, and she demanded more, wrapping insistent fingers around his cock, rubbing the head between her sweet folds.

He would've waited, taken this easy and slow had that been what she wanted, but it wasn't, and he was more than willing, more than happy to comply.

He did so then, aligning their bodies, pushing up until he found what he was looking for, driving his cock as deep as he was able. Her fingers fluttered on his shoulders where she held him. Or at least that was where she held him until she managed to get her hands on his ass and squeeze.

She gripped him hard, pulled him forward, refused to let him take the time with her he had planned. And so he changed his plans, spreading her wide there where his fingertips gouged her inner thighs, holding her open for his thrusts.

His face buried in the crook of her neck, his bent knees supporting his weight and a whole lot of hers, he let himself go, pumping at the pace she demanded. Her cries of completion weren't long in coming. He followed immediately, blown away by how overwhelmed he felt. By how hard he had to struggle to breathe.

When he pulled free from her body, she groaned as she lowered her leg to the floor of the tub. A second later she smiled. And she sighed. And she cuddled up into his body as if she would never be able to get as close as she wanted.

Then, as softly as he could, his lips buried in her sweet-smelling wet hair, his hand on her head holding her cheek tightly to the center of his chest, he mouthed the words, "I love you, too."

* * *

"Why do you think Wick assumed Julian worked for Spectra?" Natasha asked, sitting cross-legged in the center of Christian's bed watching him dress.

It was strange to see him putting on his own clothes rather than Peter Deacon's, but she understood that he needed to feel comfortable in his own skin, to shed all restrictions in order to concentrate on what he needed to do.

"I dunno, but I don't like it."

"What did Julian say?"

Christian tugged a black Henley T-shirt over his head, left the neckline snaps undone. "Just told Bow that he'd taken care of the business that had brought him here. And that he'd be back in touch."

God, but she loved watching him dress, watching his body move, the way he stretched. She shuddered, refocused. "That's got to mean Wick was expecting someone from Spectra to show up here. So"—she considered the implications—"he's been in touch with them again."

"I'm going to drive to the point, make a call, see what Kelly John found on the hard drive." The T-shirt bunched around Christian's waist as he threaded his belt through the loops on a pair of well broken-in jeans. "And I'm going to kick Tripp's ass if he's sleeping on the job. If your godfather contacted Spectra, I should've known about it long before that elevator door opened up."

"I can't imagine why he would have." She wrapped the sheet tighter around her body, shivering even though the room wasn't cold. "I would think the only reason for contact at this point would be the delivery of the money."

"In which case, *they* would be contacting *him*." Christian opened the closet door, unzipped his garment bag, pulled out a shoulder holster and gun.

Natasha watched him strap it on, swallowing the gasp tickling the back of her throat. Of course he would be armed. He'd always been armed, as she well knew. But having him draw his gun on her that morning they'd veered off the Palisades Parkway was nothing when she thought now about him needing the firearm for protection.

For saving his own life.

Tears welled and ran down her cheeks before she could blink or wipe them away. The realization that his life was in danger, that it was in danger with every mission he took on . . .

No. No way. She couldn't sit here crying and being so passively, ridiculously inept. This was her life at stake here, too. Her future, her past.

Her present.

She swung her legs over the side of the bed. "I'll check his bank accounts for recent activity. Not that he'd have the amount of money we're talking about wired anywhere I might see it."

"Still won't hurt to check." Christian pulled a sport coat from the closet, shrugged into it, making sure the gun was concealed before turning toward her. "I won't be gone long. If you find out anything, just hang tight."

She nodded, hating the thought of him leaving her alone even to make his call. "I'll be fine. Go do what you need to do."

He crossed the room to prop one hip on the mattress's edge, sitting so that he faced her. "You will be. You're tough and you're strong and you're very, very clever."

"Right. Clever's going to take me really far."

"Don't knock it." He toyed with the still damp ends of her hair brushing her shoulders. "It's a trait that comes in handy when you find yourself in hot water."

Like now, she almost said, then didn't. She was growing tired of analyzing the situation when it was obvious nothing would change without action.

The information Christian had sent to the Smithson headquarters for analysis was only half the story. That data revealed *what*. It did not reveal *why*.

And the why was the one thing Natasha couldn't leave the estate without knowing.

Getting the information out of her godfather would require too much in the way of mental machinations.

She'd start with the other side of the equation—with the genius who had the brains to steal confidential files from the government, but still stumbled over every word whenever she was around.

Twenty-four

Woody Jinks swore he'd died and gone to heaven. The empty lab was getting to him, this working underground on his own, no one around but an old geezer with wheels for legs and even then not all of the time.

He had his tunes, sure. He didn't have his games. He couldn't even risk playing under a new identity. Not when his trademark strategies were legendary and pointed too easily to him. Nope. He was stuck like Chuck, nothing to do, nothing but work, nothing but wait . . .

. . . and, oh boy, nothing to get him excited until now.

He swallowed hard, reached down and tugged at the fly of his pants, watching Natasha, in a really short skirt and really high heels, walk down the stairs from the lab's platform to the floor. He tried to meet her smile, was sure he came off looking like a fool when he pushed a hand back over the ratty hair he knew he hadn't combed.

"Hey," he said with a lift of his chin, doing his best to come off as cool when even *he* knew cool was too far out of his league to master. "What's up?"

Her answering smile actually caused his stomach to hurt. How could she be so amazingly out of his reach when they were only four years apart in age? Too bad he couldn't have met her after this whole scenario had finished playing out.

Then he'd have the money chicks dug and no one would care that he was goofier looking than Bill Gates.

"Good morning, Woody. I thought you might enjoy a bit of company."

"Uh, why?" Crap. What a stupid thing to say. "I mean, you don't come down here much at all. You must have a lot of work keeping you busy, huh?"

"I'm caught up for now." She glanced around, grabbed a chair from the workstation across the aisle from his, and wheeled it over. "Wick isn't feeling too well this morning, and I imagine you get rather bored down here by yourself when he's out of pocket."

Out of pocket. Heh. What a stupid expression, he thought with a snort. And then he shrugged so that Natasha wouldn't think he was making fun of her. He really wasn't. That would be about the lamest thing in the world he could do.

Thing was, he really kind of enjoyed having the place to himself. Dr. Bow seriously creeped him out these days; his nerves weren't exactly wired for all this secrecy. "I don't mind it much. I like not having the distraction of a lot of people around."

She'd just started to sit, and stopped. "Would you like me to leave?"

"Oh, no. No." Not in a gazillion years, no. "I just meant it's hard to work under those conditions all the time. Sometimes quiet is just the thing."

"I can definitely relate." She scooted the chair even closer to his and sat, leaning on the chair arm toward him, crossing her legs so that when she swung her foot she almost touched his jeans with her toe. "It's why I enjoy the drive back and forth to the city. Lots of quiet time."

"I guess you'll be staying in the city to work once Dr. Bow is gone, huh?"

She frowned, blinked, her lashes like paintbrushes against her cheeks. "Gone? I'm not sure what you mean by gone."

Shoot. Stupid, stupid, stupid. "I just meant"—he waved his hand around uselessly because that's how he felt, almost giving away the professor's plans—"that he's not going to be around forever and stuff."

That wasn't what he'd meant, of course, and he sure as hell hoped she bought the cover he'd scrambled to make, because if she started digging he wasn't sure he wouldn't cave.

"Well," she began, clearing her throat lightly. "Wick's death isn't imminent, so I'd prefer to take things a day at a time."

"Yeah, sure. Makes sense." Now to switch the conversation to a subject that wasn't going to make her uncomfortable or make him want to crawl into a hole and die.

Unfortunately, that meant bringing up the one thing they had in common that he wished they didn't. "You got any idea what time Mr. Deacon's gonna be around? I figured with Dr. Bow not up to working, me and Mr. Deacon could see about capturing a transmission or two. I was having trouble keeping a connection the other day when he was here, but now it's all good."

"I see," she said, watching as he brought up a window and typed in the commands that would get him into the CIA feed. "I know he had a few phone calls to make, but I imagine he'll be back shortly."

Woody frowned. "He left?"

This time it was Natasha waving a hand. "To get a better connection on his cell."

"Hmm. He must have some kind of cell. Out here? In the middle of nowhere?" Sheesh. Look who he was talking about. Of course, working for a syndicate like Spectra IT the dude would have the best equipment money could buy. Woody swore he was going to end up in the hottest of hot water if he didn't keep his big mouth shut.

But Natasha seemed cool about it. "I suppose he has what he needs to do his job. But I'm sure he'll be anxious to check out any transmissions you've been able to capture. It sounds like you've made remarkable progress."

"Yeah, it's pretty cool how this all worked out." Did she really know what was going on? "I haven't talked to Dr. Bow in years, and he contacts me like he did out of the blue."

She reached over and patted his thigh. "Honestly, I haven't seen him this excited over a project in forever. It's been good for him to have you here. And to have something this consuming to engage his mind."

"It's definitely been consuming." And it was definitely hard to keep his eyes from rolling back in his head when he thought of her touching him again. Touching him higher on his thigh. Touching him *there*. "But I did a lot of the prep work years ago. Who knew it would come in so handy, huh?"

Natasha turned her chair to face him better, the foot of her crossed leg slipping behind his calf. "I'll bet you knew it would come in handy. Otherwise, you wouldn't have thought to go to the original effort."

Oh yeah. He was the man. He was *the* man. "I've never let anything out of my hands without leaving myself a way back in. I'm kinda a control freak that way."

"Well, it certainly paid off."

"I'm still reeling over that." He shook his head. "I mean, I've always known I'd eventually be making millions. But I never figured it would come in one big fat whopping lump like this."

She nodded, gave him a wink that was like a secret handshake, like she knew exactly how cool it was what he'd done. "If you're so close to being finished here, I guess Peter won't have to stay much longer."

If the dude would show up and hang out long enough to get a full demonstration . . . "Uh, I thought you liked having him here."

"Oh, I do. But it's always a relief when visitors leave." She paused for a second, then quickly hurried on to add, "Not that I think of you as a visitor at all. You've been much more like one of the family."

He could be a whole lot more if he had a way to lock down the elevator and she would pull up her skirt and bend over. He thought of her doing just that, wished for half a second she wasn't in the room so he could adjust the goods and relieve the building pressure down there.

But then the blinking cursor he'd been watching vanished, the window filled with scrolling code, and that was all that mattered.

"Here we go," he said, pointing her attention toward the monitor. "This is what it's all about. The stuff Spectra can't get from anyone else. Hell, it's worth double what they're paying. But then putting it out there on the open market would draw too much attention. Word would get back to the Agency, and there goes the master plan, you know?"

"Right." Her voice was tight, almost a squeak. "All that work for nothing."

"Not to mention I like keeping my name out of the equation. Sorta makes me the one with the highest level of intelligence." He chuckled at the joke he'd been waiting to make. "Get it? The Agency? Central Intelligence?"

"I do believe she got it without your prodding, Dr. Jinks."

Woody's gaze shot to the wheelchair ramp. He watched Dr. Bow roll his way down to the lab's floor, wondering how the professor had gotten into the room without making any noise because Natasha seemed just as surprised to see him.

"Wick. Good morning." She pushed her chair away from the workstation and got to her feet.

She was smiling, her chin was up, but Woody swore her knees were shaking. He swore that because she kept bumping into the chair.

"I'm surprised to see you," she said. "I thought you were staying in your quarters today."

"Or are you surprised to see me because you and Dr. Jinks here were too intimately involved in conversation to hear the elevator arrive?"

"It wasn't really that intimate," Woody mumbled.

Bow rolled further into the room. "As if you would know the meaning of the word. You obviously don't know the meaning of many words common to the English language. Such as secrecy and silence."

"Uh, sure I do." Woody glanced nervously from Dr. Bow to Natasha and back.

"Then why were you talking to my goddaughter about things that are none of her business?" Bow asked, his voice rising.

"I didn't know—"

"Of course you knew. You've known for months now not to talk to anyone at all."

"Well, I thought—"

"You did not think. You did not think at all." He stopped his chair where neither one of them could get around him easily. "And now I am forced to take action I was hoping to avoid."

"Listen, Wick. Woody's not at fault here. I came down to keep him company while he waited for Peter."

"Yeah. That's all that was happening," Woody added, feeling sweat break out in his pits.

Bow looked from one to the other. "My dear, Natasha. I do wish it were so simply explained away. But your inquisitive nature leaves me no choice."

"Wick, let me call Mrs. Courtney." Natasha gestured toward the elevator. "You know she doesn't like seeing you this agitated."

"Then why would I let you call her?"

Woody slowly pushed his chair farther into the horseshoe of his workstation, praying his sneakers wouldn't squeak on the floor mat and draw the professor's attention. All he had to do was scramble beneath the table behind him, hop the railing onto the ramp, and beat it up to the elevator.

"Why would I let you do that when Mrs. Courtney will insist that I return to my room and rest?" The professor stacked his hands on the bulge of his stomach. "I will have plenty of time to rest later."

"You'll never live to see later if you don't listen to your body now," Natasha said, then pressed her lips tightly together.

The air in the room suddenly became impossible to breathe. Woody held on for dear life to the arms of his chair, his palms sweating like crazy, ready to bolt, waiting for the perfect moment and watching Bow shake his head.

"You are so very wrong, my dear. I will be living for a very long time to come."

Natasha began inching closer to the wedge of space between the workstation's corner and Bow's chair. Her chest heaved like she couldn't breathe either. "I don't understand. Your prognosis—"

Bow interrupted her, lifting one arm and weakly waving his wrist. "There's no need for you to understand. Just close your mouth and do as I say."

She gasped. "Wick—"

"Close your mouth, Natasha." Bow lifted his other hand. And he had a gun.

Oh God, please, no. Woody shot to his feet, stopped, froze. The gun was aimed his way, held in very shaky hands.

"Wick, what are you doing?" Natasha cried. She took a step forward and Bow fired. She gasped, pressed her fingers to her mouth.

Woody simply wet his pants. The bullet had zinged by his right ear and exploded behind him. It had been too close . . . he'd almost turned that way to make his getaway . . . he hadn't signed on for this crazy crap . . . he was too young to die a virgin. . .

"Dr. Jinks. Come here, please."

He inched his way toward the professor. "Uh, I really need to go to the bathroom."

"I'd say you already have." The gun was still wobbling like Woody's knees. Bow gestured with it toward the back of the lab. "Please retrieve a roll of duct tape from the storeroom. Natasha, you will accompany Dr. Jinks."

"You go to hell."

The gun went off again. Natasha yelped. Woody didn't even look back but hurried to find the tape. He turned on the light in the small room, scanned the shelves of replacement hardware and sticky notes, found the tape, and hurried back.

Natasha's eyes were wide; tears ran down her cheeks and blood ran from her shoulder down her arm. Woody turned on Bow. "You shot her? You freakin' shot her?"

"I can shoot you just as easily."

"You are out of your mind," Natasha whispered gruffly, one hand holding the bicep of the other arm, blood tunneling between her fingers. "Whatever you're doing, you won't get away with it."

"So far as I can tell, I *am* getting away with it." Bow's face was pale, his eyes wicked bright and scary. "Woodrow, please tape my goddaughter's wrists together behind her."

"How can you do this to me?" she asked, moving her hands to the small of her back when Woody shrugged and held up the tape. "You've been as much a father to me as my own. You've told me countless times that you think of me as a daughter."

She yelped.

"Sorry, sorry," Woody mumbled, winding the tape again, keeping it loose enough that she might be able to wiggle out once Bow left her alone.

"Wick, please tell me what's going on. Make me understand."

"Thank you, Woodrow. Now, please escort this . . . liability to the storeroom and lock her in."

"You bastard. You fucking bastard."

"Tsk, tsk, Natasha." Bow inclined his head, turned his chair to follow as Woody guided Natasha forward. "Obviously I wasn't much of a father figure to you at all if you can talk to me like that."

"Uh, what about her shoulder?" Woody asked, his hand on the open door. He couldn't do this. He couldn't lock her up and leave her in pain.

"A flesh wound that will be no more than a nuisance."

Natasha sobbed. Woody met her gaze, felt the tears streaming down his own cheeks, caught a breath and hiccuped as he wiped the moisture away. He tried to give her a look that said he'd be back to get her, but he didn't know what sort of look that would be.

And so he shut the door.

"Thank you, Woodrow. I realize that was an unpleasant

task, but it was quite necessary. Now." Bow wheeled back around at the sound of the approaching elevator. He lifted the gun.

Behind him, Woody jumped up and down, waving his arms to signal Mr. Deacon as he stepped out onto the platform. But it was too late, and he was too far away to do more than think about a flying wheelchair tackle.

"Good morning, Mr. Deacon," Dr. Bow said.

And then he fired the gun for the third time.

Twenty-five

"What the hell did you do?" Christian yelled, the door slamming shut behind him, the whites of his eyes showing as he advanced.

"Get the hell away from me. I didn't do anything!" She pressed as far into the corner as she could, her bound hands grappling behind her for something to use as a weapon.

She ran instead, into the empty back wall, cast a quick glance at the industrial shelving six feet to her left, wondered how fast she could get to one of the tools stacked in bins.

Not fast enough.

Christian slammed a fist into the wall beside her. He was in her face now, his wide eyes furious, his nostrils flared. "Goddammit, Natasha. What did you say to Bow?"

"I didn't say a thing." God, what was his freaking problem? Why was he blaming her? "He didn't even show up until I'd been talking to Woody for awhile."

He backed away, his hand still fisted, and turned, pacing the six-foot width of the room. "Fuck, fuck, fuck. If not to Bow, then . . . okay, what did you say to Jinks?"

"Nothing, dammit. Nothing." Her arm was on fire, burning, throbbing. She wasn't sure she'd be able to move it even if cut free from the tape. "He was doing most of the talking. I was just listening."

"And obviously Bow was listening, too," he said with a snort. One, two, three steps, turn. One, two, three steps, turn.

"I didn't see him until it was too late, so I'm sorry but I really don't know." All she knew was that she was in a world of hurt, and time wasn't making it any better. "Do you think you could stop with the ranting and the accusations long enough to get this tape off my wrists?"

It took a second for her request to sink in, but then he came back, shaking his head as he approached as if dislodging an errant thought. She turned; he cut through the tape, wrenching her shoulder in the process.

"Ow, shit." She grit her teeth, faced him again. "And where's your gun anyway? How'd you end up in here?"

"He shot first. Had Jinks disarm me." He jerked open his jacket where his empty holster hugged his side. "I wasn't about to trust that he wouldn't accidentally shoot, the way his hand was shaking. Now, tell me what Jinks was talking to you about. What might've caught Bow's attention?"

She brought her injured arm down to her side, cradled her elbow close to her body. "Shit. Uh, shit." She grimaced. "He said something about the agency and intelligence, and I'm guessing he meant the CIA."

She was working to find the least painful position, not paying any attention to Christian, so she jumped when, standing over her, he said flatly, "You're bleeding."

"Yeah. I know." Actually, the bleeding had stopped. It was like Wick had said. A nuisance of a flesh wound that bit deep and stung like a sonofabitch. "I'll live."

"He shot you. *Christ.*" That was the tamest of the oaths that followed. "Jesus Christ, Natasha. Why didn't you say something?"

"Uh, because you wouldn't shut the hell up long enough for me to talk?"

Christian growled. "We need to make you a sling. At least bind it so you don't damage the muscle moving it around."

She lifted a brow. "Dr. Bane, I presume?"

"Funny." His gaze canvassed the high-ceilinged box of a room. "Duct tape."

"Oh, if you insist." It was a two-year-old sweater after all, and glue couldn't do much more damage than the bullet had done.

Or than her godfather had done, she thought, her eyes watering anew, her chest aching with a burn that had nothing to do with the bullet he'd put in her arm—though it really had everything to do with it.

She wondered . . . glanced from shelf to shelf. Yes, there. "Hey, doc. Next to the CDs? The rewritables? You want to pass me a couple of those Advil packets?"

Christian found the pain reliever, tore open the packets, and poured the four pills into her palm. She managed to swallow them one at a time, smiling up at him once she had. "Give me a leather belt to bite on, and I'm set."

"Natasha?"

"Yes, Christian?"

"Just checking to see if you're all there."

"Yep. All here." She raised her good arm overhead when he gestured, then held her wince while he bound her bad arm to her body.

She knew she was being goofy. She couldn't help it. Or maybe she didn't care. It was just so much easier to laugh than to cry. If she let one tear fall, another would follow, then another until no dam would hold back the deluge.

And she needed to hold it back. She needed to keep the mood upbeat and positive—no matter her pain—so that Christian didn't snap to the fact that he was imprisoned again in a six-by-six cage.

"Okay." He tore the strap of tape from the roll. "That should keep you until we can get you to the hospital."

"Hospital. Right. I'll call a cab."

He rolled his eyes, tossed the tape back onto the industrial shelving, shoved his hands to his hips, and glanced around the storeroom. None of what Wick and Dr. Jinks might be doing in the lab was audible; the storage closet, like all of the basement, was soundproofed.

"What did you find out from your phone call?" she asked, grinding her jaw as she shifted position and the throbbing radiated like a starburst.

"Jinks and your godfather have somehow cracked the encryption securing the transmissions the CIA's data analysts send to their agents in the field. You know. The information those same agents use to keep our country secure from outside threats. Stuff like that." He said it while still looking around the room, just rattled it off like he would directions to Yankee Stadium.

"Christian, wait." She pushed away from the wall on which she'd been leaning. "It's true, then? The real CIA?"

"No. The one I made up." He dropped to a crouch, peered behind stacked boxes of printer paper after pushing them away from the wall, ran his hand along the seam where the floor met the wall. "Yes. The real CIA."

"Wait just a minute. You're saying my godfather is selling this technology to an international crime syndicate? That's he's a traitor?" The pain she was feeling now almost dulled that from the gunshot wound.

"That's pretty much the way of it. Spectra will now know what the CIA knows and probably before. They'll be able to warn their operatives when the Agency is closing in."

"I don't understand. Why would Wick do this?"

"The money."

"But that makes no sense." She remembered telling Christian the first night they met that he didn't know her godfather at all if he thought money factored into Wick's research.

Obviously it was a little late in the game to realize *she* was the one who needed to make the acquaintance of the real Wickham Bow. God, but her stomach hurt.

She felt so useless, watching as Christian continued to push aside shelving and storage crates when she had but one working arm and moving it sent sympathy pains shooting through the other. "Wick has always been more about theories and hypotheses than anything. Especially the last few years. This just seems . . . I want to say out of his league. Technically, I know it's not. But morally?"

"It's actually Jinks's doing." Christian grabbed a claw hammer from the shelved tool bin, bent down and ripped off the baseboard next to the heavy metal door. "Shit. Who the hell builds a storage closet out of concrete board instead of drywall?"

"They built it when they remodeled the basement walls to house the lab. What do you mean it's Jinks's doing?" she asked, trying to keep her mind off the fact that the six-by-six cage they were trapped in was made of concrete.

Bamboo would've been so much nicer.

"Jinks worked on an encryption program when enrolled at Polytechnic. You might've noticed that he pretty much lives and breathes gaming." When she nodded, Christian went on. "Seems he always has. He left strategic back doors into every program he ever designed."

That control freak thing Woody had mentioned. "He designed for the CIA?"

"Not exactly. He designed part of the program they're using to encrypt their analysts' transmissions. K.J. is pretty sure it's an amalgamation of more than a few programs. And Bow knew that."

"So he brought Jinks here to crack the encryption. And then sold the technology to Spectra."

Nodding, he shoved spindles of CDs to one side, a bin of external drives to the other, studying the wall behind. "I'm guessing that's what blew Bow's fuse. He heard Jinks telling you what they'd done."

She thought for a minute, frowned. "How did Hank find out what Wick was doing?"

"It didn't work like that." He was pacing again. Back and forth. Back and forth. "I came here to get Jinks out. Word was he was here against his will."

She gasped. "He was not! He was here as Wick's guest."

"Pretty much why I freaked that first night when you told

me he was coming to dinner." And then he stopped and rubbed a hand over his forehead. "Listen, Natasha. We've got to get out of here, and I'm all out of ideas."

"I know. I don't know . . ." She was absolutely no help.

"I can't stay in here. I mean, I can stay. If I'm busy. If you can think of something for me to do or some way for us to get the fuck out of here." He barreled into the edge of the shelving, nearly bringing it down on his head but bracing it just in time.

She watched his struggle for control, the color rise in his face, the way he breathed in through his nose, out through his mouth. All while his pulse beat like a drum at the base of his throat.

She shook her head, buried her face in her hand. "I'm sorry, Christian. I didn't mean to screw things up."

"You didn't. It's just . . ."

"Just what?" she asked when he cut himself off and moved to the front of the room.

"Nothing." He slammed his fist into the center of the metal door. "Why the hell isn't this sonofabitch hinged on the inside?"

"Christian? Tell me." Her nerves were as shot as her shoulder. Her stomach was waiting for the word to heave. Now he was falling apart and she could tell just by looking that he didn't want words of comfort from her.

He hung his head, faced away. "I shouldn't have involved you, that's all."

Somehow she knew that wasn't all. "You're not exactly the one who got me involved."

"Yeah, but I took you to Hank's. Then brought you back here."

"What were you going to do with me?" she asked with a cackle of a laugh.

He shrugged, kicked at a box of copy paper, pierced the cardboard and several reams with the toe of his boot. "We could've figured out a cover to keep you out of the way until I wrapped up things here."

She exhaled, deflating like a big red rubber ball. "So I've been in the way."

"That's not what I meant."

"It's what you said."

"I don't want to get into this now."

"Well, I do," she demanded just sharply enough that he spun on her.

His chest rose and fell so rapidly she feared he would hyperventilate. That he wouldn't be able to speak. And then when he did, she wished he hadn't.

"The time I spent in that Thai prison? A woman put me there. I'd told her the details of the op. She worked for Spectra."

Oh God. Oh God.

"Why would you tell her the details?" she whispered. When Christian said nothing but started to pace, she knew. She knew. "You loved her, didn't you?"

But he didn't answer. He whirled back around and bit off a harsh, "Fuck me. There's smoke coming in beneath the door."

Having pulled off the road at Overlook Point, Wickham Bow sat behind the wheel of his van and watched his own personal Tara burn.

He wanted to say he had no regrets but that wouldn't quite be true. He'd built his reputation on a lifetime of amazing work, yet no one would know what he'd accomplished here today. When he left the clinic a year from now healed and whole, he would not be able to return to the States.

He would be able to say nothing to anyone about his incredible feat.

Nothing about the intelligence of Woodrow Jinks and how he, Dr. Wickham Bow, had seen the potential and nurtured it, honed it, shaped it, and molded it to produce a brilliant mind capable of a feat rogue governments would kill for. He could, in fact, have had anyone killed had he so wished in return for the gift of the technology.

He preferred the money he would be receiving from Spectra hours from now.

The attaché in the seat at his side contained the hard drive backups for Dr. Jinks's computer. Examples of the captured data and the software program used to accomplish the task would be handed over in exchange for a mirror attaché filled with cash.

This morning he had uploaded the fruit of his recent labors to Natasha's university computer. Her hard drive now contained enough evidence plotting the details of his assassination—*manufactured* evidence, true—to put her and her lover away as the murderous traitors he'd set them up to be. Because whoever he was, the man she was sleeping with was not Peter Deacon.

Dealing these last months with Spectra IT, Wickham's first experience with the criminal element that operated beneath the world's stage, was indeed a new venture. But he was not a stupid man.

Though his body was failing, his mind functioned fully, as did his powers of reason and logic. And it was more than obvious, especially since Natasha's return from her weekend in the city, that her companion was more interested in what he'd found between her legs than in Dr. Jinks's work.

Yes, Wickham had been made aware of Peter Deacon's playboy reputation; learning of such had cemented the plan to set up the couple to take this fall. But Deacon was first and foremost a businessman here to conduct business, very little of which had gone on at all.

Wickham's recent contact with Spectra and their subsequent sending of Mr. Rivers to verify Wickham's suspicions of things gone awry had been the nail in the imposter's coffin. The supposed Mr. Rivers had given Wickham none of the prearranged signals establishing the truth of his identity.

Another imposter. One in cahoots with the first. He couldn't help but wonder who these men were and what they'd done with Mr. Deacon. But the wondering was idle because he couldn't say he really cared.

The deceptions made the deaths justifiable—not that anyone would ever know anything but that an accident had happened. That the two lovers had fought, one binding the other, the second caught unawares, disarmed and locked away by the man they had kidnapped and forced to facilitate their heinous, traitorous crime.

Wickham frowned as he considered the Courtneys and watched the flames lick the treetops above the house's gables. He had sent the couple into the city this morning and was working on the assumption that they were long on their way. If not, so be it. They would simply be another sacrifice he had been forced to make.

The loss of Woodrow Jinks was regrettable but indisputably preordained. Once his body was identified, authorities could link his kidnapping to Natasha and the man with whom she'd conspired to sell Dr. Jinks's brilliant and criminal coup.

Ah, yes. Natasha. His goddaughter. The fruit of the loins of his dearest friend. A complete termagant with her constant nagging over his work habits and seeming need to run his life her way.

He shook his head when he thought of the *efforts* she'd made to ease his suffering, to battle his depression, to seek out treatment—experimental, holistic, cutting edge—yet he had been the one to make the discovery that would now save his life.

Save his life while costing him more money than he'd see should he live another forty years.

He glanced in his sideview mirror as another van pulled up behind his. He would leave his wallet on the floorboard, his wheelchair tucked but not secured behind his seat.

All he needed was the attaché.

Twenty-six

Christian ran another strip of tape along the floor to seal off the cracks left between the rolls of paper towels he'd wedged at the bottom of the door. Goddamn door opened outward. Not even a freakin' inside lock to pick.

He tore the tape from the roll, knowing if they couldn't get out through the ceiling, he'd just put the lid on their coffin—unless someone in the house was alive to call in the fire. He wasn't holding his breath on that one. Not with the way Dr. Bow had gone off the deep end.

And that was the other thing. When he and Natasha got out of here, nothing in the world above would be the same. Christian had only lived here a couple of weeks. Natasha was looking at an entire life turned upside down. If her godfather wasn't already dead, he was looking to be that way soon.

"You have a clue what's above the ceiling?" Ventilation ducts were out. The fire rising from the basement would cook them inside the ducts like turkeys in tinfoil.

She shook her head, her eyes wide, tears brimming at the corners. Spots of bright color high along her cheeks stood out on her deathly white face. She'd been trying to help him by talking to Jinks.

And now here he was, showing her how he excelled at failing those who did help. The irony was hardly lost.

"C'mere." He gestured her over and tucked her behind him next to the metal door that was rapidly heating.

He was running out of time, and fast. He had to get up to the ceiling, see if there was any sort of crawl space, if the air was breathable, if there was a chance in hell they could find a way out.

He grabbed hold of the shelving, rocked it forward, back, forward, back, and forward again with one more sharp jerk. Supplies crashed every which way with a deafening clatter as it toppled against the far wall.

Christian wedged himself into the triangle of space between the near wall and his makeshift ladder. Behind him, Natasha coughed. He bit off a curse. Telling her to hang in, that everything would be all right . . . shit. Just . . . shit.

He stepped onto the edge of the lowest shelf, shook as hard as he could. Stable enough, and he climbed, edging into the center of the unit for balance. He only needed to climb up one more shelf . . .

Sonofabitch! Adrenaline coursed through him. "Natasha, what's behind this back wall?"

The back wall now sporting a deep gash from the falling corner of the shelving.

Concrete board didn't gash.

"Uh, I'm not sure. Wick remodeled the basement a couple of years ago."

"Think, sweetheart. Think." Christian inched his way in that direction. "And hand me up the hammer." He heard her scrabble around beneath him, digging through the rubble and clutter.

"Here." She slapped the handle into his hand. "I think that's the wall where the furnace was."

A furnace. A chimney. How old was this house?

He scooted within striking distance of the wall, balanced on the edge of the shelf he feared was starting to buckle, drew back his arm, and swung. The claws of the hammer bit deep into the drywall.

He pulled away big chunks, working his way to the right to reveal one-by-eight slats randomly hammered together.

As if boarding up a hole. . . .

He hooked the claws behind the first board and jerked it away from the wall. The second came free with a creaking snap. A third followed. A fourth and fifth, and there it was.

The coal chute built into the original structure.

He glanced down a moment, blinked, said . . . "This wall faces the driveway. Beneath the kitchen."

"Yes! God, I didn't even think!" She moved closer to the shelving unit. "The chute's door is beneath the hedges. It looks like a miniature cellar entrance. I can't remember the reason they built it like that, but I do know it hasn't been used in years."

His heart racing, he braced his feet, shifted to balance his weight directly beneath the chute, stuck his head into the dark opening, and sniffed.

Rotted wood. Dank earth. Oily coal residue, but no smoke.

The fire wasn't yet burning on this side of the house. Smoke would be rising up the basement stairwell and elevator shaft, but it wasn't here. Not yet.

He yanked away the last two boards. "We're going up."

"What about the fire? The smoke?"

He shook his head, drawing in a full breath. "We're good, but we've got to hurry." He turned back, held out a hand to help her onto the makeshift ladder. "You need to lose the shoes."

"Okay." She kicked off the heels and stood in her bare feet, her thigh-length skirt, and a pink and black sweater taped tight to her body. The binding restricted her movement too much; she would never be able to climb. Christian's mind whirred.

She stepped onto the edge of the lowest shelf, scooted her way toward him, moved up onto the one where he stood, and gave him a shaky smile. "Now what?"

Damn if she wasn't in more pain than he'd realized, more

than she was letting on. Deep purple half-moons colored the skin beneath her eyes, and he kicked himself a thousand times for letting Bow get the drop. "If I don't untape you, I don't think you'll be able to climb."

She nodded, swiveled so that her injured arm was within his reach. This time he went for the switchblade in the sole of his boot, cutting her free instead of jerking her around like last time when he'd had no clue she'd been shot.

Christ . . . she'd been *shot.*

"A trick of the trade?" she asked, wincing only once during the process.

"Doesn't do me a lot of good when I can't get to it." He closed the knife, shoved it into his pocket.

"You would've used it on Wick?"

"In a heartbeat."

She nodded, her eyes tearing up. "I wish you had."

God, but he loved this woman, her bravery, her belief in him, her trust. He looked down into her eyes. "This is going to hurt like hell, you know, climbing up."

"Nah. I've got that adrenaline thing going on. I'm impervious to pain."

He cupped the back of her skull, kissed her forehead. "Then up you go, soldier."

"Wait." Her voice echoed with panic. "After I'm out, then what?"

He thought. "If there's fire, hit the water garden. But if you can get to your SUV, we're outta here. You need to get stitched up."

"And you? What happens next?"

"One step at a time, sweetheart. One step at a time. Now let's go."

Natasha rolled out through the coal chute doors into the hedges and screamed.

Smoke billowed far above her head. Flames crackled and popped. Heat poured down. She scrambled around onto her hands and knees, gritting her teeth at the knife blade of pain slicing through her arm.

Climbing up, *God,* grabbing for handholds, rotted wood crumbling. She couldn't believe she'd made it. Her palms and soles felt like porcupine skin. But she was out. And Christian was right behind.

"Natasha!"

"I'm here."

"Can you get to the garage?"

She whipped her head around. "Yes. The cars are fine. Wick's van is gone. The garage door is open."

"Okay. You need to find a shovel. A hoe. An axe. Something."

"Why? What's wrong?" she cried. She could see the top of his head, and he wasn't right behind her at all. No. No! Panic welled. Her chest ached. "Christian!"

"The chute's too narrow here. The dirt's caved in."

Caved in because she'd climbed through first and dislodged the rotting wood holding it back. "Hang on. I'll be right back."

"Hurry, sweetheart. Hurry."

She shot to her bare feet and ran, heart pounding, toward the open garage. Mr. Courtney kept his gardening tools . . . where?

She whipped her gaze from the workbench of mechanic's tools, oil, coolant, transmission fluid . . . to the pegboard, the hammer, the saw . . . to the table beneath, the sander, the drill . . . to the closet in the far corner. Yes!

The padlock hung open. She couldn't believe her luck! She jerked open the door and screamed, grinding her jaw against what felt like a shark latched onto her shoulder with spikey teeth. She swore she was going to throw up, swallowed hard against the urge.

The sharpshooter shovel, the hand trowel, the hoe, the spade. She grabbed all she could and ran back, ducking and yelping as burning embers rained down from the trees above.

"Here!" She dropped to her knees, handed him down the trowel, used the hoe to chop at as much of the remaining wood as she could reach. Beneath her, Christian sputtered and disappeared from view. "Christian!"

"Down here," he called from the basement, his voice muffled by chunks of timber and dirt clods falling.

He wasn't going to make it! He was going to die!

She tossed aside the hoe and started using her hands, scooping out dirt into her lap and the ground around her. She couldn't dig fast enough. The smoke was everywhere now. Her eyes watered. She couldn't breathe. Couldn't think. Couldn't feel her limbs at all to know if she was doing any good.

But then he was there, his gorgeous face covered with dirt and old soot as he shoved his shoulders through the widened tunnel, twisting upwards until he hooked his hands over the edge of the chute's frame. He hauled himself free, rolled out onto the driveway.

She watched his chest heave as he struggled for breath on his hands and knees. She watched until she couldn't wait another moment, then launched herself forward and hugged him as hard as she could. He was out. He was alive.

She couldn't bear the thought of losing him when she'd only just now found him. "Stupid place for a coal chute, huh?"

"I wouldn't have it anywhere else." He hugged her back as if he needed to ground himself in the same reality of their survival, and then seconds later shoved to his feet.

He grabbed her by the hand; they sprinted for her SUV, ducking away from the fire debris now pouring down. Christian opened the Infiniti's front door, Natasha the back. They climbed in, slammed the doors in unison.

"You got keys? Or do I hot-wire?"

"On the visor. I leave them in case Mr. Courtney needs to move me out of the way. What about the Ferrari?"

"It's Deacon's. It stays," Christian said as the engine roared to life. He wheeled around in the drive and shot forward down the estate's private road, leaving the Ferrari behind.

That beautiful hot-bodied car suddenly was the ugliest

thing Natasha could imagine. It belonged to a man who, in absentia, had destroyed so many lives. She couldn't even bear to look back. To see her home away from home of so many years going up in flames.

And then it hit her. "The Courtneys! And Woody! Do you think they got out?"

"I don't know, sweetheart. Hang on!"

Christian whipped the wheel, sent the SUV sideways onto the main road. Natasha yelped as she tumbled across the seat and Christian picked up speed. She caught her breath, scrambled back up, glanced out the window.

"Christian! Stop!"

He slammed on the brakes, stopped in the middle of the road.

"Oh my God! Look!" She gestured wildly toward the gaping hole through the retaining wall at Overlook Point.

"Shit." Christian gunned the SUV forward into the circular turnaround, threw the vehicle into 'park,' and slammed open his door.

Natasha followed, gravel biting into her bare soles as she hurried forward. Christian stopped her with a raised arm thrown across her chest.

She cried out, pushed her way past and stared down the rocky slope toward the lake's shoreline where Wick's van lay in a mangled heap.

"Oh, Christian. Oh God. We've got to go down."

"We're not going anywhere."

"But Wick—"

"A thousand bucks says he's not within twenty miles of here."

She glanced over at him. His T-shirt was torn at the neckline and one shoulder seam, and dirt coated his jeans, his hands, his face. She remembered the first night they'd met, less than two weeks before, when they'd stood in this very spot and flirted in their finest.

Did she care if Wick was at the bottom of the lake? Did she want to know?

He had tried to kill her and Christian both. He might very well have left the Courtneys and Woody for dead, too. She turned from Christian and looked off in the direction of the house. Tears welled in her eyes as she watched the smoke billow, and the flames leap from tree to tree.

Her arm begin to ache unbearably, her knees to sag. "I don't even have a phone to call 911."

"No need," he said, his voice cold and flat.

She glanced back toward him and picked up the sound of approaching sirens, a sound that should have brought relief, but instead brought uncertainty. It was what she saw, however, that frightened her to death.

The look in Christian's eyes.

He gently took her by her good arm and returned her to the SUV. She didn't argue. She didn't fight to stay where she was. She didn't demand he release her so she could clamber down the incline to the lake.

She didn't have the energy to do more than comply. Exhaustion was rapidly replacing panic. Nothing was over. Nothing was complete. But what happened from here was out of her control.

She wasn't even going to be able to keep him around.

"Natasha, listen."

She shook her head, stood her ground. That much strength she still had. "No. I don't want to hear it. Just go."

"I have to. The authorities will get you to the hospital." He bit off a curse, shoved his hands to his hips, then scrubbed one over his head. "Fuck it, no. I'll take you."

She stepped in front of him, placed her palm in the center of his chest. "I can take care of myself. I've been doing it twenty-eight years without you."

"Fuck." He spun away, kicked out at the SUV's tire. His eyes glistened brightly when he looked back seconds later. "I can't be found here. I can't be questioned."

"I know that." The sirens were getting close. She and Christian stood in plain sight. "Go. Take my car."

He shook his head. "Where's the closest pay phone?"

She glanced to his waist, where he usually wore his cell. "He took your cell, too?"

Christian nodded. "Won't do him any good if he kept it."

"Secret spy stuff, huh?" She tried to smile. Her mouth quivered. And nothing else came out.

Christian's expression darkened. "You do know what to say, right? When they question you?"

"Of course. My godfather left me to die. That he was working with a man named Peter Deacon. That's all I know."

Finally, his eyes softened. "You know you don't make a bad spy yourself."

"Right." She rolled her eyes. "Just call me Jennifer Garner."

"I've got to go, Natasha," he said, sobering.

She nodded. "Keep on the west side of the road. There's a corner store in about five miles."

"Thanks, sweetheart." He backed away. "Be safe."

"You, too."

He glanced sharply in the direction of the sirens, looked back at her. "It's not you I'm leaving, Natasha. I'll be back for you. I will find you again."

"I know. You're a wonderful spy, Christian Bane." He was more than a wonderful spy. He was a wonderful man. Wounded and honorable. A worthy and valiant partner with whom she wanted to spend her life.

"Oh, baby." He cupped a hand to her cheek, leaned his forehead against hers. "I'm not so sure I'm more than a survivor."

When he released her, she waved him away. Once he'd disappeared into the woods, she let the tears go and walked slowly toward the road to flag down the authorities.

For so long she'd measured the men she'd known by the two who had meant the most in her life. Two fairy-tale princes created by a lonely little girl. No single man had ever gotten past that ruler to engage her heart.

Or, truth be told, she had never given one a chance, seeing as she'd been taught to suffer fools lightly and had looked for faults long before strengths. Yet if she had been so wrong about Wick, how many men had she unfairly blown off by making assumptions that were untrue?

But Christian . . . oh, Christian.

In Christian Bane she had discovered a complex man, one harder than most, more capable and worldly, yet in so many other ways lost and little-boy vulnerable. He wanted to protect her from his uncertain future when, for the first time in her life, she'd never been more sure of hers.

Now to convince the stubborn man that marrying him and living happily ever after was one fairy tale she believed in with all of her heart.

Twenty-seven

Twenty feet from and parallel to the road, Christian crashed through the underbrush, losing his footing, picking it up again, struggling to keep his balance and his mind.

Even knowing he had no choice, he couldn't believe he was leaving Natasha behind. If there'd been another way . . . if there'd been time. . . .

But there'd been neither. He couldn't risk being found at the scene and compromising SG-5. His priority now was to call the ops center and find out if Julian had returned to the city or was still in the area.

Timing was critical. The authorities would be combing the estate for evidence of all that had happened here. Bow's fire guaranteed they'd find little. Which meant using the data Christian had pulled from Jinks's hard drives to put Bow and Deacon away.

Deacon would be the easiest. Bow, not so, though the moment he resurfaced he'd be wishing he'd locked himself in that fiery basement. No matter what it took, no matter how long, Christian would make sure the old man suffered double the pain he'd caused Natasha.

The most logical place to begin setting up the trail of evidence would be Bow's office at the university—as long as that office was still intact. Tripp would be in the city; he could get started as soon as Christian got to a phone and made contact.

Sirens approached rapidly. He hit the ground, flattened himself behind a thick stand of brush. The ambulance with Natasha. He should be there with her. He slammed a fist into the dirt, waited another few minutes before setting off at a more even pace.

Thirty minutes later he came to the crossing and the rear of the corner store. Hands on his knees, he leaned forward to catch what he could of his breath before finding the pay phone, dusting detritus from his clothing as he walked from the woods out into the open.

He dialed the number set up at the ops center for unsecured calls. When the connection clicked through, he said simply, "Bane," then left the line open for the trace. Several minutes later, a computerized voice replied, "Thank you," signaling that his location had been made.

Now to wait. And to convince himself that getting back to the city was paramount, that he had no time to stop at the emergency room where Natasha would have been taken. He couldn't do anything for her now but make matters worse. He'd fucked her over too many ways already.

Once she was healed and had moved on with her life she would see that. See that she was better off without a man who hopped from frying pans into fires on a regular basis and who might not come home someday. Eventually she would see that she didn't really love him at all.

Not like he loved her but had been too blind to see.

Eight weeks later

Christian watched MaddyB circle the track and found himself grinning for no real reason but the obvious. That Hank would be flying high come racing season. The filly was two years old and chomping at the bit, ready to show her stuff. Typical female stepping into her prime.

Another reason he couldn't help but grin. The thought of a prime female turned Christian's mind in the only direction it seemed interested in heading these days. He'd told her he would find her, that he would be back. And, yeah, he knew exactly where she was.

He knew she was working out at her health club again, that her shoulder had healed with no permanent damage. He knew she had taken a new position with a brokerage firm in the financial district. He knew she spent her weekends blowing off steam with Susan, Yvonne, and Elaine.

He just hadn't yet grown the balls to go to her. He supposed he needed to figure out why.

The sound of Jackson Briggs's approaching chopper caught Christian's attention and reminded him all too vividly of the day Natasha had discovered who he really was. Funny thing, though, was the reality of that man no longer existing. And he had Natasha to thank for that.

From that very first night, he'd been entranced by her mysteriously seductive air. The way she wore her clothes, held her chin high, lowered her lashes and spoke with her eyes, had aroused both his lust *and* mistrust. A reasonable reaction considering another so much like her had sentenced him to die in a bamboo cage. No. That wasn't right. Because Malena was nothing like Natasha.

He'd come to that realization the night Natasha had told him she loved him. Those words . . . He blew out a long slow breath and thought of how many times he'd replayed them since in his mind. She'd taught him to laugh, when he never thought to have reason to, blown him away with her fun-loving spirit, her caring, selfless nature.

"She's something else, isn't she?" Hank said, moving in stealthily from wherever he'd come from to stand at Christian's side.

"Sure is," he answered, knowing full well they weren't talking about the same *she* at all.

"She's a might happier these days, too, without that stink smelling up the barn," Hank added with a snort.

Christian chuckled. Peter Deacon had long since been transferred from the vault beneath the stables and left bound and unconscious in Dr. Wickham Bow's Polytechnic office. An obvious case of a double-cross gone down.

Or so it had looked once Tripp and K.J. finished setting Deacon up, leaving the evidence, and getting the hell out with no trace of the Smithson Group left behind.

"One down," Christian said with a sigh. "Too many more to go."

"One bad guy at a time, son. That's the best we old soldiers can do."

Christian chuckled again, realizing he'd been doing a lot of that lately. "You might want to watch who you're calling old."

With two fingers, Hank snagged the cigar he held in the corner of his mouth. "You're getting there right on the money, boy, but you are sure wasting a lot of time along the way."

Well, now, wasn't this interesting, Hank gearing up for a lecture. Christian turned from the track to face the man who had saved his life. He crossed his arms over his chest and glanced down. "Spit it out."

Hank arched a thick white brow in return and gestured with the cigar. "Figured you would've sorted out a few things by now. That you might be feeling a bit restless. Lonesome, even."

He was talking about Natasha, of course. "I have been. A bit."

For the several seconds that followed, Hank looked into Christian's eyes, his own growing misty until he turned back to the track with a clearing of his throat. "I don't talk much about my Madelyn, but not a day goes by that I don't think about her."

Christian glanced down at the last of the green grass hugging the posts of the fence, shoved his fists into the pockets of his jeans, and nodded silently. This sure wasn't the lecture he'd been expecting.

He knew a lot of what Hank took on and doled out to his

operatives was in a big part to keep himself busy, his mind sharp, his thoughts occupied. And as much as Christian couldn't get Natasha out of his head but for minutes at the most, he understood. He understood more than he'd ever thought possible, this compelling need driving a man to one woman.

Hank pulled his cap from his head by the bill, smoothed back his thick shock of white hair before settling it back in place. "It's hard to think that I might never have had those forty-one years if I hadn't stopped thinking a woman like her was a lot better off without having to wrestle a hardheaded sonofabitch like me."

Christian felt the corner of his mouth twitch at the same time he realized that was exactly why he hadn't gone to Natasha. That he thought she'd be better off without him, considering who he was and what he did. He didn't want to let her down. Couldn't bear it if he did.

"Anyhow," Hank said after several quiet moments, slapping Christian on the back as he turned toward the house. "I just wanted you to know that there is always a method to my madness. You remember that now, come morning."

Christian watched him go, frowning at what had to be a reference to an upcoming mission. Or so he thought until a frisson of awareness skittered down his spine. He didn't even have time to turn before she spoke.

"Hey, spy boy. What's cooking?"

What's cooking? Spy boy?

He only made it halfway around before he heard her running footsteps. And he barely managed to open his arms and brace himself before she launched herself bodily forward.

He wrapped his arms around her and spun in a circle where they stood, his face buried in her hair because he wasn't sure he could look her in the eyes without choking up. His heart was lodged firmly in his throat.

Warm sweet honey and spiced harem flowers and everything good in the world. That's what she smelled like, felt like, and finally what she tasted like when he pulled back and brought his mouth down on hers. He kissed her with weeks of built-up frustration and need, and she kissed him right back, her hands roaming over his head and neck as she held him still.

"Oh, Christian. I have missed you so much," she said, long, hot moments later, tendering tiny kisses all over his face.

No way in hell had she missed him half as much as he had missed her. "What are you doing here? How did you get here?"

She slowed her kisses and stepped away, her eyes shining with unshed tears but her smile starting to falter. "The helicopter. Mr. Briggs brought me. Hank didn't tell you?"

Christian shook his head, brushed her hair back from her face, which was the last thing he wanted to see every night before falling asleep for the rest of his life. "Not until two minutes ago."

"That sneaky bastard," she said with a growl and a stomp of her foot.

"He's definitely that." God, but she was beautiful. She was generous. She was gorgeous and courageous—this woman who had risked her life for his, reducing the memory of his bamboo cage to ashes.

And she was so very damn much a part of him now that he didn't know why he hadn't gone to her weeks ago.

She frowned in the direction of the house. "He told me you needed me."

"I do need you."

"You do?" she asked a few seconds later, blinking curiously.

He loved that about her. One of so many things. And he nodded.

"Hmm, well. He makes a better spy than you do, then." She shoved sassy hands to sassy hips and flipped back her hair.

"Why do you say that?"

"Because he found me. You didn't."

"Natasha, listen—"

"You listen first, spy boy." She poked him in the chest. "I know who you are and what you are." Poke, poke. "How could I not? I've seen you in action"—*poke*—"at close range"—*poke*—"and I hate that someone, that *anyone* has to do what you do. And, yes. I'll be scared to death while you're away—"

"Wait a minute." He grabbed her hand, squeezed her fingers. "Away from where?"

"Away from me, silly."

He was through playing games. From now on, it was brutal honesty time. She was here and she was his and he'd live the rest of his life in Thailand before he ever let her get away. "And what are you going to be doing while I'm gone?"

"Oh, darning your socks." She shrugged, lowered her lashes demurely, toyed with the mother-of-pearl snap on his shirt, and monkeyed her finger around until she found his bare chest beneath. "Stuff like that."

He tossed back his head and laughed. "You are so full of crap."

"Oh, Christian. No, I'm not." She looked up then, her eyes brimming, tears spilling and running down her cheeks. "I'm full of love. For you."

And, at that, he had no choice. He gave up his heart and soul into Natasha's safekeeping. "Natasha, sweetheart. Oh, sweetheart. I love you, too."

Meet the men of the Smithson Group—five spies whose best work is done in the field and between the sheets. Smart, built, trained to do everything well—and that's everything—they're the guys you want on your side of the bed. Go deep undercover? No problem. Take out the bad guys? Done. Play by the rules? I don't think so. Indulge a woman's every fantasy? Happy to please, ma'am.
Fall in love? Hey, even a secret agent's got his weak spots . . .

Bad boys. Good spies. Unforgettable lovers.

Episode One:
THE BANE AFFAIR
by
Alison Kent

"Smart, funny, exciting, touching, and *hot.*"—Cherry Adair

"Fast, dangerous, sexy."—Shannon McKenna

Get started with Christian Bane, SG-5

Christian Bane is a man of few words, so when he talks, people listen. One of the Smithson Group's elite force, Christian's also the walking wounded, haunted by his past. Something about being betrayed by a woman, then left to die in a Thai prison by the notorious crime syndicate Spectra IT gives a guy demons. But now, Spectra has made a secret deal with a top scientist to crack a governmental encryption technology, and Christian has his orders: Pose as Spectra boss Peter Deacon. Going deep undercover as the slick womanizer will be tough for Christian. Getting cozy with the scientist's beautiful goddaughter, Natasha, to get information won't be. But the closer he gets to Natasha, the harder it gets to deceive her. She's so alluring, so trusting, so completely unexpected he suspects someone's been giving out faulty intel. If Natasha isn't the criminal he was led to believe, they're both being played for fools. Now, with Spectra closing in, Christian's best chance for survival is to confront his demons and trust the only one he can . . . Natasha . . .

Available from Brava in October 2004.

Episode Two:
THE SHAUGHNESSEY ACCORD
by
Alison Kent

Get hot and bothered with Tripp Shaughnessey, SG–5

When someone screams Tripp Shaughnessey's name, it's usually a woman in the throes of passion or one who's just caught him with his hand in the proverbial cookie jar. Sometimes it's both. Tripp is sarcastic, fun-loving, and funny, with a habit of seducing every woman he says hello to. But the one who really gets him hot and bothered is Glory Brighton, the curvaceous owner of his favorite sandwich shop. The nonstop banter between Glory and Tripp has been leading up to a full-body kiss in the back storeroom. And that's just where they are when all hell breaks loose. Glory's past includes some very bad men connected to Spectra, men convinced she may have important intel hidden in her place. Now, with the shop under siege, and gunmen holding customers hostage, Tripp shows Glory his true colors: He's no sweet, rumpled "engineer" from the Smithson Group, but a well-trained, hardcore covert op whose easy-going rep is about to be put to the test . . .

Available from Brava in November 2004.

Episode Three:
THE SAMMS AGENDA
by
Alison Kent

Get down and dirty with Julian Samms, SG–5

From his piercing blue eyes to his commanding presence, everything about Julian Samms says all-business and no bull. He expects a lot from his team—some say too much. But that's how you keep people alive, by running things smoothly, cleanly, and quickly. Under Julian's watch, that's how it plays. Except today. The mission was straightforward: Extract Katrina Flurry, ex-girlfriend of deposed Spectra frontman Peter Deacon, from her Miami condo before a hit man can silence her for good. But things didn't go according to plan, and Julian's suddenly on the run with a woman who gives new meaning to high maintenance. Stuck in a cheap motel with a force of nature who seems determined to get them killed, Julian can't believe his luck. Katrina is infuriating, unpredictable, adorable, and possibly the most exciting, sexy woman he's ever met. A woman who makes Julian want to forget his playbook and go wild, spending hours in bed. And on the off-chance that they don't get out alive, Julian's new live-for-today motto is starting right now . . .

Available from Brava in December 2004.

Episode Four:
THE BEACH ALIBI
by
Alison Kent

Get deep under cover with Kelly John Beach, SG–5

Kelly John Beach is a go-to guy known for covering all the bases and moving in the shadows like a ghost. But now, the ultimate spy is in big trouble: during his last mission, he was caught breaking into a Spectra IT high-rise on one of their video surveillance cameras. The SG–5 team has to make an alternate tape fast, one that proves K.J. was elsewhere at the time of the break-in. The plan is simple: Someone from Smithson will pose as K.J.'s lover, and SG–5's strategically placed cameras will record their every intimate, erotic encounter in elevators, restaurant hallways, and other daring forums. But Kelly John never expects that "alibi" to come in the form of Emma Webster, the sexy coworker who has starred in so many of his not-for-primetime fantasies. Getting his hands—and anything else he can—on Emma under the guise of work is a dream come true. Deceiving the good-hearted, trusting woman isn't. And when Spectra realizes that the way to K.J. is through Emma, the spy is ready to come in from the cold, and show her how far he'll go to protect the woman he loves . . .

Available from Brava in January 2005.

Episode Five:
THE MCKENZIE ARTIFACT
by
Alison Kent

Get what you came for with Eli McKenzie, SG–5

Five months ago, SG–5 operative Eli McKenzie was in deep cover in Mexico, infiltrating a Spectra ring that kidnaps young girls and sells them into a life beyond imagining. Not being able to move on the Spectra scum right away was torture for the tough-but-compassionate superspy. But that wasn't the only problem—someone on the inside was slowly poisoning Eli, clouding his judgment and forcing him to make an abrupt trip back to the Smithson Group's headquarters to heal. Now, Eli's ready to return . . . with a vengeance. It seems his quick departure left a private investigator named Stella

Banks in some hot water. Spectra operatives have nabbed the nosy Stella and are awaiting word on how to handle her disposal. Eli knows the only way to save her life and his is to reveal himself to Stella and get her to trust him. Seeing the way Stella takes care of the frightened girls melts Eli's armor, and soon, they find that the best way to survive this brutal assignment is to steal time in each other's arms. It's a bliss Eli's intent on keeping, no matter what he has to do to protect it. Because Eli McKenzie has unfinished business with Spectra—and with the woman who has renewed his heart—this is one man who always finishes what he starts. . . .

Available from Brava in February 2005.

We don't think you will want to miss
JUST A HINT—CLINT by Lori Foster,
coming this month from Brava.
Here's a sneak peek.

A bead of sweat took a slow path down his throat and into the neckline of his dark T-shirt. Pushed by a hot, insubstantial breeze, a weed brushed his cheek.

Clint never moved.

Through the shifting shadows of the pulled blinds, he could detect activity in the small cabin. The low drone of voices filtered out the screen door, but Clint couldn't make out any of the slurred conversation.

Next to him, Red stirred. In little more than a breath of sound, he said, "Fuck, I hate waiting."

Wary of a trap, Clint wanted the entire area checked. Mojo chose that moment to slip silently into the grass beside them. He'd done a surveillance of the cabin, the surrounding grounds, and probably gotten a good peek in the back window. Mojo could be invisible and eerily silent when he chose.

"All's clear."

Something tightened inside Clint. "She's in there?"

"Alive but pissed off and real scared." Mojo's obsidian eyes narrowed. "Four men. They've got her tied up."

Clint silently worked his jaw, fighting for his famed icy control. The entire situation was bizarre. How was it Asa knew where to find the men, yet they didn't appear to expect an interruption? Had Robert deliberately fed the info to Asa to embroil him in a trap so Clint would kill him? And why would Robert want Asa dead?

Somehow, both he and Julie Rose were pawns. But for what purpose?

Clint's rage grew, clawing to be freed, making his stomach pitch with the violent need to act. "They're armed?"

Mojo nodded with evil delight. "And on their way out."

Given that a small bonfire lit the clearing in front of the cabin, Clint wasn't surprised that they would venture outside. The hunting cabin was deep into the hills, mostly surrounded by thick woods. Obviously, the kidnappers felt confident in their seclusion.

He'd have found them eventually, Clint thought, but Asa's tip had proved invaluable. And a bit too fucking timely.

So far, nothing added up, and that made him more cautious than anything else could have.

He'd work it out as they went along. The drive had cost them two hours, with another hour crawling through the woods. But now he had them.

He had *her.*

The cabin door opened and two men stumbled out under the glare of a yellow bug light. One wore jeans and an unbuttoned shirt, the other was shirtless, showing off a variety of tattoos on his skinny chest. They looked youngish and drunk and stupid. They looked cruel.

Raucous laughter echoed around the small clearing, disturbed only by a feminine voice, shrill with fear and anger, as two other men dragged Julie Rose outside.

She wasn't crying.

No sir. Julie Rose was complaining.

Her torn school dress hung off her right shoulder nearly to her waist, displaying one small pale breast. She struggled against hard hands and deliberate roughness until she was shoved, landing on her right hip in the barren area in front of the house. With her hands tied behind her back, she had no way to brace herself. She fell flat, but quickly struggled into a sitting position.

The glow of the bonfire reflected on her bruised, dirty face—and in her furious eyes. She was frightened, but she was also livid.

"I think we should finish stripping her," one of the men said.

Julie's bare feet peddled against the uneven ground as she tried to move farther away.

The men laughed some more, and the one who'd spoken went onto his haunches in front of her. He caught her bare ankle, immobilizing her.

"Not too much longer, bitch. Morning'll be here before you know it." He stroked her leg, up to her knee, higher. "I bet you're getting anxious, huh?"

Her chest heaved, her lips quivered.

She spit on him.

Clint was on his feet in an instant, striding into the clearing before Mojo or Red's hissed curses could register. The four men, standing in a cluster, turned to look at him with various expressions of astonishment, confusion, and horror. They were slow to react, and Clint realized they were more than a little drunk. Idiots.

One of the young fools reached behind his back.

"*You.*" Clint stabbed him with a fast lethal look while keeping his long, ground-eating pace to Julie. "Touch that weapon and I'll break your leg."

The guy blanched—and promptly dropped his hands.

Clint didn't think of anything other than his need to get between Julie and the most immediate threat. But without giving it conscious thought, he knew that Mojo and Red would back him up. If any guns were drawn, theirs would be first.

The man who'd been abusing Julie snorted in disdain at the interference. He took a step forward, saying, "Just who the hell do you think you—"

Reflexes on automatic, Clint pivoted slightly to the side and kicked out hard and fast. The force of his boot heel caught the man on the chin with sickening impact. He sprawled flat with a raw groan that dwindled into blackness. He didn't move.

Another man leaped forward. Clint stepped to the side, and like clockwork, kicked out a knee. The obscene sounds of breaking bone and cartilage and the accompanying scream of pain split the night, sending nocturnal creatures to scurry through the leaves.

Clint glanced at Julie's white face, saw she was frozen in shock, and headed toward the two remaining men. Eyes wide, they started to back up, and Clint curled his mouth into the semblance of a smile. "I don't think so."

A gun was finally drawn, but not in time to be fired. Clint grabbed the man's wrist and twisted up and back. Still holding him, Clint pulled him forward and into a solid punch to the stomach. Without breath, the painful shouts ended real quick. The second Clint released him, the man turned to hobble into the woods. Clint didn't want to, but he let him go.

Robert Burns had said not to bring anyone in. He couldn't see committing random murder, and that's what it'd be if he started breaking heads now. But in an effort to protect Julie Rose and her apparently already tattered reputation, he wouldn't turn them over to the law either.

Just letting them go stuck in his craw, and Clint, fed up, ready to end it, turned to the fourth man. He threw a punch to the throat and jaw, then watched the guy crumble to his knees, then to his face, wheezing for breath.

Behind Clint, Red's dry tone intruded. "Well, that was efficient."

Clint struggled with himself for only an instant before realizing there was no one left to fight. He turned, saw Julie Rose held in wide-eyed horror, and he jerked. Mojo stepped back out of the way, and Clint lurched to the bushes.

Anger turned to acid in his gut.

Typically, at least for Clint Evans and his weak-ass stomach, he puked.

Julie could hardly believe her eyes. One minute she'd known she would be raped and probably killed, and the fear had been all too consuming, a live clawing dread inside her.

Now . . . now she didn't know what had happened. Three men, looking like angelic convicts, had burst into the clearing. Well, no, that wasn't right. The first man hadn't burst anywhere. He'd strode in, casual as you please, then proceeded to make mincemeat out of her abductors.

He'd taken on four men as if they were no more than gnats.

She'd never seen that type of brawling. His blows hadn't been designed to slow down an opponent, or to bruise or hurt. One strike—and the men had dropped like dead weights. Even the sight of a gun hadn't fazed him. He moved so fast, so smoothly, the weapon hadn't mattered at all.

When he'd delivered those awesome strikes, his expression, hard and cold, hadn't changed. A kick here, a punch there, and the men who'd held her, taunted her, were no longer a threat.

He was amazing, invincible, he was . . . *throwing up*.

Her heart pounded in slow, deep thumps that hurt her breastbone and made it difficult to draw an even breath. The relief flooding over her in a drowning force didn't feel much different than her fear had.

Her awareness of that man was almost worse.

Like spotting Superman, or a wild animal, or a combination of both, she felt awed and amazed and disbelieving.

She was safe now, but was she really?

One of her saviors approached her. He was fair, having blond hair and light eyes, though she couldn't see the exact color in the dark night with only the fire for illumination. Trying to make himself look less like a convict, he gave her a slight smile.

A wasted effort.

He moved real slow, watchful, and gentle. "Don't pay any mind to Clint." He spoke in a low, melodic croon. "He always pukes afterward."

Her savior's name was Clint.

Julie blinked several times, trying to gather her wits and calm the spinning in her head. "He does?"

Another man approached, equally cautious, just as gentle.

But he had black hair and blacker eyes. He didn't say anything, just stood next to the other man and surveyed her bruised face with an awful frown that should have been alarming, but wasn't.

The blond guy nodded. "Yeah. Hurtin' people—even people who deserve it—always upsets Clint's stomach. He'll be all right in a minute."

Julie ached, her body, her heart, her mind. She'd long ago lost feeling in her arms but every place else pulsed with relentless pain. She looked over at Clint. He had his hands on his knees, his head hanging. The poor man. "He was saving me, wasn't he?"

"Oh, yes, ma'am. We're here to take you home. Everything will be okay now." His glance darted to her chest and quickly away.

Julie realized she wasn't decently covered, but with her hands tied tightly behind her back, she couldn't do anything about it. She felt conspicuous and vulnerable and ready to cry, so she did her best to straighten her aching shoulders and looked back at Clint.

Just the sight of him, big, powerful, brave, gave her a measure of reassurance. He straightened slowly, drew several deep breaths.

He was an enormous man, layered in sleek muscle with wide shoulders and a tapered waist and long thick thighs. His biceps were as large as her legs, his hands twice as big as her own.

Eyes closed, he tipped his head back and swallowed several times, drinking in the humid night air. At that moment, he looked very weak.

He hadn't looked weak while pulverizing those men. Julie licked her dry lips and fought off another wave of the strange dizziness.

Clint flicked a glance toward her, and their gazes locked together with a sharp snap, shocking Julie down to the soles of her feet.

He looked annoyed by the near tactile contact.

Julie felt electrified. Her pains faded away into oblivion.

It took a few moments, but his forced smile, meant to be reassuring, was a tad sickly. Still watching her, he reached into his front pocket and pulled out a small silver flask. He tipped it up, swished his mouth out, and spit.

All the while, he held her with that implacable burning gaze.

When he replaced the flask in his pocket and started toward her, every nerve ending in Julie's body came alive with expectation. Fear, alarm, relief—she wasn't at all certain what she felt, she just knew she felt it in spades. Her breath rose to choke her, her body quaked, and strangely enough, tears clouded her eyes.

She would not cry, she would not cry . . .

She rubbed one eye on her shoulder and spoke to the two men, just to help pull herself together. "Should he be drinking?"

The blond man said, "Oh, no. It's mouthwash." And with a smile, "He always carries it with him, cuz of his stomach and the way he usually—"

The dark man nudged him, and they both fell silent.

Mouthwash. She hadn't figured on that.

She wanted to ignore him, but her gaze was drawn to him like a lodestone. Fascinated, she watched as Clint drew nearer. During his approach, he peeled his shirt off over his head then stopped in front of her, blocking her from the others. They took the hint and gave her their backs.

Julie stared at that broad, dark, hairy chest. He was more man than any man she'd ever seen, and the dizziness assailed her again.

With a surprisingly gentle touch, Clint went to one knee and laid the shirt over her chest. It was warm and damp from his body. His voice was low, a little rough when he spoke. "I'm going to cut your hands free. Just hold still a second, okay?"

Julie didn't answer. She *couldn't* answer. She'd been scared for so long now, what seemed like weeks but had only been a little more than a day. And now she was rescued.

She was safe.

A large lethal blade appeared in Clint's capable hands, but Julie felt no fear. Not now. Not with him so close.

He didn't go behind her to free her hands, but rather reached around her while looking over her shoulder and blocked her body with his own. Absurdly, she became aware of his hot scent, rich with the odor of sweat and anger and man. After smelling her own fear for hours on end, it was a delicious treat for her senses. She closed her eyes and concentrated on the smell of him, on his warmth and obvious strength and stunning ability.

He enveloped her with his size, and with the promise of safety.

She felt a small tug and the ropes fell away. But as Julie tried to move, red-hot fire rushed through her arms, into her shoulders and wrists, forcing a groan of pure agony from her tight lips.

"Shhhh, easy now." As if he'd known exactly what she'd feel, Clint sat in front of her. His long legs opened around her, and he braced her against his bare upper body. His flesh was hot, smooth beneath her cheek.

Slowly, carefully, he brought her arms around, and allowed her to muffle her moans against his shoulder. He massaged her, kneading and rubbing from her upper back, her shoulders to her elbows, to her wrists and still crooning to her in that low gravely voice. His hard fingers dug deep into her soft flesh, working out the cramps with merciless determination and loosening her stiff joints that seemed frozen in place.

As the pain eased, tiredness sank in, and Julie slumped against him. She'd been living off adrenaline for hours and now being safe left her utterly drained, unable to stay upright.

It was like propping herself against a warm, vibrant brick wall. There was no give to Clint's hard shoulder, and Julie was comforted.

One thought kept reverberating through her weary brain: *He'd really saved her.*